CASTLE REEF

a novel

ANDREW B. SAMPSEL

ISBN 978-1-63885-767-9 (Paperback)
ISBN 978-1-63885-769-3 (Hardcover)
ISBN 978-1-63885-768-6 (Digital)

Scripture references are taken from The Holy Bible, New International Version.

Covenant Books
11661 Hwy 707
Murrells Inlet, SC 29576
www.covenantbooks.com

To my dear wife, Susan, your unfailing love and support
encouraged me to make this dream become a reality.

In memory of my earthly father, Prem E. Sampsel Jr.,
and my father-in-law, James D. Van Brunt.

CASTLE REEF

chapter

1

The steady melodic ring tone slowly carried Julie Kerrig out of a familiar dream and into a sunny June morning. It was the summer solstice, the longest day of the year, and the sounds from Main Street below reminded her that the tourist season was well underway in the coastal town of Castle Reef.

After a big yawn, she slowly raised her cell phone to stop her alarm and check for any messages or missed calls. No messages, no calls. This was a great start to perhaps a better day, but as she glanced at the curved tattoo line on her right forearm, suddenly, a flood of unavoidable memories raced into her mind, memories from which Julie continually fought to escape. Quickly, in order to break the train of thought, she placed the phone on the nightstand, rolled out of bed in one swift motion, and groaned. "Time to make the donuts!"

Making her way through the small upstairs apartment and into the kitchen, she carefully reached for her favorite coffee mug and poured from the carafe that had been warming for over an hour. Slowly stirring in the creamer, Julie yawned again and recalled the old Dunkin' Donuts commercial from her early childhood, featuring a tired bakery worker, who being awakened early by his alarm clock, would then deliver that infamous line: *"Time to make the donuts."*

Ironically, she remembered that it was also her father's favorite go-to phrase whenever something became monotonous. Cautiously sipping from the hot ironstone mug, Julie's suppressed thoughts began to surface once more.

She whispered, "Is this my life now? I love this town, I love my job, I love my friends, and I love…" Tears began to well up in her vibrant green eyes.

Even though she desperately wanted to, she couldn't bring herself to finish the sentence.

Taking one more sip of her coffee, Julie headed to the bathroom. It was time to get ready for work. Perhaps a hot shower would allow her a brief escape from the heartache.

#

Five miles to the south, Charlie Philips carefully placed his big floppy hat and beach towel on the dry sand. He smiled as he watched the sandpipers dance along the water's edge of the white picturesque shoreline, in search of their breakfast. The eighty-one-year-old widower and retired Navy officer made watching every sunrise, along with an early swim, part of his daily routine. Today was no exception. After a few minutes of rigorous stretching, he tightened the drawstring of his brand new blue and white-striped swim trunks and plunged into the waves that were now starting to crest in rhythm with the rising tide. Despite being very alert for his age, Charlie never even noticed the unusual commotion in the water just beyond the breaker zone.

#

Trent Green turned off the rusty, white 1972 GMC pickup and leaned his back against the torn bench seat. After an extra-long sigh, he rested his head on the back window. He had made up his mind that today was the day he was going to do it. It had been over a month since he'd last spoken to the woman who had broken his heart. A brief and very cold greeting during a formal town hall ceremony was all that had transpired between the two of them. He just couldn't let things continue the way they were. After all, he had invested too much of his time, money, and energy toward the life he had always desired with the one he loved.

Five years had passed since Trent left the corporate rat race, quitting his affluent job within the financial district of New York City. He had taken his earnings and embarked on the pursuit of a dream to open a hotel and restaurant. Castle Reef was the perfect location to fulfill that dream. He had initially discovered the 160-year-old coastal town while vacationing along the east coast several years prior. Its location was unique, sitting nearly fifty feet above sea level on a large limestone base. The historic village earned its name before the turn of the century because viewing it from the water, the outline of the town buildings bore a resemblance to a medieval castle, especially at night. Many British trading ships would see the illuminated buildings and become confused, thinking they were nearing their homeland.

Trent had purchased the old boarding house on Main Street and converted it into the Green Sea Inn. He restored the building and kept many of its original features, yet updated everything to all the current commercial building codes. The majestic inn was now a five-star establishment, which served its guests gourmet cuisine and had some of the best ocean view rooms in the country. The staff of eighteen, including his best friend Mike, who maintained the facility, were all committed to making the inn a memorable and enjoyable vacation experience, which kept customers coming back year after year.

And yet, even with all of the success of his business, as much as Trent tried to convince himself that he was truly fulfilled, he felt incomplete without the woman who had captured his heart. How had he let three years go by since his intended marriage was called off abruptly after a family tragedy?

"Enough is enough," he whispered. Today he was determined to break the silence and find out if he ever had a chance to be in her life again. Grabbing his keys, he jumped out of the truck and made his way to the back kitchen door of the Green Sea Inn.

\#

Ian Reynolds pushed his way through the group of college students huddled in front of the assignment board on the west wall of the lifeguard station. His coworkers made a path for him and began loudly chanting his name in unison. He grinned, flexed his muscles in a WWE pose and looked to see where he would be stationed.

"Oh, yeah! Looks like I will be way south today, while you losers will be working up here with all the crying babies and their screaming mothers, in good ol' Castle Grief!" taunted the blond-headed twenty-one-year-old.

The bronzed, buff young man adjusted his designer visor, quickly grabbed his backpack, and gave his colleagues an obscene gesture. They all howled in laughter as he jumped on one of the ATVs parked along the wooden walkway, and then purposely spun out loose sand onto them before racing away.

This was Ian's third season working for the county recreation department as a lifeguard.

The son of a wealthy politician, and a junior at Brighton State University, Ian's main focus was maintaining his cool public image. The summer job gave him an opportunity to deepen his tan before returning to campus in August. He essentially got paid for checking out all the college girls on the beach during the day. In addition to maintaining a muscular and very tone physique, he paid careful attention to be on the cutting edge of fashion. No matter what the occasion, Ian made sure everyone noticed what he was wearing. Clearly, Ian was into Ian, and only Ian!

As he drove to his assigned location, Ian planned out, in his narcissistic mind, the strategy for the day. Upon his arrival, he would quickly climb up onto the lifeguard chair, pretend he was awake behind those expensive shades, and then sleep his eight-hour shift away.

Little did he know, an event was about to occur that would drastically change his life forever.

#

Standing in front of the hallway mirror, fully dressed after a long hot shower, Julie Kerrig fastened the last button on her uniform. The young woman stood motionless, gazing intently at her reflection. Staring back at her was the newly appointed police chief of Castle Reef. The nameplate secured beneath her badge confirmed this extraordinary fact.

It had only been a few weeks since she was unanimously voted in by the town council and recognized during a special community Memorial Day service, which paid tribute to all the fallen soldiers and law officers of Brighton County. The late Chief John Kerrig was among those honored, and Julie received an award on her father's behalf.

Wiping another tear that found itself in the corner of her eye, she then carefully fastened her leather Biachi duty belt. It was complete with a two-way radio, handcuffs, gloves, mace, extra ammo clips, a flashlight, a baton, and most importantly, her father's Colt 1911 45ACP. Julie was determined, in some way, to make her dad proud. It was still hard for her to believe that he had been gone for over three years.

"Okay, Chief… You got this," she said, sighing in a slow and steady exhale.

The sobering moment was interrupted by her cell phone on the nightstand, next to her unmade bed. She quickly answered it.

"Hello?" Julie said.

"Hey, Chief Reef!" On the other end of the call was that familiar sweet voice.

Julie quickly composed herself. "What are you doing, girlfriend?"

"I know you're probably heading to the station, I just wanted to see if you were up for lunch today?" The female on the other end giggled.

"Sure thing, Vick, let's meet at Nina's around 12:30-ish?" said Julie, twirling the damp, braided, single ponytail on the back of her head.

Having grown up together, Julie and her best friend, Vicki Stanwick, had always been inseparable. Vicki's parents, Greg and Martha, were significantly older than their daughter, who they had adopted twenty-nine years ago, after returning from a mission trip in Nigeria. Now, well into their early seventies, the Stanwicks still owned and operated *The Reef*, the small town's only newspaper. Their devoted daughter was always eager to help them with their venture by doing most of the reporting and advertising on the side, in addition to her position as an office clerk at the town hall.

"Winner, winner, chicken dinner!" Vicki said in a pretend Southern accent followed by her signature laugh.

"You're a mess. I will see you then," said Julie with a genuine smile.

"Sounds like a plan, Jules." Vicki giggled again.

Julie smiled as she ended the call and put her phone in the appropriate holder on her duty belt, sitting snugly upon her waist. Grabbing her prized blue cap off the top of the dresser and then feeding her long blonde braid through the back headband, the thirty-four-year-old chief of police made her way downstairs and across the street for another day of protecting and serving the people of Castle Reef. Today, however, would be the most memorable June 21 in the history of the town. Within a matter of hours, Julie would need to draw on everything her dad taught her, both professionally and personally.

#

Vicki Stanwick hung up her recently acquired 1984 retro wall phone. She paused and looked at it with contentment. It was a unique color red, and was complete with a rotary dial and eight-foot cord. She picked up the handset once again and dialed another familiar number. The sound of the rotary wheel was music to Vicki's ears. She loved old things, and anything that was an antique made her giddy.

"Good morning, Stanwick residence." The chipper voice on the other end sounded a little winded.

"Hey, Mom, how are ya? You sound like you have been running."

"Hey, sweets, just got back from my bike ride." Martha Stanwick inhaled long and then steadily let out an even breath.

"Did you know you are an amazing woman, and you make me look like a wimp?" Vicki chuckled as she twirled the phone cord.

"Stop that nonsense. You're a Stanwick, and you're not a wimp."

Vicki snickered and then cleared her throat and spoke in a dramatic way. "Any assignments for me at The Reef today, Mrs. Stanwick?"

Vicki's mom laughed. "I don't know, silly, just give your Pops a call. He's at the office."

"Well, I'm going to have lunch with Julie in a little bit, and if I have time, I will drop by to see if he needs any help with a story before the paper goes to press.

"Good idea, Vicki, and you're still coming over for game night, right?" Martha asked.

"I wouldn't miss it for the world!" announced Vicki proudly.

"Thanks, sweetie. I love you, my daughter. Say hello to Jules for me."

"I will. See you tonight. Sure do love you." Vicki smiled, hanging up her new vintage treasure and left her apartment.

#

Kelli shouted over the hum of the Hobart mixer, "Good morning, Trent!"

"Hey, Mrs. Davis! I see you're busy making our signature homemade bread," greeted Trent loudly, after walking through the screen door.

"I've cranked out about thirty-seven loaves since five this morning!" Kelli laughed.

"That is awesome!" Trent then turned his attention to the middle-aged woman with salt-and-pepper hair, who was working feverishly at the long center counter in the large commercial kitchen.

"What's tonight's special?" Trent asked his faithful chef Rita McGuire as he headed to the walk-in refrigerator.

"The shrimp scampi was a big hit last night, but I'm thinkin' sea bass. Fran is supposed to bring us a fresh catch from Jerry's this morning." Rita kept her attention on the vegetables she was dicing.

"Okay, that's cool. Have you seen Mike yet?" Trent asked, slowly twisting the cap off of his ginger kombucha tea he'd just retrieved.

Rita, slicing an onion carefully, paused. "Hmm, yeah about ten minutes ago. He said he was checking on a guest upstairs who was complaining about his television or something."

"No worries, just let him know I'll be in my office placing orders with one of our vendors. Thanks, Rita."

Trent stepped into his glass-windowed office, located in the back of the kitchen, next to the large pantry. He began working on his laptop, surveying the inventory that he needed but found himself unable to concentrate. He pulled out his cell phone and began to compose a message which he had memorized for weeks, simultaneously erasing it at the same rate he typed.

#

It was 8:55 a.m., and Ian Reynolds had been at his assigned post for nearly forty-five minutes. The Brighton State junior had been partying with his friends the night before and was beginning to feel its effects. Anticipating a long nap, the sound of the crashing waves was making him very sleepy. Ian gazed once to the north before he leaned back, adjusted his earbuds, and shut his eyes behind his $350 pair of sunglasses. The arrogant college student was so into his high and mighty chair, suntan lotion, and loud music, that he had failed to notice Charlie Philips swimming directly in front of him, only seventy yards away. Ian was oblivious to the aged swimmer, as well as the large, dark fin cutting through the water directly behind him.

chapter

2

It was only morning, and Mayor David Willis was already sweating. Despite being in an air-conditioned office, stationary at his desk, and wearing a short-sleeved shirt, beads of perspiration formed on his brow. The mayor was on the telephone and visibly upset. Vicki, who had just arrived, was about to bring him a cup of coffee, yet noticed not only was he busy, but obviously in no condition for a hot beverage.

"Is he all right, Joan?" Vicki asked the mayor's secretary, who was seated at her desk.

"He's been on that call for almost twenty minutes, and it doesn't sound good," whispered the neatly dressed forty-eight-year-old redhead.

"Oh my, I guess I will go find something else to do. Do you happen to know who he's talking to?" Vicki turned her back in order to hide her facial expression.

"Not sure, but I did hear him say, 'Sorry, JK,' which tells me it might be '*The* JK'," mouthed Joan. She nervously shifted in her chair and put her head down pretending to read the papers that were on her desk.

"Wow, I wonder what's up? Let me ditch this coffee and go check my messages. Get back with me if you hear any other juicy tidbits."

Vicki found herself whispering too and began to giggle. Slowly leaving Joan's desk area she acted as if she was casually passing by and desperately tried not to laugh out loud. Joan winked, then turned back to her computer, and started working again.

#

Several minutes of complete ocean bliss had passed for the muscular college student. His second Nu metal song had just finished, and he was adjusting his earbuds. Suddenly, from the surf came a terrifying scream that made Ian sit straight up as if he was electrocuted.

"What the..." he barked as he leaned forward.

He thought he heard it again amid the sets of waves. Pausing his music, Ian picked up his binoculars and looked out into the water directly in front of his chair. There was nothing but foaming waves breaking apart along the shoreline. He slowly panned from side to side and noticed a pair of seagulls bobbing in the water about a hundred yards from him. Only the drone of a small airplane several miles away competed with pounding waves on the sandy shore.

"Dude, you've been up way too long! That sounded too real. That's messed up. Those stupid gulls freakin' scared me, like for real!"

Ian dropped the binoculars into his canvas bag, twirled his whistle string twice, then leaned back and exhaled slowly.

"I gotta chill out. Remember, Ian this is the life, and you get paid to do this," he mumbled, drifting back into a sound sleep.

Meanwhile, less than fifty feet away from his lifeguard stand, a freshly torn piece of blue-and-white striped fabric momentarily floated into a tidal pool, then slowly sank, and rested on a broken sea shell.

#

The Green Sea Inn kitchen was always relatively quiet during the early breakfast shift. Most of the cooking was performed out in the front dining room in an open grill area, with serving counters flanking three sides. It was now brunch, and the servers were busy taking orders and clearing tables.

The very large dining room was filled with antique wooden tables and chairs of all sizes and styles. Even the old decorative tin ceiling still remained, along with the original wood columns. A wide staircase allowed access to the upstairs rooms. The tables along the large windows facing Main Street were always the first to be taken and today was no exception.

Patrons and room guests loved dining here because of the amazing food, fun atmosphere, and wonderful customer service.

"Welcome to Green Sea. Please feel free to sit wherever you like," greeted the teen server to a neatly shaven man.

He pointed to the corner of the room. "Thank you, I think I will sit back there."

"That's an excellent choice. My name is Kendra, and I will be your server."

"Thank you, Kendra Baker," he said, walking behind her.

"No problem," she said, as she wondered, *Did I tell him my last name?* The young waitress paused and placed a menu on the table. "Can I get you something cold to drink?"

"I will have a glass of diet root beer." The man gave a forced smile and slowly sat down.

"Yes, sir, I'll bring that right to you." Kendra hurried to the serving counter. At sixteen, she was cheerful yet a little awkward due to the fact that this was her first job.

As the man sat down, he reached into the pocket of his neatly pressed light-blue dress shirt and placed what looked like a mobile device on the table in front of him. He then slowly surveyed the room. This time, there was no expression on his face.

#

Jerry Foster, known as the best fisherman in all of Brighton County, had lived in Castle Reef his whole life. Coming from four generations of fishermen, he was the owner and operator of Ocean's Seafood Market. This seventy-six-year-old gruff character, along with his eccentric second wife Becky, ran the infamous year-round market located in the marina of Salty Dog Harbor. Ocean's sold a variety of freshly caught seafood to local restaurants, state vendors, as well as the general public. Jerry's operation looked like something out of a magazine. It was well-organized yet rustic enough to give the tourists an experience they would always remember.

"Hey, Jerry! Top of the mornin' to ya!" said the short, stocky Irish man.

"How's my leprechaun doin' today?" The weathered face of the old fisherman wrinkled with joy.

"Awful good!" Francis O'Reily laughed as he placed the large cooler on the dock where Jerry Foster was working.

"I bet you're here for more of that sea bass, aren't ya?" Jerry grunted with a smile.

"You know it my ol' pal, ya got any?" O'Reily asked.

"Good news, I got a bunch that just came in. What's city boy Trent doin' with this stuff anyway?" Jerry chuckled as he walked over to a large ice bin and lifted the lid.

"He makes the best grilled bass this side of the Atlantic fer sure, my pal." Francis used his boot to slide the cooler closer to where Jerry was standing.

"Well, he's a good man and a great customer." Jerry was now placing several large sea bass carefully into Fran's cooler.

"It's a shame he and that dote lass, Cap'n Julie, don't get themselves back together."

"There's a history there that needs fixing, for sure," said Foster.

"I may not be the native that you are, but even I can see plainly those two are sure meant fer each other, don't ya think?"

Jerry paused and looked up at Francis. "Julie's dad was a fine man and my best friend. He thought the same thing. Sure hope she comes around to realizing that."

The sound of footsteps through the gravel parking lot interrupted the men. A middle-aged and oddly dressed woman wearing a pair of large white sunglasses approached them both.

"What are you boys doing out here?"

Becky Foster, at fifty-six, still looked like a skinny teenager. She stood smiling in the sunshine with a green scarf on her head, wearing white Bermuda shorts and bright orange sneakers.

"Would ya look at that, Jerry. She's wearin' the flag of me home-land!" Francis cackled as he scooped ice into his cooler.

"Real funny, Mr. Corned Beef and Cabbage!" she shouted loudly, followed by an outburst of laughter that echoed off the water and surrounding boats.

Jerry did his trademark belly laugh as he patted Francis on the back and helped him lift the full cooler into his truck. Mr. O'Reily, the single, sixty-year-old Irishman, who had just been humorously silenced, shook his head, got in his truck, and slowly drove away.

After composing herself, Becky managed to tell her husband that he had paperwork to sign in the office. As they walked toward the office, in the distance behind them, Jerry's fishing boat moved slowly side to side, in its slip.

The *Susan Marie*, a 1963 commercial fishing boat, had a lot of history within the depths of its hull. Throughout the decades, it was instrumental in hundreds of fishing trips, hauling in thousands of commercial catches, as well as assisting in some of the most dramatic Coast Guard rescues during storms and accidents. It was a powerful craft and well maintained by Jerry's crew, who also worked at the fish market.

Sadly three years before, tragedy had struck the vessel when John Kerrig was swept overboard, roughly six miles off the coast, during a March storm. Jerry had been the last person to see John. Both were heading home after a short fishing trip when an unexpected Nor'easter began blowing in. Apparently, John had been securing the rigging on the main deck before going below and was suddenly hit by a large wave. He reportedly disappeared into the depths of the ocean. By the time Jerry came up to see if his friend needed help, it was too late. After weeks of searching the coastal waters and shoreline, all efforts were called off. The town was devastated, to say the least, and his daughter Julie even more so.

#

Ian was suddenly awakened again, this time by a loud, sobbing voice. He sat up in a rush and instantly looked down from his chair into the face of Billy Daily. Ian gasped, and he looked at his watch in disarray.

13

"Mr. Ian Lifeguard? Mr. Ian, help him!" the thirty-five-year-old man cried.

"What Billy? What's the matter? What's going on, dude?" Ian shouted.

Ian was very familiar with Billy, who was in fact beloved by many in Castle Reef. A gentle, loving, and special man with Down syndrome, Billy lived by himself and worked for the town keeping the beaches and community clean by doing trash removal. Billy's only family compromised of the folks in Castle Reef. Abandoned as a baby and raised as a foster child in several families, he was surprisingly emancipated at the age of eighteen. The city had stepped in and provided an apartment for him by working with the state's disability assistance program.

Despite Ian's self-centered disposition, he had always been kind to Billy. Even before Ian had attended college, he would often frequent the beach at Castle Reef. He found himself keeping Billy Daily from ridicule and practical jokes that others tried to play on him during the summer tourist season. Ian always made sure he was protected, and this caused Billy to trust him.

"I can't wake him up. He asleep. He... He look real bad and scaryyeee!" Billy then dropped his head down all the way into his florescent green vest and remained motionless.

Grabbing the two-way radio and jumping down off the high stand, Ian asked him very gently in a fearful whisper, "Billy, tell me where the man is. Please, Billy, tell me."

Without looking up, Billy pointed south in the direction of the jetty that was three hundred yards away.

"Stay here, dude, don't leave, okay? Do you understand me, Billy?"

"Yes, sir, yes, I will stay." Billy sighed and wiped his eyes, keeping his chin down into his vest.

Ian then jumped on the ATV and headed toward the jetty. As the breeze hit Ian's face; he grabbed the radio out of the holder and called the station.

"CR Base, hey, this is Ian at zone 1. I've just been informed by Billy that he found a man who won't wake up. I'm headed to the Jetty; that's where Billy says he is."

A serious male monotone voice responded over the radio. "CR Homebase to Ian, we copy, let us know your status when you get to him."

"10-4, Base, Ian out."

Ian closed in on the jagged rock jetty that curved south. The surf was only one third of the way up on the rocks, and the sun was nearing the center of the sky. Ian's heart began to race faster than the vehicle he was riding.

#

Upon seeing Kendra approaching the table, the man swiftly pressed a button on his strange device and moved it to the side.

"Here's your root beer, sir. Are you ready to order?" said the young waitress, placing the frosted glass and straw in front of him.

"Thank you. I will just have a cheese sandwich on white bread."

"Is that all you want, sir?" asked the puzzled, young and inexperienced server.

The blue-eyed man looked directly at her with a seemingly, painted smile on his face.

Kendra felt nervous inside. It was as if he was looking right through her.

"I think we can do that, um… Are you sure I can't get you anything else?" She avoided his eyes.

"No, Kendra," he said, sipping from his personal metal straw he had just put into his glass. Suddenly, his face became flushed. His smirk instantly turned into a scowl.

"Is something wrong, sir?" Kendra was becoming increasingly worried.

"I thought I told you I wanted diet root beer." There was a tone of anger in his voice, and he became motionless.

"Oh, my bad. I'm truly sorry, sir; I will fix that right now," said the teen in a quivering voice.

"Unacceptable!" the man retorted.

Kendra grabbed the glass and broke free from the presence of the man, who oddly made her feel sick to her stomach. In a panic, she made her way into the kitchen to find her boss.

#

"Good morning, Chief." Officer Sanchez greeted Julie with a smile.

"Hey, Chris, long night?"

"Yes, ma'am, the graveyard was pretty boring." The tall, forty-year-old cop yawned as he walked down the hall past the processing room and jail. Before he stepped into the men's locker room, he looked at Julie and yawned again.

"I don't think any of us will ever get used to that shift," Julie said sympathetically.

"You got that right!" The tired officer scratched his head and rubbed his eyes.

"Have a great rest of your day, my friend."

"See ya tomorrow, Chief."

"Don't forget to say hi to Jasmine and the kiddos for me."

"You bet. *Hasta luego!*" Sanchez entered the locker room.

Julie checked the message board and then walked into the main office of the police station. On the walls were many large framed pictures of the ocean mixed with portraits of past police chiefs. Appropriately, over her desk was a framed photo of her father wearing his signature blue cap, which now rested upon Julie's head.

John Kerrig was a tall, muscular, and broad-faced man who always looked intimidating, but was a teddy bear at heart to all who knew him. He had worked in law enforcement for several years before retiring to Castle Reef. His original intent was to just relax and spend his time fishing, but somehow, he could never keep himself from helping the police department.

Eventually, John joined the department part-time until ultimately it became his entire world.

Julie had no living relatives that she was aware of. If she had any, they never kept in touch. Her mother had died during her childbirth, with Julie miraculously surviving. As a widower, John had raised her by himself for eighteen years until she was on her own. He was a strong father who made sure that his daughter was well educated, socially adjusted, and very prepared for any of life's obstacles.

Not only was John Kerrig a great father, but he was committed to his wife even after her untimely death. John never even dated, much less considered remarrying. Yet, he always made it a point to have older women of positive influence speak into Julie's life as she grew up. One of those special ladies was Shirley Allen. A single seventy-five-year-old, Shirley was a dispatcher for the Castle Reef Police Department, and Julie loved her like family.

"Good morning to you, our dear Chief Kerrig!" said the stout and jolly gray-haired woman at the computer desk.

"Good morning, Mama Shirley." Julie looked past her and laughed.

"What's so funny?" Shirley asked, spinning around in her chair.

"It looks like Judy is stylin' this morning." Julie walked up to Shirley's desk.

"Oh, that silly Sanchez, he found those sunglasses in the beach parking lot this morning."

"You know that rescue dummy gives me the creeps, right?" Julie leaned over and hugged her tightly, laughing.

In the far corner by the evidence safe was a female mannequin, clothed in a one piece bathing suit with a pair of sunglasses on her head. It was intended for beach rescue training purposes, but thanks to all the male officers, Judy was used mostly for their practical jokes.

Julie was getting ready to ask Shirley about the delicious-looking pecan pastry sitting on her desk when suddenly a call came over the radio from the lifeguard dispatch.

"PD Dispatch, this is CR Guard, go to one," said the stoic male voice.

Shirley turned quickly, switching the auxiliary feed to channel one and spoke into the table mic, while depressing the base switch.

"PD Dispatch, go ahead."

"10-33, zone 1 reporting an unresponsive male, guard is en route."

"10-4, please advise," Shirley shook her head.

"10-12, stand by," the life guard office dispatcher's voice droned.

Julie then turned and looked outside, to the busy street, in deep thought. The word "unresponsive" meant more to her than anyone could imagine. It was the same word that always plagued an officer, a dispatcher, a citizen, and even a daughter. The same word she expected to hear while on duty three years ago on March 16. Instead, her dad had just vanished with no trace. Tears welled up into her eyes.

"Are you okay, honey?" Shirley asked, as she awkwardly attempted to get up out of her cushioned rolling chair.

"Yeah, yeah, it's just..."

Julie had the uncanny ability to instantaneously jump from the past to the present. She learned to do this every time she awoke from a dream about her father during the last three years. She turned her attention to the matter at hand.

"I wonder what that could be about?" asked Julie, quickly turning and wiping her eyes.

"I don't know, Jules, it doesn't sound good that's for sure." Shirley sighed, shaking her head slowly.

#

Vicki had spent the morning typing a few letters and filing some reports. She had contacted her father and discovered that he didn't have any work for her at the press office. With her paperwork all caught up, she found herself with nothing to do except wonder what the call was all about earlier with the mayor. The only JK she knew of in Castle Reef or Brighton County had to be JK Reynolds. She started leafing through the office call records slowly on her laptop to investigate. The door to her office opened abruptly.

"Did you find it yet?" asked the serious and trembling voice of Mayor Willis. "I know what you are looking for."

Vicki jumped and let out a short quiet shriek. "You startled me!"

"Sorry, Vicki, I need to know," asked the perspiring mayor.

"I don't know what you are asking about, sir?"

Vicki was starting to panic inside, but she didn't want to let on to the mayor. She played it cool and waited for his response.

"Joan said you were trying to find the amended transcribed minutes from last month's council meeting in order to file them," said the mayor forcefully.

The mayor looked at her with his bloodshot brown eyes. She noticed that he looked very tired even though it was still morning. Joan had never told her to look for what the mayor was inquiring about. This must have been her way of warning Vicki. She had to think of something fast.

"Well, yes, sir, I think they must have been filed under a different name or with a different document. That stuff happens all the time with the records we get from the county courthouse."

Relieved that she had come up with an answer so quickly, Vicki slowly closed the lid of her laptop. She stood up and walked over to the wall of file cabinets in the main office. Facing them, she gained her composure and then turned around to face the mayor, waiting for his response.

"Okay, well, I need you to locate that May 15 meeting transcript as soon as you can and bring it directly to me. You don't have to say anything about this to anyone else; just find the report and bring it to me directly," said Willis sternly.

The mayor exhaled slowly and wiped his brow with his handkerchief. He glanced at Vicki briefly, then hurried to his office.

Vicki turned her attention back to the file drawers, pretending to look for the report that Mayor Willis was desperately searching for. She thought to herself; *This is becoming odd very quickly. I can't wait to let Julie know about this at lunchtime. What could be such a big deal about a town council meeting transcript anyway?*

chapter

3

Julie stood looking blankly across the room, as the radio transmission from the lifeguard station finished. It was low tide, and the remains of an elderly male had been found on the rocks of the southern shore. The man was thought to be Charlie Philips, which caused her mind to race. *Why do these tragedies always happen to good people?*

"Are you okay, sweetheart?" Shirley asked tenderly.

"Yes, I'm fine. Send Kenny down there. Tell him I'll meet him in ten minutes or less." Julie's voice cracked as she moved into the corridor.

"Let me know if I can help in any way," Shirley called out from her chair.

Julie made her way to the parking lot, walking swiftly to her patrol SUV. This was the first emergency call of the season and the first for her as the police chief. She knew that this event would define how she would be perceived by her coworkers and the entire town. She had to quickly collect herself, draw on her knowledge and skills with the utmost professionalism, and most of all, it was imperative for her to respond like a Kerrig.

Opening the door of the Ford Bronco, Julie stepped up and into the vehicle in one smooth motion. She started up the truck and promptly pulled out of the station lot with lights and siren engaged.

#

"Um, excuse me, Mr. Green, sorry to bother you." The embarrassed, skinny high school student stepped into Trent's office.

"Hi, Kendra. Remember, it's Trent, please." He smiled at the seemingly upset employee.

"Yeah, sorry, um…I just messed up a drink order for this really strange guy and he is creeping me out." Kendra's voice quivered.

"Hey, hey, calm down. It's an easy mistake to make," said Trent kindly.

"I must have pushed the wrong button on the…on the…the…" explained the flustered teen.

"You mean the bar gun? The one with all the buttons?" remarked Trent, with a smile.

"Yeah, that thing. I didn't mean to mess up. I'm so sorry."

"This is all new for you, and it's all part of the learning curve," assured her boss.

"What am I going to tell him? He's really weird, Mr. Green, and he's scaring me." Kendra began to panic.

"Slow down, Kendra. It's all right. Tell me more about this customer, why do you think so he's so weird?" Trent stood up.

"Okay, I'm sorry, I just…Well, he's making me feel very uncomfortable. He's just acting like…like, um, sorry I can't explain, I know this is my first job, but I…" The teen began to cry.

"It's all good. Everything will be fine," Trent gently took the glass she was holding and set it down on his desk. He slowly walked Kendra back out into the kitchen.

"I know I'm making a big deal out of something so small. I tend to overreact sometimes." Visibly upset, Kendra began to wipe the corner of her eyes with her apron.

"Tell ya what, help Rita finish up in here, and I'll go visit Dr. Strange for you, okay?" Trent smiled and tried to comfort Kendra.

"This makes me look like a real airhead, Mr. Green." Kendra sniffled.

"No, it doesn't, you're fine. It's just a silly mistake. And please, it's Trent, call me Trent."

Trent was a man of compassion, and all of the Green Sea employees respected him for it. He carefully walked Kendra over to Rita and explained the situation to her. Trent then made his way through the double doors of the kitchen that led into the dining room.

"Hey, Wendy, could you get me a diet root beer?" Trent asked the server behind the center island, who was busily folding linen napkins.

"Sure, is there a problem, Trent?" The husky-voiced woman looked concerned.

"Well, Kendra came in all upset about a customer's drink order."

"Oh, you mean that guy sitting back there in the corner?" Wendy nodded toward the far end of the dining room as she handed him the glass. Trent turned and looked to see a thin, neatly dressed man staring directly at him.

"Yeah, I guess that's the one, thanks, Wendy."

As Trent carefully made his way through the dining room, greeting other customers, he noticed the man in the corner slowly beginning to rise from his chair.

"Hi there, I'm Trent the owner of Green Sea." Trent extended his hand as he set the diet root beer on the table.

"Hello, Mr. Green." The man stood facing Trent motionless, with cobalt eyes that never blinked.

"I understand there was a problem with your drink order?" Immediately, Trent knew Kendra was onto something: this guy was a little strange. Trent lowered his hand into his front pocket.

"Where is Kendra Baker?" The man continued to give Trent the same cold gaze.

"She's tied up helping our chef prep dinner. Kendra said you wanted a diet root beer. I apologize for the mix-up." Trent continued to smile despite the situation. The odd man just stood there with a bizarre look on his face and said nothing.

"Is there anything else I can get you, on the house?" Trent asked politely, now beginning to feel a little nauseous.

"There will be no need for that, I am finished here. Put whatever you think is fair on my bill. Now, if you will excuse me."

The man walked swiftly past Trent, through the dining room and up the wide staircase that led to the guest rooms. Trent knew that this guy definitely had issues. He glanced at the table where he had been seated and noticed that nothing was on it. It was completely empty. There was no plate, no silverware, or anything. Everything was gone. Ray, the busboy, walked up to Trent.

"I came to clear the table, and it looked just like this. Kendra served him a drink earlier, but I don't know who cleared the table."

"That's okay, Ray, I'll take care of it," he said in a warm, friendly voice.

Inside, however, Trent was now troubled even more than Kendra was several minutes ago. He resolved within himself to look into this strange character that made a simple brunch experience culminate into an awkward mystery. He made his way to the front desk to inquire about the strange guest. The clerk was busy on her computer.

"Hey, Sally, that man who just went past you, going upstairs, what room is he staying in?" asked Trent as he looked up at the second floor balcony.

The young clerk replied, "I have never seen that guy before. I don't think he's a guest, Trent."

Thanking Sally, Trent quickly proceeded up the stairs. As he reached the top, he stopped and looked in both directions. There was no one around. No footsteps, no doors closing, no voices, only the sound of the ice machine at the far end of the south hall dropping its ice cubes.

Trent had a bad feeling about this man and an urgency to find out more about him.

#

"It doesn't look good, Chief," said Officer Kenny Caldwell, walking up to Julie, as she shut her truck door and adjusted her duty belt.

"How long do you think he's been dead?" Julie rubbed her hands together as she walked toward the rock jetty.

"Maybe an hour or two. 'Rig' hasn't set in yet."

"What do you think happened?" Julie asked, slowly inhaling.

"I think it looks like a drowning, and then he washed up on the rocks and took a beating."

Kenny slowed down and allowed Julie to enter the scene first.

The body was on a plastic tarp pulled away from the water's edge near the rocks. Ian Reynolds and Billy Daily stood at a distance looking on in disbelief. Julie approached the dead man who was facing sideways. She noticed the right side was completely torn open and that a portion of his swim trunks were missing. Bending down and examining the face, she recognized that it was indeed Charlie Philips.

"Oh mercy, Charlie, what happened, my friend?" she whispered, looking at his face carefully.

"Apparently, that lifeguard over there rolled him over to get his vital signs and realized he was dead. He put him on this tarp and dragged him over here because the tide was starting to wash over his body." Officer Caldwell pointed in Ian's direction and knelt down next to Julie.

"Kenny, call the County Coroner and close this side of the beach today," Julie said sternly.

"Yes, ma'am."

"I'll talk to the guard. You give Billy a ride back to the station and have Shirley talk to him. I'll wait here for EMS until you get back."

"You got it, Chief," the officer said, standing up and motioning for Ian and Billy to walk forward.

As Caldwell escorted Billy to his patrol vehicle, Julie stood up, smiling briefly at Billy, and then turned to face Ian Reynolds. Her expression suddenly became hard and serious. She knew the individual she was about to question.

"You're JK Reynolds's boy, aren't you?"

"Uh, excuse me? I'm not a boy." Ian became immediately defensive.

"You're a twenty-one-year-old college student. You have an important summer job that you obviously don't take seriously enough. A naval veteran, who was an avid swimmer, I might add, has drowned on your watch, and you're upset because I asked you if you were JK Reynolds's boy? What am I missing here?" Julie didn't flinch as she stared down the muscular twenty-one-year-old.

"Dude, this is messed up! I don't have to take this crap!"

"Well, Mr. Reynolds, I think your attitude is crap, and you're going to have to start learning a little respect. You can begin by addressing me as Chief Kerrig for starters."

"Do what? Do you know who I am?" Ian retorted defiantly.

"Oh yes, yes, I know who you are. You're the Reynolds's boy, remember? Apparently, you don't know who I am! You are going to start giving me all the details from the moment you left the party at 2:17 this morning, up until just a minute ago when you felt you were entitled to be disrespectful to an officer of the law. Got it?" Julie's eyes shot into his soul as she stepped forward.

"How did you know about any party?" Ian questioned nervously.

Julie tilted her head from side to side in order to loosen up her neck. She was certainly ready and willing to take this punk down quickly; however, holding a seventh-degree black belt kept her self-disciplined and in control. Instead, she briefly sighed, spoke a series of numerical codes into her shoulder mic, and then crossed her arms waiting patiently for the now visibly shaken lifeguard to start talking.

"What are you looking at? This is crazy! I find an old dude who's dead, and now I'm on trial?" Ian kicked some sand as he shook his head looking at the surf. For a long moment, it was silent, with the exception of the crashing waves hitting the shoreline.

"Let's go, Mr. Reynolds. I don't have time for this!"

"It's Ian. Call me Ian." There was another long pause. "Please... Chief?"

"Okay, Ian, that's progress. Now, I need to know all the details from the beginning," Julie asked patiently.

Ian reluctantly began telling her, in-depth, the last nine hours of his whereabouts, as she waited for the EMS vehicles and Dr. Gary Hackett, the coroner, to arrive. It was almost noon, and the tourists were starting to populate the beach.

#

Mike finished putting his tools back into his canvas bag and closed the door to room 115. He found nothing wrong with the television, satellite receiver, or any connections. He had assured the guest that everything was back to normal, but it still puzzled him. Was it a VHF frequency surge from a watercraft offshore? Maybe it was a solar flare? Regardless, he had never encountered something that weird before but soon brushed it off and proceeded down the hallway.

"Hey, Trent, I'm finished up here for now. I just need to take a look at the ice machine before I go to lunch," said Mike quietly, into his two-way radio.

"Sounds good, Mike. Before you take your lunch, can you drop by my office? I need to speak with you about something."

"10-4, good buddy, hope everything is okay." Mike raised his brow as he placed the radio in his back pocket and made his way down the hall toward the ice machine. The trouble he detected in his friend's voice had him concerned.

The role of handyman was a perfect fit for Mike Rawlings. Despite being ten years older than Trent, their friendship and working relationship from the corporate world continued on in Castle Reef with the Green Sea Inn. A native New Yorker and single guy, whose marriage sadly ended after only a short time, Mike had been ready for a fresh start when Trent invited him along on this journey. Now he was stress-free and truly enjoying this season of his life.

"Excuse me, sir," came a soft female voice from behind him. Mike turned to see a beautiful woman smiling at him. He fumbled his tool bag and then awkwardly dropped his screw gun on his left foot.

"Yes, can I…can I help you?" Mike said, grimacing in pain.

"Sorry, that looked like it hurt." The lady smiled as she adjusted her sunglasses a little higher on her dirty blonde head.

"Um, yeah, a little bit…Is there something you need, ma'am?"

"Well, I'm about ready to hit the beach, and I needed some ice for my cooler, but the machine up here isn't working." She looked at Mike with a flirtatious grin.

"Yes, I was just headed that way." Mike cleared his throat and put his screw gun back into his tool bag. He then looked down the hall, away from her gaze.

"I think it does have ice in it, but maybe the door is stuck or jammed," she said as she started walking in front of Mike.

"Are you the one who called and reported it?" Mike was now obviously distracted and wishing he had answered this call sooner.

The lady giggled. "Yes, that was me."

They both made it to the vending area, and he approached the ice machine. The woman stepped back. Mike attempted to lift the bin door. It was definitely jammed. Eventually, he got it open by using a screwdriver.

"Wow, thanks so much." She smiled in appreciation.

"No worries, ma'am," Mike said politely.

"By the way, my name is Karen, and thanks again." She extended her hand.

"I'm Mike, are you enjoying your stay here in Castle Reef?" he said, shaking her hand soft and slow.

"For sure, this place is awesome and the town is beautiful," Karen said, adjusting her beach cover up.

"There's nothing like it anywhere." Mike was feeling a little more comfortable.

"My friend Jill and I arrived last night, and it is truly like something out of a movie or a novel." Karen smiled real big again.

"Yeah, I've been here for close to six years, and it never gets old." Mike's heart was starting to pound a little faster with each minute he spoke to her.

"That is so cool! Hey, maybe I will run into you again while we're here? You never know!" Karen's attractive smile had Mike smitten.

"Yup, you never know." Mike was definitely blushing.

"Well, Mike, I need to get going. Like I said, I'm headed to the beach, and I have to go grab my cooler. Thank you soooo much!" Karen winked and turned to go back to her room.

"You're...welcome... Have a great day." Mike's voice faltered.

He stood there watching her walk out of sight and wondered what had just happened.

Before Mike left the vending area, he made a quick adjustment on the ice machine, noting that the bin level was extra high. His palms were sweating, and his heart rate had increased. He laughed to himself, wiped his hands on his cargo shorts, and headed downstairs to stop by Trent's office before lunch.

#

"So I woke up and Billy was standing there upset, asking me to help." Ian finished with a big sigh and then sat down in the sand shaking his head.

"Well, Billy trusts you, and he obviously didn't know you were up on your chair, asleep."

Julie turned to the EMS vehicles arriving along with the county coroner's truck.

"Now what happens?" Ian was still feeling embarrassed.

"You get yourself up and get to work. Drag the guard tower, with those big muscles, over there about hundred yards so we can block off this area," said Julie, pointing north.

"Okay, then what?" mumbled Ian.

"After you do that, you can help the EMTs and Officer Caldwell set up a perimeter of caution tape." Julie continued to gesture with her hands as she spoke.

"I'll probably call it a day after I do that."

"No, you'll go back to work and you will sleep later. Do you understand me?"

Ian paused. "Yes, Chief." He turned away from Julie and stared at the water.

Julie sighed and then walked toward the arriving emergency vehicles, noticing the tourists in the distance, who were curiously staring at their flashing blue and red lights. She instructed the EMTs to document everything and to quickly remove the corpse as soon as Dr. Hackett was finished examining the body. Julie then motioned to the coroner as he got out of his vehicle.

"Hello, Chief," said the very tall middle-aged man.

"Hi, Gary, sorry it's never over a cup of coffee. It looks like Charlie had some trouble this morning in the surf. His body got pretty messed up on the rocks."

"Let's take a look. He was a great guy. I've known him for a long time. What a shame," remarked the doctor, recognizing the dead body lying in the distance.

Dr. Gary Hackett walked with Julie to the scene, as he cleaned his sunglasses with one of his monogrammed handkerchiefs, which he always carried in his shirt pocket. For over thirty years, his outstanding reputation had preceded the fifty-nine-year-old forensic doctor from Brighton County.

"Officer Caldwell should be here any minute to get this area marked off," Julie said, watching Gary do his examination.

Dr. Hackett opened his small kit that he was carrying and took out a pair of latex gloves.

He then stretched each glove carefully over his hands and proceeded to examine the mouth and wounds of Charlie's dead body, using his unique instruments.

"Obviously, an autopsy will tell us more, but I don't think Charlie died by drowning."

Gary's face was puzzled.

"What are you telling me, Doc?" Julie looked at his expression and silently gulped.

"He died of this large wound on his side, I believe," said the doctor, as he pointed.

"So he was swimming and happened to hit these rocks? That's impossible! He's a Navy veteran. The rocks are only covered at high tide. Besides, rigor mortis hasn't set in." Julie was more puzzled than the coroner.

"You're spot on, Chief. This man has only been dead for about four hours."

Officer Caldwell pulled up in his vehicle and got out. He quickly walked up to the two baffled officials. "Billy is giving Shirley his statement. What can I do, Chief?"

"Take Ian, tape off this area, and make sure you help the EMTs get the body off the beach as soon as Dr. Hackett is finished," instructed Julie.

"You got it, Chief," said Caldwell.

Julie turned her attention back to Dr. Hackett.

"What I'm about to tell you is only speculation. I think he was severely bitten," said Hackett as he removed his gloves and wrapped them in his handkerchief.

"You're telling me a…shark?" Julie whispered, with wide eyes.

"It appears so, but I'm not familiar with this bite pattern. The autopsy will tell us more."

The doctor appeared to be very disturbed while he finished putting his instruments away.

Julie looked at the body one more time before the zipper closed. This was the first shark attack that she had ever encountered during her time on the police force. It seemed so surreal. Julie asked Gary to notify her as soon as he had the results of the autopsy. She made her way back to the vehicle in deep thought, looking down at her feet moving across the sand.

"Kenny, make sure you get a written statement from the Reynold's boy over there. Tell him it better match what he told me." Julie somehow found herself getting angry all over again.

"Yes, ma'am," replied the officer.

"After you get this area secured, continue to patrol it. I'll be at the station," she said, approaching her SUV.

"You bet," Caldwell responded.

Before getting into the vehicle, Julie turned and faced the ocean. She knew she needed to be objective and take control of the situation. She looked out over the waves that were crashing into the white sand and took a deep breath. Exhaling slowly, the words fell softly across her lips, "Oh, Daddy, I sure could use your help right now."

chapter

4

One hundred and sixty miles northwest of Brighton, a long black limousine left a private airstrip escorted by two unmarked security vehicles. Inside sat Devin Alexander, the founder and CEO of Alexander Industries, along with State Representative JK Reynolds, chairman of the House Armed Services Committee for the United States. As the convoy traveled swiftly along the winding four-lane highway into the mountains, the two men were busy exchanging pleasantries and filling their glasses with expensive scotch whiskey.

"JK! It's delightful to meet with you once again," said the heavyset, elderly billionaire that was comfortably positioned across from JK Reynolds.

"My pleasure, Devin, and how is your wife?" Reynolds asked.

"Valerie is doing better since your last visit. The doctors say she has a better chance with the new stem cell research we are implementing."

"That's good news, and your daughter?"

"Oh yes, of course, Cortney. She is a rock star. She has caused our company to double its quarterly forecast. Although she has an unorthodox approach to our business model, I am so proud of her. She is not only our lead scientist, but I recently moved her into product development and chief of operations as well," said Alexander proudly.

Devin Alexander founded his prestigious tech company in 1994 at the start of the dot-com bubble. He had doubled its growth each year since and was beginning to move into filling large government defense contracts. Alexander Industries employed many workers that were housed on-site and paid extremely well. The majority of the work and development were underground and remained top secret.

"I sure wish my son had the same motivation as your daughter," said Reynolds with a tone of disgust in his voice.

"Well, JK, maybe he needs to be in a position of power along with his inherited money!" cackled the filthy rich executive.

"Maybe so, I can't figure that boy out. He has so much potential, but he's too busy enjoying the college experience."

"Let him go to all the parties and have all the girls he wants. Then, when he gets it out of his system, maybe he'll come around and realize it's all about making money and keeping the family name," said Devin, pouring another drink for himself.

"You make a good point, Devin. I think everyone of us did stuff like that in our younger days," insisted Reynolds.

"Indeed, as I recall, Janet has some wild stories about you!" babbled the overweight executive.

"Hey now!" laughed the politician. "We're here to talk about business, not all the skeletons in our closets!" announced JK with a forceful laugh.

Both men clinked their tumblers together in a toast, followed by a burst of loud laughter.

The limo was heading for a massive four-hundred-acre complex located in the nearby mountain range.

Representative Reynolds, now serving in his third term as a ranking member of the House of Representatives, had traveled to Alexander Industries in order to make the final arrangements on a multimillion-dollar government contract. JK, like any truly corrupt politician, was accustomed to working deals to his advantage. Born and raised in Brighton County, Reynolds came from an affluent family that had made its wealth in the textile industry. He had married his wife Janet while still in college, and they had one child at home, a son, named Ian.

#

"It just doesn't make sense. The creepy guy got up and left. Before I knew it, I turned around and Ray, the busboy, tells me there wasn't anything left on the table where the man was sitting." Trent leaned back in his chair staring at Mike.

"That is definitely bizarre, my friend," Mike said as he leaned forward and put his elbows on Trent's desk.

"Kendra was a mess after waiting on the guy," Trent ran his hands through his wavy brown hair and chuckled.

"Do we know what room he is staying in?" asked Mike.

"According to the front desk, he isn't one of our guests," Trent muttered.

"Don't worry, Trent, I'll keep an eye out for the guy," assured Mike.

"Thanks, man. He was up there before you ever went to room 115 and just disappeared."

"Yeah, about that satellite ordeal... Nothing seemed to be wrong with the receiver or television and..." Mike was interrupted by the sudden laughter from the kitchen outside of Trent's office. It was Francis O'Reily who had just returned from Ocean's market.

"All right, man, I'm going to lunch and then maybe hit the beach afterward. I met this..."

Mike stopped. Francis O'Reily stepped into the doorway. Mike grinned and rolled his eyes.

"Hey thar, bottom of tha' mornin' to ya!" said the laughing Irishman.

"So it is, my friend. How are you, Mr. O'Reily," Trent said, smiling respectfully.

"Got ya catch of the day at Foster's, and I will ice them down fer ya."

"Excellent, thank you. How are Becky and Jerry doing?" asked Trent earnestly.

"They're ornery as ever,'" quipped Francis as he shook his head.

"Guys, I need to get going. See ya, Fran. Talk to ya later, Trent." Mike winked, giving Trent a fist bump as he walked out of the office.

"I'm goin' to get those fishes iced," said Fran as he shuffled off.

Trent smiled and then glanced down at his phone. He was relieved that his screen saver had come on moments before. Finishing his text to Julie, he was just about ready to press the send button when Mike had come knocking on his door. Now, he slowly picked up the phone and stared at the screen to review his typed words. Trent was in deep thought until he caught sight of the thin, curved tattoo line on his left forearm and wrist. He carefully placed the phone back on the desk and slowly walked to the kitchen. He made a conscious decision to wait a while longer.

#

Nina's Café, a small storefront eatery nestled between the post office and the local hardware store on Main Street, was busy serving their famous soups and sandwiches. The popular and quaint place was always packed for lunch because of its simple and inexpensive menu. Nina's, was owned by Nina Lynne, a former professional gymnast who medaled in the 1990 Summer Olympics. She retired in Castle Reef, along with her husband Ben and their two poodles, to enjoy the ocean and open a small restaurant. Today was crowded, as usual, and Vicki Stanwick had been fortunate enough to get a sidewalk table for two.

"Can I get you anything to drink?" asked the young female server.

"Two glasses of raspberry iced tea, please. I'm still waiting for my friend to arrive," said Vicki cheerfully.

"No worries, here are your menus." The server smiled as she laid the small menu cards on the red plaid tablecloth.

Where are you girlfriend? Vicki thought as she texted the same question on her phone and sent it.

"Excuse me, is anyone going to be sitting here with you?"

Vicki looked up into the face of a slender man with a noticeably tight dress shirt. She sat back and looked around to see if he was with anyone else.

"Um, yes, that chair will be occupied shortly, and it won't be by you." Vicki sarcastically laughed.

"I do not understand." The man was clearly taken by surprise.

"I'm sorry that was rude of me. My friend will be showing up any minute." Vicki was trying to be sincere and save face after her snarky comment.

"Apology accepted," said the man, as he straightened his posture and adjusted his shirt cuffs.

Vicki's thoughts began rolling through her mind, as she took in the sight of this strange character. *Why would anyone be wearing a long sleeved dress shirt in the summer at a beach town? He also has some real creepy bright blue eyes that are blankly staring at me.* She managed to smile and pretend that she wasn't freaked out.

"Another table may open up real soon, hopefully," said Vicki optimistically.

"No, that is not likely," he said.

The server came and set a tall glass of tea at each place setting, then smiled and went to the next table. There was an awkward silence.

"Well, lookie there! Jules!" Vicki jumped up and squealed after spotting Julie.

"Hey, girl, so sorry I'm late." Julie hugged her best friend tight and extra-long.

"Not a problem, I was just talking to…um sorry, I didn't catch your name?" asked Vicki.

"No, you didn't, because I didn't give it to you," said the strange man.

Julie quickly turned and moved within inches of the man's face, placing her hand on his shoulder. "I'm Julie Kerrig, police chief of Castle Reef," she said, looking at him directly.

The man stood quiet and motionless. The silent moment seemed to last for several minutes but in reality was only a few seconds.

"Are you here on vacation or business?" Julie asked with a forced smile, then turned and sat down. She was beginning to feel a little nauseous but didn't want anyone to notice.

"Just taking a few days at the beach to work on my research." He seemed to carefully choose his words.

"So what are you researching?" Vicki asked as she raised her left eyebrow.

"I'm an independent market researcher," the man said, as he started to turn away.

Julie saw right through his evasiveness and asked, "Well, enjoy your stay here. Mr...?"

The policewoman began popping her knuckles as she waited. Finally, she slowly got up and once again, leaned in very close to the odd man's face.

"What...is...your...name?" asked Julie with a slow, relentless and stern voice.

The man stepped back in shock and his facial expression changed from arrogance to surprise.

"Do you want to answer me now or shall we take a trip over to the station and you can answer me there?" Julie did not flinch.

"I know my rights. If you are arresting me, then do it Chief Kerrig. Otherwise, I will be leaving," snapped the thin man, slowly walking away. He eventually disappeared into the crowded sidewalk traffic.

Julie stood there for a minute watching and then recalling every detail of the man she had just confronted. She made a mental note of his conversation, what he was wearing, his hair, his hands, and those strange eyes. She then turned back to Vicki and shook her head.

"How long was that fruitcake here? I'm in no mood for another goofball today," she said, exhaling slowly.

"He was only here for about five minutes. He was just looking for a seat, I guess."

"Yeah, I bet. He's a creep and I'm going to make sure we find out all about him." Julie rolled her neck to each side, a gesture she performed an hour ago with Ian Reynolds. She was feeling a little dizzy. *It must be low blood sugar*, she thought, taking a drink of her iced tea.

"Is everything okay, Jules? What's bothering you?" Vicki asked.

The server arrived at the table and topped off their drinks. "Did you gals need more time, or are you ready to order?" she asked.

"Two cups of bisque and two house salads with balsamic." Julie managed to smile as she spoke to the young lady.

"Excellent choices. I will have that out to you soon," said the young lady, picking up the menu cards and making her way back inside.

"Some things never change. It's how we roll, we are the soup and salad express!" Vicki giggled, as she placed her napkin on her lap.

Julie leaned forward and whispered in a serious manner. "Keep this between us."

"Sure, sure, what's going on?" Vicki quickly changed her expression as she noticed her best friend wasn't in a laughing mood.

"Charlie Philips was found washed up on the rocks at the South end this morning."

Vicki gasped. "Oh my, you got to be kidding me? That poor old man, I really loved him."

"Well, we all did, but it gets worse." Julie looked around to see if anyone was listening.

"In what way?" asked Vicki.

"It may have been a shark attack." Julie adjusted her blue cap.

"What? That is pretty scary stuff, Jules." Vicki reacted with big eyes and nearly choked on her raspberry tea.

"I will know more soon. Keep this quiet until I learn more of the details. Your dad can call Shirley in the morning for the press release," whispered Julie.

Julie then nodded toward the server who was coming out the café door. Vicki winked at Julie, and they both stopped their conversation. The energetic girl arrived and gently placed the two bowls of Nina's signature crab bisque and garden salads in front of them. She carefully topped off their glasses again.

"You're all set. Is there anything else I can get you ladies?" she said with a cheerful smile.

"No, thanks so much," Julie said, while Vicki nodded in agreement.

They both waited a few seconds for the server to leave, and then they simultaneously leaned in toward each other.

Vicki looked from side to side and said in a hushed tone, "Hey, I wanted to tell you about my strange morning too."

"What's going on?" asked Julie.

"Mayor Willis was a little unhinged because he couldn't seem to locate the amended minutes of last month's town council meeting."

"That's strange," Julie said as she finished a bite of salad.

"Uh-huh, Joan and I noticed he was really amped up after a call with JK Reynolds…we think."

"Don't get me started on the name Reynolds," said Julie as she rolled her eyes.

"Really not sure what is going on Jules, but he was pretty nervous," Vicki said as she started on her crab bisque.

"Something about that guy has always troubled me. You're the only one I can say this to. I think the mayor isn't who we think he is," Julie said with a look of concern.

"What? That is freaking me out Jules," said Vicki, with a slight tremble in her voice.

"I don't know…I can't put my finger on it now, but something isn't right there," said Julie, as she sipped on her tea and looked out into the sidewalk, bustling with people.

They both realized that they needed to quickly change the subject and finish their lunch together with only small talk and pleasantries, due to the risk of others hearing their conversation, because the café was becoming increasingly crowded. Vicki also wanted to be sensitive to her best friend because she knew it had been a rough morning, and she needed some space.

Unbeknownst to Vicki, Julie was carefully reviewing and making detailed mental notes of all the events and information from the previous five hours. She was well trained in her profession to compartmentalize and multitask while hiding it from others. She did this with ease as she listened to Vicki cheerfully talk about the new additions to her vintage record collection.

Julie had a lot to think about: first the disturbing discovery of Charlie Philips, then the weird man who made her feel sick when she touched his shoulder, and now the mayor's strange behavior.

Julie finished her meal, and as she reached for her glass, she caught another glimpse of the tattooed line on her wrist. This was something she couldn't hide. Vicki stopped in the middle of the description of her newly acquired Moody Blues album. She reached across the table and gently touched Julie's arm and smiled.

"You miss him, don't you?" Vicki asked.

"Yes… Yes, I do," Julie said as she sipped from her glass with tear-filled eyes.

chapter

5

It was two o'clock, and nearly all of the local fishermen in Salty Dog Harbor had finished cleaning their boat decks and dock areas from the morning catch. Several boats, mainly pleasure crafts, were slowly passing through the calm waters and heading out to sea. Couples were walking hand in hand, families laughing together, and many other people were having a good time with their ice-filled coolers and picnic lunches. As the busy summer afternoon continued to play out above the waters, tourists and locals alike were blissfully unaware of the ominous figure swimming fifteen feet below them. The large dark form was circling in a uniform pattern. It measured over nine feet long and was almost four feet wide with distinct triangular pectoral fins.

Oddly, the predator appeared to be uninterested in the remnants of the fish heads, organs, and blood that made its way into the depths of the water. On the contrary, it seemed as if it was searching for something, or perhaps someone, specifically. After several trips around the harbor, it darted toward the inlet and then quickly disappeared between the two large pilings marking the channel leading into the ocean.

#

Lunch had ended and the entire kitchen was in clean up and dinner prep mode. The dining room was empty of all customers. Only the staff members were present performing their assigned duties. Trent was proud of his shift crews and serving staff. Green Sea was more than an inn and restaurant; it was a family.

"Great job, everyone," Trent said, as he went to his office.

He was still troubled by the man that he had encountered earlier and even more so by the unsent text. He sat down and stared at the phone lying on his desk. This time, without giving it a second thought, he swiped the screen to wake it up and then hit the send button.

"What did I just do?" Trent gasped with wide eyes.

Now his stomach was full of butterflies and his palms were getting a little moist. It was time to get some fresh ocean air. He grabbed his keys and headed for the back door.

"Um, hey, guys, I will see you in a couple hours. If you need anything, I've got my phone." Trent waved, as he quickly walked outside.

Sliding his feet across the warm gravel parking area, he got into his truck and drove around the building onto Main Street, heading south to the beach access. The warm breeze was gentle, but his heart was racing, as he recalled the text message he had just sent.

> *Dear Julie, There isn't a day that goes by without me thinking of you. It has been way too long. Can you give me just a moment of your time to talk? Thanks, Trent.*

After parking his truck, Trent made his way down the narrow wood walkway that opened wide onto the beach. It was fairly crowded, but relatively quiet. He noticed a group of children building sandcastles, an elderly couple rinsing their feet off at the foot wash station, and a mother and daughter feeding the seagulls. The sun was reflecting its radiant heat off the sand.

Remarkably, Castle Reef Beach wasn't a wild party type of beach. It was very much family-friendly. Trent looked around and noticed that the warning flags were up, even though there wasn't any high surf. He thought it was odd but quickly dismissed it after being startled.

"So you're down here too?" a familiar voice resounded behind him. Trent turned around to see Mike standing behind him holding a hamburger in one hand and a large drink in the other.

"What are you doing here?" Trent laughed.

"What do you mean? The question is, what are we doing here?" Mike chuckled, sipping on his straw.

"I just needed to see the ocean and get some fresh air, and you?"

"The same, I guess?" Mike took a bite of his burger and adjusted his sunglasses.

After a long pause, Trent cleared his throat. "Well, my friend... the truth is, I finally texted Julie about twenty minutes ago."

"Wow, that took some..." Mike suddenly paused and swallowed hard.

Both men were alarmed to hear the loud warning siren, followed by distant screams and commotion occurring about a hundred yards to their left at the water's edge. A large group of people were frantically running and pointing toward the water.

Suddenly, as if it were in slow motion, everyone in the immediate vicinity witnessed what happened next. A helpless female swimmer thrashed in waist-deep ocean water. Her hands were trying to stop something as she violently shrieked. In an instant, she vanished under the small waves. A large dark dorsal fin appeared for a second and then disappeared where she had been standing only seconds before. Terror gripped everyone on the beach.

#

"I am really anticipating great news from those test results today," remarked the congressman, as he finished his short putt on the eleventh hole of the Alexandria Industries private golf course.

"We have put a lot of effort into its development, and I'm happy we can keep this technology in the United States instead of selling it to other foreign assets." The proud tech company founder removed his glove to adjust his visor.

"I sure hope it stays that way. When can I expect to see the prototype demonstrated?"

"Not quite sure, JK. I will have to ask Cortney and get back with you on that."

"Perfect, I'll have my assistant check my calendar when we get to the clubhouse and inform you of the dates I'm free," said JK, slowly sitting down in his golf cart.

"And the generous donation you and Uncle Sam gave to the Solar Defense Initiative project will definitely speed up the process too. If you know what I mean?" Alexander deviously grinned.

"Absolutely, my friend, absolutely." JK was smiling ear to ear.

The two men drove off to the next hole on the scenic 180-acre course, which was privately nestled in the mountainside. They boastfully exchanged many details of their exotic vacations, expensive homes, and hobbies.

The day had been a great success for both of them because their illegal scheme was beginning to take shape. Devin Alexander was able to secretly funnel more money to a project started by his daughter Cortney and then use the remainder of funds on another slow moving government project known as *The Solar Defense Initiative* or *SDI*.

JK Reynolds, on the other hand, planned to return to Washington and deceive the House Armed Services Committee into thinking that their leading defense contractor was making great progress on SDI. He would falsely report that all military vehicles will be solar powered within five years.

Furthermore, the trusted state representative would continue to invest as an anonymous shareholder in the Cortney Alexander project, expecting to make millions of dollars without any trace of wrongdoing. Two government-funded projects, two different purposes, both under the same name. It was genius.

One mile away and 108 feet below the main level of Alexandria Industries, Cortney Alexander was finishing a private teleconference call. Her sweet, innocent, and loyal scientist persona had all those around her fooled. Ms. Alexander far surpassed that of JK Reynolds's and her father's financial greed. She had an agenda. It was a global one, and her final project would soon make it a reality.

"Thank you, Dr. Zeleny, I will be in touch with you very soon," said the attractive, brown-eyed, and slender woman, proceeding to end another successful meeting.

"Exlent! You velcome, Miz Alexander," the young male said in his broken English.

They both nodded and exchanged cold and empty smiles. Cortney turned off her laptop and quickly put it into her black leather bag. She opened the sliding doors to the soundproofed lab and walked down the hall to the elevator. Pushing the upward arrow button, she thought to herself, *Yes, today was a great success, and now phase 3 will soon be complete.*

#

The station was quiet. Julie was finishing up her report on Charlie Philips and processing his belongings. Across from her, Shirley was busy transcribing the statements given by Billy Daily and Ian Reynolds. Suddenly, a 911 call came in on all frequencies. Shirley turned and looked at her monitor.

"Medical emergency, north end of the beach!" Shirley called out.

Julie jumped up and grabbed her cap. "I'm on it!" She jogged down the hall, turning her radio on, in her belt.

"Let me know what I can do for you sweetie!" shouted the faithful dispatcher.

Outside in the parking lot, Julie opened the SUV door, moved her phone she had left on the driver's seat, and hopped in. Upon starting the vehicle, her eyes fell on the illuminated screen.

She quickly picked up the cell and read the text on the screen.

"There's not a day I don't think of you either Trent," whispered Julie, pulling out of the parking lot with her cruiser's siren blaring toward the beach.

Inside, the station telephone rang. Shirley made her way over to take the call after saying a silent prayer.

"Castle Reef Police Station," Shirley answered, using her normal friendly greeting.

"Is the chief of police available?" said the unusually calm male voice.

"May I ask who is calling?" Shirley asked politely.

"Obviously, she isn't available, Shirley, or you wouldn't have deflected my initial question," the arrogant sounding man responded.

"Sir, may I take a message for the chief? What is the nature of your call?"

"The nature of my call, Ms. Allen, is that I wish to inform Ms. Kerrig that today is just the beginning of the end."

"I'm not sure what you are talking about, sir?" Shirley slowly asked, making sure the call was being digitally recorded.

"Things are only going to get worse for this community and the last remaining Kerrig."

The man's voice suddenly became silent. Shirley realized there was no longer anyone on the other end of the call. Slowly hanging up the phone, she made several notes and finally let out a long sigh.

"Oh, John Kerrig, if only you were here right now."

#

"Quick! Somebody help me!" The young lifeguard shouted, as the small wave splashed and swirled red saltwater around him. He managed to pull the victim up out of the surf and hold her until several others came to assist.

"Hang in there, sweetheart, it's going to be okay," said a young nurse calmly, who happened to be vacationing in Castle Reef. Upon hearing the screams, she had immediately called 911 and then ran to help hold the lifeless woman's head up, as they began to carry her.

Trent and Mike also ran to the water's edge and joined the many stunned onlookers, who were aghast watching the severely bleeding woman.

"No, no, no!" shouted Mike. "It can't be! It can't be!" He frantically stepped in to help them bring her up to the dry sand. Once the woman's body was laid down, he took off his left shoe and quickly began to remove the lace out of the eyelets. Meanwhile, the nurse wrapped the woman in several beach towels to prevent shock and shouted out first-aid orders to those around her.

"Good job with the tourniquet. Make sure you go as high as you can on her thigh," she directed Mike.

"Where is the ambulance? Oh dear God, please help her," whispered Mike, beginning to sob.

Trent knelt down and put his hand on Mike's back. The sounds of sirens in the distance were now moving closer.

"Help is on the way, buddy, she's going to make it, Mike." Trent attempted to console his friend.

Mike's bloody hands tightened the lace on the upper right thigh of the pale young lady who was missing the rest of her leg. The crowd had now been moved back by the lifeguard and several other men. Many people nearby, who had witnessed the horrific scene, began to pack up their beach supplies and take down their umbrellas, creating a chain reaction everywhere else.

"Everybody out of the water!" shouted the lifeguard as he jogged down the shoreline blowing his whistle.

The EMS and the police SUV entered through the emergency vehicle access next to the lifeguard station. People scrambled as the sirens and lights prompted them to make a path.

"They're here, Mike, it's going to be okay," said Trent softly.

"I just met her before lunch, Trent," Mike cried.

"I'm praying, man." Trent continued to reassure his best friend who was now sitting in the sand helpless.

"Why, Trent, why does crap like this happen?" Mike blurted out in his anger.

The paramedics jumped out of their vehicle and quickly got to work on the female victim.

The large group had moved out of the way. Only the nurse remained to help take vital signs as they placed the stretcher into the ambulance while working frantically to save her life. Mike slowly stood up and walked over to a tidal pool, washing his bloodied hands. Trent looked past his friend to see Julie step out of the police cruiser. Their eyes met. The moment was awkward.

It seemed like it lasted for an hour but was quickly interrupted by the loud siren of the EMS vehicle as it pulled away en route to Brighton General Hospital, about fifteen miles away. Trent watched it leave and then turned back only to look into the face of Julie, who now stood only three feet away from him. He gazed into her green eyes that were shaded by the brim of her hat.

She hadn't changed. Her hair, cheekbones, nose, lips, and freckles were just the way he had memorized them. Trent's pulse was starting to race again. He needed to focus.

"Tell me, Trent, what exactly happened?" asked Julie in a serious tone.

"Ah… Hi, um, Mike and I had just gotten down here and then we heard people screaming. We looked over and saw it," Trent said nervously.

"Saw what exactly?" Julie adjusted her cap and ponytail.

"This lady was in the water fighting off a shark. We saw the big fin, then, it pulled her down under. It was terrible, Julie."

The moment Julie heard Trent say her name, something was rekindled inside of her. A knowing in her heart that this was the man she was supposed to marry three years ago.

She was the one who, for all intents and purposes, had left him standing at the altar. Trent was the only man she had ever deeply loved and she walked away. She had to exercise self-control and not give in to what was flooding into her heart and mind. The last time they spoke was at the town hall ceremony, when she was sworn in as police chief. It was only a short and cordial greeting that left a dull ache in her stomach that still remained. Now she had to gather her emotions that were beginning to rise up. This was an emergency rescue scene not a trip down memory lane. It was time to compartmentalize. Julie took a deep breath, sighed, and gently cleared her throat.

"Has anyone sighted the shark again?"

"No, the lifeguard got everyone out of the water, but we haven't seen it again," Trent explained.

"Okay, what did Mike see?" Julie put her hands on her hips.

Trent answered, "The same thing I did, it was so horrific. She was trying so hard to fight it off."

Julie gave Trent an affirmative short nod and walked over to Mike, who was facing south, wiping his hands off with a nearby beach towel. She elected to ask him more detailed questions in order to keep her emotions in check.

"Are you okay, Mike?" asked Julie, after briefly speaking into her shoulder mic, letting Shirley know her status.

"Yeah, I guess so," he said, shaking his head.

"Trent said you guys saw the fin. How big was it in relationship to the woman?"

"Her name is Karen…" Mike said, as he blankly stared at the sand.

"So I take it you know her?" she carefully asked.

Julie could see the familiar pain in Mike's eyes. She remembered that same look in Trent's eyes the day she returned her engagement ring. It caused her to briefly shiver in the summer heat.

"It was pretty big and angular. Maybe two feet or so, but the shark itself was huge!" interjected Trent, walking closer to Julie.

"Interesting…" Julie paused. There was a long silence between them. Only the sound of the waves and people murmuring in the background prevailed.

Julie spoke up, "You better take care of Mike, he looks pretty upset. If I need any other information, I'll call the Green Sea. Thanks, Trent."

"You're welcome…It was nice speaking with you… Chief, sorry it had to be under these circumstances," Trent said respectfully.

"Take care, guys," she said with a professional tone and walked to her vehicle.

Trent carefully watched her leave the beach area and drive slowly south, along the shoreline. He wondered if she had ever read his text. He knew how good she was at hiding her emotions. As he observed the cruiser until it was out of sight, he thought to himself, *Maybe, just maybe, this was a small step toward reconciliation.* He could only hope. Trent shook his head slightly and turned to his troubled friend.

"Mike, this day has to be one of the craziest days of my life."

"Trent?" Mike finally spoke.

"Yeah, buddy, you okay?"

"I want to go to the hospital and check on her."

"Do you think you're fit to drive, big guy?"

"Yeah, I'll be fine. I met her just before lunch when I was working upstairs. I tried to tell you about it earlier."

"I figured something was up when I was talking to you in my office. I know you, man."

"I came to the beach because I was hoping to find her and maybe talk some more. Boy, this went another direction, that's for sure. I pray she makes it." Mike wiped his eyes as he spoke.

"It's gonna be all right. We'll get through this, bro," said Trent, hugging him from the side.

As the two men made it to the parking lot, the lifeguards behind them taped off the beach access and continued moving people out of the area. Castle Reef Beach was officially closing until further notice.

chapter

6

"I understand; keep me posted." The mayor hung up the phone and then sat still staring at the floor for a few seconds.

"Is everything all right, sir?" asked Joan, who had been getting briefed on all the calls to make for him.

"That was Chief Kerrig. She said there were two possible shark attacks today with one fatality. Charlie Philips died this morning, and just a while ago, a female tourist was badly injured. The beach is closed for the rest of the day." Willis stood up and put his arms behind his balding head, exposing his soaked armpits.

"That's terrible, sir," said his secretary, as she turned her head to look outside, purposely avoiding the mayor's repulsive hygiene.

"Is Vicki in her office?" asked the mayor, walking over to his desk.

"I think so. She was about ready to leave the last time I saw her. That was about ten minutes ago." Joan was puzzled by his expression.

Mayor Willis punched the intercom button on the desk. He paced as he waited for a response. He was visibly becoming very angry. After a few seconds, the friendly voice of Ms. Stanwick answered.

"Hi, Mayor, I was just going out the door," remarked Vicki.

"I have been waiting for you to answer! Did you find what I asked you to look for earlier?" the mayor asked impatiently.

Joan watched, as the mayor paced like a caged animal. She did her best to appear as if she didn't know what the conversation was about. She thought back to earlier in the morning and knew it had to be in regard to finding the amended minutes of last month's town hall board meeting. The observant redhead had overheard the intense phone call between Willis and presumably JK Reynolds. After the call, the visibly shaken mayor had asked Joan to find the documents. Instead, she told the mayor that Vicki had already been looking for them in order to complete her monthly filing report. This was Joan's clever way of keeping Vicki in the loop without giving the impression that both ladies knew what was going on, and it seemed to be working.

"Not yet, sir, but I think I can get them to you tomorrow morning," Vicki said softly.

"Very well then, I will see you tomorrow, first thing." Willis forced himself to be cordial as he pressed the intercom button quickly.

"Did you need anything else, sir?" Joan asked politely.

"No, just make those calls before you leave, and if any of the news trucks or reporters show up, just tell them we will have a statement tomorrow morning." The mayor looked at his watch and noticed it was almost five o'clock.

"I will, Mayor. Have a good evening," said Joan, closing the mayor's office door behind her.

Mayor Willis stood with his hands on his hips staring outside at the busy street for a long time. He was feeling the pressure from a man named JK Reynolds who clearly wanted to control Castle Reef. An only child who had everything handed to him by his now deceased parents, David Willis never had never held down a real job. Growing up in Brighton, he hadn't been very popular and barely made it through college. David never really accomplished anything except for his willingness to head up a few select environmental projects at the beach. He ran unopposed for town council and eventually was appointed mayor when his predecessor, Mayor Frank Tibbets, suddenly died of a heart attack. David loved the prestigious position of mayor until today. Now he was filled with dread at the very thought of what he had to do tomorrow.

#

51

"Gary Hackett called to say he is sending you his preliminary findings in the morning," Shirley said, as she poured Chief Kerrig a cup of coffee.

"Thanks, Shirley," said Julie, who was finally sitting down in her office chair. "What a day!"

"Coast Guard is on their way as we speak, and they will be running the coastline to see if they can find that bugger!" the spunky white-haired woman informed her, slapping her desk in frustration.

"Anything else, my favorite dispatcher?" Julie exhaled to relieve some of her stress.

"Yes, there is. I also got a weird call right after you left for the beach," Shirley spoke cautiously.

"Just add it to the list. This whole day has been weird and full of surprises," Julie said as she stirred in the creamer.

"You can listen to it now if you want to. I saved it on a flash drive and sent you the file." Shirley sat down in the chair next to the chief's desk.

"Nah, if it isn't urgent, believe me, it can wait." Julie yawned as she adjusted her uniform shirt.

"Actually, I think you better give it a listen because it's pretty scary and, quite frankly, threatening." The tone in Shirley's voice let Julie know it was serious.

"Really?" Julie leaned forward to her laptop, clicked on the attached file in the e-mail, and it began to play. The moment she heard the voice, she immediately knew who it was. The strange man had escalated the confrontation at Nina's Café. He was clearly breaking the law by making a threat against the community and officers of the law. Julie felt her adrenaline surging once again.

"So eerie and stalker-like," scoffed the chief. "I ran a voice analyzer over the recording, and it had no reading whatsoever. He must have had some unique equipment."

"That guy is a bad egg!" Julie said, swiftly standing up and grabbing her cap.

"That was one of your father's favorite sayings when he knew someone was a criminal," noted Shirley.

"I know, and he was always right, wasn't he, Shirley?" Julie scowled, getting ready to leave.

"Where are you going now, Jules?" The troubled look on Shirley's face made Julie stop.

"I'm going to take a look around town and then go to the hospital and check on the lady who was attacked. I also want a 10-66 sent out to everyone. Tell the guys to keep a lookout for a tall thin man. He's wearing blue dress slacks, a long-sleeved, light-blue dress shirt, and he has steel-blue eyes with sharp facial features, no rings, no watch, no visible tattoos or birthmarks."

After Julie reeled off her photographic memory list, she adjusted her gun in its holster and rubbed her hands together.

"You got it. Is there anything else, Chief?" Shirley smiled slightly, feeling a little less stressed after seeing Julie take charge.

"Yes, get a hold of the county sheriff's office and have them put out an APB on that creep too."

"Okay, Jules, just be careful," Shirley said, scribbling on her notepad.

"One more thing, I want Sanchez to follow you home tonight when he comes in."

"Now that will not be necessary. The Stanwicks live right down the street, remember?" insisted Shirley.

Julie raised her eyebrows, tilted her head, and then smiled at her faithful friend and dispatcher. "That's an order."

"Yes, ma'am," said Shirley sheepishly.

"Also, keep the electronic locks activated. See you tomorrow, Mama Shirley," said Chief Kerrig, quickly walking out the double doors of the station.

On the outside, Julie wanted to give Shirley the impression that everything was under control. Deep inside, however, there was a turbulent uneasiness that she couldn't seem to put her finger on. Julie left the station and drove slowly through town observing every storefront and singling out every male walking alone. There was a lot to ponder on the way to the hospital, but before leaving town, she wanted to make sure the strange individual wasn't nearby. Yes, she was great at compartmentalizing, but it seemed that every section in her heart and mind was rapidly filling up. After her second pass down Main Street, Julie headed west to Brighton General, beginning to pick up speed with blue lights flashing.

Things were quickly intensifying in Castle Reef. A longtime resident had died of an apparent shark attack and another was left with a life-threatening injury. The mayor was acting peculiar, and now there was this strange visitor who made several people, including Julie, feel uneasy. It was rapidly becoming a powder keg of anxiety and stress inside the thirty-four-year-old police chief, who was trying to hold it all together. To make matters more intense, another combustible element was added to the mix. Trent Green had showed up in person. There was no more avoiding him. She had to confront the guilt and shame of breaking his heart because of a tragic event, over which he had no control over. Driving down the highway at 85 mph, tears formed in the corners of Julie's emerald green eyes.

#

After seeing that Mike was stable enough to drive, Trent had made it back to the Green Sea just in time for the final dinner preparations. His staff was moving like busy ants all throughout the restaurant. The dining room was almost completely set up for the arriving guests.

In the kitchen, the entrées were cooking slowly inside the large wall oven and upon the two large stove tops. Rita and Kelli were discussing the menu with the wait staff. Francis and the dishwashers were stocking shelves and organizing the walk in cooler.

"Hey, everyone, sorry I'm late, did you hear?" Trent said apologetically. Everyone looked up and paused.

"Yes, we did. We heard it was horrible," said Rita, wiping her hands on her apron and looking intently at Trent.

Francis added, "It came over yer police scanner in the back." He continued placing cans of olive oil on a lower shelf.

"Did you see anything?" Kelli asked, slowly mixing salad greens.

"Sure did, both Mike and I and practically the whole beach saw the attack. It wasn't good. Say a prayer for the young lady. She is one of our guests. Pray for Mike too; he was pretty shook up."

"You got it, Trent!" affirmed the staff collectively.

"She's at the hospital, and he went to check on her."

Trent paused and then asked, "Do you guys need anything from me?"

"I think we're all good here, Trent," Rita said.

"Did anyone call for me? Any messages?" asked Trent.

"Nope. We're just getting a big crowd tonight due to the beach closing," Kelli chimed in.

"Ther was one thing, Trenty ole lad. The couple stayin' in room 115 is havin' trouble again with ther tellyvision," said Francis, as he finished lifting his last box.

"Thanks, Fran, I'll be sure to check it out. Thanks again, guys, for all you do."

Everyone smiled and went back to their duties. The Green Sea staff knew Trent well enough that they could tell he was troubled. They gave him his space and prepared for a night of hungry guests who were coming for a well-anticipated dining experience. Trent walked into his office and noticed the glass of root beer that Kendra had been holding earlier sitting next to his laptop. It was now room temperature and very full from the melted ice. He grabbed a napkin nearby and picked up the glass carefully by the bottom, slowly carrying it to the prep sink where Kelli was now peeling carrots.

"Excuse me, Kelli, can I have a jar to pour this into and a plastic ziplock bag to put the empty glass in?"

"Sure thing, boss," Kelli said as she reached up to the shelf and handed him a jar. "I'll be right back with the bag."

"Thanks, Kelli," Trent said, as he carefully poured the contents into the empty car and sealed it.

"Here ya go." Kelli Davis returned with a large bag and opened it up for Trent. He then dropped both items into the bag, and Kelli sealed it.

"We are the Green Sea Crime Lab," Trent said jokingly, though inside he was serious.

"What are you doing?" asked Kelli, slightly confused.

"We had a guest this morning that was a little strange to say the least," Trent spoke softly.

"Yeah, that was the dude that gave Kendra the creeps, right?" added Rita.

"Oh yes, it was and it's time to find out who this guy is, maybe with some help from the chief of police," said the determined inn owner, carrying the bag and jar to his office.

Trent shut the door to his office and began his call to the police station. Kelli and Rita looked at each other and smiled. Both ladies knew Trent very well and were fully aware of what he had endured for the past three years. They, along with their husbands, gave him the love and support he needed during the rough several weeks after his wedding was canceled. Somehow they all knew Trent and Julie were meant to be together. Could this be the start of the long-awaited answer to their prayers?

"Castle Reef Police Department," said the pleasant voice on the other end.

"Hey there, Ms. Shirley?" Trent immediately recognized the friendly tone.

"Well hello! Is this Trent? How are you doing, my dear?" Shirley asked excitedly.

"I'm fine, I know it's been a while since we've spoken, I sure do apologize. I bet you are about to leave?"

"No, not yet. Don't you think a thing about it. I know you are a busy man."

"You can say that again." Trent softly cleared his throat. "Is the chief in, by any chance?"

"Oh, Trent, you missed her by a few minutes." Shirley sighed.

"Okay, maybe I can try her tomorrow?" said Trent sheepishly.

"You can do that, or I can leave a message. You can try her on her cell phone too. You still have that number don't you?" Shirley slowed down as to hint the latter suggestion strongly.

"Um, yeah, I still have it. I just wanted to be a little more professional and call the station directly," said Trent, feeling a little embarrassed.

"Give her a call. She's probably at the hospital by now."

"I'll do that, Shirley... Thanks."

Shirley softened her voice. "Trent, she told me you were there with Mike when it happened."

"Yes, Mike and I were there. It was pretty bad. That was a first, for sure. I've never experienced anything like that before." Trent glanced at the glass and bag on his desk.

"Well, I'm here for you, Trent, and more importantly, our Heavenly Father is always here for all of us," said Shirley.

"Yes, I know, Shirley. Thank you for that. I hope I get to see you soon. Come by and have lunch sometime, on the house." Trent changed the direction of the conversation so he wouldn't become emotional because he knew how close Shirley was to Julie.

"I will sure try and take you up on that," remarked the dispatcher.

"Well, I'll talk to you soon. Thanks again."

"Call her, Trent, call her..." Shirley let the silence extend.

"Yes, ma'am," Trent cleared his throat.

"Bye, dear."

"Bye, Shirley." He ended his call, took a deep breath, and then exhaled. He grabbed his truck keys along with the evidence and waved to his staff on the way to the back door. Trent was determined to make it to Brighton County Hospital to catch Julie before she left. In his haste, he failed to notice a dark-blue sedan with tinted windows parked in the driveway of a residence only fifty yards away.

chapter

7

As the sun set, a gentle westerly wind bent the dune grass toward the quiet surf. It was now high tide and only the distant sounds of the busy Main Street prevailed. Nearby, all the lifeguards sat on the wooden benches that were located around the perimeter of the station.

Only a little more than eight hours earlier, everyone had been in the same exact spot, laughing and tolerating the insults hurled by the arrogant college student, Ian Reynolds. The mood had definitely changed from levity to seriousness.

"Ian, did you see anything else that seemed strange today after finding the body down in your assigned area?" asked Tom Martin, the beach director.

"No, man. Everyone just stayed away from the area we taped off, and it ended up busy as usual for the rest of the day." Ian was still feeling guilty but didn't want anyone to know it.

"Okay, I want everyone to report here tomorrow. If the beach is closed, we will all pick up trash and do needed maintenance work," said the stoic Martin, walking back into the lifeguard building.

The somber guards lingered for a moment and then dispersed in different directions, with one exception. Ian sat alone on the long, empty bench. He leaned back against the building and crossed his tan, muscular arms. He didn't feel like partying with his friends tonight. The realization that Charlie Philips would no longer be showing up for his routine early morning swims was starting to set in. Ian was beginning to see that his life was miserable, and he didn't know why. It was a gnawing feeling inside of him that he couldn't ignore. Suddenly, he was startled by a loud voice.

"Hi, Mr. Ian! You...you look sad, very sad."

"Huh? Oh, um, hello there, Billy, I didn't see you walk up," Ian said to the stout short man dressed in bright, flowered shorts and a neon yellow polo shirt.

"Did that man...that man sleep? Did that man go...go to sleep?" Billy stuttered as he slouched looking at the sand.

"Well, Billy, not quite. He..." Ian paused. He searched for a way to tell Billy Daily the truth about Charlie.

Then Billy suddenly straightened up and spoke clearly. "He died today, didn't he, Mr. Ian?"

"Yes. Yes, he did, Billy, and I'm sorry you had to see that this morning, dude." Ian stood up, adjusted his tank top, and slid his feet back into his sandals.

"You, my friend, Mr. Lifeguard Ian." Billy walked over to hug Ian.

Ian awkwardly hugged Billy briefly and quickly looked around to see if anyone was watching. He then picked up his backpack and put it over his left shoulder.

"Come on, Billy, let's go grab a burger. I'll buy you dinner," Ian said, walking toward Main Street with his arm on Billy's shoulder.

#

"Hi, sweets!" said Martha Stanwick, hugging her daughter who had just entered their historic house, built in 1907.

"Hi, Mom." Vicki kissed her mother's cheek and gave her big trademark smile.

"How was your day? Your dad is in the den watching the news."

"It was crazy, as you've probably heard."

"Yes, it was indeed! We were just watching Channel 6 describe the attacks."

"Bad news travels fast. Tomorrow, this place will be swarming with news trucks, reporters, and every kind of social media driven outlet." Vicki sighed. She placed her purse on the foyer table and walked into the den with her mother by her side.

"Hey, hey! There she is!" said the jolly silver-haired man, sitting in a wingback chair holding a television remote.

"Mr. Editor in Chief of The Reef!" Vicki said as she hugged her dad's neck and giggled.

"Glad you made it for dinner. We made the news tonight!" said Greg Stanwick, stroking his mustache.

"Yes, we did. Julie told me about Mr. Philips at lunch, and Joan told me about the lady before I left the office."

"Really?" mused Vicki's father.

Vicki sat down on the couch next to her dad. "Pops, I'm sorry I didn't get a chance to drop by the office to tell you, but it got really crazy today everywhere."

"That's okay, Vicki. The word gets around this town fast, you know?" Greg chuckled and winked at his wife.

"I'll go get the table set while you guys catch up on the details," said Martha, walking into the kitchen.

"I will probably be calling Shirley at the police department and Tom Martin at the lifeguard station, first thing in the morning to get more details," said Vicki's dad.

"Do you want me to get ahold of Julie or Mr. Hackett concerning the body?" asked Vicki.

"That would be great! We need to contact the hospital and see how the young lady is doing too."

"What a story, Dad! I sure hope this doesn't ruin this summer season though," said Vicki with wide eyes.

"I'm afraid it will. There's part of me that doesn't even want to run this story."

Mr. Stanwick turned off the muted television, stood up, and began walking to the kitchen.

Vicki sighed. "Can't blame you there, but it's news and we can't just ignore it."

"Vick, I'll let you know what I find out as soon as I can."

Vicki jumped up and followed her father into the kitchen. This was family night for the Stanwicks, a tradition they began when Vicki first came into their home as a little toddler from Africa, over thirty years ago. They played games, laughed, told stories, and prayed. Tonight was no different. It would be a night of Uno, fellowship, and Martha Stanwick's signature dish linguini and clam sauce, in a beautiful home admired by the many tourists who passed it on their way to the beach.

#

"Yes, sir, I will get it tomorrow. I promise," said the mayor with a tremble in his voice.

Mayor Willis ended his call, locked his office door, and continued to walk down the hall.

Everyone was gone except the janitor, who was busy buffing the lobby floor. Willis exited at the side entry and made his way to his luxury car. The parking lot was empty with the exception of the mayor's Lincoln Town Car and a dark-blue sedan parked in the distance.

The sun had fully set, and it was slowly becoming dark outside. David, however, was rapidly falling into a different kind of darkness. He had finally given into political pressure, greed, and the quest for power over a year ago, shortly after he was elected. He wanted it so badly, and in order to get it, he had to submit to the ugly forces, now at work both within him and upon him. David Willis was a puppet. A shell being gutted weekly in order to achieve the perceived power, at the expense of others. Castle Reef had always elected upstanding community members that carried on a tradition of family values, economic responsibility, and the protection against corruption. This had all changed suddenly when his predecessor, Frank Tibbets, unexpectedly died in his office chair from cardiac arrest. Almost conveniently, David had been handed the opportunity because it was an election year for Brighton County and all of its municipalities.

"Good evening, David Willis." The hollow-sounding voice of a man came from directly behind the mayor.

"What? Excuse me. You startled me. How can I help you?" Willis answered, fumbling with his briefcase.

"I assume everything is running smoothly here in your city?" The man was now visible under a dim parking lot light. He stood tall, thin, and motionless.

"Um…I believe so…and may I ask who you are?" the mayor said with a noticeable tremble in his voice.

"That's not relevant. The important thing for you, David Willis, is to get ready for tomorrow."

"What do you mean by that? Are you a reporter? If so, I have no time for questions!" said Willis abruptly, continuing to walk to his car. The mayor was becoming angry.

I'm going to find out who this guy works for, and I'm going to let whoever it is have a piece of my mind, he thought to himself, unlocking the car door with the key fob remote.

Willis turned to tell the man to politely get lost but was stopped short in mid-sentence. He gasped for air as he found himself being lifted by his neck with a tightly gripped large hand.

In shock, his keys fell first, and then the briefcase released from his hand and bounced off the parking lot pavement. As his feet dangled a foot off the ground, he was swiftly drawn into the face of the one forcefully holding him in midair. The unforgettable bright steel blue eyes were now only inches from his face. The mayor felt as if he was ready to vomit. He could only gurgle and stare directly into what felt like a nightmare.

"David, you will be ready for tomorrow," commanded the unchanging voice of the man—or beast—that seemed to look right into the soul of Willis.

Suddenly, the freakishly strong man released the mayor. Willis stumbled back against his car and tried desperately to catch his breath. He placed both hands on his thighs and bent over, wheezing like an injured animal. All he could do was listen, as the sound of rhythmic footsteps walked away. Once he had composed himself, he lifted his head just in time to watch the car at the far end of the parking lot drive away.

The shaken mayor managed to make it to his townhouse. He dreaded the thought of what "tomorrow" would bring. He couldn't erase the image of the dreadful eyes that were still looking at him when he tried to sleep. David Willis would not find rest tonight.

#

The minister put his arm around the visibly shaken man seated in the waiting room of Brighton County General Hospital. "Mike, we prayed and now we need to trust God."

"You're right, Pastor, thanks for the reminder."

After several minutes, Pastor Hollins noticed that Trent Green had arrived. Trent motioned for him to come over to the hospital snack bar, where he stood holding two bottles of water. Hollins excused himself and walked over to meet him.

"Hi, Trent, there's good news. She's going to make it. The doctors said that they were able to stop the bleeding in time. She made it through surgery."

"That's so good to hear. I have never seen Mike like this before, ever."

"Most of the time, a crisis brings things to the surface in all of our lives," said the pastor of Brighton Community Church.

"He had just met her before lunch," said Trent. Glancing over the pastor's shoulder, he watched Mike rub his forehead with both hands.

Suddenly, the automatic entry doors opened, and Julie Kerrig walked in. Pastor Denny and Trent immediately stopped their conversation and watched her greet Mike before proceeding to the front desk.

"Well, I better get over there and see if Mike needs me," said Trent, with a nervous grin on his face.

"Yes, you *need* to be there for him and…" The pastor paused. "And for her too."

Trent turned and looked at the front desk and back at Pastor Denny. Nothing more needed to be said.

"Will I see you both tomorrow?" asked Denny.

"Tomorrow?" Trent paused and looked at his pastor, puzzled.

"We're having a special 10:00 a.m. prayer service for both communities, in light of Charlie's death and Karen's injury."

"Oh, yeah, sorry. Yes, Mike and I will be there. If not, I know I'll be there," Trent said, reaching out to give his pastor a quick handshake.

"God bless you, Trent," said Denny warmly.

Pastor Denny then called out softly to Julie, "Hey, Jules, thanks for all you do for us." He then exited the hospital after briefly speaking to Mike.

"I didn't expect to see you here," Julie said, as Trent walked up to the counter where she was reviewing paperwork.

"I got here as soon as I could. Mike took it pretty hard, and I knew you would…"

"Would what?" asked the attractive police chief.

"You would be here too." Trent smiled and looked into Julie's eyes.

Quickly Julie looked away. "Well, I was supposed to be here sooner, but I had to check on something in town before I headed this way."

"I really need to talk to you," said Trent softly.

"And what does that mean?" Julie was trying very hard to maintain a tough exterior. Her heart was starting to melt beneath the authoritative image she was so desperately trying to maintain in front of him.

"Well, I have something in my truck I want to show you before you leave," said Trent awkwardly.

"That sounds interesting, the old white truck, huh?" Julie finally allowed a smile to come across her face.

"I know it sounds weird, but…" Trent was feeling like this whole scene had the potential to fall apart right before his eyes.

"Trent…" Julie said with a wavering voice. She finally realized that she had not spoken his name out loud in a very long time. It was so freeing for her to actually hear her own voice say his name. *Trenton Rowan Green*, it was a beautiful name, she thought.

"Yes? What it is is it, Julie?" Trent asked, leaning in.

Julie snapped out of her daydream. "Um, I got your text." Julie's eyes began to slightly well up with tears.

"I'm sorry, I didn't mean to…" apologized Trent.

"It's fine, Trent, I'm okay with it. You're right, we need to talk." Julie felt her heart was going to explode because it was racing so fast. Suddenly, the intensity of the moment was broken up.

"Excuse me, sir, excuse me, Officer." The receptionist interrupted both of them politely.

"Yes?" Julie was blushing, and Trent noticed. She quickly wiped her eyes and turned toward the counter.

"The doctors said it would be fine for you to go into the recovery room now if you'd like," said the elderly receptionist with a smile.

"Yes, please, thank you," said Julie, as she turned to Trent. "I will be right back. Give me about fifteen minutes."

"Sure thing…um, Chief." Trent felt like he was now blushing too.

#

Two figures walked to a parked sports car near the hardware store. The taller and more muscular one was sipping on a milkshake and the shorter and more round silhouette was eating french fries like a baby robin eats worms.

"Good night, Billy," Ian said, as he got into his BMW and put the top down effortlessly with the push of a button.

"Cool, Mr. Ian," said Billy, watching the ribbed vinyl fold into the back compartment of the trunk area.

"Be careful, dude. Don't go down to the beach."

"No, beach bad, beach bad place now," said Billy, shaking his fist.

"I gotta split, Billy, see you around, man."

Ian started his car, pulled away with a short squeal of the tires, and headed to the family beach condo located on the upper dunes, north of the town. Billy watched the car disappear into the darkness. He then turned and walked slowly down a side sandy lane, away from the busy night activity on Main Street. This path led to the Salty Dog

Marina. He always loved to sit on the benches by the dock during the summer nights, watching the boats move with the tide and seeing all of their reflections dance on the water. He made it a routine to stay until his digital watch beeped punctually at 10:00 p.m. Billy would then retreat for the night to his small apartment.

Tonight seemed different. The water appeared to be stirring in different spots. Billy stood up and walked to the edge of the dock. Suddenly, he saw it.

"No, no, that bad! Really bad!" cried Billy. He stood and pointed into the water, attempting to call out again, but this time to no avail. Billy was frozen with fear. The only things moving were the tears rolling down his rosy cheeks and the dreadful figure below the water's surface.

#

"Dispatch, CR88, 10-37 or 38, I have a dark-blue sedan, late model Chevy, with tinted windows, license plate 613NHJ, headed west toward the county line."

"10-4, 88," said the Brighton County dispatcher Officer Chris Sanchez had been on duty for only thirty-eight minutes patrolling the beach access areas, when he caught a glimpse of an unfamiliar vehicle leaving Castle Reef city limits and heading west on Highway 61. The car was currently driving within the speed limit and not exhibiting any noticeable violations. Sanchez called in the license plate and kept his distance, waiting for the county dispatcher to run the plate in the system before he made any attempt to investigate. After about two minutes, the return call came in.

"CR88, negative on the 10-37 and 10-38." There was a long pause.

"Repeat, Dispatch?" Officer Sanchez was confused.

"There was another long pause. 10-22, disregard 88," said the female's voice with no inflection.

"10-4... CR88, 10-10," he finally responded in an obviously disappointed voice.

Chris Sanchez hung his microphone on the dash in disgust and shook his head. He pulled his cruiser over to the shoulder of the highway. He knew something wasn't right because the Brighton County Sheriff's Department had worked in cooperation with the Castle Reef Police Department for many years, sharing mutual investigations and criminal cases. It was very odd to get a disregard code on a vehicle without providing any further information. Chris made some notes on his laptop, then turned his cruiser around, and headed five miles back to Castle Reef.

chapter

8

The indigo sky glowed behind the western range. Below it sat an illuminated brick mansion nestled in the base of the nearby mountain. The Alexander residence was located only two miles from the family's enormous industrial complex. Inside the sixteen thousand square foot house, the three family members were served by a staff of thirty-eight people.

The words "extravagance" and "luxury" were understatements in describing the structure both inside and out. And yet, although this place had everything imaginable, it was missing the main ingredient for any healthy home, the presence of love.

"Hello, Father. How was your day with Congressman Reynolds?" asked the thin and well-dressed daughter of Devin Alexander.

"Cortney, my dear, it was splendid!" Alexander chuckled, while pouring his favorite aged scotch over the silky ice cubes in his tumbler.

"So are we getting more funding for my project?" asked the forty-year-old, only child.

"Yes, indeed!" Devin laughed as he sipped on his second drink.

Cortney knew how to get what she wanted from people, especially her father. She had learned the skill at an early age from her mother, who was heavily medicated and shut away in a remote room of the Alexander mansion due to her illness. Ms. Alexander had the uncanny ability to ask a stranger a few questions in a certain way and then lead them on a deceptive journey that would ultimately end in private information being forfeited or something of great value given up. Her father was always an easy target after several drinks, especially in the evening. He was completely unaware that he was being played, and his devious daughter wanted to keep it that way. She squeezed tighter with each passing moment like a python, working her charm to obtain finances, favorable board decisions, and other inside information, which would help further her secret agenda.

"We are making great progress with the SDI project as well, and we should have the solar prototype ready for demonstration in about two weeks," said Cortney convincingly.

"Excellent, my dear, you are so talented and certainly know how to get things done," said the drunk billionaire.

She began to rub her father's shoulders after he sat down in his expensive recliner while cradling his third drink.

"Well, Cortney, my baby girl, tell me what you need and I'll make it happen." Devin's speech was starting to slur.

"Well, Father… There is another favor I wanted to ask of you." Cortney leaned over her intoxicated parent with rehearsed puppy dog eyes.

"What is it my, my dear?" mumbled Devin as he closed his eyes.

"Father, can you have JK pull some more strings for me?" said Cortney in a sickeningly sweet voice.

Now that Mr. Alexander had reached intoxication, he was putty in the master manipulator's hands. He was a blank check for his twisted daughter, whose terrible motives he never suspected. Before he passed out from his inebriation, he instructed her to tell his secretary to give her whatever she needed. Cortney slowly slipped off her father's shoes, pulled his chair back with the mahogany lever, and put his glass on the white Statuario marble counter. She had succeeded in record time in getting exactly what she needed and was thrilled that her plan was quickly taking form. It bore resemblance to an intricately crafted web which was constructed by a woman who should have been born with a red hourglass birthmark on her back.

#

In the hospital waiting area, Trent stepped aside from Mike and made a call to his inn.

The front desk connected him to room 115. He had forgotten to touch base with the guest who was having satellite reception issues in his room again. It was only after listening to Mike describe how he had met Karen on the second floor earlier in the day that Trent remembered he needed to make the call.

"Hello, this is Trent Green, owner of The Green Sea. I'm so sorry for calling this late."

"Hi, it's fine, Mr. Green. We just got back from dinner," said the guest, in an appreciative manner.

"It's been a very long day. Thank you for your understanding, and I do apologize for not getting back to you sooner. I hear you're having difficulty again with your television reception?" asked Trent.

"Yes, it's the weirdest thing, Mr. Green. The TV will be working fine, then suddenly there is a long burst of static on the screen, followed by a long shrieking noise for about three seconds and then it quits."

"Well, Mike, our guest services manager told me that he couldn't find anything wrong when he stopped by earlier today. Does it happen often or only on one particular channel?"

"All channels, sir. It's random when it happens. It scares the crap out of you because you never know when it's going to go haywire," explained the guest.

"Wow, that is so strange. Tell you what, we will get it looked at first thing in the morning," assured Trent.

"Thanks so much. We just put it on for the kids, especially now that the beach is closed."

Trent paused a few seconds. "I want to give your family a complimentary stay for all the trouble this has caused you," said Trent apologetically.

"Wow, thanks. I wasn't expecting anything. We just wanted to let you know."

"Sir, it's on us. You have a good night, and we will see you around ten, okay?" said Trent in his usual friendly and professional manner.

"Yes, and thanks again. Good night."

After the guest hung up his room phone twenty-two miles away, Trent lowered his cell phone and stood facing the window that over-looked the parking lot. He was puzzled by the mystery of the television. His thoughts were suddenly interrupted by an authoritative, yet kind and familiar feminine voice.

"Hey, guys, is everything all right out here?" asked Chief Kerrig.

Mike looked up to see Chief Kerrig standing directly in front of him with both hands on her hips, smiling at Trent.

"Uh, hi! Yes, we are doing just fine," said Trent, swallowing hard as he turned around.

"Julie, how is she?" asked Mike with concern in his eyes.

Julie grabbed a nearby chair, spun it around, and sat down in it backward. Trent marveled at how seamlessly she did things like that. He knew that she was very athletic and well-trained in the martial arts, but he had always been amazed at her fluid movements when-ever she took a decisive plan of action. Although Trent was physically fit and worked out three days a week, he knew he couldn't hold a candle to Julie. It never intimidated him though or made him feel the need to prove his masculinity. He accepted the fact of who she was and how nicely it all fit with her personality and occupation. He loved Julie dearly for a lot of reasons, and this was just one of many.

"Well, Mike, she's stable which is a good thing."

"Is she awake?" Mike's eyes were wide with anticipation.

"No, oh no, she will be out for a few days the doctors said."

"I can imagine with the trauma and the surgery, right?" added Trent.

"Yes, but she's going to pull through." Julie reassured Mike by reaching out to his arm.

Trent looked down and noticed the tattoo on Julie's arm. Tears flooded his eyes. He quickly turned and wiped them away. Julie looked up and gave him a strange look.

"Are you okay, Trent?" asked Julie, looking a little confused.

"Yeah, yeah, it's nothing, just kind of tired. All this stuff hap-pening, it's kinda crazy."

Trent cleared his throat a couple of times and then faced them both.

Julie looked at Mike. "Jill is here. She's Karen's friend. They allowed her to stay with Karen, so she does have somebody with her whenever she wakes up. Her family has been notified, and they are on their way."

"Any chance I will be able to see her myself?" asked Mike hopefully.

"Right now, it looks like it's her best friend and family only."

"Will she be able to function after this? I mean, I know I'm asking stupid questions, but I'm just trying to process all of this after seeing it happen in slow motion over and over in my head." Mike sat back and exhaled with both arms behind his head.

"She's going to be fine, Mike. Just let the doctors and professionals do their jobs. In time, you'll get to see her," Julie assured Mike.

"Tell you what, buddy, leave a message at the desk for Jill to give to Karen when she wakes up or give Jill your cell number or something," suggested Trent.

"Great idea!" Julie stood up and spun the chair around again like a top and slid it gracefully back into place.

"Mike, I gotta show Julie something I brought. It's in my truck. I'll meet you outside after you finish giving the receptionist your message for Karen and her friend," said Trent.

"Sounds good, guys. Sorry I'm being this way." Mike stood up and headed to the desk.

"Good move, Trent. He's got to get back to reality. I know it sounds cold, but in spite of the circumstances, Mike has to get on with his life and have some sense of normalcy," mentioned Julie, her voice charged with emotion.

As soon as the words left her lips, the realization of what she'd just said hit her. Her face became flushed, while looking into Trent's eyes. The irony that she would verbalize the very statement fitting to her own life—right in front of the man she had hurt so deeply several years ago—and all because of her wounded heart. There was an uneasy pause. They both stood staring at each other; a silent understanding was shared between them.

"You are so right, Julie. That's a great point." Trent broke the moment to free them from their awkwardness.

"What is it you want me to see?" asked Julie after letting out a brief sigh. She began walking toward the automatic doors.

"Well, I was wondering if you could run fingerprints off of a glass and get DNA from a jar of root beer?" Trent walked outside and caught up with her.

"Sure thing, as long as they haven't been compromised by too many people handling the evidence."

"I think it's just two people. One is a server from our dining room, and the other is from a stranger. And I do mean *strange*. This guy acts weird and is very stealth-like. I've seen it myself," Trent said jokingly.

Julie stopped abruptly. She looked at Trent with a serious stare. The last time he saw that look was the night she returned her engagement ring. Trent shivered. He didn't like that look at all.

"Say that again?" asked Julie in a higher-pitched voice than usual. It was obvious she was troubled.

"Yeah, it was Kendra, a high school student, who works the lunch shift and this customer guy, who is skinnier than me and has a beard trimmed close to his face with crazy eyes."

"Trent, I put out a call to look for that same guy tonight. He's bad news. I met him today also. Something isn't right there, I can feel it." Julie turned to look for Trent's familiar truck.

"Wow, that's insane!" Trent paused. "I'm parked over here." Trent pointed to his left, walked in front of Julie, and unlocked his door. He reached across the bench seat and slowly pulled out the large ziplock bag containing the glass and jar.

"The ice has melted obviously, but I left it all in there for DNA purposes," said Trent proudly.

Julie carefully took the bag. "Thanks, I will drop this off at the county lab before I head back to the beach."

"Sure glad I could help," said Trent earnestly.

Trent looked into those beautiful eyes. He studied her ponytail that was resting slightly on her right shoulder. Although she had been through the terrible loss of her father, Julie hadn't aged one bit. Her face had no wrinkles or lines. Her mannerisms were exactly the same as he remembered. This was the woman he wanted to spend the rest of his life with. This was his bride-to-be.

If only she could see it that way, he thought.

What Trent didn't know was that Julie was thinking the same thing about him. She longed for his company and his unfailing love. She knew her past hurt made him hurt more. If only she could break through the seemingly thick and protective wall she had constructed around her heart for three long years. Yet tonight, that barrier was feeling very thin and fragile to her.

Trent, I miss you more than ever, Julie cried out from the inside.

"Hey, it's all good, the receptionist will give Jill my message tonight," said Mike, walking up in the middle of their silence, completely oblivious.

"That's great Mike," Trent said, smiling at Julie.

Both of them gave each other another gaze of mutual understanding before they turned their attention to Mike, who seemed to be acting more like himself.

"We will come here again to see her, don't worry," Trent reassured his friend, glancing at Julie again.

"Keep me posted, you guys. It's getting late, and I need to get to the crime lab before they close," said Julie walking toward her cruiser.

"Thanks for stopping by," said Mike sincerely.

"Yeah, Jules, I mean, Chief, thank you for looking into that."

Julie turned to look at Trent once more before leaving. A large genuine smile spread across her face. "I will be in touch real soon, Trent. Feel free to text me anytime."

Trent smiled and nodded his head. He cherished this meeting. The wall between them was officially coming down.

#

Vicki was driving back to her apartment, less than five blocks from her parent's home, when she suddenly slammed on her brakes. In the middle of the road stood a husky-bodied man with his head down facing the pavement. She quickly rolled down her window and shouted from the yellow antique car.

"Billy? Is that you?"

"Yes, ma'am," said Billy, still motionless, in a low voice.

"I could've hit you, buddy." Vicki's voice was soothing to Billy, who now looked up into the headlights. "Come on, Billy, get in, and I'll drive you home, my friend."

"Thank you, Ms. Vicki." Billy began to walk fast and then opened the passenger door, gladly getting into her '71 VW Super Beetle.

"Why were you standing in the road, buddy?" Vicki shifted and proceeded slowly down the back street toward the center of town.

"I like your car, Ms. Vicki. I like color yellow," said Billy as if he purposely changed the subject.

"Well, thank you, Billy. You scared me, I just about to hit you."

"I live right up here, Ms. Vicki!"

"I know, and you sure do have a nice place, Billy."

"I don't like scared, Ms. Vicki," said Billy, as he put his head down into his chest.

"Oh, Billy, I'm sorry, I heard about everything today. You must have really been scared," said Vicki tenderly.

"Bad! Everything bad and scary!"

"It's okay, Billy, you'll be safe in your home."

"Safe! Thank you, Ms. Vicki." Billy raised his head up and smiled.

Vicki's Volkswagen approached Castle Reef's only traffic light as it turned red. Slowing to a stop, Billy leaned forward and looked up through the small windshield with wide eyes and his mouth fully open.

"Are you okay, Billy? What do you see?" asked Vicki, perplexed.

"Red light! Big red light! No small light!"

"It's our traffic light, Billy, you know that. Are you being silly with me?"

Vicki let a whisper of nervous laughter out from under her breath. She had never seen Billy act like this. Something was troubling him.

"Big red light good. Little red light bad," said Billy, as he put his head back down into his chest.

Vicki had a chill run down her back. She stared at Billy and wondered what he was referring to. A car that had pulled up behind them beeped its horn and snapped her out of the trance of deep thought. The light had turned green. Vicki pulled away and drove into Billy's shared driveway next to the small public library.

"Here you go, Billy. You are home." Vicki smiled at Billy who raised his head and quickly opened the door.

"Thank you, Ms. Vicki. I like your car. I like color of your car."

"You bet, Billy. I like my car too. I like the color yellow."

"My favorite color was red. Now my color yellow."

Vicki felt that she was onto something. Billy, like most Down syndrome adults, was very loveable and kind. However, if something changed his routine or scared him, he became very upset and would self-talk himself through everything.

"Billy, why did you change your mind about the color red?"

"Little red light scared me, that why."

"What little red light, Billy?" asked Vicki carefully.

"The one in the water."

"Water? What did you see, Billy?"

"Little green light, then little red light on big, big, scaryyee fish!"

Billy shut the VW passenger door and walked away quickly down a short sidewalk. He took the lanyard from his neck and used the attached key to unlock his house door. He then turned and waved at Vicki, and she slowly waved back. Billy shut the door fast and turned off the porch light. Vicki sat in her car as it idled and wondered what had just happened in the last fifteen minutes. She took a deep breath, let out the clutch, and pulled away slowly. She needed to get home and get some sleep. Vicki knew that tomorrow was going to be intense at city hall. Maybe a hot bath and *Days of Future Passed* played on her 1977 Lafayette Stereo would be the best remedy.

#

"No, Dad! I'm staying on the beach!" Ian said, as he plopped his massive muscular body on the living room couch of his family's large three bedroom luxury condo.

Earlier, Ian had received several calls from his friends who wanted to go out and party.

Although the opportunity to get drunk, smoke some fresh weed, or possibly sleep with a different girl was tempting, tonight he would decline all invitations. He finally realized, for the first time, that those things would only give him a temporary escape from his miserable life. The police chief's question *"You're the Reynolds boy, aren't you?"* kept playing over and over in his mind. Why? His misery was now escalating due to the fact that JK Reynolds, his father, was on the phone.

"Son, the beach will not be open anytime soon," said Congressman Reynolds.

"People come to this beach to vacation! They love this place!" shouted Ian.

"Ian, I'm telling you to come home. The beach will be closed because of safety concerns until that shark is caught."

"You can't do that! This is my life!" Ian shouted again.

"It's already done, Ian. Safety is our main concern. Your mother and I want you back in Brighton!"

Ian put his phone on speaker and then tossed it on the glass coffee table. JK paused a few seconds and then purposely changed the subject like a true politician.

"Hey, guess what, son? I scored a 91 today golfing with one of our best clients. Do you want to play a couple rounds tomorrow with me and some of my staffers?"

Ian sighed long. "Good night, Dad. Tell Mom if you ever make time to see her that her son said hello."

Ian reached for the phone and pressed the red circular button at the bottom before his father could pitch another insincere offer his way. Truth be told, he had hung up on his parents a long ago. There were countless birthday parties, recitals, football games, and award ceremonies that were missed by both of them. They placed their social activities and themselves over quality family time with their only child. They had made sure he had the best of everything, but the nannies, housekeepers, and private tutors knew Ian better than his own parents. He was wretchedly unhappy with his life. Ian Reynolds was a train wreck waiting to happen.

#

Julie had already finished her takeout dinner from Ocean's Seafood Market. The long and crazy day had finally come to an end. After a much-needed hot shower, she lay in bed staring at the ceiling. She quietly watched occasional shadows move slowly across the room that were projected from passing car headlights on Main Street below. Hundreds of thoughts from the day now raced through her head, but she was taking the time to address each one of them, make mental notes, and then prioritize. Julie had done this nightly ever since she was a child. In the beginning, it was suggested as a way to fall asleep by her dad. He called it the productive version of counting sheep. As she grew older, it became a habit in order to map out the next day.

Looking back, Julie knew that her father was always preparing her for life's challenges. This technique was a great example and just one of many disciplines he had introduced in order to keep her focused, leading to a healthy and balanced life. Tomorrow was already mapped out in her mind. No stress. No worries. Just follow the plan. This was the textbook John Kerrig approach.

Julie took a deep breath and spoke the words out loud like she had done so many nights before. "Good night, Daddy, I love you."

She suppressed the hurt that was still tangled inside. The reality was, her father was gone, but so many questions continued to haunt her. Her father's life resembled a giant book, which she was reluctant to close, because the story was never finished.

In the silence, Julie felt a tugging on her heart. For the first time, she realized how miserable she had allowed herself to become. Quickly sitting up, she reached over to the nightstand and lifted up the worn leather Bible that was buried beneath several magazines.

"What have you been doing, Julie Kerrig?" she asked herself out loud.

Distant memories of singing in church with her father began to trickle into her mind as she opened it. Studying the first few onion skin pages, she could vividly remember giving her life to Jesus on her fourth birthday. She remembered seeing the tears in her father's eyes when he scooped her up and hugged her tightly after praying. *"Never forget He loves you. Never forget John 3:16. I love you, Jules."*

"I will never forget. I will never forget you either. I love you, Daddy," she whispered.

She looked at her father's handwriting of that same Bible verse and noticed how it bled through to the next page. Falling back upon her pillow, tears rolled down the sides of her face.

Julie shut her eyes and managed to do something she hadn't been able to do in three long years.

She began to pray. "Heavenly Father, I am sorry for blaming You. Please forgive me for turning my back on You. I need You Jesus, I can't do this alone." Julie began to weep bitterly.

Her hardened heart was becoming softened. Layer by layer, the hurt and pain was slowly beginning to dissolve.

After a long and precious time in the presence of God, Julie noticed her phone on the nightstand silently lighting up. Letting a few minutes pass, she wiped her eyes and picked it up to see that she had received two text messages. As she began to read them, she sat up in bed. The first text was from Vicki.

Hey there, girlfriend! Talk to you tomorrow…
WEIRD stuff going on around here! Love ya sista!

Julie smiled and shook her head as she let out a long cry sigh. She then scrolled down and read the next and most recent text that had come from Trent.

> *Hey, Jules! (There, I finally said it, unashamed!) Today was a bad day for Castle Reef, but a good day for you and me… I hope. Can we do lunch tomorrow?*

Once again, Julie allowed more tears to find their way into her now tired green eyes. She inhaled slow and long, filling her lungs to their fullest. Finally, she spoke the five words that had been trapped inside of her for such a long time.

"I love you, Trent Green!" Julie exhaled in relief.

After reading his text again, she typed a simple "Yes" along with a smiling emoji and placing the phone back on the nightstand, laid her head on the soft pillow. Tonight, Julie would sleep peacefully without any troublesome dreams.

chapter

9

The morning sun rose over the glassy sea and bathed the beach, now only populated with sandpipers and hermit crabs. It should have been another perfect summer day with many people enjoying the white sand and light green surf. On the contrary, hundreds of tourists were packing up and leaving because of yesterday's shark attack. The commotion of the exiting traffic and the stir of the local news trucks filling the streets began to create an uneasy feeling that there could be more unrest in store for this quaint community.

Meanwhile, several miles away inside the city of Brighton, Pastor Dennis Hollins concluded his short sermon after many community leaders had read Scripture and prayed. As he looked out over the large crowd that filled the pews of Brighton Community Church sanctuary, he realized how well-knit and connected this community was. Charlie Philip's funeral and burial would be at Arlington National Cemetery in Washington DC, but he was still honored by a chaplain of the United States Navy. Furthermore, Karen Anderson's parents were flown in by the United States Coast Guard and given free lodging by several local charities.

At the conclusion of the service, the young pastor, with his signature long hair and mustache, stood in the front lobby and greeted people as they exited.

"Hey, Pastor Denny. Great service, we needed that," said Trent, firmly shaking his pastor's hand.

"Thanks, Trent, glad you made it. Where's Mike?"

"He decided to stay in town and catch up on some service calls."

"Please tell him to let me know if he needs to talk. I'm here for him," said the minister sincerely.

"I will. I know you have always been there for me." Trent smiled.

"It sure looks like your prayers are finally being answered," Denny said quietly, with a curious smile on his face.

Trent nodded at his pastor, looking a little confused. He then exited the building from the side door and into the parking lot. As he turned to hold the door open for the person directly behind him, he saw that it was Julie.

"Oh, hey there!" said Trent, being taken by surprise.

He immediately began replaying Pastor Denny's words in his mind from only seconds ago. Yes, maybe his prayers were being answered. Julie stood smiling and looking very attractive in her police dress uniform.

"This really felt good to be here today," said Julie, walking up to him.

"I agree. Glad to see you again." said Trent warmly. He noticed how beautiful she was and also that something seemed different about her today.

"I'll admit it was a little hard being here, given the situation, but it's not about me, it's about praying for Karen Anderson and respecting Charlie and what he meant to our community."

Julie put her sunglasses on and started walking to her cruiser.

Trent caught up beside her. "It's still hard to believe this happened. Do you think the same shark that attacked Karen is the one that…"

"I hear all the social media platforms and news outlets are reporting it that way, despite the fact that our investigation has only just begun," said Julie, in an almost annoyed tone, as she stopped and surveyed the parking lot.

"That must be frustrating. How do you think this will affect Castle Reef?"

"Well, the tricounty coastlines are now on high alert and our beaches are closed until further notice. Hopefully, this will only last a couple of days."

"Sorry, Julie, you must be stressed," stated Trent compassionately.

"Mr. Green, it comes with the territory. Nobody said this job was going to be easy, right?" Julie eased up, adjusted her uniform, took a deep breath, and then looked over at the man she loved.

Trent smiled cautiously. "You must have a busy day ahead of you."

"Yes, I do, but what are we doing for lunch?" teased Julie with a big grin.

"Oh yeah, um, are we still on for our...I mean, lunch?" Trent asked sheepishly.

"Sure, I said yes last night, remember?" Julie joked.

Trent was embarrassed. "Yes, you did, and I'm sure you don't want to eat at the Green Sea, right?"

"Right! We don't want people to start talking now, do we?" said Julie, smirking and then continued toward her vehicle.

"Well, where do you want to go?" asked Trent, moving closer to her.

"Tell ya what, I will text you around noonish and let you know where we can meet. I've got some things to check on. One of them being that evidence you gave me last night," said Julie.

Trent opened her door. "Sounds good. I look forward to hearing from you, Jules."

Julie sat in the driver's seat; Trent shut the door and bent down to look into her open window. Julie's first instinct was to lean out and kiss him, but she stopped herself. Instead, she was transported back in time to the day when they first met. It had been five years since that routine traffic stop when she pulled over a large rental truck that ran a stop sign entering Castle Reef. After the truck's driver saw the blue flashing lights, he managed to pull into a nearby parking lot. She recalled walking up on the right side of the vehicle, cautiously inspecting the truck. Then she hopped up on the side step and carefully leaned inside the open passenger window with one hand on her weapon. Looking in, she saw a man fumbling with his license and rental paperwork. He was visibly upset and praying out loud as he looked into the driver side mirror. She remembered startling him by asking him where he was headed to. As soon as he turned and faced her, their eyes met. At that moment, she knew her life was never going to be the same.

Within a short period of time, she learned about his move from New York, his recent purchase of the old boarding home, along with many other random subjects. Everything seemed fine until her father pulled up in his patrol car. Being concerned for her safety, he wasn't too happy about the fact that she neglected to radio back to the station after calling in the traffic stop.

Needless to say, she never forgot the lecture Chief Kerrig gave her that evening once she was off duty. He told her emphatically, "I always need to know where you are Jules, as an officer and as my daughter." All of this had made for an interesting start to their relationship. Things changed through time though, as soon as her dad got to know him. John Kerrig and Trent Green eventually became very close friends.

Two years had passed like the changing of the tide. Time quickly rolled along during their dating process, Trent's marriage proposal, their engagement announcement, and finally, the wedding plans. Then tragedy struck. The turbulent waters of life pulled on her for three long years. She couldn't seem to move forward despite the postmortem honor given to her father and the promotion she received at the large community event weeks ago.

However, everything did seem to change the previous night when Julie found herself broken before God. She gave all of her hurt and the unforgiveness to Him. Today's service also seemed to provide her some closure. She knew that she needed to move forward with her life and with the man that she wanted to spend it with. She was more in love with Trent than ever before.

Stay focused, Julie, she thought, as she glided back into the present.

"Are you okay?" asked Trent, with a puzzled look on his face.

"Yes, Trent, I am definitely all right. I will touch base with you in a little bit," said Julie softly.

"That sounds great, Jules."

Julie started her cruiser and slowly drove away. She gave a quick glance in the rearview mirror and saw the love of her life still standing there watching, so she waved out the window for him to see. Trent's heart leapt.

#

"Becky!" yelled the old fisherman frantically at the top of his lungs.

His eccentric wife, dressed in a football jersey, pajama bottoms, and yellow knee-high boots, was busy packing ice around shellfish in the display case inside the market. She quickly dropped her small bucket and scoop and ran to meet him.

"What's the matter, babe?" said Becky with a look of terror on her face.

"Has anyone been aboard the *Susan Marie* since last night?" asked Jerry Foster in a rare, angry, and elevated voice.

Becky gulped. "Why no, dear, what's wrong?"

"Looks like she's been ransacked!" shouted Jerry, throwing his hat across the small gravel parking lot.

"What do you mean?" asked Becky, heading to the dock.

"Stay put, woman! We gotta call the police! We can't touch anything!" screamed the old sailor.

Jerry mumbled a curse word and then sat on the bench nearby. He ran both of his broad hands through his gray wavy hair in anguish. Becky fumbled for her cell phone and frantically began to press numbers on the screen to get help.

As they both gazed at the port side of their fishing boat in disbelief, they noticed that the exterior and upper deck appeared untouched. However, inside the aged craft was an entirely different story. The helm, the mid-cabin, and cargo holds were all destroyed and the electronics had been burnt beyond recognition.

"Shirley, this is Becky. I'm calling you instead of 911, like you've always told me to do. We've got a problem. You better send someone over here right away!"

#

Mike Rawlings walked slowly into his small side office at the Green Sea Inn. He shut the frosted glass-paneled door and sat down in his soft leather chair. Leaning back, he stared at the wall that was decorated with over a hundred pictures. The eclectic collage contained portraits of family, friends, and notable celebrities that he had met throughout his lifetime. They were arranged haphazardly in all types and styles of frames on the pine paneling. One picture caught his eye in particular. It was one of Trent, himself, and his previous wife skating in Rockefeller Center, taken about two years before his divorce. Mike recalled how devastated he was when she decided to leave him. That was over seven years ago. He had never really dated or even taken an interest in any woman since that time. Until he met Karen, that is. She was special.

He needed to find out more about her.

Mike got up and headed out to the front desk. He noticed an elderly couple busy at the counter so he stood in the distance and waited patiently until they were finished.

"You folks drive safe. So sorry you couldn't finish your stay. Please come back and see us," said Mary, the other front desk clerk.

"Hey, Mary, how's it going?" asked Mike quietly.

"Good morning, my friend. How are you today?" she said cheerfully.

"Better than yesterday, that's for sure." Mike leaned on the counter and began fidgeting with the front desk bell.

"Yes, I heard. I'm so sorry about that. That must have been terrible."

"It was, believe me. That's all I saw in my mind last night when I tried to sleep," said Mike, shaking his head.

"It really rocked the town that's for sure. Half of our guests checked out already, including that family from room 115," said Mary, finishing her computer entry.

"Really? I was actually just heading up there to check things out again."

"It was weird, Mike. Did you know that it was the only room that we had an issue with this week?"

"Strange, huh? I'm going to go up to check it out anyway," Mike muttered.

"Is something wrong, Mike? I get the feeling you want to ask me something," said Mary, tilting her head to one side.

"Kind of." Mike shuffled his feet and then leaned on the counter.

"I know it's against our policy, but can you give me the contact info for the two guests that were involved with the...you know... the..." Mike said in a hushed voice.

"The attack?" said the clerk compassionately.

"Yes, I was at the hospital last night and never got her or her best friend's numbers."

"Given the circumstances, Mike, I don't think it's a problem," said Mary, scrolling through the guest software program.

"Jill Sullivan and Karen Anderson, both are from Forked River, New Jersey."

"Thanks so much," Mike said, with a little more life in his eyes, watching Mary quickly scribbling on a notepad.

"You bet. Here ya go."

"If you need me, I will be upstairs figuring out that mystery in 115." Mike took the note and stared at it closely as he walked to the back hall maintenance closet. He wanted to make sure to remember to call Jill and see how Karen was doing if he didn't hear anything by lunchtime.

#

"Has Vicki gotten here yet?" asked the frantic mayor.

"Yes, sir, she's been working on getting you that paperwork," Joan said calmly.

"I've tried her office twice, and she's not picking up," said Mayor Willis, who was pacing like a caged animal.

"Well, sir, she's in the records room, and she said that she would bring it to you as soon as she finishes." Joan almost laughed out loud at the sight of the mayor and his behavior.

"Okay, just keep me posted!" Willis shut his office door and immediately got on the phone.

Joan noticed that the mayor turned his high back chair around and faced the window away from her. She immediately leaned over and called Vicki on her cell phone.

"You better finish with that addendum to last month's meeting or Willis will become unglued," whispered the secretary.

Joan rubbed her left temple and looked over her reading glasses toward the mayor's office.

"Uh-huh, about that…I found something very interesting, plus a real zinger that's gonna rock this town!" Vicki said.

"Shh! Tell me about it later. Just get that thing here because he is acting worse than yesterday!" Joan whispered more dramatically to prove her point.

She ended the call and slipped her cell phone into her purse, which was sitting on the floor next to her desk. As the secretary sat up and turned around, she came within six inches of a strange man's face with crazy eyes.

"Hello, Joan Bradford. I am here to see Mayor David Willis," stated the tall thin man, slowly inching back and keeping his bright blue eyes gazing upon her.

Joan swallowed hard and then composed herself. "Excuse me, sir, you startled me. Do you have an appointment with the mayor?"

"I believe he is expecting me." The man's expression did not change as Joan rose to her feet.

"Your name, sir?" asked the secretary in a professional tone, hoping to mask her fear.

"I assure you, he knows who I am."

"Let me see if he is available. I'll be right back."

Joan got up and crossed in front of the strange intruder, making her way to the mayor's office. She knocked on the door, while noticing in her peripheral vision that the odd man was studying her carefully.

"Yes, Joan, what is it? Is Vicki here?" asked the mayor from his desk.

"No, sir. Not yet. However, there is a man here to see you."

"Who is it?" asked the mayor, spinning his chair around to look out his interior office window.

"He didn't give me a name," said Joan in an annoyed tone.

Joan watched as the mayor's face turned pale while he fidgeted in his seat. His eyes grew big as he let out a gasp.

"Tell him that I am busy!" pleaded the mayor.

"Yes, sir," said Joan with a raised brow. She could see the terror in David Willis's eyes.

"Hey there, Joan! Is the mayor busy?" said Vicki loudly, as she walked past the strange man, not noticing him.

"Uh, yes, he is, Vicki," said Joan uncomfortably, as she closed the mayor's office door.

"Is everything all right?" asked Vicki.

"Yes, Vicki, everything is ALL right," responded Joan, looking past her coworker and over her shoulder.

Vicki Stanwick felt a pair of eyes drilling into her back.

"Um, Vicki, where are we going to lunch today?"

Joan was now trying to divert Vicki, who realized that something was wrong. Vicki turned around to face the man who was now sitting in the chair next to Joan's desk. He was just the way she remembered him: wearing the *same* shirt, the *same* pants, with the *same* trimmed beard, and those *same* weird eyes.

"Hey, Mr. No Name!" said Vicki boldly, walking up to the stranger.

"Excuse me, Vicki Stanwick?" said the man, moving his head slightly.

"She said that she didn't catch your name." Joan laughed nervously.

Joan reached out and grabbed Vicki's arm. Vicki turned and looked at Joan in surprise.

The odd character began to methodically flip through the screen of his mobile device. He seemed preoccupied momentarily. The ladies decided to take advantage of the situation.

"We've got to get going, girl, we have a *reservation*, remember?" Joan said loudly, giving Vicki an intense look and then a fake smile to the man.

"Oh yes, you are so right! How could I forget?" Vicki winked at Joan.

"It looks like you have what the mayor is waiting for, right?" said Joan in a lower voice.

"Yes, yes, I do, Joan," said Vicki as she held the folder tight to her chest.

"Aren't you going to give it to him?" whispered Joan angrily.

"Not until Julie sees it. If you're nice, I may let you in on it too," Vicki whispered back, giggling.

"Well, let me get my purse and we will head out," Joan said quickly.

She went back to her desk to retrieve her purse, all the while, keeping an eye on the man who was still busy with his mobile device. The man sat in the chair expressionless. He just watched the small screen and never moved. Then he carefully slipped his device back into his shirt pocket and looked forward. The ladies slowly walked away afraid to look for fear of seeing the creepy guy trailing behind them. They made it to the office hallway and realized that they were free from his sight.

"That is the same guy I saw yesterday! He tried to ruin my lunch with Chief Kerrig," Vicki whispered, looking over her shoulder.

"Well, he just appeared out of nowhere and scared the crap out of me!" Joan whispered.

She took off her glasses and rubbed the bridge of her nose. Vicki peered down the hall behind her.

"That guy is a freak show, and I need to tell Julie that he's here."

"Let me come with you, please? I am not staying here."

"Sure thing. Come on. I have to show her these documents," said Vicki, clutching the folder.

"What's the deal? You can't take those out of the building!" Joan whispered louder.

"Watch me! I'll tell you all about it in the car," remarked Vicki, walking faster, heading for the exit doors.

"Wait for me! This is just great! I'm a criminal now," exclaimed Joan, while trying to catch up.

Once they made it outside, Vicki walked swiftly to her VW, and Joan quickly followed.

Meanwhile, inside his office, Mayor Willis had received a phone call. He was sweating again. This time, it wasn't because he was talking to JK Reynolds. Fear itself was sitting fifteen feet away, just outside his office.

#

Moving swiftly through the warm ocean water, with its large dorsal fin only inches below the surface, the intimidating eating machine headed directly toward the Sentinel Class patrol boat, positioned less than a mile off the coast. All the US Coast Guard officers were up on the bridge of the 104-foot craft, studying the digital coastal chart and, totally unaware of the giant creature's intentions.

"This looks like the best course to stay on, sir," said the ensign navigator, while pointing to the screen.

Rubbing his chin, the captain said, "I agree. Steady ahead. I think if we follow this school of dolphins we may find our shark."

"Do we need to call in a Jayhawk, sir?" asked the lieutenant commander.

"Not yet. This shark has only been seen once. They usually move on with the current. Just keep me posted."

"Yes, Captain!" the second-in-command affirmed in a loud voice.

The captain left the deck and headed to the galley for lunch. He was annoyed at the inconvenience of having been called to the present assignment and missing an officer's appreciation luncheon in Washington.

"Tell me, Ensign Bailey; you're from the Brighton area, when was the last time you remember a shark attack?" said the lieutenant commander.

"Never, Commander Lee. I'm only twenty-four, but even my father has never heard of any in his lifetime," the ensign said, looking across the bow.

"Well, I guess there is a first time for everything."

The words had just finished leaving the lieutenant commander's mouth when it happened. They both felt it. The ship continued to cut through the ocean water, but everyone onboard felt the large vibration move through the entire boat. The ensign saw the red light flashing on the com phone and quickly picked it up.

"Bridge… Yes, sir!" said the young officer, listening with wide eyes. The ensign slowly hung up the phone.

"What is it, Bailey?" asked Officer Lee in a guarded voice.

"We've been hit, sir, not sure by what, but we are taking on water."

"Slow us to five knots," said Lee with authority.

"Aye, sir," said Bailey, pushing the tandem throttle lever forward.

The lieutenant commander quickly called on his private line to the galley in order to speak to the captain. He removed his cap and ran his hand through his salt and pepper crewcut while he waited. When the captain came on the other end, Lee quickly placed his hat back on his head.

"Sir, our status is unknown at this time. We have slowed to five, and I will make sure all hull pumps are engaged and our ballasts are stable."

"Find out if we hit something. This is a clear channel and nothing should be here except fish," the captain said in a perplexed voice.

"Sir?" said the ensign, waving to get the lieutenant's attention. He had his binoculars out and kept bringing them up to his eyes and away while he looked across the ocean water in disbelief.

Lee nodded to Bailey and said, "I will get back with you right away, Captain." He hung up the phone. "What is it, Jeff?" asked Lee.

"You're not going to believe this, sir," said the shocked ensign, handing Commander Lee the pair of binoculars.

As the lieutenant commander raised the glasses up to his eyes, focusing carefully in the direction officer Bailey was pointing, he saw it. Its fin was cutting through the calm water like a ship's rudder, about five hundred feet away, and heading straight for Castle Reef.

chapter

10

The Brighton County Coroner sat behind his desk looking intently at the chief of police who was still in her formal uniform. Julie had made it a point to stop and see him on her way to the crime lab since both offices were in the same complex.

"The bite pattern is inconsistent with any kind of shark in our area," Dr. Hackett continued.

"So what are you saying, Gary?" asked Julie.

"Hit-and-run and bump-and-bite attacks occur mostly from bull sharks on our coastline," said Hackett, looking over his glasses.

After several seconds of silence, he got up with the report in his hands and placed it on the desk in front of Julie. He then put his hands in the pockets of his lab coat, walked over to the office window, and looked outside.

"This is different, Julie. I have never seen anything like this before."

"In what way?" Julie inquired.

She began to examine the close-up images of the bite patterns on Charlie Phillip's abdomen.

"There appears to be no evidence of ingestion of any flesh, and the teeth patterns are identical in size and pressure all around each wound," remarked Hackett.

The doctor turned around, stepped forward, and removed his glasses. He then leaned against the front corner of his large desk and sighed.

"This attack wasn't from a shark, as we know it."

Julie's eyes widened, in anticipation of the doctor's next sentence. "Go on, Doc, you're freaking me out, but go on," said Julie, her palms now faintly perspiring.

"I think Charlie was killed by a mechanical device or perhaps something that simulated a shark jawbone."

"Wow! That's great. Someone killed him by hacking him up with a sharp object that looks like shark teeth?" asked Julie in disbelief.

"No, there's more. As you can see in the toxicology report and in the autopsy, Charlie was definitely swimming at the time of his death."

"Which means someone killed him in the surf to make it look like a shark attack?" Julie questioned in a puzzled manner.

"No, whatever killed him has a massive force in its mandibles. Charlie died of the pressure first and then the puncture wounds and the severed tissue followed."

"I'm trying to wrap my head around this, Dr. Hackett!" exclaimed Julie.

"I would like to examine the young lady's injured leg at the hospital today and see if we are dealing with the same entity," stated the doctor, as he stood and put his glasses into his shirt pocket.

"Sounds like we have ourselves a situation much bigger than Chief Brody had in *Jaws*." Julie closed the folder and quickly rose to her feet.

"It appears so, I'm afraid," said Dr. Hackett, turning back to his desk.

"The EMTs and lifeguards searched the entire beach and coastline yesterday, and I'm sure this morning as well, but didn't find any trace of the rest of her leg."

"That makes it very odd indeed," Gary said, grabbing his key ring off of his desk.

"Please call me as soon as you find out. Right now, I'm headed to the crime lab to get some results from yet another bizarre situation I'm looking into." Julie sighed, making her way to the door.

"I sure will, Chief."

Gary held open the door for her as he followed Julie out into the hallway. She stopped and turned to the doctor who she respected and trusted.

"Gary, my dad always said you were a straight shooter. I want you to be honest with me. Do you think something strange is going on in Castle Reef?"

"Julie, your father and I had this saying from the great Arthur Conan Doyle, 'There is nothing more deceptive than an obvious fact.'"

"Sherlock Holmes, right?" Julie attempted an educated guess.

"Precisely! John Kerrig loved his books as you know, and he loved using quotes and stories to teach others," assured Hackett with a sincere smile.

"He always told me to *just follow the facts*, and that is what I try to do, but I'm afraid this is going to be a little more difficult," Julie said quietly.

"Maybe not, Jules. You were trained by the best, and you have a lot of people that support you. And don't you forget that!" exclaimed the doctor, shaking her hand firmly.

"Thanks, Gary, that really means a lot. Talk to you soon!" Julie turned and made her way down the hall, determination in every step.

#

Seven miles away, the mysterious sedan crept along the gated residence of JK Reynolds.

A reflection of the large French provincial home glided across the tinted glass windows, as the dark-blue vehicle drove slowly past the house and eventually out of sight. Inside, the wealthy middle-aged politician finished his phone call with the state governor. He had spent most of the morning making sure his plans were finalized before leaving for his scheduled golf outing. His wife, Janet, was busy gossiping with her girlfriends by the pool, playing their weekly game of bridge.

"I'm headed to the country club, darling!" exclaimed JK, stepping outside onto the patio.

"What time will you be back, dear?" Janet replied with a painted smile on her face.

"Well, it's hard to say. You never know with those fellas." Reynolds chuckled, shutting the door and making his way to the garage.

As JK got into his Bentley Bentayga and drove out of the gated residence, the women sat sipping on their wine coolers and discussing all the latest neighborhood news.

"JK's a piece of work, Janet!" said Cheri, one of Janet's best friends.

"Nothing has changed since the day I met him." Janet laughed smugly.

"Does he really go golfing, or does he have a mistress?" Cheri giggled, covering her mouth and trying not to spill out the wine she just guzzled.

"I can't get even Tom out of the house so that I can have an affair." Carla cackled, with a forced laugh.

"Ladies, men will be men," sniped Mrs. Reynolds, shuffling the deck of cards several times.

"Speaking of men, where is that hunk of a son of yours, Janet?" asked Amber, the oldest of her three friends.

After a long pause and a drink from her wine glass, Janet's expression changed. "Not sure, he might be headed home now since the beach is closed. JK never tells me where Ian is," she said in a somber voice.

"Is everything all right?" asked Amber.

The rest of the women chimed in all at once, badgering her for any information they could gather. Finally, Janet stood up.

"Yes, yes, everything is fine!" shouted the politician's wife.

Janet's so-called friends stopped and looked at each other in shock.

"Does anyone want some more wine?" deflected Reynolds.

The ladies took her cue, quickly changing the subject, and began to talk about their shopping sprees. They also continued their card game while slowly getting pitifully drunk in the summer heat under the large patio umbrella.

#

"Trent!" yelled the trusted kitchen worker.

"Kelli! How are you?" Trent Green removed his sunglasses and surveyed his busy kitchen.

"I'm fine. We are ready to roll out our lunch special. It looks like we're getting a lot of to-go orders, unfortunately," said the dedicated kitchen worker.

"I scaled things back, Trent," Rita chimed in, as she walked past him with a pan of fried shrimp.

"We'll be fine, ladies. I appreciate all you're doing," Trent said, looking through the mail that was left for him on the large maple butcher block.

"A lot of people are leaving today that's for sure. The dining room is pretty empty," remarked Kelli.

"I didn't see Francis when I came in," Trent said, looking around.

"Didn't you hear?" Rita questioned Trent in a serious manner.

"Hear what? No, Rita, what's going on?"

"He went over to Ocean's. The Foster's boat was vandalized last night."

"Oh my! Are they okay?" asked Trent as he pulled out his cell phone.

"Not sure. The police should be over there by now," whispered Rita, washing her hands.

"Also, Mike is upstairs looking at the satellite thingy," Kelli said, trying to recall the proper word.

Trent managed a smile, despite the news about the Foster's boat, and wasted no time in calling to check on his friends. "Hi, Becky, this is Trent Green. Are you guys okay over there?"

"Yes, Trent, thanks for asking. Jerry is really upset, but we will be fine."

"The ladies here said your boat was vandalized?" Trent asked, leaning against the counter.

"It looks like it was. I haven't seen inside it yet; only Jerry has. Boy is he mad!" exclaimed Becky.

"I bet he is. Is there anything we can do for you guys?"

"No, dear, I think we can rent a boat from one of the marinas up north."

"Are you sure?"

"Yes, sweetie. Besides, Fran came over and is trying to calm Jerry down."

"Please let us know if you need help," offered Trent sincerely.

"We will, Trent. I think the police are here, so I gotta go!" Becky began to speak more urgently.

"Okay, sorry to keep you, Becky. I will stop by later." Trent ended his call and shook his head, looking up at the ladies.

"Is everything all right?" asked Kelli, moving closer.

"As good as it can be, given the situation," Trent exhaled.

"What's the matter?" questioned Rita.

"Yeah, what is it, Trent?" Kelli chimed in.

"Is it just me or do both of you notice a string of events happening around here that are just coming out of nowhere?" Trent looked at the two women with an expression that made them shiver, in spite of being in a warm kitchen. They both slowly stepped forward with fear in their eyes.

"Now that you mention it, I do," Kelli whispered lightly.

"I think you're onto something, Trent. Sharks, a weird customer, vandalism… What's next?" Rita sighed.

"No reason to freak out. I'm just saying some strange things are going on," said Trent calmly.

Kelli gasped, crossing her arms and holding both of her elbows close to her sides. "I'm already freaked out."

"Well, don't worry. I'm sure things will return to normal. Let's not stress about it now. We'll finish our lunch shift and regroup this afternoon," reassured Trent.

"Sounds like a plan, boss!" Rita said firmly, followed by a fist bump to Trent.

"I'm into no stress, that's for sure," said Kelli timidly.

"Hey, my Aunt Betty had a saying that always helped me," said Trent, with an odd grin on his face.

"And what would that be?" asked Rita sarcastically.

"Stressed spelled backward is desserts!" Trent burst into laughter, and the ladies followed.

"Speaking of dessert, I gotta get the blueberry cobbler out before it burns!" Rita shouted, running to the wall oven.

"I'm going upstairs to see how Mike is doing with the *satellite thingy*," said Trent, winking at Kelli while walking into the dining room.

"Hey now!" Kelli laughed as she began slicing bread.

"I'll be back around two o'clock so we can discuss the dinner plan. Make sure all the staff is here, okay, Rita?"

"You got it, Chief," Rita agreed and smirked in order for Trent to see.

"We'll meet in the dining room," Trent added.

"You got it, Chief," repeated Rita, removing her oven mittens.

Trent smiled really big and shook his pointed finger at Rita. "I heard you the first time and don't ask."

"I'm not saying anything. We just noticed you seemed to have an extra kick in your step today." Rita removed the foil from the cobbler, avoiding eye contact.

Trent grinned and shook his head before leaving the kitchen. "Talk to you later, Detective McGuire."

#

"Okay, I will see you then," said Vicki, quickly putting the cell phone into her purse.

"What did Chief Kerrig say?" asked Joan.

Ms. Stanwick held the file folder tightly to her side. "She wants to meet at one o'clock, at Abletti's Deli."

"I'm supposed to be back in the office by then!" shouted Joan in disbelief.

"Oh, you're not going back there today!" Vicki's eyes widened as she spoke.

"Why not?" Joan studied her face.

The traffic light turned green. Vicki gave Joan the folder as she shifted her little yellow German car.

"We have a game-changer in that folder, and you won't want to be working at city hall anytime soon. Trust me!"

"What did you find Vicki?" asked the secretary, looking down at the folder marked *March Minutes*.

"Oh, Joanie, Joanie, Joanie! You're not going to believe it!"

"What? You're scaring me! I'm just a divorced redhead from Massachusetts! I don't need to get involved in any criminal investigation!"

"Too late, Ms. Bradford. You're in this with me!" Vicki laughed nervously.

Joan sat numb, looking forward and afraid to move. "Great, Vicki, just great!"

"This traffic is unreal!" Vicki sighed as she glanced in her rearview mirror.

"Please don't tell me it's something creepy about the mayor," said the petrified secretary.

"Oh yeah, Joanie! There's a lot in that folder. I also stuck a copy of another unrelated bombshell I found in there."

"Can you tell me what's going on, so I can honestly say to the judge, when we are on trial, that I never looked at any of the evidence?" Joan said frantically.

Vicki slapped her hands against the steering wheel as she laughed hard. "Girl, you won't be on trial, trust me!"

"I came to Castle Reef like so many, to get away from the crazy city, crime, traffic, and weird people. Now where do I find myself? In traffic, with weird people and holding a file folder that my coworker stole from the local government I work for!" Joan shouted nervously in her Boston accent.

"Oh, Joan, you crack me up! It's going to be all right. God has got our backs. He always does," Vicki said confidently.

"I sure hope so," said the redhead, rubbing her forehead.

The VW sat at a stop sign for several minutes. The picturesque town was becoming congested with dozens of cars trying to maneuver through the narrow side streets in order to get onto the main highway outside the city limits. News trucks were setting up remote broadcasts in the beach parking lot. Despite all the confusion, the shops and restaurants still remained open. The summer was beginning to heat up in so many ways.

#

"Hi, Chris! Thanks for covering extra shift time," said Shirley, patting the tall officer on the arm.

"No problem, Ms. Shirley. Are you sure you don't need me over at Ocean's?" asked the tall officer.

Officer Sanchez put his gear away in his locker and sat down at his small desk, located next to Shirley's dispatch area.

"No, Chris, I sent Kenny and his partner over there. The rest of the guys are doing traffic."

"It sure is crazy out there."

"That's an understatement. Can I get you something to drink before you go?" Shirley walked over to the small refrigerator next to her chair.

"No, thank you, ma'am. I'm sure Jasmine has something for me at the house."

"Becky said that their boat was vandalized pretty severely. It's real strange that the inside of a fishing vessel would be ransacked like that." Shirley spoke softly while staring across the room in deep thought.

"Speaking of strange, I saw a suspicious vehicle last night driving out of town on Highway 61."

Shirley snapped out of her daydream and looked at Sanchez with a surprised expression. "Really? What did it look like?"

Officer Sanchez opened his laptop and scrolled through his report log. "It was a dark-blue sedan, early 2000 model maybe, with a local plate."

"Did you make the stop?" asked Shirley curiously.

"After calling the plate in as suspicious, County Sheriff Dispatch responded by giving me a 10-22."

Shirley hesitated. "A 22 disregard, huh?"

Chris leaned in. "Si, *señorita*, the car wasn't breaking any laws, but the long pause on the license plate inquiry puzzled me. Also, the fact that I've never seen a car like that around here before."

"Tell you what, Chris, write the plate number down on a sticky note and put it on the chief's desk. I'll have her look into it when she gets here," replied Shirley.

"Nah, it's no big deal."

"No, seriously, I can't stand when Brighton County does stuff like that to us. It's our community and we need to know."

"You've got a point there, Ms. Shirley." Chris scribbled on his notepad and stood up.

"Please enjoy the rest of your day, Chris. Give your wife and kiddos a big hug for me," said Shirley in a tender voice.

Sanchez placed the note on Chief Kerrig's desk and then turned back to Shirley. "Gracias, Shirley. You're the best!" said the faithful, tall policeman.

"Stop it, you'll make me blush!"

"Nah, the only girl that blushes around here is Judy!" said Sanchez, pointing to the expressionless mannequin standing quietly in the corner.

Shirley grinned, watching Chris walk out the double doors, and then she glanced over at Julie's desk. Pausing for a moment, she pulled out a small electronic device from her uniform shirt pocket.

#

State Police Commissioner Neil Hillsdale had just finished his call with Governor Riddick. The executive order was now issued. Reluctantly, Hillsdale summoned his secretary to his office.

"Linda, we have an executive order from the governor to take over the jurisdiction of Brighton County and Castle Reef municipalities. Can you send out text memos to our lieutenant colonel, and to all the mayors, as well as all the other authorities in Brighton County, with one exception?

"Yes, sir, and who would that be, sir?" asked the secretary.

"I assume the governor knows what he's doing, but every top official is to be notified with the exception of the chief of police in Castle Reef," stated Hillsdale as he adjusted his necktie and then stood up behind his desk.

"I will get this completed right away, sir. Is there anything else?"

"Apparently, the governor does not want the news media in Castle Reef either."

"Does this have anything to do with yesterday's shark attacks and today's Coast Guard incident?" inquired the secretary, standing in the office doorway.

"I'm sure it does, Linda. Please keep me in the loop throughout the day."

"I will, sir." Linda closed the door carefully.

Neil Hillsdale walked over to his bookshelf and surveyed all the framed pictures arranged neatly on each shelf. The photos of his wife and children managed to bring a smile to his face.

He then gazed upon several portraits of himself throughout his distinguished career. His expression became somber. Memories of all the hard work and danger he had faced through the years raced through his mind.

Something was missing from the job that he used to be so passionate about. He recently found himself at odds with the present administration after several laws had been passed that were contradictory to his core values. The mission of the state police was to assist the local police and county sheriff departments while upholding and enforcing the state laws. Hillsdale now felt that his department was being forced to neglect its purpose. The governor's order didn't sit well with Neil. This was yet another example that put the commissioner in an awkward position and made his job very frustrating. He knew there needed to be a change.

chapter

11

Trent called out across the flat gravel roof. "Mike, are you up here?"

"Over here!" shouted a distant voice in the warm salt air breeze.

The panoramic view on top of the Green Sea Inn was breath-taking. You could literally see for almost three miles in every direction. Trent had only surveyed the roof about a dozen times since he purchased the inn. He had always wanted to make an easier access to the roof in order to make repairs on the air-conditioning, or even to set up a stargazing spot with his eight-inch reflector telescope which he had inherited from his father.

The satellite dishes were strategically located in the center of the roof in order to be out of sight from the ground level. You needed to use a large step ladder in order to reach the fixed steel one on the north side of the building to which it was attached, ten feet from the ground. It was a lengthy process, to say the least.

"Hey, my friend, how are things going?" Trent asked, out of breath from the climb.

"I think I found our culprit," Mike revealed.

"What in the world is that?" Trent stooped down to where Mike was kneeling among a myriad of cables.

"This, my friend, is a high-frequency transmitter," replied Mike proudly.

"And…so?" Trent said slowly, in anticipation.

"It has nothing to do with the LNB that is on the satellite dish."

Trent furrowed his brow. "Not to sound stupid, but what is an LNB?"

"Actually, it stands for low noise block down convertor. It gathers the radio frequencies and it—" Mike was interrupted.

"Ha! Okay! Ground Control to Major Tom! So why did the satellite company mount it on this particular dish antenna?" Trent looked over Mike's shoulder at the device carefully.

"Great question! The lead wires are tapped into a little solar cell here and then the transmitter was mounted alongside of the LNB," explained Mike, pointing everything out with his long screwdriver.

"Okay, Mike! You're losing me, buddy," Trent inserted before Mike could continue.

"This little piece of equipment is from someone else. It has recently been installed. I took a picture of it before I removed it. This device must have either moved from the wind up here or was mounted in a hurry because it was touching the LNB."

"Which caused the signal to get scrambled in room 115," Trent concluded, standing up.

"Bingo!" Mike spoke in an animated voice, putting the contraption into his tool bag.

"What do think we should we do?" asked Trent.

"Well, I'm going to send the picture to Jim Renaldi in New York and ask him to have his guys look at it."

"Jim?" Trent looked at Mike puzzled.

"Yeah, you know my friend who runs the security company? He has all those contracts on Wall Street, remember?"

"Good idea, Mike!"

"Thanks, I'll let you know as soon as I find out something. In the meantime, I'm gonna put this in the old safe in your office."

"Sounds like a plan. I'm waiting to hear from Julie anytime now. We're supposed to meet for lunch, and I'm hoping to get her insight on everything."

"Wow, that's fantastic. So glad you two are talking again."

"Me too, it's been way too long." Trent stood up.

"I'm gonna to call Karen's friend here in a minute to see how she is doing."

"Awesome man, so glad you're doing better today, Mike," Trent added.

"Yeah, me too, for sure," Mike said as he arranged his tools.

The two men started walking toward the ladder at the end of the building when suddenly they saw a helicopter rapidly approaching from the south. They both noticed it was a US Coast Guard Jayhawk as it passed swiftly overhead.

#

"Young man, I've been fishing two times longer than you've been alive!" snapped Jerry Foster.

"I understand that, sir, but can you tell me again how you discovered the condition of the boat?" asked the officer politely.

There was a patrol car parked sideways in front of the marina. One auxiliary officer was taping off the scene while Officer Kenny Caldwell was attempting to get details from the Fosters.

"What part of I stepped onto the *Susan Marie* this morning, around 10:30 to get my extra pair of gloves, and I found her destroyed—plain and simple—don't you get, young man?" Jerry blurted out.

"Mr. Foster, we are here to help you. We have to get the facts first and then combine them with any evidence we find here at the scene."

"I understand that, I'm just a little irked to say the least."

"We will most likely call in assistance from the sheriff's department to help on this one. You can be sure we will do everything we can to find out what exactly happened and hold whoever did this responsible," assured Caldwell.

Becky Foster, wearing red nylon athletic shorts, an Ohio State Buckeye football jersey, and pink flamingo flip flops, walked up to the officer and offered him a glass of iced tea.

"Kenny, here's some fresh mint tea."

"No, thank you, ma'am. I'm fine. Did you guys notice anyone lingering around the pier last night or early this morning?" the officer inquired, while taking notes on his cell phone.

"Nope, not a soul," interjected Jerry. "I was the last one here yesterday evening and the first one to arrive this morning."

As the Fosters were speaking with the police, Francis O'Reily came walking up with Billy Daily. Billy had his head down, and Fran had one hand on his shoulder.

"Pardin me, folks," insisted their Irish friend.

"What is it, Fran?" asked Jerry.

"I was a lookin' a da boat, when I be noticin' from afar, lil' Billy Daily a standin' there lookin' scared."

"I thought I saw Billy watching us, over there by the shed," recounted Becky.

"You don't have to be scared, son," said Jerry in a concerned voice.

"Billy, are you okay, sweetheart?" Becky put her arm around him.

"I'm a thinkin' da lil' guy know somethin'," Fran whispered to Officer Caldwell, with one hand to the side of his mouth.

"What did you see, Billy?" the officer asked calmly.

"You can tell us, Billy. It's all right, you're not in trouble," Jerry assured him.

"That's right, we just want you to help us, Billy." Becky gently put her hand under his chin and slowly lifted his head that was pressed against his plaid shirt.

"Tell you what, Billy, I will give you a ride in my police car after we are finished here," promised Kenny, genuinely smiling at Billy.

"Police car ride for me?" Billy exclaimed.

"You bet! I will even buy you an ice cream cone."

"Wow, that sounds fun, Billy!" reassured Jerry.

"A fine treat if I do say so meself," chimed in Francis.

They all stood quietly as the water lapped against the bulkheads. Several seagulls cried out circling the nearby dumpsters that were recently emptied. Becky removed her hand slowly from Billy's chin.

"It's okay, Billy. Go ahead," whispered Becky.

"Ian got me supper last night and he...he went...went home," Billy stuttered.

"That sounds fun, Billy. Where did you go after supper?" Officer Caldwell kneeled down and looked up at the visibly shaken man.

"Right here! I was right there." Billy pointed at the bench next to the dock.

"Did you see anybody last night, Billy?" asked Jerry, in a child-like voice.

"No, Mr. Jerry, I saw green light, red light down in water, and then…and then a great big mean face!" Billy began to cry.

"It's okay, Billy," consoled Becky.

"Don't worry, you're safe with us, buddy," Caldwell interjected.

"I ran fast, and Ms. Vicki pick me up in funny yellow bug car." Billy sighed, wiping his eyes.

Officer Caldwell finished entering the notes quickly on his smartphone and then stood up and spoke in a calm voice, "Mr. Daily, you earned yourself an ice cream cone and a police car ride!"

"Good job, Billy!" Becky cheered.

"C'mon, fella, I'll take ya ta getcha that ice cream cone," O'Reily insisted.

"When do I ride in police car, Mr. Policeman?" Billy asked intently.

Kenny Caldwell chuckled. "Tell you what, Billy, when I am finished here and I give all my important stuff to the police station, I will meet you at your house before supper, at five o'clock. Then, I will drive you around town in my police car, and maybe we can even stop and get some pizza at Umberto's."

Billy's eyes lit up and a big smile came across his face. He started to laugh and look at Fran and the Fosters with pure delight. Fran gently put his arm once again on Billy's shoulder and slowly walked him to the parking lot.

"Let's go, me lad. You got an ice cream cone to get. Let the lep-rechaun walk ya there," Francis proudly said, winking at the Fosters.

As Officer Caldwell and the Fosters watched Billy and Francis O'Reily walk past the patrol cars toward Main Street and then out of sight, they turned to face each other.

"What do you think he meant by flashing green and red lights?" Jerry asked, with a baffled look on his bearded face.

"The *mean face* part made the hair on the back of my neck stand up!" interjected Becky.

Caldwell spoke professionally, "We will look into this thoroughly. I am going to have this area blocked off from traffic until we get a diver down there to look around your boat. The sheriff's department should be here soon, and I will inform Chief Kerrig."

"Thanks, Kenny," said Jerry, exhaling deeply.

Officer Caldwell summoned the assisting officer, and they discussed their notes and began to document the vandalism with pictures while they waited for the Brighton County Sheriff's Department.

#

"Make sure the second team meets me on the lower level after they have finished the batch of solar cells for the SDI Project," Cortney Alexander commanded her supervisor.

"Yes, Ms. Alexander," said the fair-skinned woman, in a thick Slavic accent.

"Keep me posted on the progress of both projects, too."

"Yes, I vil, Ms. Alexander. Also, Terry is vaiting in yur office."

"Thank you, Natalia," replied the powerful tech genius.

She turned and walked down the long labyrinthine corridor of the giant industrial complex, heading for her office. Inside sat Terry Warren, waiting patiently. Warren was Alexander's personal and corporate computer programmer, a mutual childhood friend, who had lived at home until a critical car accident claimed the lives of Terry's parents. Cortney then hired and housed Terry shortly afterward. This made Terry extremely devoted to Alexander, always making sure all of her scientific research was successful.

The white steel door opened. "Terry, it looks like you are patiently waiting," said the forty-year-old billionaire's daughter.

"Dear Cortney, no need to worry," Warren said cheerfully, after quickly standing up.

"When M2 contacts the main interface, make sure you instruct it to finish locating our asset and then transmit at the eighteen-hour mark," Cortney said emotionless, approaching her blank desk that was essentially an enormous, flat touchscreen.

"That's in a few hours. What about our dinner plans tonight?" Terry hesitated.

"There are more important things pressing right now, Terry."

"Like what, Cortney?" asked the visibly frustrated assistant.

"Did I detect an ungrateful tone in your voice?" snapped Alexander as she glared across the room.

"It's just..." Terry said in disbelief.

Cortney quickly interrupted. "You best keep your feelings to yourself!"

"But I..."

"Without me, you are nothing!" barked Cortney.

"That's not fair! You know how I feel about you. I thought we had something special together!" Terry began to sob uncontrollably.

"Shut up! You do what I say or else! Do you understand me?" screeched Cortney inside the soundproof, bleached-white office.

Sitting down, Terry's head hung in submission. The two strange individuals sat in silence for over two minutes. Only the sound of Warren's sniffles and the steady puffing breath of Alexander, resembling a medieval dragon, filled the room.

"Terry?"

"Yes?"

The alpha Alexander sighed. "Have you controlled yourself?"

"Yes, Cortney, I apologize," babbled the manipulated Warren.

"That's better. Now, I am going to be very busy on the lower level tonight, and I want you to carry out what I asked you to do this afternoon and evening," Cortney stated evenly, acting as if nothing happened.

"I will," said Terry, continuing to have no eye contact with the dominating witch of a woman.

"Look at me," demanded Alexander in a softer voice. "I have come too far to let this opportunity slip from my hands. When we are successful in phase 3, then maybe we will have our time to celebrate. Is that clear?"

Warren sat upright. "Yes, I apologize once again. I was being selfish."

"I receive that apology, Terry. If I hurt your feelings, you know that was not my intention. You need to learn to be more understanding," the conniving Cortney said, moving toward the door.

Warren rose from the chair, slowly looking up. "I will make sure M1 and M2 carry out their plans."

"Excellent! Thank you. You know I care for you very much, Terry."

With that brief statement, Alexander quickly exited, leaving the emotionally disturbed Terry Warren alone once again in the solitary office, which ironically mirrored both of their lives.

#

"Yes, sir, I will inform the rest of the crew." Lieutenant Commander Lee hung up the ship's intercom phone.

"We have the rupture contained, sir," reported Ensign Bailey.

"Excellent job. The captain has instructed us to make a one mile turning circle at five knots," instructed Commander Lee.

"Aye, sir, and, Commander?" asked Bailey.

"Yes, Ensign?"

"About what we saw, sir?"

"We didn't get the picture in time from the bridge, but our 3D sonar data imaging did get a reading, and we sent it to Washington," assured the commander.

"Sir, have Castle Reef and Brighton County authorities been notified?"

"Affirmative, air support is in our region as well," added Lee.

"I have never seen a shark that size before," inserted the serviceman.

"Young man, in all my years on the ocean, this was a first for me too," admitted the commander.

"What do we do now, Lieutenant?" asked Bailey.

"Wait. Plain and simple, we wait, son, until we get our orders.

The vessel tossed slightly as the warm, westerly wind blew across the water. Most of the crew aboard had their attention on the port side of the ship. They were watching a Coast Guard Jayhawk fly north up the coastline, in search of the massive man-eater, which had been spotted earlier.

chapter

12

"You are not going to believe it, Mama Shirley!" Julie came out of the ladies' locker room fully dressed in her street uniform. She slowly began to put her gear on.

"What's going on, Jules?" asked the senior dispatcher sincerely.

"It has been one thing after another. I feel like I'm on a gerbil wheel," said Julie apologetically.

"You are a busy bee that's for sure! I'm sure we have a lot to discuss," insisted Shirley, picking up a chocolate nonpareil from her candy dish and dropping it in her mouth.

"Indeed, we do! Thanks for holding down the fort here." Julie smiled as she fastened her duty belt around her waist and checked her firearm.

Ms. Allen gave Julie a hug and motioned her over to her desk. "Have a seat and tell me what's happening."

"What's this?" Julie asked, picking up the sticky note that was fastened to her day planner.

"Well, Chris left it there for you. It seems he called in an 11-54 or a 10-38 last night on a vehicle that looked suspicious."

"Really?"

"Yes, and Brighton County stalled at his request."

"Did he call it in correctly?" Julie studied Shirley's face and then looked down at the note in her hand.

"Yes, and the county dispatch had him waiting for a while and then told him to disregard." Shirley cleared her throat.

"That's odd. Then again, what isn't odd around here these past two days?" declared Julie.

"That's exactly what I thought too." Shirley looked away and began organizing papers on her desk.

"Did he say anything about the vehicle? A description of the driver?"

"Nothing about the driver, but I think he did say it was a late model sedan with heavily tinted windows."

"He should have stopped the car." The chief sighed.

"Sanchez said there was no probable cause at the time."

"Tinted windows, he could have stopped the car for the windows. The glass can only be tinted at 28 percent in our state," Julie said, opening her small backpack.

"Really? I didn't know that. He said it was pretty dark," remarked Ms. Allen.

"Yup, unless the car's tag was from Michigan, but it wasn't, so I would have made the stop."

"Why Michigan?" Shirley asked curiously.

"That state has no restrictions on window tint."

"Wow, I didn't know that either."

"You learn something new every day," recited Julie.

"Spoken like a true Kerrig." The dispatcher smiled.

"You bet!" The chief put her hands on her hips. "Guess what?"

"What is it, Jules?" answered Shirley, looking intently at her.

"The autopsy showed that Charlie may have been killed by something other than a shark," said Julie, picking her small backpack up off the floor.

"What are you telling me?" Shirley was startled.

"The bite marks were inconsistent with a shark. It may have been something else bigger or stronger," Julie revealed.

"What? Oh my!" Shirley appeared surprised.

"We'll find out from Dr. Hackett as soon as he examines the lady at the hospital. Her name is Karen Anderson." Julie pulled an evidence bag out of her pack and set it on her desk. Shirley tilted her head and looked over her reading glasses to see what was in the bag.

"What in the world is that?" asked the puzzled senior.

"Well, this is a glass from the Green Sea Inn," remarked Julie casually.

"I see it's a glass, but I didn't know it was from the Green Sea Inn?" Shirley spoke with a strange grin on her face.

"Why are you smirking? This is serious evidence!" Julie was astonished at Shirley's reaction.

"What? Go ahead tell me." The stout dispatcher leaned in to look and placed her hand on her chin, in order to hide her grin.

"The strange man, you know the creepy guy Vicki and I saw at Nina's Café' and the one we think called here and threatened us?"

"Yes? Did he drink from that glass?" asked Shirley intently.

"Yes, he did according to…" Julie slowed her sentence midway to a pause. She suspected Shirley's attention was somewhere else ever since she mentioned the Green Sea Inn.

"What?" Shirley asked, like a child who got caught stealing a cookie from the cookie jar.

"You knew I talked to him, didn't you?" Julie caved in with a smile.

"Well…" Shirley laughed heartily and finished with a slight cough.

"When did he call?" asked Julie, squinting her eyes with suspicion.

"Last night, before I left to go home, he called and wanted to speak to you."

"Well, yes, we saw each other at the beach after the attack and…"

"And? Go on!" Shirley slid her reading glasses up on her short gray-haired head.

"We spoke, and then we spoke again at the hospital. After you told him where I was going last night, obviously." Julie pretended to playfully reach over and slap Shirley with a mimed stroke.

"He still loves you, Jules. I think he loves you now more than ever," Shirley said seriously, rolling her office chair closer to Julie's desk.

Julie got very quiet. She sat back in her chair and then after a short pause began to break down and cry. Shirley was caught off guard.

"Oh my, honey. I'm so sorry I started all this," said Shirley remorsefully.

"No, no, Shirley, it's okay. I've been doing a lot of this lately."

"You guys have fought this for far too long."

Julie sobbed. "Yes, I know. It's all me. It's just hard to let go of the fact that my daddy isn't coming back."

Shirley stood up and went over to console her. She moved the long-braided ponytail and softly rubbed her shoulders while looking over at some of the portraits of John Kerrig. Julie wiped her tears with several tissues. Shirley took a deep breath and gently spoke to the young lady whom she loved like her own.

"God has a way of turning our darkest moments into something beautiful, dear child."

Julie exhaled. "I know. I've blamed Him and become bitter. I prayed for the first time in years last night."

"That's wonderful, Jules."

"Wasn't much, but it was a start, I guess."

"Things are all going to work out. As crazy as they may get, I think we have to keep the big picture in mind," Shirley said confidently.

"You sound like my dad." Julie composed herself with a few sniffles.

"He left an impression on all of us, Jules." She kissed Julie on the forehead and walked back to her desk.

The room was quiet with an occasional interruption of radio checks from the units on duty. After a minute, Julie sat up and performed her signature neck roll from side to side.

The chief now spoke more intensely. "Oh boy! Now, where were we?"

"You were talking about the glass?" Shirley grinned.

"Yes, that's right! Trent gave me the glass, and I had it analyzed. It came back with no fingerprints or DNA," continued Julie.

"It must have been compromised somehow," Shirley insisted.

"Trent said they took great care to make sure it wasn't," Julie added.

"Odd, very odd." Shirley shook her head as she sat down.

"Just the root beer, water from the melted ice, and a trace of biodegradable food material." Julie carefully wiped her eyes in order to not smear her eyeliner.

"Well, I'm sure you're going to hang on to it, right?" urged Shirley.

"You bet! Let's put all our findings and evidence regarding this weird guy in the evidence safe, and then we will build our case." Julie gathered the evidence bag, sticky note, and a thumb drive containing the man's voice recording, and walked across the room to the large safe door.

"I'm sure you also heard about the rumblings over at the marina with Jerry's boat?" asked Shirley.

"Yes, Caldwell called me and told me about the vandalism. He also said that the sheriff's department was going to assist with their diving team," Julie spoke slowly, while punching in the vault code on the keypad.

"Becky called me first. She was pretty upset."

"Add it to the list!" exclaimed the chief from inside the vault.

Julie closed the vault door and proceeded to walk over to the large dry erase board that was mounted on the wall between the bathrooms. She picked up a marker on the tray and proceeded to draw a circle and then connect six spokes to it. She wrote *Events* inside the circle and then listed *Shark, Charlie, Karen, The Man, Jerry's Boat*, and *The Car* next to each individual spoke. She then placed the marker on the board tray and began to organize her pack.

"That's interesting, Jules," Shirley remarked, studying the board.

"I'm going to finish it after I get back from my late lunch," suggested Julie, looking at her watch.

"Who are you meeting?" asked Shirley with a Cheshire cat smile.

"For your information, Ms. Matchmaker, I am grabbing a sandwich with Vicki and Joan at Abletti's," Julie shot back sarcastically.

"Is Trent invited?" the dispatcher timidly asked.

"He's going to be, but he doesn't know the other two ladies will be with me!" blurted out Julie who then began giggling.

"That poor guy. Just when he thought he was having a private date," chuckled Shirley.

The ladies began to laugh together simultaneously. The sound of their outburst echoed throughout the police station. Julie wiped her eyes once again, but this time, she realized the tears were due to the true joy that she was now feeling for the first time since losing her father.

Their hysteria slowly subsided with a lot of breaths and giggles. The veteran dispatcher also dabbed the corners of her eyes with a light-blue monogrammed handkerchief and returned it to her sleeve.

"It's so good to see you getting back to being the Julie we all know and love," said Shirley carefully.

"Thanks for being patient with me." The young chief adjusted her uniform and duty belt and gave Shirley a big hug.

"I need to get going. The traffic is crazy out there due to this whole shark scare." Julie pulled out her phone and began texting Trent.

"How was it coming back from Brighton?" asked Shirley, watching Julie curiously.

"Bumper to bumper, on the westbound lane, of course."

Chief Kerrig finished her message with a smile and looked up and met Shirley's eyes.

They both knew without any verbal exchange that Trent was now invited for lunch at Abletti's Deli.

Julie added, "I did see a couple of HPs, but there was only radio silence on all channels, which I thought was odd."

"I heard the county dispatching the highway patrol, but no bulletins or calls came into us from anyone. I thought that was strange too," said Shirley, with some unease in her voice.

"It sounds like we may need to include another spoke on our circle, along with the mayor, who is acting strange according to Vicki." Julie took the dry erase marker and added two spokes labeled *Mayor* and *HP* to the circle on the board. She then closed her laptop, pushed in her chair, and put her sunglasses on.

"Be careful, young lady," said Shirley, watching Julie walk toward the hallway.

"No worries, Ms. Shirley. If you need me, you know where I'll be."

Shirley raised her voice because Julie was now quickly moving down the hall, "Okay, Chief, but watch your back, Jules!"

"I'll be back. Remember to keep these electronic doors locked," Julie shouted, walking outside into the hottest and second longest day of the year.

Julie pulled out into the congested Main Street traffic and drove away from the station.

Across the street undetected, in a narrow alley between buildings, sat the elusive mysterious blue car. It remained motionless.

chapter

13

The Eastbound lane was completely closed to any incoming traffic headed for Castle Reef, as both lanes were now open all the way to the interstate highway, roughly three miles outside of Brighton. The state police kept the steady flow of traffic moving as they continued following orders to evacuate the beach town. Many people were now panicked after seeing the flashing lights and patrolmen waving the traffic, along with flares and signal cones. Several curious motorists stopped to ask about the shark attacks and if the beach would ever be open again this season. They were greeted with stern looks and commands to keep moving.

"How are things going down there, Lieutenant Roth?" asked Superintendent Hillsdale.

Roth firmly held the microphone and responded, "As directed, sir, we have all traffic moving west, and we are about to clear Castle Reef when given the green light."

"Send four units to the town station in order to pick up the subject," directed the superintendent.

"Does the city police chief know our intentions, sir?" asked Roth.

"I'm afraid we have to move in unannounced on this one."

"Yes, sir, I will touch base when we make the arrest."

"Make sure every news outlet is vacated from the area before you go in," Hillsdale ordered.

"We are clearing them out now, even as we speak, sir."

"Keep me posted. This operation has to go down under the radar without the press, networks, or even the local authorities knowing about it," Hillsdale insisted.

"Affirmative, sir, we will report as soon as it's secure there," said the sergeant, hanging his mic on the dashboard of his unmarked patrol car.

Neil Hillsdale hung up his phone after speaking to Lieutenant Roth and threw his notepad across the room in frustration. Just minutes before, the superintendent received another order given to him by the governor to clear not only the beach, but the entire town of Castle Reef due to a credible threat given to him by the state bureau of investigation. Neil always trusted his gut more than the system he worked within. Something was bothering him, and he just couldn't put his finger on it. He reached for the intercom to call his trusted secretary.

"Linda? Do you have a minute?"

"Yes, sir, I will be right there."

Thirty seconds passed, and the door opened to Hillsdale's office. Linda Saunders walked up to Neil's desk, picking up his notepad along the way. She carefully placed the pad on the desk and stepped back, looking intently at her boss over her reading glasses.

"Hey, Linda, sorry to bother you again." The superintendent sighed uncomfortably.

"No problem, sir. How can I help?" said Saunders.

"I'm going to need you to do me a big favor, off the record," said Hillsdale.

"Sir?" gasped Linda.

"Nothing illegal, Linda, just a ten second phone call, that's all."

"Not to sound disrespectful here, sir, but if it is only a ten second call…Why am I the one making it?" Linda was perplexed and slowly folded her arms.

"Trust me on this one. I got your back, Linda," assured Neil.

"What is going on, sir? Things are a bit strange today. I mean, I am sending out orders that make no sense and everything seems cryptic and just…just…"

"Wrong?" Hillsdale finished her sentence.

The two state police employees, who after working together for fourteen years trusted each other implicitly, exchanged glances for a long moment.

"I will make the call, sir," said Saunders confidently.

"Thank you," Hillsdale said, as he scribbled the number and the message on his notepad.

"Anything else, sir?" asked his secretary with a faint smile on her face, taking the paper in hand.

"Yes, when you're finished, take the rest of the week off and go somewhere with Jim and the kids. Get out of Dodge. Things are going to get a little ugly around here."

"Thank you, sir!" Linda winked at her boss while leaving his office.

Neil Hillsdale felt a burden lift from his shoulders, but the uneasy feeling still remained.

He sat back in his office chair and slowly turned around to look at his family and career portraits once again. He was definitely ready for that change.

#

Vicki gasped, staring out the delicatessen's large window. "Will you look at all the cars, Jules!"

"Believe me, I noticed. I haven't heard anything from the county or state as to what the deal is." Julie checked her radio frequencies after speaking.

"Things are really getting weird here. I gave Billy a ride home last night, and he started flipping out about the traffic light."

"How so?" Julie asked, finishing her sandwich.

"We pulled up to the traffic light, a block from the marina, and he started getting excited and said something like, big red light good and little red light bad."

"Interesting." Julie gazed out the window in a long thoughtful pause.

"We've been on the world's longest lunch break that's all I know," Joan interjected.

The three ladies sat at the center round table inside Abletti's eating their sandwiches. The deli was normally very busy, but today the staff and the ladies were the only one's present. Music from the Rat Pack quietly played overhead.

"Trent's on his way," Julie remarked as she scrolled through her phone.

There was a brief awkward pause. Vicki looked at Julie with one of her infectious smiles. Joan looked over at Vicki and then back at Julie trying to figure out what exactly was going on.

"Um, that's good, Jules. Will we have time to show you what we brought with us?" asked Vicki.

"It's all good, Vick. He's in the loop. Besides, it's only Trent, right?" Julie gave Vicki a quick wink and a brief smile while Joan wasn't looking.

"I found out some pretty serious stuff, and you might want to be in the right frame of mind before you look at it," suggested Vicki cautiously.

Joan was looking at her phone with wide eyes. "Vicki? I got three calls and two texts from Mayor Willis wondering where we are," she whispered, leaning over the table.

Vicki seemed to ignore Joan's comment because she noticed Julie was now looking at her cell phone too. She could tell something was wrong by the expression on Julie's face.

"What's the matter, Jules?"

"According to all the news outlets, it seems that Castle Reef is being evacuated," said Julie as she began popping her knuckles.

"I know I heard the tourists were leaving because of the beach being closed, but we didn't hear anything about an evacuation at city hall!" Vicki exclaimed.

"Maybe that's what the mayor was calling about. Should I call him back?" Joan asked nervously.

"No, not yet, Joan," Julie spoke firmly.

"Oh, okay, sorry," Joan retreated.

"Vicki, what's in the folder?" asked Julie, glancing out both windows.

"Well, things are going to get a little interesting when I show you this," stated Vicki, slowly opening the folder in front of her.

Julie wiped her mouth with the napkin on her lap. "What do you mean?"

"Well, we left town hall with this folder because we were being watched."

"By who?"

"Remember Dr. Strange Eyes?" Vicki imitated the odd man they both encountered yesterday.

"Yes, and?" said Julie, expecting more details.

"He scared the Boston Tea out of me!" Joan blurted out.

"He showed up at the mayor's office," Vicki added.

"Interesting," said Julie, taking a sip of her lemonade. *Something just doesn't seem to add up.*

"Here's the bombshell along with another extra page of goodies for your eyes to feast on," Vicki said, sliding the open folder across the table in front of Julie.

Joan gulped her drink and then coughed. "Heaven help us all!"

Julie started reading the copied documents. She turned the pages and examined every detail while finishing her drink. Her eyes raced across the pages and the expression on the police chief's face never changed. Vicki and Joan sat staring at Chief Kerrig in awkward silence. Only Frank Sinatra's "New York, New York" was playing in the background, which made Vicki nervously giggle to herself.

Suddenly, the restaurant door opened and startled the ladies, with the exception of Julie who continued reading. The noise from the traffic and people murmuring outside was quickly silenced when the door closed. Trent Green had walked in and was approaching the table.

"Hey, there," said Trent, looking a little confused.

"Hi, Trent!" Vicki jumped up and gave him a big hug.

"Hey, Vicki, I didn't know you were going to be here," said Trent quietly.

Joan stood up and extended her hand to Trent. "Hi, I'm Joan Bradford. I work with Vicki."

"Nice to meet you, Joan." Trent shook the secretary's hand firmly.

Everyone turned back to the table and looked at Julie, who was still engulfed in the documents that were inside the folder. She leafed through the pages and began to tilt her head side to side with a neck rolling motion. Trent and Vicki knew exactly what that mannerism meant. Julie was slowly becoming angry. Vicki cleared her throat loudly to get her attention.

"Oh, hi, Trent, have a seat," said Julie, glancing up quickly and then back down at the papers.

"I'm sorry I was late. I had to park my truck three blocks down and walk. Pretty congested to say the least."

"It is getting crazier by the minute," said Joan.

"We already finished our lunch, Trent. Sorry, I had no idea you were meeting us or Julie," said Vicki in a loud voice, in order to get the police chief's attention.

Julie held up her pointer finger to signal that she was just about finished and not to interrupt her. Vicki laughed out loud then covered her mouth.

"Nah, that's fine, I'm not really that hungry," Trent remarked, sliding his chair up to the table.

"Let me get you something to drink. What do you want?" asked Vicki, walking to the counter.

"I think they have Vernors here, if not just get me a cream soda. Thanks, Vicki," Trent said cordially.

"Well, Trent, it's been an interesting day so far for me. I feel like I'm in a movie," Joan said sarcastically.

"I know what you mean." Trent folded his hands together, grinned at Joan, and then looked over at Julie.

Julie took a deep breath, piled all the pages together in a neat stack, and shut the folder. She pursed her lips and slowly exhaled.

"Are you okay?" asked Trent tenderly.

After a long pause, Julie looked into Trent's eyes and stated, "No, I'm not, and this would be a good time for all of you to pray."

Vicki walked up and set a bottle of cream soda in front of Trent. They both, with the exception of Joan, recognized a look in Julie's eyes that they had seen three years ago when she first got the news of her father.

"Vicki? Joan?" Julie spoke in a quiet yet intimidating voice.

"Yes," they both replied in unison.

If the moment wasn't so serious, Vicki thought to herself, she would be laughing hysterically because together they sounded like robots.

"I want you to go back to work and pretend you never obtained this folder or met me for lunch," said Julie evenly.

"Jules, we can't do that! Willis is expecting me to give him the first set of documents you just read," Vicki pleaded.

"These are copies, right?" asked Julie.

"Yes, they are," agreed Vicki.

"Willis has been demanding these meeting minutes since yesterday," Joan cut in.

"Exactly, and you are going to go back to City Hall and give him what he was asking for." Julie looked at both of the ladies with a serious stare.

"That's all? I mean what you read is blatant corruption, and that's all that you're going to do?" Vicki whispered intensely, as she leaned in.

"I will keep the folder and will be visiting Mr. Willis shortly. You gals head back and tell him that the traffic and confusion today was the cause of your delay," Julie instructed.

"I trust you, Jules. I'm sorry for all this!" Vicki had tears in her eyes.

"It's not your fault, girlfriend. Trust me, this is literally just a spoke in the big picture of what is going on around here right now," exclaimed Julie, looking over at Trent.

"Joan, now I feel like I'm in that same movie you were talking about earlier," Trent announced.

"For sure, I just hope it's over soon." Joan stood up and adjusted her dress. "We better get going, Ms. Stanwick."

"If anything changes, please text me, Jules?" Vicki pleaded gently.

"It's going to be all right. You both better walk there and leave Bumblebee parked here," suggested Julie to break the tension.

"Okay, I will see ya soon. Bye, Trent," Vicki smiled nervously and left the deli with Joan.

Trent and Julie sat quietly at the table for the remainder of Sinatra's "I've Got You Under My Skin" that serenaded them as they watched the traffic slowly move past the large window. Only moments ago, after reading the contents of the folder, Julie was hurt and angry, but now, in spite of it all, she felt a wonderful peace knowing Trent was next to her.

They gazed into each other's eyes after the song finished. Trent moved closer to hold Julie's hand. Looking down at their joined arms, they noticed the thin ink lines that formed a perfectly shaped heart. The memory of getting the tattoos together after their engagement announcement silently raced through their minds.

"Jules?" Trent looked into her eyes.

"Yes?" Julie welled up.

"Things aren't too good, are they?" he softly asked.

"No, Trent, it seems as though the recorded minutes, from last month's board meeting, may have been altered. My appointment to be the chief of police was a temporary assignment at best, and they never told me otherwise," Julie said calmly, followed by a sigh.

"What does this mean?" Trent's face became alarmed.

"I'm not sure yet. Trying to put it all together." Julie moved her hands slowly away from Trent's, adjusted her ponytail, and then finished her drink.

"You were nominated and duly elected to the office, Jules," insisted Trent.

"I thought so too. There is something fishy going on here in Castle Reef, and I intend to get to the bottom of it," said Julie firmly.

"What about the DNA from the weird guy? Did you find anything out?" asked Trent.

"There wasn't anything found on the glass or in the fluids. The results also came back negative for prints too, but trust me, he is involved in all of this that's for sure!"

"What are you going to do, hon—" Trent stopped and caught himself.

"It's okay, you can call me honey again." Julie gave Trent a genuine smile and then continued. "I'm going to go visit the mayor after I look around town and put an end to all of this nonsense."

"Do you want me to go with you?" urged the man she adored.

"No, Trent, take this folder to your office and lock it up in that old safe. Just keep your eyes open and call or text me if you see anything going on." Julie stood up and put on her sunglasses.

"Can we meet later?" asked Trent expectantly.

"How about my place?" Julie gave Trent her beautiful smile.

"Deal! Please watch your back," said Trent with great concern.

Julie reached out and took Trent's hand. "I will."

The couple suddenly stopped when they heard the song that was now playing in the empty deli: "Love and Marriage."

"What are the odds?" Trent laughed, walking her across the room.

"I don't know, but I think those odds are increasing every minute," said Julie, placing her cap on and adjusting her firearm within its holster.

As Trent slowly turned toward the door, Julie leaned over and kissed him on the cheek. "See ya soon, Mr. Green." She winked.

Julie left and jumped into her Bronco cruiser, turning on the flashing lights and using her siren intermittently, in order to make the traffic yield to her presence. Meanwhile, Trent stood inside Abletti's Deli, looking out the large window and taking in the remainder of Frank Sinatra's song with a smile. Julie was back in his life, but certainly not the way he had expected.

chapter

14

Bubbles were surfacing as the last diver made his way to the top of the Salty Dog Harbor.

The Sheriff's Department Diver Rescue Team spent nearly two hours searching beneath the *Susan Marie,* looking for any evidence that would corroborate with Billy Daily's story. Officers Caldwell and Hill were standing on the dock waiting for the team to give their results.

"We're all done here, Blue!" declared the dive captain climbing up the ladder.

"Nothing huh?" asked Caldwell.

"Nope, it's all clear down there. I guess we're calling it a day."

Both divers began removing their tanks and putting their gear into their pickup.

"I heard a call come in earlier on your channel, when you both went down. Something about you all being called back to base?" inquired Caldwell.

"Yes, not sure what that was about. I think they might have been talking about turning it over to the HP. Apparently, the situation here is running hot," explained the sheriff's deputy.

"What situation? The shark attack?" asked Officer Hill.

"We never heard anything from our dispatch," Caldwell inserted.

"It's been pretty quiet. I think I heard a code 6 for Castle Reef," the other sheriff's diver added.

"Really? I wonder what's going on, that would keep you guys away from the beach?" asked Hill.

The diver captain sighed. "Not sure, Five-O, I will let you know if we hear anything."

"Thanks, County. Keep us posted," Caldwell replied.

The divers had finished loading their gear into the truck and were ready to leave.

Caldwell and Hill both thanked the deputies and walked over to Jerry Foster, who was organizing his fishing gear.

"Mr. Foster, we are all finished here for today," said officer Caldwell.

"Well, what did you find? I see the divers are leaving," asked Jerry, who was still grumpy.

"There wasn't anything below the boat that looked suspicious. We'll keep the area secure tonight and try to get the crime specialists from Brighton in here tomorrow," assured Hill.

"I'm sorry, Mr. Foster. We will be sure to thoroughly look into this," added Caldwell.

"I don't think you'll be able to give Billy a ride in your car today or even tomorrow boys. The word is out that the town is being evacuated." Jerry scoffed, picking up a couple of baskets and rope.

Both officers looked at each other.

"Excuse me, Mr. Foster?" asked Hill.

"Becky heard on the scanner that they now have both lanes open outbound all the way to the interstate," Jerry mumbled as he continued to finish his work.

"Mr. Foster, I will contact you in the morning." Caldwell gave Hill a nod and motioned him to head to out.

"Just a kindly reminder fellas, I won't be leaving the town without a fight, so tell that to Chief Kerrig!" Foster called out, walking under the covered dock area.

The officers nodded, making their way to their patrol cars and eventually drove off, maneuvering through the back streets as they headed for the station.

#

Ian cracked open one of the cold beers from his backpack and staggered down the beach with his college friends. It was time to party. The girls were coming later, but now it was time for Ian to unwind, forget about who he was and somehow escape the prison from which he lived inside. He had tried so hard the day before to walk away from all the vices that fed his disintegrating life, but the depression was too much for him to handle.

The beach was all his with the exception of Randy and Jake, fellow guards who had tagged along in hopes of meeting some of Ian's girlfriends. Nobody was going to tell him that it was closed. It was time to show everyone that Ian Reynolds was his own man and that he was the most popular, richest, and best-looking lifeguard around.

"It's gettin' dark soon, Ian. Are you sure it's okay for us to be out here?" asked Jake.

"Yeah, dude, I think the beach is off-limits even to us lifeguards. That's what boss man said yesterday," interjected Randy.

"Shut your faces, boys, or I will take both of you for a walk into the ocean." The drunken Atlas laughed, clad in his red swimming trunks.

"Let's head north to the rocks so we can see if the shark is up there eating all the fish guts from the marina," shouted Jake, running away from Randy and Ian.

Reynolds, the star quarterback, grabbed a beer can from his sack and hurled it like a pigskin into the center of Jake's back. The skinny twenty-year-old fell to the ground rolling, in pain.

"Why did you do that, Ian!" screamed Jake, turning over on his back.

Ian kicked sand into his face. "Because I'm Ian Reynolds and I run the show down here on this beach!" slobbered the drunken politician's son.

"Hey, let's go to the north rocks and wait for the hotties to meet us instead!" begged Randy.

"Now that's a plan I can get behind!" Ian shouted.

The three tanned, obnoxiously drunken men made their way up the beach singing and shrieking obscenities in the setting evening sun. They were too inebriated to notice the large fin seventy yards out, cutting through the shallow ocean waters parallel to them, leaving its long, thick, dark back exposed.

#

Pacing in his small office after his initial phone call greeting, the concerned and lovestruck maintenance man finally sat down in his office recliner.

"She's awake and doing so much better," sighed the loyal friend, looking over at the hospital bed.

"I was really concerned about her, and I just wanted to call and check to see how she was doing," said Mike gently.

"I'm sorry, who is this again? I'm kind of tired," Jill said apologetically.

"No, no, my bad, so sorry, Jill. This is Mike Rawlings. I'm from the Green Sea Inn."

"Oh my gosh! You're the Mike that Karen was telling me about?" said Jill.

Mike's heart skipped a beat. "Uh yeah, I guess, that's me."

"She was so excited to finally meet someone, for the first time, who she instantly connected with. You know what I mean?"

Mike cleared his throat. "Yeah, I know, me too."

"She really likes you, Mike. I wish she could talk, but she is still sleeping a lot," said Jill regretfully.

"Is her family there yet?" asked Mike, pacing again.

"Yep, her parents came in yesterday. They went out to catch an early dinner. They'll be back pretty soon to give me a break."

Mike took a deep breath. "Can you tell Karen I called and asked about her?"

"I sure will, Mike. She was saying something about blinking red lights," reported Jill.

"That's interesting. I wonder what she meant?" inquired Mike, switching the cell phone to his other ear.

"That was also the first thing she mumbled when she woke up after the operation on her leg," recalled Jill.

"This is a terrible thing for her, you, and everyone." Mike winced after making the comment.

"The doctor from the county coroner's office...I think his name was Dr. Hackett, he came by, talked to the other doctors and asked Karen some questions. All she could really remember was the blinking red lights."

"Strange, huh?" said Mike awkwardly.

"Very...I'll tell her you called when she wakes up," assured Jill.

"I appreciate that. You get some rest too," Mike added.

"I'll try. So much for that relaxing beach trip." said Jill, with a soft laugh.

"I'm really sorry this happened."

"Maybe if I had been there it would've been different. Well, I gotta let you go, Mike. It looks like Karen's family is here. Thanks again for checking in."

"You bet, Jill. Talk to you soon." Mike ended the call and held the phone to his chest. He was both thankful and puzzled at the same time. He was so happy to find that Karen had survived a horrific event and had mutual feelings for him. However, the blinking red lights statement kept racing through his mind.

Suddenly, Mike was startled by his phone vibrating. He looked down and saw that it was an incoming call from New York. He was about to reject it as spam when he recognized the number. It was Jim Renaldi, his friend, the security expert.

#

After receiving the incoming data, Terry quickly typed nearly 115 lines of code along with exact coordinates on the touch screen glass surface interface. Unaware that Cortney had provided a job, a place to live and an unhealthy codependent relationship for the sheer purpose of Terry's excellent computer programming skills, Warren worked feverishly to make sure the commands were sent to M1 and M2, in order to make Alexander happy.

"We received the data you asked for, and I just sent the final instructions to M1 and M2 as requested," announced Warren over the intercom.

"Excellent! All we need is the one remaining piece of the puzzle, and phase 3 will begin at once!" celebrated Alexander's voice, piercing through Terry's headphones.

"M1 and M2 will now be working in tandem temporarily. We lost connection to Port 46 this morning," Terry reported sheepishly.

"Reroute the signal on tier 7261 and we should be fine," directed Cortney.

Warren paused and took a drink from the bottle of diet soda that was on the glass desk.

"Your father was looking for you earlier," said Terry, cautiously changing the subject.

"Oh? What did he want?" asked the probing, manipulative voice.

"Well, he said to tell you that Mr. Reynolds has taken care of everything as promised," assured Terry proudly.

"That is very good news indeed," said Alexander.

"I told him that you were very busy in the lab working on the Solar Defense Initiative cell tests."

"Well done, dear Terry!" Cortney said in her sickening, syrup sounding voice.

"Thank you. That means a lot to me, Cortney," Terry said timidly.

"You will be rewarded." The intercom signal ended abruptly.

Terry was now relieved that approval was once again gained with Cortney. The fragile adult, with the emotional intelligence of a young teenager, smiled in great satisfaction. Warren continued to check on all the moving data on the large flat desk screen, while sipping on a steel straw inserted in a bottle of diet root beer.

Meanwhile, several floors below, the thin arrogant woman stood with her hands crossed, admiring her final design in the sterile lab. It was here, in this cloaked, top secret room, that Cortney Alexander had spoken with Dr. Zeleny less than twenty-four hours before. The global terrorist group was ready to advance at a moment's notice.

Cortney's hate for America grew stronger with every stage of the project's advancement.

However, this loathing had begun many years prior when she was only twelve years old. Her father, as always, made friends and connections with many politicians and people of influence.

For several years, a close friend of the family who was a United States Senator, vacationed, and visited often with the Alexanders. Like all pedophiles, he groomed his victim by gaining her trust. Seizing an opportunity to act, the deviant senator stole a young girl's innocence and abused Cortney. As most monsters do, he threatened her not to tell anyone.

In time, she found the courage to disclose the event to her parents. The senator was eventually confronted, but instead of taking responsibility for his actions, put the blame on one of his security guards. Cortney tried to tell everyone the truth but was ignored and instructed by her parents to never bring up the subject again. The innocent guard was convicted and sentenced to fifteen years in federal prison. Upon his release, he was never seen again. Eventually, the senator was involved in another sexual abuse scandal and was forced to resign. He had been found dead four years earlier, hanging in his garage in an apparent suicide.

All these injustices and violations from her past were fueling the fire of hate inside of Ms. Alexander. This became the driving motivation to fulfill her cause. The world would soon experience a new alignment and revolution, as soon as the last piece of the puzzle was found and put into place with the completion of phase 3. Nothing would stop Cortney Alexander now.

chapter

15

"Is everyone here?" asked Trent, walking into the dining room.

Rita McGuire responded, "All present, Trent, except for Mike. We sure don't want to be outside in that traffic."

"I guess it's pretty obvious we won't be open tonight. I'm sorry, guys," said Trent, looking at all of his kitchen and server staff.

"What exactly is going on, Mr. Green, I mean, Trent?" asked Kendra, the young server.

"Yeah, me, boss man, what's happenin'?" asked Francis O'Reilly.

"Honestly, I don't know the full story. We know the town is clearly being shut down. It's strange to say the least. I have never seen anything like this before," expressed Trent, shaking his head.

"Ever since the shark attacks and that freaky customer showed up, everything started going crazy," Kelli Davis spoke up.

The staff all began nodding in agreement among themselves. Trent looked around the room and noticed that a sense of anxiety was starting to build. Some workers were pointing at the traffic outside, while others were texting or looking at the news reports on their phones. He was just about to quiet everyone down and speak when the front door opened. A state highway trooper entered and walked directly up to Trent.

"Mr. Green?" asked the patrolman.

"Yes, Officer? How can I help you?" responded Trent respectfully.

"By order of the governor, I'm going to have to ask you and your staff to vacate the premises and leave town," ordered the trooper.

"Do what?" asked Trent in disbelief. The staff started murmuring among themselves.

"I really hate to do this, but we have orders to inform all the residents and business owners that Castle Reef is under a mandatory evacuation," said the officer, in a kind manner.

"Not to be disrespectful, but that doesn't make sense. There isn't any weather event or health hazard that we are aware of."

"Just doing my job and following my superiors, sir."

"Why evacuate the entire town because of two shark attacks?" implored Trent.

"Sir, I'm sorry. You guys seem like really good people, but I have my orders. There may be other reasons, but I'm just doing my job. Okay?" said the state patrolman, handing Trent the emergency eviction notice.

The entire staff got quiet and looked at both Trent and the patrolman in disbelief. The busy inn which had been filled to capacity the previous night was about to be abruptly vacant.

"How much time do we have, Officer?" asked Trent.

"I'm afraid, the order is effective immediately," said the patrolman, adjusting the chin strap of his large brimmed hat.

"Okay, sir, we'll do our best. I guess we have no choice." Trent stood up and walked the trooper to the door.

"Most of the traffic is moving steady in two lanes. It's blocked off at the interstate. Hopefully, you guys will be back here soon."

Trent forced a smile while shaking the officer's hand, then closed the door. He turned and looked at his trusted staff. No words needed to be exchanged. They slowly got up and quietly began closing down the Green Sea Inn. Trent's phone vibrated in his back pocket. He pulled it out and saw that it was a text from Mike Rawlings.

We need to talk ASAP! the text read.

Something was definitely wrong everywhere.

"I'm a goin' to Jerry and Becky's, lad, after I'm a dun here." Fran's Irish dialect interrupted Trent's thoughts.

"Sorry, Fran, I just got a text. Are you going to stay there?" asked Trent.

"If they a stayin', I will or perhaps I'll get me self one of them boats to sleep en. I'm not a leavin' the Reef, boss man!" said the Irishman firmly.

"I understand, Fran. Just be careful and don't do anything foolish," pleaded his employer and friend.

"I'll be keepin' me self outta sight fer sure."

O'Reilly made his way to the kitchen to secure the inventory and lock the coolers. Trent pulled out his cell phone and speed-dialed Julie. It rang several times and went to voicemail. He left a brief message for her to call him. Next, he speed dialed Mike's number.

"Hey, Trent! Where are you?" Mike hastily answered.

"I'm here in the dining room and walking into the kitchen. What's going on? I got your text," replied Trent, as he made his way into his office and closed the door.

"Some weird crap is going down, my friend!" blurted out Mike.

"Where are you, man? The state police just came by and ordered everyone off the beach!"

"What? That's nuts! I'm upstairs, and I'm searching the rooms and halls for more of those little transmitters."

"Transmitters? Like the one we found on the roof?" Trent asked in surprise.

"Exactly! My friend Jim Renaldi from the Big Apple called a while ago and told me some freakin' scary stuff!"

"Well, the notice I just got from the state police to evacuate the premises is scary stuff!"

"You gotta be kidding me!" Mike slowed the conversation down and then paused.

"Mike?" Trent heard a thud and then the sound of something crunching.

"You better get up here, Trent," said Mike slowly.

"On my way!"

Trent ended the call and quickly put the folder Julie had given him along with the eviction notice into the old safe and shut its door. He ran from his office, through the kitchen and into the dining room. The staff was too busy locking down the restaurant to notice him race past them and up the wide staircase.

Upon reaching the top, Trent turned and looked down the south hall. Mike was near the end, holding an outstretched arm with something dangling from his fingertips. His silhouette was backlit from the window at the end of the hall. It looked as if he was clutching a mouse by its tail. Yet, as Trent walked closer, he could see it was another small transmitter that Mike had discovered, identical to one from the roof.

"Found this in the middle of the ice machine covered up and wired into the compressor," said Mike, with a baffled look on his face.

"Oh my, this isn't good," said Trent with great alarm in his voice.

"Yeah, and that's not all," Rawlings said, directing Trent's attention to the floor.

He followed his friend's gaze, looking at the area in front of the ice machine. There on the floor, mixed in with ice cubes was a pile of items including plates, silverware, wallets, purses, credit cards, cell phones, and keys.

"All this stuff was in there too. Now it all makes sense, Trent."

"I can't believe what I'm seeing."

"Remember all those guests over the past few months who were asking us about their lost items?" inquired Mike.

"Yes, I do! People who lost car keys, wallets, and personal items that were never found," recalled Trent.

"Normally, the ice bin is always full, and the unused ice melts and drains. These items were hidden underneath and shifted, thus partially blocking the water drain," explained Mike.

"I get it. They were possibly stolen and put here in the ice machine, but I'm not following you with the blocked drain." Trent stood there, confused.

"Do you remember when I met Karen yesterday?" asked Mike in a calmer tone.

"Yeah, I do, right before we saw each other at the beach." Trent stood there, thinking for a moment.

"Do you remember what I was doing up here when I radioed you?"

"Oh man, now I see! You were fixing this ice machine! It was jammed or something, right?" Trent's adrenaline was now pumping.

"Right! It was producing ice, but the door was jammed because it was too full. The drain at the bottom of the bin was covered with all these things," expounded Rawlings.

"What were they?" asked Trent impatiently.

"Right here. This cloth napkin, plate, all the silverware, and a table centerpiece from our dining area," said Mike, bending down and pointing to the items clumped together with melting ice around them.

"Good grief, that's everything that was missing after that weird guy left the restaurant yesterday morning all upset and…" Trent stopped and stared at Mike, as goose bumps formed on both of his arms.

"It gets better, bro." Mike stood up and proceeded to scroll through his phone, finding pictures.

"In what way?" asked Trent, as he moved next to Mike to see what was on his phone screen.

"This is what I wanted to show you just before I found another one of these transmitters behind the ice machine."

Mike slowly swiped his phone to advance some pictures for Trent. "These are government photos, of foreign EHF transmitters, that Jim Renaldi sent me."

Trent gasped. "Those look just like the one you are holding!"

"They transmit a signal that operates at a frequency that is so high it's measured in the *terahertz* realm. That's just under the speed of light." Mike held up the device in his hand and looked at it carefully after his explanation.

"So is the strange guy we are all suspicious about, a foreign agent that's setting up some sort of attack here in Castle Reef?"

"Jim said that the transmitters have been spotted in some foreign embassies, as well as several Middle East military conflicts. Our special US forces have retrieved them from battle theaters, but they never could find the receiver or the second part of the system. Renaldi also stated that they are very costly and the electronics inside are mind-boggling."

"Maybe that's why the state police are here and we are being evacuated," Trent remarked.

The two men stood in the vacant hotel hallway for a while, not saying a word, but only pondering their findings. The sound of muffled sirens outside added to the mounting tension building inside of both Trent and Mike.

"I haven't heard from Julie."

"She's probably really busy with all of this going down."

"Maybe, but I don't have a good feeling in my gut, Mike."

Trent checked his phone again and then texted Julie. *Please call or text me and tell me you're okay. I love you.*

#

The police cruiser pulled into a visitor parking space at the town hall municipal building.

Chief Kerrig quickly got out and started walking toward the office entry. Entirely focused, she purposely used her cell phone, instead of the police radio, to contact Shirley. During their call, several notifications came in, Julie ignored them, quickly swiping them away, while she explained what she had found out from Vicki, at Albetti's. The trusted dispatcher listened intently and then warned Julie that the governor had just issued an evacuation order for Castle Reef and to watch her back because something was definitely going down. She assured Shirley that she would keep in touch after confronting the mayor.

The automatic sliding doors opened and Chief Kerrig entered. She swiftly walked down the entry hallway, observing the many empty offices and several employees who were gathering their personal items as they prepared to leave. She made her way to Vicki's office space located in the center of the building. Julie surveyed the area and saw that Vicki was alone in the room. Walking up to her desk, she pretended not to notice a corner security camera that was slowly panning in her direction.

"Hey, girlfriend, how is it going?" asked Julie, sitting on the corner of her desk.

"It's crazy around here as you can see," whispered Vicki, cautiously leaning in.

"Did Willis finally get the folder he was demanding?" inquired Kerrig, lowering her voice slightly.

"Yep, and he is becoming unruly. He literally yelled at us when we got back here," Vicki answered with a louder whisper.

"Is the blue-eyed wonder boy still here?" Julie looked down the hall.

"No, he was gone when we got here," said Vicki cautiously.

"Where's Willis?" asked Julie.

"He's been in his office ever since I gave him the folder and he has been on his computer a lot, according to Joan," explained Vicki.

"As soon as I leave here, text Joan and tell her to let the mayor know that JK is here. Got it?" urged Kerrig.

"You bet, Jules," answered Vicki quickly.

Vicki Stanwick didn't want to ask any questions. She could tell by the look in Julie's eyes that her best friend was becoming super focused. The tension was building and she feared the situation with Mayor David Willis was about to escalate into something ugly.

"Please be careful," urged Vicki, with a troubled look on her face.

"No worries, Vick. Just get your stuff together quickly and go to your parent's house. Please stay there," instructed Julie calmly.

The police chief got up and walked down the hall. She could see past the large glass interior window into the mayor's office area. Joan Bradford was in the process of hanging up her phone as Julie proceeded through the entry. Joan nervously smiled, then nodded. Chief Kerrig moved past her desk and opened the door to Willis' office. The mayor was facing away from the doorway in his high-back office chair and wiping the beads of perspiration from his forehead.

"JK, I'm sorry, I didn't know you were going to be in town today," said the startled mayor, in a fake cheerful voice.

"Sir, I live in this town," answered Julie sternly.

Willis spun his chair around quickly and gasped in embarrassment. The color from his sweaty face drained momentarily and then returned as scarlet.

"You're not JK!" Willis shouted.

"I'm JK, Mr. Mayor, a.k.a., Julie Kerrig, or were you expecting someone else?" taunted the young chief.

"What! What are you doing here?" demanded Willis.

"I'm here to talk to my superior about my position as chief of police."

Julie did not flinch. The mayor was at a loss for words. He knew that somehow he had been exposed. He sat for a moment in shock, just staring at Julie, who was now standing in front of his desk with both arms crossed.

"Perhaps Ms. Stanwick let you in on something, but this day was going to happen, Kerrig, no matter what!" barked Willis, trying to hide his humiliation.

The mayor promptly stood up and bent over his desk to get into Julie's face. Julie remained expressionless. She could see the fear in his eyes and in his body language.

"You lied to the board members, the police department, and to the people of Castle Reef by swearing me in as the chief of police and not making it official," stated Julie firmly.

"You'll never prove it. That's politics, Kerrig. We can *do* anything we want, in order to *get* what we want," sniped the mayor with an evil grin.

Julie did a slight neck roll and then controlled her temper. "Mayor Willis, you are corrupt. You've been bought, and things are about to get really complicated for you."

"You're fired, Kerrig! Get out of here!" roared Willis.

"I was never hired in the first place, David. You and JK Reynolds fixed the election results and the minutes from the council meeting last month for a specific reason." Julie reached over to her left shirt pocket, unfastened her badge, and laid it carefully down on the mayor's desk.

"This could have been handled differently, Kerrig, but you had to be difficult and stir things up! You were never cut out for the job anyway!" jeered the corrupt mayor.

"I know I've been a pawn for the last month in something you, Reynolds, and possibly others have been cooking up. I haven't figured it all out yet, but when I do, it's not going to turn out good for you people."

The mayor pointed his finger in Julie's face almost touching her cheek. "Is that a threat, Kerrig?" he snarled.

"Nope, just a promise, David," Julie said candidly without flinching.

"Well, that's too bad because everyone is going to learn that the town is being evacuated due to the poorly handled shark attacks by you and your worthless department. I'm now the acting police chief and just because you're John Kerrig's daughter doesn't mean squat. You'll never stop us!" squawked the angered mayor hoarsely.

"Thank you, Mr. Willis," said Julie with a smile on her face.

"For what? You lousy..." Willis cut his sentence short. He slammed both hands on the desk and continued to mutter several curse words under his breath.

Julie stood grinning at his foolish antics. "You just told me a lot, Dave. For that I thank you. Your unrestraint and weak character saved me so much time."

She turned around and began to leave. The mayor suddenly threw his coffee mug, barely missing her head by a few inches. It hit the wall and shattered. Julie stopped, bent down, and selected a piece with her fingertips. Carefully placing it in her shirt pocket, she left the room.

"You have until five o'clock to get everything that belongs to you out of that station! Do you hear me, Kerrig?" the mayor screamed.

Julie calmly walked past Joan's desk and gave her a wink. Joan stood up and watched her proceed down the hall and then glanced over at the mayor's office. Willis slammed his door and quickly got on his phone. The startled secretary rapidly gathered her belongings and chased after Julie.

"Wait! Wait up!" pleaded the Bostonian redhead.

Julie stopped. "Joan, you're going to be safer over at the Stanwicks tonight. Do you know where they live?"

"Yeah, yeah, the historic house, right?"

"That's the one."

"What was that all about back there?" asked Joan, panting in fear.

"Just calm down. It's going to be all right, Joan," assured Kerrig.

As several cars and news trucks passed by the town hall, Julie heard sirens in the distance. Purposely showing no concern in front of Joan, she thought it was strange that there was still only silence on her radio frequency. The sirens sounded like highway patrol vehicles. She made her way outside and down the sidewalk with Joan following.

"I want you to do me a favor. Go to the Stanwicks as soon as you can. Tell Vicki these words *teddy bear in a basket*. She will know what they mean. Do you understand me?" urged Julie.

"Yeah, yeah, bear in a basket," repeated Joan nervously in her noticeable accent.

"Just tell her, she'll understand. It's several blocks from here, so get moving, Joan. Remember, don't leave the Stanwicks!" ordered Julie.

"You got it, Chief!" shouted Joan. She began to mumble under her breath both the Lord's Prayer and "bear in a basket," as she quickly walked toward the historic district.

Julie unlocked her police cruiser and then removed its key fob from her key ring. After grabbing her backpack, she took the cruiser key, put it under the light rack on top of the roof, and headed to the police station. Her mind was now in hyperdrive. She began reviewing the last two days, all the evidence, how the mayor reacted, and what he had said just moments ago. As Julie walked quickly through the side streets, she suddenly heard a set of uniform sounding footsteps, about fifty yards away, following her. She was able to catch a glimpse of the individual in a parked car's sideview mirror. It was the elusive, tall strange man, who was now rapidly advancing behind her.

Julie spoke into her shoulder microphone. "Dispatch, 10-18, I'm headed your way on foot. Unlock the door when you see me in the security camera!"

"Affirmative, Chief," said the dispatcher calmly.

If only Shirley knew what was going on right now, Julie thought, walking briskly and fully aware of the man following her. Pretending not to notice his presence, she approached the station and crossed the street. Julie realized there wasn't any traffic on Main Street and all the squad cars were neatly parked in the lot.

What is going on? This isn't right!

Julie suddenly had a lump in her throat. It felt surreal, as if everything that was happening was a giant practical joke or a surprise party gone wrong. She battled thoughts of panic and utter failure. Walking up to the front doors, oddly enough, Julie no longer heard the footsteps behind her. She looked around in every direction. The strange man was gone. The sound of the station door locks disengaged and alerted her that it was time to go in and break the news to Shirley.

chapter

16

As the sun slipped below the western horizon, several pelicans glided along the water's edge. The ocean was calm, and the beach had lain undisturbed for another day, with the exception of the three young men sleeping in the shade of two large cypress trees that were entwined in the rocks on the north shore. The sound of feet quickly moving across the dry sand came to an abrupt halt.

"Mr. Ian, you all dirty and smell bad!" shouted Billy Daily, who was standing over the half inebriated twenty-one-year-old lifeguard.

"What! Huh? Go away!" grumbled Ian as he belched and rubbed his eyes.

"No, no, no, I won't go way. You veree bad, Mr. Ian!" yelled Billy in anger.

"Hey, man, we're tryin' to sleep here! What's your problem?" Jake growled.

"Dude, leave him alone man, or Ian will put a hurtin' on both of us if anything happens to him!" interjected Randy, who was still feeling buzzed from his six-pack.

Ian groaned. "Billy, go back to your house."

"Mr. Police with big hat says I must leave town now!" said Billy, picking up an empty beer bottle and smelling it.

"Tell that cop to go, um...go fly a kite." Ian rolled over on his stomach. His face was practically buried in the sand.

"Dude, you mean the police told you to leave your home?" asked Randy, scratching his beard.

"I no go home now." Billy put his head down to his chest and dropped the bottle that was in his hand.

"What?" Ian managed to sit up slowly. "What time is it?" asked the groggy lifeguard, wiping his face.

"A little after seven," Randy said as he started flipping through his sand-covered phone.

"Can you all just go somewhere else? My head is killing me!" Jake moaned.

"Ian, man, you're not going to believe this!" exclaimed Randy.

"What's going on, Randy? This better be good or you're going to feel my wrath," answered the young Reynolds. He brushed the sand off his red swimming trunks and spit.

"Dude, Castle Reef *is* being evacuated, man!" announced Randy.

"Where are the girls?" yelled Jake before he passed out again.

Ian stood up, rubbed his head, and looked toward the town. It seemed as though he was instantly sober.

"Can I have burger and french fry, Mr. Ian? I hungree," asked Billy.

"Not now, Billy. Where are the police?" asked Ian, squinting.

"Not same police, look not same! White cars! Big hats!" Billy shouted again.

"Dude, you're scaring me! What is it, Ian?" asked Randy.

"Not sure. Just shut up and let me call my old man!" Ian barked.

Ian Reynolds shuffled in the white sand over to his backpack. He dug feverishly inside it and eventually pulled out his cell phone. Billy watched Ian call his father. In the meantime, Randy kept scrolling on his phone for more news and Jake was on his back fast asleep.

"Come on, man, where are you?" Ian paced, waiting for JK Reynolds to answer.

The call went to voicemail, and Ian hung up. He then swiftly used his thumb to call another number. He ran his hand through his hair several times as he waited.

A woman's voice replied, "Hello?"

"Can you tell me what the heck is going on?" shouted Ian.

He put his call on speaker due to the pounding headache he was now experiencing. Billy sat down next to Randy, both remained silent as they watched and listened.

"Ian? Are you okay? Please tell me you're okay?" The female voice on the other end sounded unusually alarmed.

"I'm fine, just a little hungover thanks to you and Dad," sneered the young college student.

Mrs. Reynolds paused. "Where are you, Ian?"

"I'm on the beach! I'm here in Castle Reef, like I said I was going to be," answered her son sarcastically.

"I didn't know that, Ian. Your father never told me. I have been busy all week doing important things." Janet Reynolds searched for something to say.

"I bet you have, Mommy dear! Real busy playing freakin' cards and sipping on those wine coolers." Ian laughed disrespectfully.

Janet Reynolds suddenly got quiet. The ocean breeze blew across the phone's microphone as Ian paced and rubbed his eyes. The conversation Ian was now having with his mother was an eye-opener for Randy, who pretended to be busy on his own phone. The egotistical lifeguard was nothing more than a hurting boy, like Randy, who also found himself in a dysfunctional home. It didn't matter what income bracket your parents were in or where you grew up, Randy concluded, a bad home is a bad home.

"Where's dear ole Dad?" asked Ian, taunting his mother.

"He's golfing. He won't be back." She paused again. "Until later."

"So what else is new?" scoffed her son.

"I'm sorry it has to be this way every time we talk, Ian," said Janet with an obviously shaken voice.

"Look, I just want to know why the whole town is being evacuated. Now, if you happen to find out anything, or if our wonderful state representative does, you can call me." Ian hung up the phone and tossed it at his pack. He began walking toward the water and eventually ran and dove in.

Billy stood up quickly and watched in total confusion. "Where he go?"

"He's a little upset right now, Billy. He'll be back. Just keep an eye on him," said Randy, as he began to text his parents.

Billy slowly walked to the water's edge and watched Ian's every move. Ian was very important to Billy, and he wanted to make sure that he was going to be safe.

#

Joan Bradford finally reached the home of the Stanwicks. Martha greeted her at the front door after she knocked and rang the doorbell simultaneously several times. Martha calmly invited her inside after noting that Joan was visibly upset. Vicki heard the commotion and came quickly, reaching out to give her a much-needed hug.

"Oh dear, you poor thing. Do you want something cold to drink?" Martha said compassionately.

"Joan, this is my mother, Martha," said Vicki.

"Nice to meet you. Oh, brother, it is just nuttier than a fruit-cake out there, I'm tellin' ya," proclaimed Joan.

"Are you okay, Joan?" asked Vicki tenderly.

"Not exactly, I got lost. I panicked and walked the wrong way. All the houses started looking the same." Joan exhaled.

"Bless your heart." Martha Stanwick embraced her.

"Everything is going down the tubes!" exclaimed the distressed redhead.

"Come on in the living room, my husband, Greg, is watching the local news."

"Hi there, you must be Joan, right?" asked Greg Stanwick, standing up from his recliner.

"Nice to meet you, sir," replied Joan, shaking his hand hard and fast.

"Why are you a nervous wreck, Joan, what is going on?" Vicki asked again.

Greg grabbed the remote and muted the television. Martha and Joan sat down on the sofa, while Vicki found a place on the corner of the coffee table.

"What happened at the office to make you come here?" questioned Vicki.

"It was horrible! This whole town is horrible!" Joan began to cry.

"Is Julie okay? Oh my gosh! Please tell me she's okay?" begged Vicki.

"She's fine, she's fine. Willis went nuts! Julie drove him nuts!" Bradford sobbed, wiping her eyes.

Greg Stanwick studied her face and then looked at the reports on the muted television. His gaze caught Vicki's attention. Without saying a word to each other, they both knew that something big was happening in their little seaside town.

"You're safe here, Joan," said Martha, handing her a tissue.

"I'm not sure about that, Martha," said Joan, swallowing hard.

"What do you mean by that, Joan?" asked Vicki with wide eyes.

"Julie told me to tell you something about a bear in a basket?" Joan wiped her eyes and looked at Vicki, and then back at both Martha and Greg. The room went silent.

"Let's go everyone! We may not have much time," ordered Mr. Stanwick, as he turned off the television and headed for the kitchen. Martha helped Joan to her feet, and Vicki grabbed a flashlight next to her father's recliner.

"Where are we going? Now what? I should have never moved here!" declared the Massachusetts native.

"It's going to be fine. Come with us, and we'll explain later," Martha Stanwick said, leading Joan into the kitchen.

Vicki pulled out her phone and attempted to text Julie, but there was no signal available.

Suddenly, the electricity went out.

#

Trent and Mike used their phones to take pictures of the items that were found buried inside the ice machine at the end of the upstairs hallway. Afterward, they went directly to Trent's office in order to secure them in the safe. On their way through the kitchen, the men noticed only Kelli and Rita remained.

"Is everybody gone already?" Trent asked in surprise.

"Yep, Kendra walked home with two of her friends, and everyone else got picked up by their husbands," Kelli remarked, wiping down the steel kitchen work table.

"They're probably all headed to Brighton by now," Rita added.

"Good grief! That was quick," Mike huffed, dropping the garbage bag inside of Trent's office doorway.

"What's in the bag?" Kelli inquired suspiciously.

"It's…" Mike winced.

Trent looked at his best friend, who was searching for words. "Just lost and found items our guests left behind," he said rapidly.

"Yeah, there's a bunch of stuff in here, that's for sure," said Mike, sounding relieved, as he picked up the bag and brought it inside the office.

"What about you guys? Where are you going tonight?" asked Trent, casually changing the subject.

"Kelli called Jeremy, and it looks like they will be officially staying at the McGuire hotel tonight," announced Rita.

"She is too kind, and besides, she knows I'm a basket case." Kelli laughed nervously.

"We'll all hunker down together. Both Ed and I will take good care of the Davis family," Rita said confidently, hugging Kelli from the side.

"Please be careful," Mike interjected, standing in the office doorway.

"Don't worry, the McGuire's will be locked and loaded," said Rita with a wink, taking off her apron.

"Stay hidden. We're not supposed to be here, remember?" Trent warned.

"We will!" both ladies said in unison, grabbing their purses.

"I love you, guys, and I'll be praying for you," whispered Trent, hugging the ladies goodbye.

Rita and Kelli made their way out the back door and into the twilight coastal town that had become hauntingly silent. The Green Sea Inn was dark, with the exception of Trent's office.

The men placed the ice machine items into the large old safe, located in the corner of the room. Trent reached inside and pulled out his .357 magnum revolver, shoulder holster and proceeded to gear up.

"Whoa! Dirty Harry!" Mike quipped.

Trent frowned. "That's not funny, man."

"Sorry, I couldn't resist. Come on, lighten up. What's wrong?"

"I haven't heard anything from Julie. I thought she would've called me back by now or at least sent a text message."

Mike could tell Trent was worried. "Do you have any idea where she is?"

"She was headed to the mayor's office several hours ago."

"Maybe she's busy with all the evacuation nonsense and helping the state police."

"Julie was going to confront the mayor about her position as police chief."

"Do what? Is something wrong?" Mike's facial expression changed, watching Trent finish tightening his shoulder strap. "Julie is still, um, the chief of police, isn't she?"

"Not sure, my friend, not sure about anything right now," said Trent, followed with a sigh.

"What *is* going on, Trent? I didn't know her job was in jeopardy."

Trent called out in frustration. "Something evil is going down. Can't you feel it?"

The small office got quiet. Trent rubbed his face with both hands. "I gotta find Jules."

Mike looked out into the dimly lit kitchen and then back at Trent. "We'll find her together, okay?"

Trent turned and locked the safe. "You need to go and be with Karen, I'll be fine."

"Nope, I called the hospital earlier and was able to speak with Jill, she said Karen is doing great, but she's sleeping a lot. I won't be any good just sitting in a waiting room, when I can be helping you find Julie," insisted Mike.

"You don't have to, but I do appreciate it. You've always had my back," acknowledged Trent. Rawlings patted him on the shoulder and then walked to the doorway. Trent locked up his desk and gathered his laptop.

"You never told me why they are evacuating Castle Reef? Is it because of the shark attack, or do you think it's something else?" asked Mike with curiosity.

"The patrolman who came by didn't say why the evacuation was taking place, just that he was following orders," said Trent with a puzzled look on his face.

"Are you thinking what I'm thinking?" Mike furrowed his brow.

"Like, the transmitters and the illusive, weird guy are all part of this scenario somehow?" suggested Trent.

"You know it, bro!" Mike agreed.

"We need to get moving," said Trent, with a short exhale.

"Do we need to bring anything else with us, other than your gun?"

Trent paused. "Can you grab a couple of our two-way radios over there on the shelf?"

"Sure thing, boss." Mike moved fast and pulled the radios from the chargers.

The two men secured the inn and walked outside. It was hard to believe that Castle Reef was no longer the busy vacation town they had grown accustomed to. The summer season had instantly come to a halt. The town was empty and very quiet with only an occasional short siren burst being heard in the distance.

"Let's take my truck and head to the police station," suggested Trent.

"Sounds like a plan," said Mike, popping open the trunk of his car.

"What are you doing?" asked Trent cautiously.

"Since I'm riding shotgun, I might as well have one with me." Mike grabbed his tactical Remington 87 shotgun and checked the safety.

"We really are in a movie, aren't we?" Trent shook his head, walking to his truck.

"We're definitely not in New York City any longer, that's for sure, Mr. Green!"

"By the way, Mike, it was a .44 Magnum that Harry Callahan used," quipped Trent, starting his truck, with a nervous grin on his face.

Mike laughed hard and hopped into the passenger side of the old white GMC. As they pulled away, the undetected blue sedan with tinted windows crept slowly into the side street and out of their view.

chapter

17

Randy was preoccupied talking to family on his cell, while Jake was fast asleep. Ian, meanwhile, was in the surf way too long for Billy's liking. He watched his friend swim against the small rip current, nearly fifty yards from the shoreline and about a hundred yards from the inlet, on the other side of the jetty. All of a sudden, a faint blinking green light appeared out of nowhere in the dark water. Billy rubbed his eyes and looked again in disbelief.

"Friend of Ian? Hey, you! I see big scareeey!" yelled Billy, without moving his attention away from the now distant swimmer.

"Hey, chill out, dude, what's the deal?" Randy lowered his phone to see what Billy was pointing at.

"Not safe! Mr. Ian come to beach here now!" screamed Billy, as he pointed frantically.

Randy looked out and saw that three hundred yards beyond Ian, in the dim ocean water, was a fast approaching large dark fin. Ian, who was oblivious, watched both Randy and Billy waving and jumping and down.

"Oh, Billy, you're so lucky! You never knew what it was like to have bad parents!" he shouted, too far out for them to understand him.

As the massive beast rapidly advanced, Ian suddenly turned and saw it pass within only six feet of his body. It continued in a straight line toward the inlet with its back only inches under water. He noticed a blinking light, directly behind the dorsal fin, turn from green to red before the creature abruptly submerged. The young lifeguard was now instantly sober.

"Oh no! It's true! It's freakin' true!" Ian immediately began swimming to shore as fast as he could.

By this time, Billy, Randy, and even Jake were on the shoreline cheering Ian on as if he were in an Olympic event. Finally, Ian made it to shore, collapsing in the wet sand.

"Big scareeey almost got you!" Billy shouted.

"Chill, Billy," Randy said, helping Ian onto the dry sand.

"That, that was…that was, oh, man." Ian gasped for every breath.

"That was trippy, man!" Jake belched and then sat down.

"You don't look good, Mr. Ian," said Billy as he backed up.

"That was a big shark! Are you all right, Ian?" asked Randy.

It could have been a combination of the alcohol and fear, but nevertheless, Ian Reynolds vomited.

#

"So that's what happened to your fired police chief today. Sorry I talked your ear off," said Julie, as she finished recounting the town hall incident in detail to Shirley Allen.

"What a mess. So sorry, sweetie," consoled Shirley.

"You know, Willis is running totally scared and out of his mind as we speak."

"I'm sure he is, Jules," said the seventy-five-year-old dispatcher.

Julie sipped from her water bottle and swallowed slowly. "I should have throttled him, but somehow, I kept my cool."

"You did the right thing, Chief. You've been trained well."

"Um, it's ex-chief, remember?" Julie reminded her trusted friend.

"You'll always be the chief to me and to this town, Julie Kerrig," said Shirley tenderly.

"Thanks, Mama Shirley." Julie grimaced. "Here's a piece of evidence you can put into the safe, along with the other items."

"What is it?"

"It's DNA from the honorable David Willis." Julie pulled a small evidence bag out of her duty belt pouch and placed the broken piece of coffee cup into it, then set it on her desk.

"I will see to it that it's secure," guaranteed Shirley.

"Thanks, speaking of secure, that strange bozo who called you yesterday was following me here, and that's why I radioed the 10-18."

"Are you sure it was him?" Shirley looked perplexed.

"Yes, it was definitely him. He wasn't anywhere to be seen after I crossed Main Street."

"How odd," remarked Shirley.

Julie got quiet. She removed her hat, adjusted her braided pony-tail, and then looked at her longtime trusted friend and coworker. Something was different about the way the dispatcher was acting. It was time to find out.

"I also noticed that all of our cruisers are in, yet nobody is here?" asked Julie.

"They all came in early, filled out their reports, and headed to Brighton with their families," responded Shirley timidly.

"What gives? How is it that I wasn't notified? There has been nothing but radio silence all day."

"I really don't know," Shirley said softly.

"All these bizarre events are linked together somehow, and we need to get to the bottom of it," Julie insisted.

"Trust me, Jules, I'm with you."

"Are you, Mama Shirley? Why wasn't I told about the evacuation from the start?" said Julie, with slight agitation in her voice.

"Trust me, Jules. Sanchez's shift was over, and I found out about the beach evacuation from Caldwell and Hill, when they got back from the Foster's boat vandalism call."

"Really? How did they know?" Julie paused.

"They were working with the county diver team, and those guys were called back to HQ in Brighton," answered Shirley.

"Not even a mention on our radio frequency or on the county channels?" wondered Julie.

"No, ma'am, the guys said they heard it from the sheriff's deputies, and they told me about it for the first time when they came back."

Julie sighed. "I wish you would've called me, Shirley."

"I assumed you already knew and were tied up with Vicki and Trent. I'm so sorry, Jules."

"This has the smell of JK Reynolds and Willis all over it!" announced Julie as she put her hat back on.

Looking across the room, Julie noticed the whiteboard that she had drawn on earlier was completely erased. Surveying the rest of the office, she noticed that everything was put away and locked up as if the station would be closing.

What is going on? I never noticed this when I first got here, Julie thought.

She turned to Shirley who was now gazing at a small electronic device she removed from her uniform pocket. The dispatcher's expression had changed into a look of seriousness that she had never seen before. A feeling of dread suddenly came over Julie.

"Mama Shirley, I don't like what I'm seeing right now."

Shirley stood up from her desk, walked over to Julie, and motioned for her to go the ladies locker room. Julie instantly knew Shirley was very troubled and that something was terribly wrong. They the both remained silent until they entered the restroom area. Shirley turned on the faucets at one of the sinks and began to speak in a low, hushed voice. "They may be listening to us. I'm not sure who it is, but you need to get out of here as soon as you can."

Julie whispered. "Who, Shirley? What is happening in Castle Reef?"

"I will explain later, but you need to go hide somewhere safe, Jules, and fast."

"What's going on? Please tell me, I noticed you erased the whiteboard? What's that device you have in your pocket?"

"This is all bigger than you think. The state police want to arrest you, Julie."

"What? Why? For what reason?" Julie pleaded. Her eyes began to fill with tears.

"It will take too long to explain, but…" Shirley hesitated.

"What, Shirley? Please tell me something."

"This goes way back to your daddy, Jules. It involves your father," said Shirley remorsefully.

Julie covered her mouth and stepped back in disbelief. She was just beginning to heal from the tragic loss, and now those familiar feelings came rushing back full force in an instant.

"My dad? In what way?" said Julie, now in shock and pacing the floor.

"There is no time, sweetie! You need to change into your street clothes. The state police are on their way now. You have about five minutes, at best, to get out of here!"

"I can't believe this is happening!" Julie raised her voice in anger.

"Shh! Trust me on this, Jules! Please trust me," whispered Shirley loudly.

Julie removed her firearm from its holster, took off her duty belt, and in a fury, whirled it across the room. It hit the block wall causing several items to fall out and scatter on the floor.

Julie released a whisper-shout. "Unbelievable! This crap is unreal!"

She quickly went to her locker and began changing clothes faster than a fireman during a five-alarm call. She pulled up her blue jeans and put on a black t-shirt. Shirley was amazed how fast the woman was moving. In her rage, she wadded up her uniform, dumped it in the trash receptacle, and began tying her sneakers. She then picked up her cap, gave it to Shirley, and proceeded to undo her braid. Julie shook her head and allowed her golden blonde hair to fall upon her shoulders.

"Please put my dad's hat in a safe place," pleaded Julie.

Grabbing the Colt 1911 from her belt, she quickly put it in the waistband of her jeans and pocketed the extra clip she had grabbed. Julie bent over to pick up her cell phone, which had fallen during her wardrobe frenzy. Upon reaching for it, she noticed something on the tile floor reflecting in the bathroom light. Slowly picking it up, she discovered it was a miniature rectangular object. It was the size of a TV remote control button, but flatter, and contained a miniature flashing amber light in its center. Julie was briefly mesmerized.

"We don't have time to waste," insisted Shirley, who was still in awe of the one-minute transformation process it took for the uniformed police chief to turn into an attractive female citizen.

"It was in my duty belt. I wonder how long it's been in there." Julie held the object between her fingers in front of Shirley's face.

Shirley's eyes widened as she realized what Julie was holding. "Take it with you Jules! Don't ask. Just hide it. We will talk later!" said Shirley urgently.

Julie scrambled and retrieved another small evidence baggie from her belt on the floor. She dropped the strange miniature item inside and quickly sealed it. She then folded it up, put it inside her cell phone case, and slid the phone into her back pocket.

"Where can I meet you?" asked Julie frantically.

"I'll find you, baby girl. You have to leave quickly."

"What about Trent? I'm supposed to meet him at my place," pleaded the visibly upset Kerrig.

"Don't worry, sweetie, I'll tell him, and we will all meet up later." Shirley walked over to the sink.

"Please tell me where," begged Julie.

"I'll find you. Stay focused, Julie. Your father taught you well. You have all the pieces to this crazy puzzle. Now, it's time for you to put it all together."

"I love you, Mama Shirley." Julie's heart was racing.

"I love you too. More importantly, God loves you." Shirley kissed her on the forehead.

"I know that, and I need Him now more than ever."

"Remember, just follow the facts, Jules." Shirley gave Julie a serious look and then turned and shut the water off at the sink.

The locker room was now quiet. Julie slowly opened the door and looked out into the station office carefully. She hugged Shirley, and then they looked at each other one last time.

The athletic blonde woman walked down the hall and outside into the dusk of night. She turned around and saw Shirley wiping her eyes. The sounds of multiple sirens were getting louder. Julie gave a short nod and then began to run down the northeast alley toward the ocean.

#

Inside the dimly lit and tiny cellar of the historic Stanwick house, the four adults had been huddled for nearly two hours.

Vicki whispered to Joan, "During a bad hurricane, when I was about seven or eight years old, Julie and I were down here hiding from the violent winds that were ravaging Castle Reef. My parents were above us, along with Julie's dad, trying to get the windows boarded up."

"It's pretty tight down here, Vicki," breathed Joan.

"Yeah, but nobody knows this cellar is here. Anyway, let me finish—"

The nervous secretary couldn't keep herself from interrupting. "So what does 'bear in a basket' have to do with a safe room in the floor of your kitchen pantry?" asked the redhead, who was now sweating.

"Well, it used to be a fruit cellar made of dirt and gravel," Martha Stanwick added.

"Actually, they used it for refrigeration back then too," added Greg Stanwick who was enjoying his daughter's story."

"Vicki, finish your story quickly because I think we need to get quiet," whispered Martha.

"Yeah, keep going, it helps to distract me from getting claustrophobic and the fact that I have to pee!" Joan whispered louder.

"Anyway, groundwater from the extremely high tide started seeping into this cellar."

"There's going to be more than ground water in here if I have to be down here much longer," warned Joan.

"I had all my toys with me including my favorite stuffed bear, which ended up floating in a wicker basket," continued Vicki.

"Is that it? That's the big mystery story? Bear in a basket?" Joan asked in a sarcastic whisper.

"Well, it was funny at the time. Julie and I never forgot it. Besides, I—"

"Hush! Did you hear that?" Martha covered their mouths.

Everyone heard the sound above and froze. The door to the house opened and shut slowly. Footsteps made a rhythmic sound as they moved throughout the house until they stopped directly overhead. The silence felt like an eternity. The four adults, who were crammed into the small cubicle, eight feet below the kitchen floor, remained motionless. Whoever was up there was now listening carefully.

After several minutes, the person's feet began to shuffle in a strange manner and then began running in place. Suddenly, there was a loud crash followed by silence. Joan quietly sobbed, while Vicki held her tightly. Martha motioned for everyone to stay quiet while Greg held down firmly on the handle of the cellar hatch.

#

"It's about time you got here!" scolded Janet Reynolds with another glass of wine in her hand.

"I told you, the boys like to have a few drinks after a round of golf," slurred JK, plopping down on the leather sofa.

"You're drunk, JK."

"Well, look who's talking! The closet wino has spoken!"

Janet stomped off into the kitchen and dumped her glass into the sink. She returned to the living room and sat down across the room from her husband, who now had his shoes off and was ready to sleep.

"Look at me, JK!" shouted Janet.

"Well, well, well. Aren't we a little mouthy tonight?" muttered JK.

"Why didn't you tell me where Ian was?" scolded the politician's wife.

"You knew he was on the beach! C'mon, he's a lifeguard!"

"You never told me you spoke with him, and you never told me that Castle Reef was being evacuated!"

"Now hold on there, woman!" JK sat up and glared at his wife.

"He called me almost an hour ago, drunk and upset."

"Well now, that makes three of us doesn't it?" laughed the intoxicated politician.

"We are pathetic! He was angry at us again, JK. Do you blame him?"

"So what else is new?"

"Why is the whole town being evacuated?"

"I have no idea. Governor Riddick made that call, not me."

"Bull! You know why!" barked Janet.

"You don't have a clue how the real world works, lady!"

"Secrets, secrets, secrets, and more lies! That's all this marriage has been built on!"

"I have given you everything and made you important! Don't you ever forget that!" garbled JK loudly.

"I can't live this way anymore, JK. I'm done," muttered the distraught wife.

Janet got up and left the room. Soon, the master bedroom door slammed. JK cursed under his breath and then leaned back and fell asleep. The large suburban house grew silent and even darker than nightfall.

chapter

18

As the white pickup truck crept through the back streets of Castle Reef, not only was the town void of people, it seemed unnaturally bleak. The mounting sense of urgency for Julie to return his call or text was growing by the minute inside of Trent. Mike suggested checking her apartment first before going the police station. Trent pulled his old GMC behind the row of shops on Main Street located directly across from the police station. He purposely parked next to a dumpster that was hidden by a lattice fence and an old sycamore tree. The stores, which were now all closed, had several apartments above them. Julie's was over an antique store and its entrance was behind the building, close to where Trent parked.

"I'm going up to check things out. Keep me posted if you see anything out here." Trent got out and quietly shut the truck door.

"You got it, man. Be careful up there, bro," whispered Mike, carefully holding his shotgun.

Trent made his way up the wooden staircase and reached the top. He was stopped abruptly at the sight of Julie's apartment door that was ripped off its hinges and wedged across the hallway. Fear rushed through his entire body as he moved past the broken door and entered the apartment.

The entire place was in shambles. Furniture was overturned with everything else scattered upon the floor. Trent used the flashlight on his cell phone as he scrambled through the mess in desperation looking for Julie's body. His heart didn't want to believe what his mind was trying to convince him of. Waves of numbness shot through his legs and arms. He fumbled with his radio and managed to call Mike.

Trent gasped. "Get up here quick, Mike, and bring my flashlight!"

"I'm on it!" Mike replied.

Trent stood in silence horrified, as a glaring question raced through his mind. *Who would do something so destructive as this?*

Mike raced up the stairs and climbed over the piles of rubble. "What in the world? This is unbelievable!"

"We have to find her, Mike." Trent said in desperation.

"Okay, calm down, man. Let's look, okay?" spoke Mike softly, pointing the flashlight downward.

"This can't be happening!" Trent held his head with both hands.

The two men turned over shelves, the kitchen table, a bookcase, the bed, and multiple piles of debris without finding anything. Julie wasn't in the apartment.

"At least she's not in here or wounded. There's no blood," said Mike, wiping sweat from his brow.

"Thank you, Jesus. I pray she's all right," whispered Trent, wiping tears from his eyes.

"Who do you think would do something like this?" Mike shook his head.

"I have a feeling it's that guy we've been talking about."

"But, Trent, this looks like five people did this."

"I know, but I have a gut feeling he had a part in this."

"Whoever it is, I'm ready to take him, or all of them, out." Mike held his shotgun up to his shoulder.

"I hear ya." Trent turned off his phone light, stepped over a pile of books, and looked out the front windows, after hearing the sound of several vehicles below.

"What is it, Trent?"

"Turn the flashlight off."

"Is someone out there?" Mike froze.

"Strange. Four state patrol cruisers just pulled into the police station across the street."

"What does that mean?"

"It means that Julie is probably over there. Unless they are looking for her, like we are."

"Hey, Trent. Check this out." Mike had a wall clock in his hand.

"What's wrong?" asked Trent, glancing out the window again.

"The time stopped at 3:45 p.m. In fact, the stove, the stereo, and all the other electronic stuff are dead."

Trent stepped over broken dishes to look at the open refrigerator that was still plugged in, but not running. "It's as if there was a dirty bomb or something that neutralized everything in this apartment."

"Those transmitters Jim told me about?" asked Mike.

"You might be onto something," agreed Trent, returning to the window and making sure he wasn't seen by any of the officers who were now entering the station.

"What do you want to do?" Mike slid next to Trent and looked over at the station in disbelief.

"I think we need to stay here and wait until we've heard from Julie or Shirley," Trent said decisively.

"Why would the state police be here? They have their weapons drawn," Mike wondered.

Both men stood silently, with many different scenarios running through their minds. The sudden reality of all the strange things going on was too difficult to comprehend. With the sound of the police car radios echoing off the vacant buildings, minutes passed as they quietly watched for any sign of Julie Kerrig.

Mike sighed and spoke first. "I think they are after Julie. What if she isn't over there, and they come here next to look for her?"

Trent nodded in agreement. "Good point. I think you're right, my friend. We're toast if the troopers find us here."

"Where do you want to go?"

"Let's get to the truck and we'll…" Suddenly, Trent stopped. He bent down and picked up an open Bible with a photo sticking halfway out of it.

"What is it?" asked Mike.

"It's her Bible and a picture of Vicki, Julie, and me the night before I proposed to her." Trent's eyes welled up as he tucked the photo in his shirt pocket.

"I'm sorry, man." Mike reached out and placed his hand on Trent's shoulder.

Trent opened the old brown leather cover. "This was her father's."

"What's wrong with someone that would trash an apartment like this?" Mike shouted in a whisper.

"We just have to keep looking for her." Trent rubbed his eyes, placed the Bible carefully on the window sill, and then made his way through the rubble and to the door.

"Where are you going?" asked Mike, following close behind.

"I think I know where we need to check first." Trent was determined.

The men pulled away carefully in the old white truck, without headlights, and proceeded south down an untraveled, dune grass-covered alley which ran parallel to Main Street.

#

One hundred yards across the street from Julie's trashed apartment, four state troopers were searching the station extensively. Shirley Allen was snacking on some pistachios as she watched them look around for a hiding Julie Kerrig.

"She's not here, boys. You can search this station high and low, but you won't find her," said Shirley confidently, standing with her arms crossed.

"Ma'am, we are just doing our jobs," stated Lieutenant Roth.

Three state troopers walked through the station and into the jail area looking for the former chief, while Roth continued to question Shirley.

"What time did she leave here, Ms. Allen?"

"Several minutes ago, and no, she didn't say where she was going."

167

"Sir, we found these in the ladies locker room." The patrolman held up Julie's duty belt and uniform in both hands.

"Looks like she's on foot dressed as a civilian," pressed Roth.

"Yes, she is, and no, I don't know where she went." Shirley was now becoming weary.

"Are you trying to make this hard on purpose, Ms. Allen?" said Lieutenant Roth with a tinge of cynicism.

"Young man, I'm not making anything hard. You are the one making things difficult."

"I beg your pardon, how so?"

"You came barreling in here with the intent to apprehend an innocent woman. You boys don't even know what you're arresting her for, do you?"

Roth lost his temper. "Excuse me, lady, we have our orders!"

"Wow, Lieutenant, you really should set a better example in front of these guys who are under your authority." Shirley grinned as she defiantly stood her ground.

"We are going to take you in as well, so let's get going. I've lost my patience. I don't have to listen to an old, retired, town dispatcher lecture me on the law."

"You obviously were not raised to respect your elders or even your fellow law enforcement family," the feisty white-haired lady retorted.

"Let's go, Ms. Allen." Roth started moving in her direction.

"Before you get so hasty young man, I would really think it over."

The lieutenant chuckled and looked at the other troopers, who were equally amused with the resilience and confidence which the stout, elderly woman displayed.

"Come with us, Ms. Allen. Help us find Ms. Kerrig," said Roth in a condescending tone while reaching for his cuffs.

"Lieutenant Roth, I'm afraid Commissioner Hillsdale will be having your big city dispatcher calling you any minute with a code 10-24."

"Our assignment isn't complete yet, ma'am, so let's go!" Roth started pulling his handcuffs out of his belt, when a call came across his radio.

"Units 30, 36, 57, and 59 please be advised 10-24, report to HQ. Repeat, 10-24."

The lieutenant froze, along with the three other troopers. They were all dumbfounded. Roth muttered a few choice words under his breath and placed the cuffs back into his belt case.

"Lieutenant Roth, please don't speak like that in our station. It is very unprofessional, especially for a man of your rank," instructed Shirley, still standing with her arms crossed.

"Who are you, lady?" asked one of the troopers.

"Don't sweat it, gentlemen. I won't tell Neil you've been difficult." Shirley slowly pulled a black leather case from her pocket containing an ID and held it in front of Lieutenant Roth.

His face immediately became flushed with embarrassment. "I am sorry, madam, please forgive my unprofessionalism," groveled the lieutenant.

"I forgive you. Now, let's pretend you guys came in here and found what you were looking for."

"Yes, madam. Guys, let's get moving back to Brighton." Roth nodded to the troopers.

Shirley folded the ID, tucked it away, and then pulled out the small transmitter from her shirt pocket. She pressed a red button on it and then put it back.

"There, now we're all set." Shirley smiled at the surprised lieutenant.

"Again, I apologize. Can we help you with anything before we leave?" asked Roth nervously.

"Like I said, you came here for Ms. Kerrig, correct?" inquired Shirley.

"Uh, yes, madam, we did," answered the lieutenant quickly.

"Well then, I think you need to take her out of here with her uniform on, a prisoner hood, and hogtied." Shirley looked at the lieutenant and then nodded in the direction of the safety mannequin standing over in the corner.

"Pardon me, ma'am, but what do you mean?" asked Roth regretfully.

"Judy needs to get dressed," snickered Shirley.

Lieutenant Roth stood looking at her for a couple of seconds and then realized what she was requesting.

"Trooper Hale! Get that uniform of Kerrig's over here and start dressing the mannequin."

"Yes, sir! Hey, Brett, Bobby, give me a hand."

"I'll put the boots on," said Bobby.

"I'll grab a capture hood for her head," added Brett.

Shirley gave a slight grin and wink to Lieutenant Roth, who was still in shock. The men finished their work in minutes. In their arms was a mannequin that would resemble an arrested unruly police officer. She carefully fastened an extra button on the shirt, then scribbled on a sticky note, and placed it firmly on the mannequin's mouth. With that, the men finished placing the hood over the head.

"Good job, fellas! Make sure you carry it like it's 120 pounds. Don't tell Chief Kerrig I said that." Shirley laughed.

"Yes, madam," said the troopers.

The electronic doors opened, and the officers quickly brought the seemingly tied-up police officer outside and into the back seat of one of the cruisers. They secured the seatbelt around the dummy and shut the car doors. Fortunately, the windows were tinted, but from a distance, the improvised mannequin looked very lifelike and believable inside the state patrol vehicle.

Shirley spoke privately to Lieutenant Roth and gave him specific instructions on what to do once they arrived in Brighton. After a few minutes, Roth joined his fellow troopers, and they all left with their lights flashing, heading west.

#

Walking along the darkened shoreline, Julie was feeling somewhat frightened, yet not alone. Earlier, she had prayed and asked God to help her get through the nightmare that was unfolding. If she was ever going to have clarity of mind, in order to objectively look at the facts, she was going to have to rely on the Holy Spirit to lead her into all truth.

Feeling His comfort, Scriptures she had memorized as a teenager started rising up from the depths of her heart. As she began to recite them out loud, the weight of the circumstances seemed to almost physically fall off her shoulders. She inhaled the salt air and continued walking and praising her heavenly Father. The fear was being replaced with gentle waves of peace.

For some reason, the image of the license plate number *613NHJ*, which Officer Sanchez had made a note of, kept coming into her mind. She knew she had seen it somewhere before, yet it was puzzling that she couldn't remember where. All of a sudden, she was startled by the vibration of her cell phone. Julie pulled it out and noticed all the notifications and missed calls she had received over the past several hours. Her heart sank.

Responding to cell calls and texts had always been one of her weak areas. As a millennial, she was comfortable using technology but really didn't like it. Working on her laptop in her patrol cruiser was about as advanced as she ever wanted to get. She was her father's daughter. John Kerrig had never used anything but a two-way radio and a telephone to communicate remotely.

Julie groaned. "Ugh! Just great, a call and a text! Sorry, Trent! He must be worried sick!" She was about to call him when she noticed another text had just popped up on her screen. She scrolled down and saw it was from the coroner, Gary Hackett.

Confirming Karen Anderson and Charlie Philips have the same lab results.

"Now that's very interesting," Julie said to herself.

At this point, only the luminance of the white sea foam could be spotted on the seascape. Julie walked along the north beach engulfed in her screen, its glow highlighting her face. She didn't see or hear the approaching figure, within six feet of her.

"Interesting? I think you're pretty interesting, babe, if I say so myself," said a husky voice directly in front of Julie.

"Whoa!" exclaimed Julie. The startled young woman stopped and looked up, sliding her phone in her back pocket.

Standing directly in front of her was Jake. He had wandered away from the others because he saw her silhouette walking toward them a hundred yards away. Jake was under the intoxicated delusion that she was one of the girls, supposedly coming to party and get wild with all the boys.

"Dude, you really need to get off the beach and go sleep it off before you get hurt," said Julie authoritatively.

"The only sleep I'm going to be doing is with you, hot stuff!" taunted the skinny young man.

"I think you're sadly mistaken, and I would watch what you're saying not only to me as a woman, but also as an officer of the law."

Julie realized that what had just come out of her mouth wasn't true. She was only a citizen now. The young man gazed at her up and down, and then, like an animal, he lunged to grab her shirt. In one swift motion, Julie pulled his arm into her right shoulder and spun him away, kicking him hard directly between his legs with her left foot and then driving her right elbow into the base of his neck, rendering him unconscious. She turned to see two other figures were now running up to her, while one remained stationary several yards behind.

"What the heck!" Randy shouted as he stopped.

"Looks like the foxy lady put a hurt on the little stick man Jake!" Ian laughed, circling around Julie.

"Boys, I am in no mood for games tonight," remarked Kerrig, walking past them and keeping her distance.

"Will he be okay?" asked Randy who was now kneeling over Jake.

"He'll live. When he wakes up in about a half-hour, he'll have a headache and some massive groin pain." Julie kept walking.

"Hey, I know you! You, you, you're the police chief!" bellowed Ian Reynolds.

"I think you're mistaken." Julie immediately recognized who was speaking to her.

"Yeah, it's you. You're sure a hottie without that uniform on," slurred Ian.

"You're pretty drunk with just your red swimming trunks on."

"Touché!" Reynolds mimed a sword fight.

"Go home, Ian." Julie walked on with her back turned to both of the men.

"Ian was just about eaten tonight by that shark you guys are trying to find!" yelled Randy.

"Randy's right, Chief Kerrig! You should've seen that big beast. He missed me!"

Julie was intrigued but kept walking. "Good for you. The beach is closed, and you, of all people, know the waters are not safe," Julie spoke loudly so they all could hear.

"I swam as fast as I could after it passed me. Mr. Jaws was headed straight for the inlet! Dang!" yelled Reynolds.

Julie did not answer and continued walking. She processed what the obnoxious lifeguard had just said. The shark was still present in the waters of Castle Reef and was now near the inlet.

"Get back here, woman! I'm talking to you!" bellowed Ian.

Turning her head to the side, she shouted, "Stay out of the ocean, boys, and head home!"

Julie walked east toward the lower sand dunes that separated the inlet from the rock jetty. On her right, she noticed Billy Daily innocently standing by, watching her carefully.

"Billy, what are you doing out here, buddy?" Julie called out.

"I come here to get Ian. Town is not open, Ms. Julie."

"I know, Billy. It's sad. We want you all to be safe."

"Big Meanie just about eat Ian!"

"I heard. That's terrible. Ian is a strong guy and swam fast. He's safe now though," assured Julie.

"Yes, yes, I take him home to sleep. He being silly."

"Yes, he is, Billy. Please do that for me. Thank you."

"I not like when people drink silly juice, Ms. Julie."

"Neither do I, Billy. Please be careful and go to his home, okay?"

"I will go tell Mr. Ian now."

"Bye-bye, Billy." Julie waved and thought to herself, *Ian really needs you, and you really need him, Billy.*

She suddenly heard a set of running footsteps approaching fast behind her in the sand. By the sound of the individual's gate, she could determine the weight and stature, and it wasn't Billy. She could tell it was Ian Reynolds. Julie stopped and remained with her back to him as he advanced.

"Don't walk away from me when I'm talking to you! Did you hear me?" Ian howled in his buzzed stupor.

"Ian, I'm only going to say this one more time. Please go home with Billy," Julie said very calmly.

She instinctively knew what was going to happen next and dreaded the outcome. Julie remained with her back turned as Ian moved aggressively to grab her. In another quick and polished karate motion, Julie raised her right arm and hand into the Seiken position and brought both legs into a Fudo Dachi stance, which made her immovable. In a split second, she turned her wrist and struck Ian in the nose with a short hard jab, causing him to drop to the sand instantly.

"Ahh! What did you do? You broke my freakin' nose!" cried the incapacitated lifeguard.

"Ian, I could have done worse. Don't ever try anything like that again on me or anyone else," Julie warned.

"What are you? A stinkin' black belt or something? Ahh! It hurts!" Ian cried.

"You're better than this, Ian Reynolds. Be the man you were created to be, not the one you think you need to be."

Ian was astonished at what had just happened. Julie still remained with her back turned and then relaxed her stance. She did a quick neck roll and began walking again.

"Wait! Ugh! It hurts!" Ian pinched his bloodied nose and sat up with his head leaning back.

"Good night, Ian. Take Billy to your condo," said Julie, looking up into the starry night sky.

"Don't go! I need a doctor!" said Ian as he gurgled on the blood now trickling down the back of his throat.

"You'll be fine. The town is evacuated. Don't get caught by the state police, or you'll have to explain all this to your father."

Within minutes, Julie made it up to the seagrass dunes and turned to look down at the faint images of the college boys and Billy. Knowing that the shark was nearby, she had to investigate the inlet.

She thought, *If the shark was feeding on fish scraps, it would make sense for it to go in and around the Salty Dog Marina, but why not attack Ian first?*

It was time to start putting all the puzzle pieces together. She needed to make sense of what was happening. She found herself repeating "just follow the facts" in a soft whisper while she descended down the west side of the sand dunes. Julie purposed to call Trent when she got to the marina. She realized now more than ever that she needed his wisdom, and most of all, his unfailing love.

chapter

19

Greg Stanwick was just about to open the hatch of the fruit cellar when he heard the sound of footsteps once again. This time, they were moving slower and more unevenly. It had been quiet for nearly an hour, and they all had agreed that it was probably safe for them to come out of the tight dark space beneath the Stanwick home.

"Shh, be real quiet," Greg whispered to the ladies.

"Greg? Is someone up there?" Martha said in a hushed voice.

"I think so. Don't anybody move," he breathed.

Joan Bradford began trembling and suddenly lost her footing, hitting an empty bucket that was near the old narrow staircase. The noise above them stopped. Vicki whispered a prayer with her eyes tightly closed. The footsteps resumed, becoming quicker and seemed to move toward the pantry. Whoever it was, stood directly overhead. The latch was now being turned from the other side. Greg grabbed hold of the handle on the door and held on as tight as he could. Finally, he lost his grip and the door flung open.

"Don't hurt us! We decided to stay instead of evacuating!" said Mr. Stanwick, shielding his eyes from the beam of the flashlight shining on his face.

"There are four of us and this is our house! We aren't armed, so please don't shoot!" said Martha, sobbing.

"Hey! Hey, it's me! Are you okay?" said the friendly voice.

"Who is that? Trent Green, is that you?" shouted Vicki.

"Sure is, Vick! Come on up out of there you guys!" Trent lowered his flashlight and proceeded to help everyone out of the cellar. The entire Stanwick family hugged him.

Joan interrupted, "Um, I really hate to break up your little lovefest, but can I please use your bathroom, Martha?"

They all laughed. Martha quickly took Joan down the dark hall to the guest bathroom.

"What exactly is going on, Trent? What is happening to our beautiful town?" asked Greg.

"Yes, please tell us," Vicki interjected.

"I don't know yet, but it sure is strange. Mike and I stayed to try and get to the bottom of it," said Trent, who then looked at Vicki in anticipation.

Vicki answered his silent question. "I haven't seen Jules since she went to see the mayor, but Joan did."

Trent sighed. "She hasn't answered my call or text."

"Julie told Joan to come here, and that we all needed to hide." Vicki started looking for candles in a nearby hutch.

"Hide? From who?" Trent was puzzled.

"Or what?" interrupted Mr. Stanwick.

Everyone stood silent. The hair stood up on the back of Trent's neck.

"What do you mean?" Trent asked, moving closer.

Martha spoke up. "When we were down in the cellar, we heard the strangest thing. The front door opened, and a single set of footsteps seemed to be almost marching throughout the house. Then, all of a sudden, the sound of the feet went crazy as if running in place, and then we heard a crash. After that, it was quiet until you came. Your footsteps were noticeably different."

"Well, your front door is out in the yard in several pieces." Trent motioned to the foyer with his flashlight.

Vicki gasped. "My word, who could have done this?"

"Something not human, that's for sure," answered Greg, as he began examining the front door frame.

Mrs. Stanwick continued. "Just before we went down into the cellar, Joan was telling us how horrible the meeting with Julie and the mayor went. Then the power went out and everyone's cell phone stopped working."

Outside on the front porch, Mike Rawlings startled Mr. Stanwick when he stepped up behind him with his shotgun over his shoulder. "Sorry to scare you, Mr. Stanwick. I was checking around back. There's nobody here; it's just us."

"Why thank you! Yes, you did rattle me a bit," Greg replied.

"Come on in, Mike, thank you for checking for us," greeted Martha.

"No problem, Mrs. S, it looks like the power is out only on this side of the street," Mike stated as he walked inside.

"Hey, Mike! Is the lady you met doing better at Brighton General?" asked Vicki sympathetically.

"Yes, she is. Thanks for asking. Her name is Karen. Karen Anderson."

"I know a Karen Anderson who lives in New Jersey," said a voice from the hallway with an unmistakable Boston accent.

"Pardon me?" asked Mike politely.

Joan came into the kitchen where everyone was standing. "I didn't know a human being could urinate for almost ten minutes straight, but I think I just did. I mean honestly!" They all broke into much-needed laughter again, with the exception of Mike, who didn't understand what was so funny. He just smiled cordially until they finished.

"Hi, I'm Mike Rawlings."

"Nice to meet you, Mike, I'm the much relieved Joan Bradford."

Mike snickered. "I'm sure there's a lot of Karen Andersons in this world, but yes, she's from New Jersey."

"If it's the same Karen Anderson I'm thinking of, my daughter and her are besties."

"Is that so?" said Rawlings, lowering his shotgun down to the floor.

"Yeah, she's originally from Brookline, just outside of Boston. I used to work with her mother years ago at Fenway. We're all big Sox fans."

"What does Karen do for a living?" asked Trent, who was now probing.

"She graduated from MIT with a master's degree and works for a company called Barrington Scientific."

"I had no idea. I just met her a couple of days ago." Mike ran his hand through his hair and sat down in the dark kitchen.

"She's a cute girl. Are you two dating?" asked Joan loudly.

"Um, no, Joan. We just met." Mike's eyes looked at the floor.

"Would anyone like something to eat or drink?" inquired Martha, who knew by her keen hostess instincts that this gathering was going to last a lot longer than anyone anticipated.

Trent and Greg pulled up chairs to the kitchen table, as Vicki lit a beeswax candle and began helping her mom prepare snacks and drinks.

"Small world, isn't it?" Joan remarked.

"Apparently so. You do know she's the one who was attacked by the shark yesterday?"

Mike sighed, leaning back in his chair.

"I heard about that, Mike, my daughter—" Joan was interrupted.

"Excuse me, is everyone ready to eat?" Greg Stanwick asked politely.

Martha and Vicki brought the food and iced tea to the kitchen table and began arranging it for everyone. Trent quickly got Mike's attention and motioned for him to step into the living room.

They both got up and went into the adjoining room.

"We gotta to make this quick, Mike. Are you thinking what I'm thinking about Karen?" whispered Trent.

"You mean the scientific company and the shark attack connection?"

"Yes! That's it! I bet there is also a connection between those transmitters I found and that company in New Jersey as well. Do you still have cell phone service?" Trent asked.

Mike pulled his phone out to look. "I sure do."

"We better hurry before your signal goes down," Trent insisted.

"You bet. I'm going to call Jim, get all the info I can about those transmitters, and see if they are made by the company Karen works for as well."

"You should go to Brighton and ask Karen yourself, or maybe her friend Jill can help you?" suggested Trent.

"What about finding Julie?"

"God has our backs, Mike. The Stanwicks and Joan can stay at Green Sea. I'll find her."

"Trent, are you sure?" Mike asked intently.

"Yes, I will be fine. We can take them to the inn with the truck. Greg and Martha can sit up front with me and everyone else can lay low in the back. That way, you can get to your car and head to Brighton."

"I can't just leave you here," demanded Mike in a hard whisper.

"I will remain out of sight as much as possible and try to locate Julie. You have to go find out what you can, and call Jim Renaldi on the way," pleaded Trent.

"Okay, man, I'll go, but please be careful."

"No worries, Mike. If the state troopers stop you, just tell them that you were detained by some crazy guy."

"And who would that be?" smirked Mike.

The best friends concluded their conversation with a fist bump and went back into the candlelit kitchen to share their plan with the others. Meanwhile, outside on the dark and vacant street, the mysterious blue car crept past the historic home undetected.

#

David Willis was feeling a sense of confidence that he never felt before. The state police were doing his work for him, and Julie Kerrig was out of the way once and for all. This was the easiest thirty thousand dollars he could have ever imagined making in his life. All that remained was one phone call to JK Reynolds.

"Come on! You're always pestering me, pick up the phone!" Willis was perspiring even more than usual as he waited for the state representative to answer.

With the sound of the continual ringing, it was becoming apparent that he would have to leave a voicemail. Willis ended the call and looked at his watch, noticing how late it was.

Where is this jerk? What if he's hanging me out to dry? The state police may be coming for me too!

David began to panic. He stood up from his chair, in the dimly lit office, and began to pace the floor, like a caged carnivore. While wiping the beads of sweat off his forehead, with his already damp handkerchief, the office phone buzzed. Willis scrambled to answer the call.

"This is Mayor Willis." He cleared his throat in an attempt to sound authoritative and professional.

"Has she been notified?" asked the gruff-sounding male voice on the other end.

"Yes, sir, she's probably in custody now, even as we speak," Willis quickly responded.

"Did it go smoothly?" The voice now became more recognizable as the caller continued.

"Yes, I think so, for the most part," said Willis in a shaky voice.

"What do you mean 'for the most part'?"

"Um, she was here…" The weakening mayor sank into his chair.

"The documents were not compromised were they?"

"I don't think so. She… She just seemed too calm about everything as if she knew something we didn't," explained Willis quickly.

"David, you're paranoid. She has no clue. Relax. You're the chief of police and mayor now. Thanks to me."

"Yes, sir. Thank you, JK. I'm sorry. She just made me lose my temper when she challenged me."

There was silence on the phone. Willis was beginning to panic. He heard a series of door slams and curse words being shouted in the background.

"Are you there, sir?" asked the mayor in a sickly and timid voice.

"How did she challenge you, David?" Reynolds now sounded not only impatient but greatly irritated.

"She suspects something is going on, I guess," replied the petrified mayor.

"You better hope this turns out good for you."

"What do you mean, sir?"

"Let's just say, if anyone finds out that you altered the records and caused great corruption in the city of Castle Reef, you'll never survive!"

The click on the other end of the phone call was the exclamation point that sent David Willis over the edge. He felt physically sick and had to use the restroom immediately. All he could do now was to wait and hope that the plan he was entangled in would indeed come to pass.

He had no clue what the plan was, but even if he did, he felt certain that he wouldn't want any part of it. However, it was too late. The rising tide was now over the mayor's head.

chapter

20

Terry's fingers were moving feverishly, adjusting levels and sequences on the large touchscreen desk. The steel door opened quietly, and into the sterile white office Cortney Alexander emerged. Behind her were two other workers, in protective gowns, taking notes as she dictated instructions to them. Once finished, they left, and Cortney turned around facing Terry Warren, with both hands on her slender hips.

"We have a problem," stated Alexander in a calm, yet sarcastic tone.

"I know. I am making the necessary changes right now to redirect the interface in order to enhance the levels to both M1 and M2." Terry never looked up from the intense work being performed on the glass interface.

"I'm not talking about the transmission interface, Terry."

Terry paused and glanced at Alexander. "What is it then?"

"The asset has been compromised and our initial recovery mission has failed." Cortney sat down in a white, circular chair and rubbed her temples.

Terry could tell it was serious and stopped moving. "What do you mean? I've executed everything with precision."

"It's not your fault this time. It's the incompetence of everyone else."

Warren chose to respond carefully in order to not set off a firestorm of rage from Alexander. "Cortney, what can I do to get us back on our scheduled deadline?"

"Well, it's very clear that we have to execute my original plan. Although it was altered because of some mindless local hero years ago, we will resume the plan and get what we need."

"When do you want it initiated?" Terry asked reluctantly.

"Immediately!" Cortney jumped up from the round, white chair.

"Can we start it first thing in the morning? I'm a little tired, and it's getting late," Warren asked sheepishly.

Cortney leaned into Terry's face and instantly went into a tantrum. "Do you even realize what's at stake here?" shouted the crazed woman.

"It isn't that simple, Cortney. Can't you understand that?" pleaded Warren.

"Nothing will stop Cortney Alexander! Do it now and then you can sleep!" roared the domineering woman, less than a foot away from the frightened programmer.

Terry meekly replied, adjusting the lopsided headset. "As you wish. I'm sorry." Warren went back to work on the touchscreen, now with even more intensity.

Alexander stood up straight and adjusted her pants suit. She wiped the corners of her mouth with her boney tan fingers, while keeping her talon-like black-colored nails away from her face. Her bright-red lipstick had extended itself further onto her face, which often occurred during her fits of rage. Cortney's mouth would widen considerably, showing off her perfectly bleached-white teeth with each rampage. If you combined this, along with her animated, dark eyes, it was not only intimidating, but extremely frightening.

#

As she walked through the sea oats at the bottom of the dunes and into the east side of the Salty Dog Marina, Julie stopped to survey her surroundings. Jerry and Becky Foster's market was locked up and their neon Ocean's Seafood Market sign was turned off. The dark and empty parking lot was a sure indication that no one was around. Only the sound of water lapping against the boat hulls and an occasional clang from the inlet's bell buoy, a quarter of a mile away, broke the silence.

Julie quietly walked to the waterfront. She noticed the *Susan Marie* tied off securely and bobbing slowly in the boatyard. As she approached it, she had a brief flashback of seeing it come into the harbor three years before in the pouring rain, the day after her father was lost at sea. She had since avoided the boat because it brought back too much pain. Fighting through those memories, Julie sat down on the bench nearby and stared across the inlet.

This was a perfect time for her to gather her thoughts and start putting the facts together from all the strange and terrible events currently happening right in her own hometown. She carefully watched the water for any suspicious movement. Everything seemed calm, so she began to mentally analyze the mapped-out areas she had drawn on the whiteboard earlier in the day at the police station.

Several minutes passed. All at once, Julie saw the water stir in a long, circular pattern, about fifty yards away. The nearby dock lights illuminated the water enough for her to see that something large was moving through the inlet. She stood to see where it was headed, and then it happened. A large explosion from beneath the water's surface sent a shockwave that rocked all the boats and splashed a three-foot swell over the bulkhead. A large circle of bubbles surfaced, and then the water subdued, returning to calm ripples.

What just happened? Am I seeing things? thought Julie. A rush of panic came over her. She needed to call someone about what she had just experienced.

"Just great! What's my problem? I forgot to answer Trent!" exclaimed Julie.

She fumbled her phone to speed-dial the man she loved. The call started to connect, then immediately went dead. Julie heard a faint, buzzing noise, which began to increase in volume until she had to pull the phone away from her ear. Suddenly, it became too hot to hold, forcing her to drop it on the dock.

All the pier lights went out, and the nearby soft drink machine flickered and then quit. It was totally dark and silent, except for the rhythmic footsteps that were striding on the wooden walkway approaching the bench where Julie was sitting. The cadence came to a halt. Julie shut her eyes. She knew exactly who it was, standing directly behind her.

"Ms. Kerrig. We meet once again," said the measured voice.

Julie stood up and turned around to face the man. He stood straight with no emotion on his face. His eyes seemed to glow a bright blue, even without any natural light present. In this moment, she immediately knew that he was after what was hidden behind her cell phone in the small evidence baggie.

"I never did get your name, so I'll call you, Frank. Just like old blue eyes himself," Julie taunted the man.

"Move away from the device that is next to you, Ms. Kerrig."

"Frank, how is it that you know everyone's name, yet you always refuse to identify yourself?"

"Move away from the device that is next to you, Ms. Kerrig."

"I don't know what you people are up to, but we won't be part of your game any longer, Frank!" Julie started running both hands through her hair to distract the stoic slim individual in front of her, as she simultaneously moved her right foot toward the cell phone.

"Move away from the device that is next to you, Ms. Kerrig." repeated the strange, male figure in the same repetitive voice pattern.

Julie started to do her signature neck roll. She surmised that she had only seconds to act first before he initiated any movement. Placing her right shoe on top of the phone, she quickly pivoted around and moved into a Hangetsu Dachi karate stance.

"Okay, Frank, let's see whatcha got."

The strange man advanced until he was just out of Julie's reach. Lifting his right hand and then performing a fast deliberate push motion, he flung Julie backward into the air without even touching her. She tucked her legs in and did a perfect summersault landing on both feet.

Adrenaline now flooded throughout her body. She flung herself sideways and proceeded to kick his extended arm with her left foot multiple times. He effortlessly blocked each blow. Julie instantly felt weak and nauseous after making contact. She remembered the same thing had happened yesterday when she first encountered the weird man at Nina's Café, but tonight the feeling was so much stronger.

"You were warned, Ms. Kerrig, now you must be eliminated," said the abnormal man, as he reached down to retrieve her phone without losing eye contact.

It was now apparent to Julie that she was not battling a human being. On the contrary, he seemed robotic or alien. Thoughts of *The Terminator* ran through her head as she decided her next move. She gathered her strength and then threw a swift throat punch just as he was standing up. He never blocked it. Julie's hand went straight through his neck and out the other side. It felt like she had penetrated a large bowl of Jell-O. She stood in shock at what had just occurred.

Quickly, she pulled her arm back; it was numb and began shaking. She instantly became weaker.

Julie gasped. "Frank, what are you?"

The strange being squeezed the cell phone tightly, and it disappeared into his large hand right before her eyes. "You were warned, Ms. Kerrig, now you must be eliminated," repeated the odd entity as it aggressively advanced.

In one quick fluid movement, Julie drew the Colt 1911 from behind her back, after racking it on the top of her waistband, and opened fire until the eight-round clip was empty. The bullet holes in the odd man's dress shirt exuded a clear slime, and he kept advancing toward her.

She maneuvered quickly to keep her distance, but it stretched out its arm unnaturally and picked her up by the neck, almost two feet off the ground. She slowly dropped her weapon and held tightly to the thing's arms, which felt like rubbery octopus tentacles, in her now queasy state.

Julie looked down and caught a glimpse inside the life form's shirt neckline. As it gripped her tightly, she noticed that the entity's face was somehow printed or tattooed on a clear human form. Only its head, neck, and hands were flesh-colored and looked like a natural human. The clothing covered not skin, but a translucent gel-like body.

Julie managed to take a deep breath. The thing's eyes, all at once, illuminated a brighter blue and its grip tightened, causing her to begin to lose consciousness.

As she slipped away, she managed to whisper, "Lord Jesus, help me."

The strange being continued to hold Julie's limp body by the neck, as it walked over to the edge of the bulkhead. In an effortless motion, it dropped her into the bay. Her lifeless body slowly sank into the calm brackish water. The manlike form then turned around and stopped. Suddenly, it began to run in place.

The speed of its legs became faster and faster in short increments until it turned to face the parking lot, while running in place, at an unnatural rapid rate. Within seconds, it lunged forward in a full sprint and quickly disappeared into the darkness, heading west.

#

Only a mile away, Trent Green had already dropped off the Stanwicks and Joan Bradford at the Green Sea Inn. He made sure they had access to the kitchen and any supplies that they needed during their stay. They were all instructed to keep the lights off and the doors locked.

Mike gave Greg his shotgun, and Vicki his radio before leaving for Brighton. Trent and Mike agreed to tell the state police, if stopped, that he was late closing down the Green Sea Inn due to a shortage of staff. They promised to stay in touch.

Trent was now driving as fast as he could, in his old, white GMC to the town hall. He had just received a one ring call from Julie and immediately tried to call her back, but it went directly to voice mail.

"Where are you, Jules?" he wondered out loud, speeding down Main Street.

He gave up on staying hidden from the authorities because he just knew that something was wrong. Julie was in trouble; he could feel it. The swell of uneasiness and dread started to find its way into the pit of Trent's stomach. He wanted to see if anyone was at the mayor's office before returning to the police station.

"Dear God, please protect Julie from any danger," Trent earnestly prayed.

The moment those words left his mouth, his cell phone rang. He picked it up off the bench seat and looked to see who was calling. It was Shirley Allen. Trent quickly answered just as he pulled into the town hall parking lot.

#

Twenty seconds had elapsed since Julie was dropped into the water by the entity disguised as a man. Sinking deeper into the bay, she was now totally unconscious. Her body was experiencing a drowning phenomenon known as laryngospasm. This involuntary reaction occurs when water enters the larynx and the vocal chords constrict, sealing the airways to the lungs. The condition would only last for a short period of time. Eventually, if not revived, she would experience brain damage or go into cardiac arrest and die.

However, Julie felt no pain and was completely unaware of her surroundings. She hovered in a dream-like state and began to experience her life as scenes from her past moved chronologically in front of her. Decades were relived in milliseconds. She traveled from her first memory as a two-year-old on Christmas morning, all the way to the day she joyfully said yes to Trent's marriage proposal.

Instantaneously, her life events continued to play out in front of her. She could feel every emotion, and all her senses were engaged in each memory. The flash of years, months, and days started to slow down and then move into a real-time replay of the very day she hugged her father for the last time. It was the sixteenth of March on a chilly morning. After the long hug, John Kerrig spoke, *"I will always be here for you, Jules."* She had never understood that until now.

Everything was becoming clearer.

"Is this oxygen deprivation, or am I dying?" she asked herself.

"Just follow the facts," echoed the faint sound of her father's voice.

Bits of segmented information floated in a spinning vortex in front of her. She reached out, grabbing words and arranging them into statements, in a bright white open space. She could hear herself speaking the words as they echoed.

"John is my father."

"He disappeared in March."

"March is the third month."

"On the sixteenth day."

"John 3:16"

"For God so loved the world that he gave his one and only Son, that whoever believes in him shall not perish but have eternal life."

Julie again vividly remembered her father reading those powerful words to her from his Bible. It was a summer evening, and she was four years old. He explained God's simple plan of salvation and led her in a prayer to receive Jesus as her Lord and Savior. John 3:16 became her favorite Bible verse. She always thought it was special because God's love is for everyone, no matter who they are or what they've done. Furthermore, the disciple of Jesus who wrote those words had the same name as her father. She felt a wave of peace flood over her entire being.

The scene began to fade before her. Instantaneously, everything went black. She began to feel herself being pulled upward with a great force. A blaring swoosh filled her ears. Everything around her became clamorous. She could hear loud voices and was beginning to feel her body ache. An acrid smell of pungent gastric acid filled her senses as she realized that she was forcefully coughing and gasping for air.

Julie awoke and found herself on her side, wrapped in a blanket, breathing heavily and shivering on the wooden walkway of the marina.

"Julie! Julie, look at me. Julie! You're going to be fine," said Becky Foster gently.

"Take it slow, lass," Fran O'Reily calmly added as he put another folded blanket under her head.

She was wet, on the dock, and people with flashlights were talking and causing a lot of commotion. Julie slowly gained awareness of her surroundings and remembered what had just happened.

"Chief K, we thought you were a goner. So thankful you made it." Jerry Foster brushed his weathered fisherman's hand across her cheek.

Julie slowly sat up and coughed up more saltwater. She looked around to see that there were others near her in addition to the Fosters and Francis. Julie wiped her eyes and noticed the dock lights were illuminated once again.

"If it wasn't for this young man right here, Julie, we would have lost you," whispered Becky holding back tears.

Julie slowly looked over to her right, her eyes focusing on another person like herself, wrapped in a towel with his head down and breathing hard too.

"Thank you," she managed to say.

The individual raised his head and looked at Julie. It was Ian Reynolds. Julie's eyes widened in disbelief, and she gulped.

"Hi, Chief," said the tired young lifeguard.

"Why are you here? I thought I told you to take Billy home?"

"He's here too, along with the guys," he said, short of breath.

"Why Ian? Why did you follow me?"

"I don't know. I felt bad and wanted to apologize. I ran up the dune and saw you getting dropped into the water by some guy who quickly ran off."

"You saved my life."

"It's what we do! We're lifeguards, right?"

Billy Daily interrupted their conversation and stepped in closer. He was holding both hands over his mouth and giggling. Julie looked up and smiled.

"Hi there, Billy."

"Mr. Ian kissed you, Ms. Julie. I saw him kiss you over and over!" shouted Billy.

Everyone around Julie started to chuckle, including Ian, as it grew into hearty laughter.

Julie became horrified. She began wiping her mouth, realizing that Ian Reynolds had performed mouth-to-mouth resuscitation on her. She could still taste and smell the sour beer. She wanted to gag but held it together and pulled the blanket over her head in total humiliation.

chapter

21

"I don't see any lights on, Shirley. The only vehicles in the parking lot are Julie's police cruiser and Willis's car," observed Trent, walking from his truck to the front doors.

"Hmm... So Willis must still be there," Shirley surmised.

"Ms. Shirley, I'm really concerned about Julie."

"Don't worry, Trent. I spoke with her just a few hours ago. She left the cruiser and walked here. She was at the station for a while, and then she had to leave." Shirley's voice on the phone seemed more authoritative to Trent.

"Why? What's going on? Mike and I saw a bunch of state police at the station."

"I'll explain later. It's complicated. She won't be meeting you at her apartment tonight," inserted Shirley.

"Her apartment is trashed."

"What? Oh mercy!"

"The whole place was destroyed, and everything looked like it was overturned and opened, as if someone was looking for something."

"When were you there?"

"Like I said, Mike and I checked there earlier. That's when we noticed the four state troopers pulling up to your station."

"I know this is confusing to you right now, Trent, but what is happening in Castle Reef is far bigger than you can imagine. Unfortunately, Julie is right in the middle of it."

"What do you mean? Where is she? I don't know where to look, Shirley."

"Don't waste your time. Hold on, my last intel tells me…"

Trent was starting to panic at her pause. "Shirley? What is it?"

"Sorry, Trent, her current location is at the Salty Dog Marina."

"Is she okay?" he asked with a tremble in his voice.

"Go to her quickly and then meet me at the Green Sea in thirty minutes!"

"You got it!" said Trent frantically, ending the call.

Hopping into his truck, Trent turned on the headlights and pulled out onto the empty street with tires screeching. He headed north, speeding through every stop sign along the way.

#

"Maximize M2 now!" Alexander barked the order to Terry, who was on the verge of an emotional meltdown.

"I terminated M1 as you directed, and I followed through with every programming interface protocol. I can only do so much!" blurted out Terry.

"Get M2 here now! Do you hear me?" demanded Alexander.

Terry continued to work on the touch screen desk, while tears rolled down the face of the highly intelligent programmer. Warren's hands quickly moved across the screen performing calculations that only a team of scientists could accomplish.

"I'm doing the best I can. If I push the interface any harder, we will reach critical mass."

Terry grew silent, then looked up at Cortney, and just stared. A new type of anger began to build inside the forty-year-old computer geek. The hostile Alexander sensed the challenge and paced back and forth looking at the large, holographic image that was emanating from the touchscreen control surface. She stopped and rubbed both of her hands together and then turned back to Warren.

"Keep working or you will be joining your parents," warned the black-widow-like woman.

The data processor looked down, crushed with fear. Terry began working frantically once again to make sure that M2 would arrive as soon as it could, without destroying its structure.

"ETA two hours and six minutes," said Warren, in a monotone, defeated sounding voice.

"Excellent! I will be on the lower level for recovery. Notify me as soon as it is nearing the complex." Cortney exited the bleak office with a demonic grin on her face and walked down the low-lit concrete and glass hallway toward the elevator door.

#

"Yes, Daniel, my sources say that they have her in custody now and are heading this way." JK Reynolds paced as he poured himself a strong cup of coffee, while holding the phone to his neck.

"So our guys arrested her at the Castle Reef station?" asked Governor Riddick.

"That's what I have been told. Willis said she was being difficult, and he gave her until five to get her belongings."

"She had no clue we were going to be there." Riddick laughed.

"What's next, Dan?" asked JK jokingly.

"Well, when she gets to Brighton, make sure you see her… Let's just say before she tries to escape."

"What do you mean by that?" Reynolds changed his demeanor.

"We can't let this deal go south, JK," the governor reminded.

"I have to keep my distance. It's one thing to keep it local, but it's another when I have some federal officials already asking me why the SDI project with Alexander Industries is taking so long," explained the corrupt representative.

"They are paying us very well, I might add," stated Riddick.

"True, but I think we should keep her in jail for a while until everything settles down. You have some judges that need favors, right?" asked the tainted congressman.

"We've come too far to get sloppy, JK. Just make sure you contact Captain Wilkes when they bring her in. He'll take it from there," the governor directed.

"You do realize you will be wiping out a family legacy, Daniel? The Kerrigs have done so much for the community in Castle Reef."

"Representative Reynolds, we can't take any chances. Three years is a long time to wait to become multimillionaires."

"I guess. Heaven knows I could use a change of scenery. I might just retire next term."

"We need to make sure that nobody gets even a hint about our involvement, or we are history."

"Devin is supposed to call me tomorrow. He has no clue what we are doing or even what his daughter is up to for that matter."

"I never heard that, JK. Your connection must be bad. Hello, JK? Are you there?" Governor Riddick laughed sarcastically before hanging up.

JK Reynolds sat numb on his couch, holding his cell phone. His sandcastle world was eroding. The deep, dark abyss he had danced around for so many years had just become much bigger, and he finally fell in. In addition to the larceny and misappropriation of government funds for the past three years, Reynolds was about to lose his family. Oddly enough, it occurred to him that in reality he had lost his wife and son a very long time ago.

#

The group huddled by the dock looked up when they saw the lights and heard the old pickup skidding into the parking lot of the Salty Dog Marina. Fran and Jerry brandished their shotguns. Everyone else, with the exception of Julie, raised their hands to their brows to cut the glare from the high beams shining on them.

"Who goes there?" shouted Jerry, holding his single-shot twelve-gauge.

"Ya don't be messin' with us here folk, ya understandin' me?" Fran's voice echoed off the water.

"Hey, guys! Easy does it! It's me, Trent Green."

As soon as Julie heard his voice, she stood to her feet and let the blanket fall. Still feeling dizzy, she managed to quickly walk and then run toward his voice.

"Trent? Trent, is that you?" Julie began to cry.

"Jules!" Trent ran to her and she fell into his arms. He held her tight and kissed her repeatedly on the face.

"I'm sorry I never called you back right away, and then when I tried, I…" Julie broke down and wept into Trent's chest. He felt her wet clothes and immediately knew she had been in the water and probably in some sort of trouble. "I'm sorry I wasn't here for you, Jules."

Julie sobbed, and then she kissed the man she loved. "No, it's my fault. I'm the one that walked away, Trent! I thought I was going to die without you."

"I'm here, Jules, and I will never leave you." Trent smiled and carefully hugged her. "Do you need to go to the emergency room?"

"No, no I think I'm okay. Can we just get out of here?" Julie kissed Trent again.

"Let's get you a hot shower and some clean, dry clothes."

"Yes, please, that sounds amazing."

Trent and Julie stopped talking. They turned to look behind them and realized they had an audience. To make matters worse, the Fosters, Francis, the lifeguards, and Billy all began clapping and cheering, which made it even more awkward. They were all so happy to see the couple together again. Trent walked Julie over to them, holding her to his side. He noticed Francis and Jerry had lowered their guns and that the Reynolds boy had a towel around his neck and was wet too.

"Hi, everybody," Trent managed to say.

"Trent, she is lucky to be alive," said Becky Foster with a big smile.

"That's for sure. We saw the rescue after hearing all the commotion. There was a big rumble, like an earthquake. We knew something was wrong so we came out to see what was going on," explained Jerry.

"The good Lord was sure lookin' out for yer lassie, Trenty ole boy," O'Reily added.

"Dude, your hottie is bad to the bone!" exclaimed Randy, standing next to Jake, who was still quietly recovering from his injuries.

"Mr. Ian kiss Ms. Julie on the dock!" blurted out Billy once more in his loud cheerful voice.

Julie did a face-palm. Trent looked around at everyone confused. Ian stepped forward.

"Mr. Green, Julie was drowning. I dove in and pulled her up. She was unresponsive, so I had to do rescue breathing."

"You mean artificial respiration, as in mouth-to-mouth?" asked Trent.

"Yeah, she was almost dead. I never had to do that for real, until tonight," said the now sober Ian Reynolds.

"You're a hero, my friend." Trent put his arm on Ian's shoulder.

Reynolds sighed. "Hardly."

Julie cleared her throat. "There's a lot that happened between the time I was thrown into the water and when Ian pulled me out," stated Julie.

"In what way, sweetheart?"

"Hopefully, I can put it all into words someday." Julie shut her eyes.

"Are you okay?"

Julie sighed. "I'm fine. This all started on the beach."

"Say again, Jules?" asked Trent, completely puzzled.

"I was down on the beach, and I walked here because these guys saw the shark and told me it was headed toward the inlet."

"Why were you on the beach?" Trent was confused.

Jake, the extremely sore lifeguard, spoke up in a shaky voice. "We were drinking and wanted to party with Chief Kerrig."

"Ms. Julie go like this!" Billy made exaggerated punching and kicking motions.

A hush suddenly fell on the marina dock. It was an uncomfortable silence. Trent lowered his head and looked at Julie.

"It's hard to explain. It's so far beyond comprehension. I don't know where to begin." Julie took several deep breaths to slow her anxiety.

"It's okay, honey, we can talk about it later," reassured Trent.

There was another awkward pause. Julie began to squirm.

"Chief, you said something that made me follow you here after you decked me on the beach," Ian declared.

Trent raised his eyebrows and winced. Fran and the Fosters looked at each other confused. Julie did another face palm. "I'll explain later, Trent," Julie said, shaking her head. "What do you mean, Ian?"

"You said, 'Be the man you were created to be, not the one you think you need to be.' How did you know?"

"Know? Know what?" asked Julie.

"I have nothing inside me. That I'm an empty shell going nowhere."

"Ian, you have so much potential, but you're seeking fulfillment in all the wrong places."

The once arrogant lifeguard lowered his head and began to cry. "After hearing what you said, it made me want to know what you meant and that's when I ran to the top of the dune."

Randy cut in. "That's when we saw, whatever it was, throw you in the water."

"What in the world?" Jerry Foster blurted out.

"Saints alive!" O'Reily crossed himself.

"Ian outran us all and dove in," explained Randy.

"This is crazy," said Trent in amazement.

"Seeing you just about dead and now breathing again, it's given me… You've given me hope." Ian wiped his eyes that were now filled with tears.

There was another moment of silence. This time, it was heartwarming. Everyone looked at each other and reflected on Ian Reynolds' words. They all knew who his parents were and how he was raised, with the exception of Billy. Ian Reynolds was a young man, who was realizing for the first time that life is a precious gift.

"We are here for you, Ian," Becky interjected.

Jerry piped up, "Come on, you guys, it's getting late. You boys can stay with us tonight."

"We've got plenty of room, and we even have some ice cream for you, Billy," Becky added, rubbing his head.

"I'm going to take Julie to the Green Sea. We'll be in touch. I'm sure there's a lot to talk about later," stated Trent, after shaking Ian's hand.

"Thank you, Ian. I'm sorry I hurt you earlier," Julie told him and then fist-bumped the lifeguard.

"No worries, Chief, I deserved it." Ian dried off his wet head with a towel that Becky Foster handed him.

The Fosters walked with the lifeguards and Billy to their house, which was attached to Ocean's Seafood Market.

Francis O'Reilly lingered behind and approached Trent and Julie. "Here's your pistol, dear lassie. I found her under da bench," said the punchy Irishman.

"Thanks so much, Fran." Julie took the Colt 1911, racked it back, and checked the chamber.

"Empty?" asked Trent.

"Yes, but it didn't matter," Julie admitted.

"What do ya mean?" Fran was intrigued.

"You and Jerry just keep an eye out tonight and stand guard. The thing that threw me into the water might be back," said Julie, running her hand through her wet hair.

"Come again?" questioned Fran with a puzzled face.

"Yeah, what do you mean, Jules? Who did this to you?" asked Trent.

Julie realized it was going to take some time to explain everything thoroughly. She wanted to tell Trent and Shirley as soon as she could. The facts were lining up into a scenario she dreaded to conclude. This was bigger than she ever could have imagined.

"Never mind, it's complicated. Just keep your eyes open, Fran." Julie pulled the extra clip from her back pocket, dried it off on the blanket, and exchanged it in her gun. She then carefully slid it in her waistband.

"I hear ya, Chiefy," winked the Irishman, as he walked away.

"Are you okay, Jules?" Trent embraced her.

"Yes, now that you're here with me. Can we go to my place?"

"Well, let's go to the Green Sea. We have to get you some dry clothes."

"I have dry clothes at my apartment." Julie was perplexed.

"We can't go there right now. I'll explain later. Shirley's waiting for us."

"She is?"

Trent hugged her gently, but Julie was now deep in thought. *Why was Shirley waiting for them at the Green Sea Inn?*

They slowly walked to Trent's truck. The moon was now over-head, illuminating the Salty Dog Harbor, which had returned to its calm state. The boats rocked gently with the tidal change. However, below the surface, at the bottom of the bay, dozens of crabs were feasting on the skin of a severed appendage that hadn't been there an hour before.

chapter

22

Outside the Brighton Highway Patrol Headquarters, three interceptors arrived and quickly parked near the back entrance. Captain Wilkes met the troopers and approached Lieutenant Roth, who was overseeing the transfer of a fully-hooded and handcuffed prisoner.

"Well, well, well, who do we have here?" said Wilkes, smugly adjusting his hat.

"It's her, sir, the one we were ordered to arrest and bring here from the Reef," said Roth, holding the entry door.

Wilkes scoffed. "Looks like she's not moving much."

"She's been difficult the whole time, and maybe she finally gave up," remarked the lieutenant.

"Too big for her britches, I hear."

"I wasn't aware of the case details, sir, but we got her as ordered."

The other troopers carried the seemingly lifeless, hooded body into the building, down the hall, and into an interrogation cell. They entered the windowless room and quickly shut the door.

"Have two of your guys stand guard and don't let anyone in the room after they get her settled," instructed Wilkes.

"Yes, Captain."

Lieutenant Roth entered the cell and ordered two of the troopers to stand guard outside, instructing the remaining one to move the vehicles back to the front of the barracks. Roth returned to Captain Wilkes, who was busy texting.

"Excuse me, sir, if you need me, I will be in my office doing paperwork until my shift is over."

"Thank you, Roth," said the distracted captain.

As Roth walked down the hall, he glanced over his shoulder and noticed Wilkes stepping away from the cell door. He was no longer texting, but talking to someone on his phone. After several minutes, the troopers exited the room, locked the steel door with a keypad code and stood by it. Wilkes ended his call and quickly walked outside. Roth's assignment was complete.

#

Terry Warren pressed the intercom button with excitement. The programmer's eyes danced upon the glass interface with glee. Thrilled to see the results of M2's mission, Terry currently found relief from an internal war that plagued the tormented soul. The success of many hours of intricate computer programming finally paid off and yielded the results Cortney wanted.

Knowing the reprieve was always short-lived, Warren cherished its temporary solace anyway.

"Yes, Terry," replied the cold, domineering voice.

"M2 is less than forty-five minutes from engagement."

"Thank you, Terry. Inform me when it arrives at the portal."

"Yes, I will, Cortney." Terry paused. "I'm sorry, once again, for angering you earlier. It was entirely my fault."

"I receive your apology, Terry."

"Am I still your favorite?" begged Warren.

"Why of course you are, Terry. You and I will do something special together when our mission, is complete, okay?" said Alexander in her fake assuring voice.

Terry bought into the lie once again. "That sounds wonderful."

"Keep me posted. I have many things to do before M2 arrives." Cortney ended the transmission.

The fragile Warren felt as if Alexander Industries was truly home. Even though, in reality, it was all a rouse, the emotionally disturbed genius believed every word that the manipulative scientist presented. The programmer was being programmed.

#

"My sweet baby girl! Are you all right?" asked Shirley tenderly.

"Oh, Mama Shirley," cried Julie, embracing the seventy-five-year-old woman.

Trent and Julie had just arrived at the Green Sea Inn and entered the kitchen. The Stanwicks and Shirley were all there to greet them.

"Jules!" Vicki ran to her and hugged her tightly.

"I was worried sick about you, Jules," Shirley spoke softly.

"We were praying for you," whispered Vicki, through her tears.

"Thank you, all of you. I love you, guys," Julie wiped her eyes with the blanket she was wrapped in.

"You need a hot shower and some dry clothes," Martha Stanwick spoke up after handing her a tissue.

"Exactly! She's right, Jules. Here's my master key, Vicki. Take her on up to the gold star suite," remarked Trent proudly.

"You mean your apartment, Trent?" Vicki giggled, taking the key.

Everyone in the room began to snicker. Trent put his head down, completely embarrassed.

"Okay, stop. Yes, it's my place," said Trent, blushing.

"I guess I missed a lot of the remodeling over the last three years," said Julie softly.

"He kind of kept it a secret, and so did I until now," Vicki admitted with a wrinkled brow.

"Vick?" Julie reprimanded her best friend humorously.

Vicki winced. "Sorry, my bad."

Trent cleared his throat in an animated manner. "Can you please take Jules upstairs?"

"Sure thing, Trent, sorry," acknowledged Vicki, with a wink.

"Everything you will need is up there, Jules." Trent kissed her gently on the lips.

The onlookers smiled as they witnessed the couple gazing into each other's eyes.

Once again, Trent and Julie realized that they were being watched. Abruptly, the moment was broken up by Joan Bradford, who barged in through the kitchen double doors.

"Is this the happenin' place or what? I'm starving!" voiced the loud redhead in her east coast accent. Everyone roared in laughter at Joan's untimely, awkward entrance.

"Trent, do you mind if Gary and I make some eggs and bacon for everyone?" asked Martha, strategically redirecting the conversation.

"Of course not! Help yourselves everyone. Are you hungry, Jules?" asked Trent.

Joan interrupted, "I'll answer for her. Yes, she is hungry, and so am I!"

More hearty laughter filled the restaurant kitchen. Shivering slightly, Julie responded with a polite nod.

"I will bring some dinner up to you in a little while." Trent held her face in his hands.

"That sounds great," said Julie in a hushed tone.

Trent kissed her on the cheek and walked to his office. Shirley stepped forward and held Julie's hands.

"My sweet, Jules, you have been through a lot today." Shirley gave her a long hug and whispered in her ear, "We will meet in the morning privately and sort all this out as promised. Just try and get some sleep."

"Okay, Mama Shirley," whispered Julie in return.

Vicki and Julie left the kitchen and headed upstairs to Trent's suite. Martha and Gary, along with Joan, moved to the work area and began getting the stove and utensils ready to cook the late meal for everyone.

Meanwhile, Shirley made her way into Trent's office and closed the door behind her. He was removing his shoulder holster and placing the revolver on the desk.

"Excuse me, Trent. I am so sorry about all this." Shirley walked over and hugged him.

"It's okay, Shirley, why are you apologizing to me?" Trent offered her a chair, and they both sat down.

"Well, it's all my fault, Trent. I let my guard down." Shirley took her glasses off, wiped the lenses, and returned them to her face.

"What do you mean, Ms. Shirley? How so?"

"When Jules gets up in the morning and is finished eating, we will all sit down and talk this over. I have a lot to explain."

"Everyone?"

"No, just the three of us. We'll meet here in your office." Shirley's countenance became very serious.

"I'm kind of getting a scary vibe from you right now," said Trent, lowering his voice again.

"It's okay, don't worry," assured Ms. Allen, patting Trent's hands and looking into his eyes confidently.

"It's a miracle Julie is alive. She said that creepy man, or thing, tried to kill her," said Trent quietly.

"What do you mean by *thing*, Trent?" asked Shirley with a troubled look.

"On the way over here, she told me that the strange man that tried to kill her wasn't human. It's some sort of superhuman or strange entity, she thought."

A distressed look came over Shirley's face. "Did she give you any more details?"

"No, but I'm sure she will."

"Indeed she will, but we definitely need to save it for when we talk first thing tomorrow." The intense gray-haired woman was now deep in thought.

Trent covered his face with his hands. "I should have stayed with her after lunch, and maybe this never would have happened."

"It doesn't matter, Trent, I think it was inevitable. I should have known long before this."

"Known what?" Trent looked at her confused.

"I'll explain everything to both of you in the morning. Please do me a favor? Don't bring any of this up when you bring Julie her food."

Trent smirked. "I'm sure those wheels are busy turning inside her head, and she probably already has some of this figured out, knowing Jules."

"Maybe so, but she just needs to rest and be ready for tomorrow."

Trent's grin left his face. "I too have plenty to add to the conversation, that's for sure."

"Yes, Trent, I'm sure you probably do."

"You have my word, Shirley. I will make sure we save it for the morning."

"We'll get through this and Castle Reef will hopefully be back to normal," encouraged the uniformed senior.

"I sure hope so." Trent straightened up in his chair and leaned forward slightly. "What about the state police and this town evacuation?"

Shirley smiled slightly. "Don't worry about that, it's all been taken care of."

"If you say so. I trust you."

"That means a lot to me, Trent."

After a short pause, Trent stood up. "I'm going to get that omelet and see how Chief Kerrig is doing."

"Thank you for being such a great man," said Shirley, reaching out to hug him.

Trent smiled after their embrace and left the office to join the others. Shirley took a deep breath, walked over near the doorway, and looked out into the kitchen. She observed the people that she loved dearly, preparing a midnight meal, oblivious to what was happening behind the scenes. The madam secretary pulled out the small device from her uniform pocket once again, pressed several miniature buttons and tucked it away. She tried to hold back her tears as she silently prayed under her breath, "Dear Lord, please help us all get through this mess."

#

"Let's make this quick," JK Reynolds muttered.

Captain Wilkes escorted the state representative through the back entry of the headquarters. The politician was dressed in a dark, red, warm-up suit and wearing a black, ball cap in order to hide his identity. Wilkes approached the troopers standing guard by the holding cell.

"You guys can go take a fifteen-minute coffee break. I got you covered," said Wilkes, who was now standing between JK Reynolds and the troopers.

"Yes, sir," they both replied in unison.

The two highway patrolmen walked down the long hall and entered the break room.

Meanwhile, Wilkes punched in the code to unlock the door. He opened it and stepped back.

"After you, Congressman."

JK stepped into the room first, followed by Wilkes who shut the door behind them. In the corner of the empty room was an individual who was handcuffed and sitting upright, almost unnaturally. The female was in her police uniform, wearing black boots and a black prisoner hood. The two men looked at each other, and then they both advanced.

"Ms. Kerrig, you should have never rocked the boat down in Castle Reef," taunted JK Reynolds.

The body sat motionless.

"Do you have anything to say before I shoot you for trying to attack us?" Wilkes moved closer.

"I don't have time for this crap, Kerrig. They should have killed your father a long time ago, but that nor'easter did it for us," announced Reynolds.

The corrupt captain looked at the unmoving subject and became suspicious. He walked over to examine the prisoner.

"What the... She's not breathing," exclaimed Wilkes, pulling off the hood.

Both men stood in shock. On the mouth of the now obvious female mannequin was a small sticky note with one word written in black marker: *BUSTED!*

"What is the meaning of this?" Reynolds demanded.

"What do you mean?" The captain's face lost all color.

"You brought me here for this?" yelled Reynolds.

"I was told to wait for you!" Wilkes barked back.

"Where is she? I thought your troopers were bringing her in!"

"I was told that you were supposed to confirm her arrest here in person before I took care of her!"

"You set me up!" shouted JK.

Wilkes gasped. "Not me! We were both set up!"

As the words left the captain's mouth, the door to the cell flew open. Both men turned around and faced several bright tactical lights from assault rifles on their faces.

"Get on the ground! Get on the ground now! Hands in front of you!" screamed several voices giving the commands. The two baffled and defeated men slowly went the floor.

JK Reynolds looked up into the lights with disgust. "You all are finished! Do you hear me? Do you know who I am?" hollered the angry politician.

"Yes, we do, JK, and so will all the world. Everyone is about to know who you really are," said a calm and distinct male voice, in the distance.

Lieutenant Roth and the other three troopers stood near the doorway watching. Both Wilkes and Reynolds were strip-searched and cuffed by a tactical team. One of the unidentified team members removed a button from the mannequin's uniform and gave it to the man who was standing behind the brilliant white lights.

chapter

23

"Isn't this place beautiful?" Vicki asked, standing in the middle of the living room totally in awe.

"It sure is. He certainly has great taste." Julie surveyed the room with wide eyes, smiling.

"He told me last year that he was going to finish it despite what happened between you guys."

Julie smirked. "Oh did he?"

"No matter what, he has always been in love with you, Jules."

"I know, I don't even want to think about how I must have devastated him." Julie walked through the dining area and into the large bedroom. Vicki followed behind her, admiring the furniture and furnishings.

"Oh my word! Julie, look at this! It's beautiful."

"He sure has great taste." Julie was in awe.

Vicki laughed. "Um, Jules, you just said that a minute ago."

The women stood and marveled at the antique queen-sized sleigh bed, complete with a canopy, along with matching dressers and a vanity. Trent had gotten everything Julie mentioned she wanted when they were planning their life together. The items had been purchased from local antique stores and even from New England. Julie began to shed tears and laugh at the same time. Vicki hugged her.

"Girlfriend, welcome back," beamed Vicki.

Those words sunk deep into Julie's heart. She recognized that God had spared her life this very night and had been there for her all along, even if she didn't feel His presence. He had waited patiently for her to return to Him. And now she realized Trent had done the same. He remained faithful to her despite being shunned and ignored. Julie finally understood that people were never designed to go through life alone.

"Thank you for always being there for me despite my drama. You are truly my best friend," said Julie, holding back more tears.

"You are mine too and always will be." Vicki hugged her again tightly. "Girl! You are still all wet! You need that shower."

"Yes, I do." Julie walked into the large tiled bathroom.

"Now that shower and tub will rock your world! Old school, yet so modern!" Vicki did a little dance as she giggled.

"Okay, okay, Vicki, you need to chill." Julie shook her head, laughing heartily.

"You're right, Jules, I better quit. I will see you tomorrow. Trent will bring up your omelet in a little while."

"That'll work. Thanks, Vicki. Love you, girl."

"Love you, sista." The two best friends hugged once more and Vicki made her way back down to the kitchen.

I could really get used to living here. Julie shut her eyes and smiled.

#

Meanwhile, approximately 118 miles west of Castle Reef, Tim and Ann were fast asleep inside the rooftop platform tent which sat upon their 1959 Land Rover. It had been a long, fun day of hiking in the foothills of the large nearby mountain range. The moonlit field where they parked was exploding with hundreds of fireflies. It was a perfect night for camping because the gentle night breeze lulled the tired couple into a deep slumber.

Suddenly, a loud rhythmic sound came rushing past the Rover and was gone within seconds. Tim woke up and zipped open the tent to see what had caused the commotion. He looked in both directions and saw nothing. Ann rolled over in her sleeping bag behind him and opened one eye.

"What's the matter, Tim?" she mumbled, then fell right back into a deep sleep.

"Probably a deer or a bear, perhaps?" Tim wondered aloud.

Not satisfied, he got out and stood on the hood of his vintage truck. Tim could see the vast field in detail, illuminated by the nearly full moon. He noticed a swath of grass that was cut approximately two feet wide, in a perfectly straight set of parallel lines, on the opposite side of the vehicle. This path stretched east as far as he could see. He then turned toward the mountain range and noticed that the grass was continuing to be carved by a dark figure, moving at a high rate of speed.

"Ann is never going to believe me," he whispered to himself.

#

Cortney Alexander slithered into the living room to find her father in his regular evening spot. She carefully removed the tumbler from his hand and kissed him on the cheek. Devin Alexander awoke and slowly turned to focus on his daughter's face.

"Hello, Father, I'm here. How was your day?" said Cortney, in her saccharin, sweet voice.

"Hey, it's my girl. Where have you been, my dearie?" sloshed the befuddled, alcoholic billionaire.

"Well, working, of course. You have me slaving around the clock on all these projects, you know?" Cortney laughed, walking to the ornate bar.

"I'm sorry, Cortney baby," replied Alexander, whose eyes were fixed straight ahead at a giant television that was flashing multiple financial ticker tapes, reports, and programs on its display.

"It's all for you, Father. Everything I do is for you."

Cortney put two more ice cubes in the glass from the ice bucket on the bar. She removed a small vial from her front right zipper pocket with a napkin, poured it into Devin's glass, and then filled it with his favorite scotch whiskey. She stirred it and brought it to him, placing it back into his hand. The empty vial remained upright on the counter.

"Thank you, my dear." Devin sipped the drink several times and smacked his lips in delight.

"Just the way you like it, right?" asked the deceptive daughter with a smile.

"Indeed, dear Cortney. By the way, I got some bad news."

"What is it, Father? Has Mother taken a turn for the worse?"

"Your mother is resting comfortably like always. It involves JK Reynolds."

"What happened? Is he okay?" Cortney's eyes became big dark saucers in anticipation.

"I'm afraid he was taken into custody tonight, along with another law enforcement official, according to my sources." Devin took two more gulps of his drink.

"Oh no, that's horrible," she said, with her great acting skills.

Devin's eyes became heavy as he leaned his head back into the recliner. Cortney walked over to his chair and leaning over, whispered in his ear.

"It seems like all your politician friends end up in trouble. Tonight, it looks to be your turn, Father. You shouldn't have let some maniac poison you and your wife tonight."

The billionaire opened his eyes one last time and barely managed to get one word out.

"Why?" he gasped in his paralysis.

Cortney finished with her final verbal dagger. "Because you never believed me twenty-eight years ago, that's why! But thank you for making me your primary beneficiary. It's the least you could do."

Devin wheezed his last breath, as his only child walked away. She left and headed to the secluded room on the other side of the large mansion to visit her only living parent. Another small vial, in her front left pocket, awaited her cold, bony fingers to pour directly into her mother's sleeping mouth.

#

Ian Reynolds was lying on a futon, staring at the ceiling in the Foster's crowded guest room. His friends, Randy and Jake, were both asleep in their sleeping bags on the floor next to him. Across the room in a twin bed, Billy Daily was quietly sleeping with a smile on his face.

But for Ian, sleep was elusive because he was still shaken and thinking over his life.

Hours before, the Foster's had fixed the boys and Francis O'Reily some fresh fish sandwiches and coleslaw. Now, they were all sound asleep including both Jerry and Becky in their bedroom and Francis on the living room couch, snoring.

Ian leaned over, pulled out his phone from his backpack, and unlocked it. Several text messages were on his screen. There were five from girls who had canceled their beach party plans earlier and one that caught his eye immediately.

I'm sorry, I love you Ian, please call me. XO Mom.

He read the message several times. Finally, he couldn't hold it back any longer and began to cry. Ian dropped his phone, covered his face with his pillow, and emptied out his hurting heart.

He sobbed. "God, if you're real, I need you to show me a sign."

Startled by someone touching his arm, Ian removed the pillow to see Billy kneeling over him with a sad look on his face. As tears rolled down the sides of Ian's face, Billy touched his shoulder gently.

"It okay, Mr. Ian. Don't be sad. It be okay."

The broken young man tried desperately to collect himself. "Thanks, Billy. I wish I could be as kind and innocent and as you are," sniffled the young Reynolds.

"I get sad too. I sometime want what you have good. I get sad."

"Billy, you have way more than I'll ever have. You're a lucky guy."

"Me lucky? You mean that, Mr. Ian, to me?" Billy grinned.

"I do, Billy. Thanks for being my friend." Ian got choked up again and managed to swallow.

"You my bestist friend ever all time!" called out Billy.

Randy and Jake stirred in their sleeping bags. Ian put his finger to his mouth to quiet the excited man.

"Shh, Billy, easy, buddy. We gotta get some sleep, okay?"

"Soree, Mr. Ian. I go back to bed now, I go," said Billy as he abruptly turned and walked back to his bed.

"Night, Billy," Ian said softly.

"Night night, don't let the bed bugs bite," Billy said in a voice just above a whisper.

Ian smiled, wiped his eyes, and arranged his pillow. It occurred to him that for the first time, he felt something inside he had never ever felt before. He was determined to call his mother in the morning.

#

The bacon and cheese omelets were a welcome sight and much needed treat for the tired and hungry adults in the Green Sea Inn kitchen. However, it was very late, and the charming inn, which had been brought back to life momentarily, was becoming quiet once again.

Greg and Martha Stanwick had already gone to their room for the night. Vicki and Joan were washing the remaining dishes, and Shirley Allen was busy drying all the silverware and placing it neatly into the holder tub, near the dining room entrance. Meanwhile, Julie was fast asleep upstairs in Trent's master suite.

Trent, sitting at his desk in his office, was staring at the wall in deep thought about the woman he loved. Earlier, he had brought dinner up to Julie. She had finished her long hot shower and was wearing his pajamas. They both ate together in the small open dining area, looking into each other's eyes and catching up on lost time. Afterward, they sat on his white leather couch, in the living room, holding hands and adoring each other in silence. Trent wanted so badly to stay the remaining hours of the night with her, but always wanting to protect the honor of the woman who had captured his heart, realized it wasn't the wisest thing to do. So he reluctantly went to the door, but then turned before leaving and held her close.

"Jules, I love you more than ever."

Julie responded in tears. "I love you so much and I can't wait to spend the rest of my life with you." She nestled her head under his chin.

After a long embrace, Trent kissed Julie good night. He went downstairs almost floating, knowing that God had brought them back together again through the strangest of circumstances.

#

Thirty-seven miles away, outside the Brighton city limits, a dim light glowed behind the curtains of a beautifully restored farmhouse window.

"Keep all roads blocked off that go to the beach until further notice," Hillsdale ordered, scribbling on his notepad next to his bed-side phone.

"We have several troopers at all access points. We are only allow-ing the list of authorized vehicles you gave us to enter and exit, sir," Lieutenant Roth explained.

"Did the operation go as planned?" Hillsdale rubbed his eyes and looked at the clock on the nightstand.

"Yes, sir, they have the two subjects in their custody now. I will give you a full report in the morning, sir," Roth replied.

"Thank you, Lieutenant. I will touch base as soon as I'm in the office." Superintendent Hillsdale hung up the phone, turned over on his back, and stared at the ceiling intently.

His wife rolled over and kissed him on the cheek. "I'm sorry, Neil. That was probably the hardest thing you ever had to do."

"No, I think tomorrow is going to be more difficult."

"In what way?" his loving wife asked.

"The dominos have begun to fall, and I think there are going to be a lot of surprises for Brighton, our state, and even our country."

"You mean it's that big?" She moved closer and rested her head on his chest.

"I'm afraid so, my dear." Hillsdale kissed his wife's forehead and then tried his best to sleep. The sunrise was less than six hours away.

#

"Knock, knock." Vicki popped her head into Trent's office. Trent snapped out of his love trance.

"Oh, hey, Vicki. Heading to bed?" answered Trent, still distracted.

"Yes, Joan and I are headed up to room 112. Mom and Dad are next door in 110."

"Okay, great, thanks so much for all your help, Vicki."

"No worries. I'm sorry I embarrassed you earlier about your private suite."

"No harm, no foul. I remodeled that room in hopes that one day Jules and I could live here, remember?"

"Well, Mr. Green, it looks like that day is quickly approaching. She loves it, and you did good up there, real good!" stated Vicki, with one of her signature winks.

"I sure hope so. I'm glad she's here and safe."

"About that, what exactly is going on, Trent?"

"Well, it's complicated. I'm sure Julie will fill you in after this whole ordeal is all over."

"I get it. That's code for 'Ms. Stanwick, stop asking questions and go to bed,'" laughed Vicki.

"You're good, you caught that, huh? Am I that obvious?" Trent asked.

Vicki giggled. "I know people!"

"Hey, can I ask you a favor?"

"Sure, Trent, what's up?" inquired Vicki, moving in closer.

"Julie's place was trashed today, and she hasn't seen it yet."

Vicki gasped. "Oh, my word! What happened?"

"Not sure yet, maybe a break-in. Just add it to the list of oddities around here."

"You can say that again."

"I was wondering if you and Joan could help me gather some of Julie's things and bring them here, in the morning?"

"Absolutely! What time?"

"I know I'm stretching, but can we get over there around six?" asked Trent with a scrunched face.

"For Jules anything, for you, eh!" jeered Vicki, slapping her thighs.

"Thanks so much, Vicki; it means a lot," said Trent sincerely.

Vicki giggled. "Now I just have to convince Joan!"

"See you around six?" asked Trent with a grin.

"You bet, Mr. Green Sea." Vicki pointed at Trent.

"Good night, Ms. Stanwick. Here, take one of these." Trent, still smiling, handed her a two-way radio from the charger.

"Awesome, now we're talkin'. I will be sure to let you know if Joan is snoring," teased Vicki, as she started to leave.

"See you in few hours," said Trent, shaking his head.

Trent stood up and waved at Joan from a distance, watching the two ladies leave the kitchen and go into the dining room. Shirley finished drying her last pan, threw the towel over her shoulder, and walked into his office.

"I'm going to my room too, Mr. Innkeeper."

Trent chuckled. "Ha! You are? Why, the night is young."

"I wish. Thanks for everything here. You have a wonderful place, and I think there's someone very special upstairs in your suite that needs to share it with you."

Trent started to blush. "Thanks, and I agree with you, but only time will tell. You're in room 111, right?"

"Yes, I am."

"I am going to be sleeping down here in Mike's office in his recliner. If you need anything, let me know." Trent handed Shirley a two-way radio from the charger.

"I should be fine."

"I'm the only staff member here, so don't ask me for extra towels," teased Trent.

"Ha! Thanks. I think we'll all be fine. I will see you in the morning, say around eight?" suggested Shirley.

"That sounds good. I'm sure Julie will be up by then."

"I'll make sure she is. Besides, I brought her things from her station locker. I'll make sure she's up and dressed." Shirley winked at Trent.

As they exchanged their good nights, Trent turned off all the office and kitchen lights and secured the doors. They both made their way to their respective rooms. Tomorrow would be a defining moment in all of their lives.

chapter

24

It was late. Terry Warren tried to notify Cortney several times for over an hour that M2 had arrived at the lower level portal. Warren, worried, finally closed the program interface in Alexander's office and went down to the lab, where Cortney was supposedly working, in hopes of finding her. Terry had never been allowed to visit the lower level before, so this risky decision made the programmer very anxious.

"Cortney?" Warren called out into the dimly lit hallway.

The elevator door slowly closed, and Terry stood alone. Noticing that all the technical and research offices were dark, Warren walked to the end of the hallway, after seeing the light from the main lab bathing across the tile floor. Turning the corner, the main doors were wide open, and Terry walked into the bright white lab. The walls were lined with computer touch screen terminals and holographic monitors.

Large workstations surrounded a giant robotic arm in the center of the room, which had cables and tubes extending from it on a circular mounted ceiling track. Inside this centerpiece sat a raised rectangular platform. It had many other smaller automated machines mounted on its sides. These robotic arms were quietly working on something that was located on the other side and out of view.

Surveying the room, Warren saw a large, thick plexiglass chamber in the far corner of the lab. Inside this chamber, stood two familiar figures which Terry adored: Cortney Alexander and M2. Walking up to the door, Cortney motioned for the computer programmer prodigy to enter the airlock door.

"Well, I see you took it upon yourself to come down here," said Alexander in her normal sarcastic tone.

"You never responded. I called for you all over the complex. I had to shut down all the programs and engage the cyber security protocols."

"Of course, I wouldn't expect anything less. I knew you would come here eventually."

"I was worried."

Terry slowly walked toward Cortney, now standing next to the strange-looking M2. A sick feeling began to settle heavily upon Warren. Cortney looked at Terry defiantly and gave M2 a verbal command.

"Turn and face zero eighty-eight."

M2 slowly turned with shuffling steps toward the stunned programmer. The tall, unclothed, translucent, and genderless body glistened, except for its face and hands, which remained human in appearance. It's bright azure and intimidating eyes fixed themselves on Warren.

"He responds to your voice commands too? I thought I was the only one in control of M2." Terry was astonished and shaking.

Alexander smirked. "Yes, isn't it fascinating?"

"You're not a programmer. How did you do this?" moaned Terry, avoiding eye contact with the synthetic android.

"It's been almost four very long years, and I would never give away all of my secrets, especially to you," bragged Alexander.

"How come you never told me?" Terry's voice was trembling.

"Terry, I used you. I learned your skills and now I'm finished with you."

"I am the one who built the interface! Only I can run it!" snapped Terry.

"You just thought you were in control of M1 and M2!"

"I built the programs, I gave the commands. It was me!"

"Terry, many of those commands were overridden by me."

"What do you mean?"

"I made sure M1 and M2 did all the things you would never do," boasted Alexander.

"Like what? This doesn't make any sense. How can you possibly know how to run these complex entities?" said the bewildered Warren.

"Anything you did was carefully monitored and recorded on the interface and everywhere in my labs. Do you think I'm that stupid, Terry?" taunted Cortney, pointing to several cameras in the ceiling.

"This isn't fair! M1 and M2 are my projects! I risked everything to help you with your crazy plan!"

"I really don't like you saying that my plan is crazy. I have revolutionaries from all over the world that think otherwise," boasted Cortney.

Warren gulped. "What are you talking about?"

"The beautiful revolution is finally here, and it's time to for it to commence!"

Terry was bewildered. "What revolution?"

"Terry, I have grown weary of you. I brought you into my empire to get everything I needed from you. I allowed you to use your skills to develop M1 and M2, but now it's over for you."

Terry swallowed hard. "Why are you saying that? I thought we were in this together? What about Phase 3?"

"We were never in this together. You're just a forty-year-old little child who is very gullible and needy."

"Are you forgetting that I'm the one who instructed M2 to get that priceless microchip back for you?" Terry's face was flushed.

"You did all the basic programming, but never really completed the task, as usual." Alexander gave a belligerent wink.

"You're insane! I shut down M1 like you requested and then programmed M2 to retrieve the chip at the coordinates you gave me!"

"You just think you did. M1 has been destroyed."

"How could you? That isn't possible!"

"Did you ever hear of the word 'override,' Terry?" Cortney leaned into Terry's face and laughed forcefully.

Warren cowered. "Please stop it, Cortney!"

"Furthermore, I knew you wouldn't terminate the targets, so I took care of them too!" bragged the diabolical woman.

"Terminate the targets? I had complete control over M1 and M2. I saw it on the interface!" exclaimed Warren.

"You just thought you were in control, but you were never in control, Terry," jeered Alexander.

"You are crazy! You mean you killed and hurt people for your so-called revolution?" yelled Warren.

"You don't understand, and you never will, Terry."

"You killed people! I want no part of this anymore!" screamed Warren.

"Shut your mouth!"

Terry's lower lip began to quiver. "Stop, Cortney, this isn't funny."

"You're weak, Terry, and that's why I don't need you any longer," said the expressionless evil woman.

"You won't get away with any of this!" Terry turned to leave quickly.

"M2, detain zero eighty-eight!" ordered Alexander.

Instantly, the semitransparent figure placed its left hand firmly around Terry's neck.

Cortney nonchalantly wiped off the sticky residue on the cell phone she had retrieved from M2 and placed it in her lab coat pocket.

"M2 will now perform the same directive I gave it to take care of Ms. Kerrig." Alexander was laughing as she made her way to the airlock door.

Terry gasped. "What are you saying? Who is Ms. Kerrig?" she demanded in a hoarse voice.

Cortney raised her long, pointer finger to her cherry red lips, so as to silence the programmer, who was now losing the ability to breathe.

"Tomorrow's news report will say something like this: 'Terry Warren, a rogue computer programmer at Alexander Industries, used technology as a weapon in order to kill two innocent people and maim one in Castle Reef. One of the victims was Police Chief Julie Kerrig, the daughter of the late John Kerrig.'"

Terry was struggling to breathe. "No, that's not true!"

"Furthermore, they will broadcast for the whole world to hear: 'Our sources say that Terry Warren also poisoned CEO and founder Devin Alexander and his wife Valerie and then held their daughter Cortney hostage in a test lab at Alexander Industries,'" continued the maniacal woman, as if she was reading a script.

"I'll do anything you want. I'm... I'm...sorry... I..." shrieked Terry.

With dead eyes, Cortney continued on, "Warren's body was found in an explosion chamber within the test lab, several floors below the research facility. The programmer was thought to have committed suicide. Cortney Alexander, the CEO and lead scientist, was restrained by Warren and rescued by the lab staff this morning."

"You're sick, Cortney. All I wanted was for you to love me!"

"Love you? I never even liked you. I used you and that's the only thing I loved about you." Alexander laughed hysterically.

"Love me! Please love me," begged Terry in a forced whisper.

"M2, self-terminate in sixty seconds!" commanded Alexander coldly.

"Cortney, please! *Please!*"

The translucent droid extended its left arm and grabbed the struggling programmer even tighter. Cortney left the chamber and sealed the door behind her. She turned around, smiled, and waved goodbye to Terry Warren, who was now frantically trying to escape the grasp of the opaque monster.

Above ground, at the main level, and inside the sturdy and soundproof industrial structure, came a slight rumble and vibration. Two on-duty security guards noticed a shudder near the elevator shaft, which led to the lower levels. They glanced at each other, shrugged, and then went back to playing video games on their cell phones. Alexander Industries would look totally different in the morning.

chapter

25

It was now 1:38 a.m. and one dozen black unmarked vehicles had swiftly descended upon the governor's mansion. The state's security detail was rapidly relieved of their duties and escorted off the premises. Several plainclothes agents exited their vehicles and set up a perimeter around the residence while the remainder entered the mansion.

"What is the meaning of this?" shouted Governor Daniel Riddick, standing in the ornate entryway.

"Come with us, Mr. Riddick," said the female agent, showing him her identification tag.

"Who are you people? I reject this!" demanded the enraged governor.

"Daniel? What is going on?" asked Riddick's wife, looking over the balcony to the foyer below.

"Call security, Lucy! Get these people out of here!" snarled Riddick.

"Ma'am, come down the stairs with your hands up!" ordered a male agent, who was standing at the bottom of the stairwell with his hand on his sidearm.

"I will have your all of your jobs for this! Do you hear me?"

"Mr. Riddick, you need to calm down," directed another agent.

"You people are—"

The governor was stopped short of firing the concealed pistol he had quickly pulled out of his robe pocket. Another agent, behind him, saw the weapon and quickly deployed his Taser.

"That will only make things worse, Mr. Riddick. Please don't fight us."

Daniel Riddick whimpered, as his body quivered on the tile floor. Four agents zip-tied his hands and feet, along with Lucy, his wife. Using their searchlights and detection devices, the remaining three armed persons cleared the large home in less than three minutes.

"I have done nothing wrong. There must be some mistake," whimpered the defeated governor.

The unidentified female agent muttered into her wrist microphone. "Sir, we have the subject and his spouse in custody. The mansion is now clear."

She nodded after receiving instructions in her earpiece and quickly motioned the rest of the team to head outside. "Affirmative, sir, transporting in less than zero point zero eight."

Within five minutes, the majority of vehicles exited swiftly through the automated front gate. Two vehicles remained behind in the circle drive and awaited further instructions.

#

At one thousand feet in the sky over the center of Castle Reef, two stealth helicopters hovered in whisper mode, monitoring two teams of special operations and maritime security forces that were moving rapidly and undetected. The teams were confiscating EHF transmitters, cameras, and other devices that had been located. This precise covert operation would last several hours and finish just before dawn.

"I'm going to try and get four hours of sleep just like our commander in chief gets each night," mused Shirley on her private cell line, inside room 111.

"Thank you for all you are doing despite the drastic change in plans," said the kind voice on the other end.

In her comfy bed, Shirley propped herself up with two pillows and continued. "Honestly, it moved a lot faster than anticipated. Teams Beta and Gamma are fully engaged, right?"

"Affirmative. Operation Iscariot is underway."

"Excellent, tomorrow morning, I am meeting with Mr. Green and Chief Kerrig. It will all be revealed to them."

"Do you think they are ready for that discussion? Is she ready for it?"

Shirley paused. "I think so. Either way, she holds the key to a lot of the intel that we need. I hope I'm ready."

The voice softened. "I think you both are."

"She's come into her own. She's a strong woman," Shirley stated proudly.

The caller remained silent for a moment and then gently cleared his throat. "Madam Secretary, I will touch base with you at fifteen hundred hours."

"That will be great. Let's both try and get some sleep."

"I'm not sure I can." He paused again.

She sighed. "Good night, 613."

Shirley held the phone to her chest after finishing the call and then placed it on the nightstand. Despite the room being illuminated by the moonlight and the myriad of things on her mind, she pulled a blanket over her head and went to sleep. She felt confident knowing that outside in the streets, and on top of the buildings, her team members were securing Castle Reef.

#

Janet Reynolds had just finished speaking with the family attorney after being awakened inside the interstate hotel. She found herself about three hundred miles from Brighton, on her way to her sister's home in Ohio indefinitely. The call was to inform her that JK was in deep trouble and was asking for her help. Janet declined to assist and informed the attorney that he was to start divorce proceedings immediately on her behalf.

She rolled over in the familiar half-empty bed and stared at the reflection of the red traffic light flashing on the wall. All of the hidden secrets, lies, and pain that began to surface during the six-hour drive earlier became clearer. Janet knew it was time to get help and end the charade she'd been living for decades. She needed a place to start and didn't know where.

Suddenly, her phone vibrated and broke the daze she was in. She reached and flipped it over to see Ian's picture on the screen.

Mom, I'm sorry. Can we talk tomorrow?

Tears instantly filled the fifty-year-old's tired eyes. The decision to reach Castle Reef in the morning was made in seconds. She would face her past and present and hopefully build a future.

Yes, Ian, I'm coming your way. Please meet me for lunch? she texted carefully.

Janet nervously awaited a response for more than twenty minutes. Finally, a vibration and light came from under her pillow. She quickly grabbed her phone and wiped her eyes.

Yes, I will try and call you.

The digital clock on the nightstand read 3:09 a.m. She got up and poured the two unopened wine coolers down the bathroom sink drain, undressed, and then started the shower.

A faint glimmer of hope dropped into her heart. It was time to make things right.

chapter

26

It was already after eight o'clock, and the sunny June morning was well underway for Trent, Vicki, and Joan. They had been awake and busy for nearly two hours working at Julie's apartment. Upon arriving, the ladies were horrified to see what had happened and quickly began helping Trent box up Julie's personal items.

"This still blows my mind. Who would do something like this to Jules?" Vicki stood with her hands on her hips shaking her head.

"I don't know, but it's kind of creepy, like last night in my opinion," said Joan in a gruff tired voice.

Trent purposely kept his suspicions to himself. "It may have been some looters looking for money."

"You got a point there. This used to happen all the time in the central part of Boston. A lot of B&Es there by a bunch of idiots," remarked Joan in her noticeable accent.

"Well, whoever it was he must be pretty strong because this place is a mess," observed Vicki, stacking her last box.

"The door, for Pete's sake, looks like the same thing that happened at your parents, Vicki!" exclaimed Joan.

"You're right, it does!" Vicki raised her eyebrows.

"I do see the similarities, Ms. Bradford. I'm sure Julie will investigate and get some answers. Let's finish up here, I need some coffee," said Trent, changing the subject.

"That sounds like a great idea." Vicki smiled.

"It's Joan, Trent, call me Joan. Coffee, nothun betta than coffee," acknowledged the redhead.

Vicki giggled. "Trent, this was a great idea. Julie will be so happy you did this."

"I hope so," shrugged Trent, who neglected to notice that the brown leather Bible was missing from the window sill.

They quickly finished their task and brought everything over, in Trent's truck, to the Green Sea Inn. They unloaded the boxes and quietly stacked them upstairs by Trent's suite door. After thanking the ladies who had gone to their rooms to shower, Trent went to the kitchen to make coffee and toast some bagels.

#

Hiding in his office all night with the window blinds pulled, David Willis finished his ninth shot of whiskey. Sleepless and paranoid, like a cornered rat, Willis was so pleased that he had remembered the hidden bottle behind a copy of *10,000 Leagues Under the Sea* on his office bookshelf several hours earlier. This was the only comfort he could find during the long and stressful night. He was alone, full of fear, and intoxicated, yet after waiting until sunrise, he had finally managed to phone his puppeteer. The call had gone to voicemail.

"JK, this is Mayor Willisss, are you there?" slurred the drunken mayor, shouting into his phone.

The befuddled Willis continued. "Hey! JK! I'm talkin' to you! You think yur thiss big time powerful man, well, I wanna tell you sumthin'. I'm more powerful then you'll ev'r be! I'm mayor and cheeef, chief of police!"

Willis fell from his office chair onto the floor. Picking up the phone and trying to untangle the cord, the pathetic mayor resumed his rant until JK Reynolds's voicemail beeped and cut off the inebriated David Willis.

"I'll show ev'rybody! Yess, I will. I will show ev'rywone whut yu made me doo!" Willis belched before passing out.

On the office floor lay the honorable mayor and self-appointed police chief of Castle Reef.

#

"We have the green light to move back to port, sir," said Ensign Bailey, hanging up the handset.

"Well, that's a relief. We can finally go home now," stated Lieutenant Commander Lee.

"Did they capture the shark, sir?"

Commander Lee looked across the bow of the ship and then surveyed the morning coastal waters with his binoculars. "That I don't know, Ensign Jeffery. It's a mystery. The word down in the galley, from the boiler room to the captain's table, is that we were under a terror alert on our coastal waters."

"Terror alert? I never heard anything on the radio, sir!"

"Neither did I or the captain. We were told to remain in our current pattern until we received further orders."

"I beg your pardon for my asking, sir, but is it fair to ask the superiors for further information?" said the ensign cautiously.

"Son, sometimes its best you don't. I've learned in all my years of service, there are some things you're better off not knowing. The more you know, the more you're responsible for."

"Yes, sir." Bailey remained silent.

"Take us back to port, Bailey. You are a good man, Jeff," said Lee, patting the ensign on the shoulder.

As the Coast Guard patrol boat increased its speed and changed course, both men looked westward toward Castle Reef. They silently agreed that what they both had witnessed the day before was something more than a shark.

#

"Knock, knock, room service," spoke Trent, with a bad English accent, gently tapping on the suite door.

The door quickly opened and there stood Julie fully dressed in uniform. It shocked Trent so much that he nearly dropped the tray he was holding.

"Good morning, Trent," Julie cordially said as she motioned him inside.

"You scared me. You're up and dressed already?"

"Of course I am! Mm…that really smells good," remarked Julie, smelling the fresh coffee.

"We're going to need lots of coffee today. I toasted some bagels too, with real butter, just the way you like them." Trent laughed. He set the tray down on the kitchen counter and turned only to be met with a warm embrace and a long kiss from Julie.

"Someone stacked some boxes outside the door with all my personal belongings in them. You don't happen to know anything about that, do you?" inquired Julie, with squinting eyes and a grin.

"Well, maybe?" beamed Trent, looking over her shoulder at the stack of eight large cardboard boxes in the corner.

"That was a thoughtful surprise. Thank you, Mr. Green." Julie kissed him again.

Trent gulped. "Oh boy, what a way to start my day."

Julie walked over and faced the boxes. "So how bad is my apartment?" She slowly turned around with her arms crossed and raised an eyebrow, staring at Trent.

"Um, yeah, about that…" He searched for his next words.

After letting him squirm for a moment, Julie broke into a giggle. "You can chill out, Mr. Green. I called Vicki just before you got here and made her tell me all about it, in detail."

"I'm so sorry, Jules. I was waiting for the right moment to bring it up. The boxes were kind of an ice breaker to get the conversation started."

"Well, it worked." The uniformed Kerrig laughed.

"Not the way I pictured it though. I'm truly sorry," said Trent regretfully.

Julie stepped closer. "It's all good. You know, I thought about you all night," whispered Julie as she held his hands.

"Oh really?" Trent cleared his throat and sighed.

"I had to focus on you because if I didn't, I would see those creepy eyes of that thing that tried to kill me."

"Well then, that's okay with me." Trent smiled, sat down, and slid a cup over to Julie.

"Yeah, I didn't sleep so well." She stirred the creamer into her coffee.

"I'm sorry, honey, you must be so tired. You don't look it though," complimented Trent.

"There certainly wasn't an opportunity for productively counting sheep." Julie quipped.

He laughed and noticed that she didn't have her hair in the usual ponytail. Instead, it was loose and resting beautifully on her shoulders.

She continued. "Maybe adrenaline, I guess. Plus, Shirley dropped this off an hour ago," Julie patted her chest and hips.

Trent raised his brow. "I see. You know, I think last night was the first time in three years I saw you dressed as a civilian."

"Really? Get out of here! Seriously?"

"Sure, every time I would see you, either you were on duty or in a special town service or parade. You were always dressed in your blues, toting all the gear." Trent shook his head with a big smile.

"You're probably right. Most of the time when I get off duty, I just wear sweatpants and a T-shirt while watching college football or old Christmas movies."

Trent looked into her beautiful eyes. "All by yourself?"

"Of course, there isn't any room in my heart for anyone but you."

He leaned in and kissed her. "I love you, Jules."

"I love you too, Trent."

They sipped their coffee and enjoyed their bagels, silently exchanging flirting glances for a few minutes.

"So Shirley came by? What did she say?" Trent changed the subject on purpose.

"Well, she knew you would be coming by and asked if we could meet here, instead of your office."

"Okay, that will work, but what about the others?" Trent was curious.

"I asked the same thing, and she said she had it taken care of."

"Well, I must say Shirley Allen is surprising me every minute."

"I know. It's as if she's pulling rank or something." Julie laughed, savoring her last bite of the buttered bagel.

"Hey, I do want to ask you more about last night before Shirley comes."

"What do you mean?" Julie looked down into her coffee cup.

"The Salty Dog Marina and what happened there." Trent placed his hands on her arm.

"Well, to be honest, I didn't sleep not only because I would see those lifeless bright-blue eyes staring right through me, but I couldn't shake what I experienced while I was drowning."

"You should have called me, Jules."

"I thought about it, but I didn't want to wake you. So I kept thinking about you instead, and that really helped." Julie placed her hands on his hands and caressed his thumbs.

"Are you okay now?" Trent asked compassionately.

Julie slowly removed her hands and leaned back in her chair. She took a deep breath and exhaled with a long sigh. "Trent, what I experienced when I was underwater and dying is something I can never fully explain to anyone accurately."

"How so? Try me, Julie. I'm listening," urged Trent.

"It's so multilayered. My father's death, his Bible, and of course, my salvation, seemingly all linked together." Julie stared across the room blankly.

"Wow, that's deep." Trent was intrigued.

Julie turned back to Trent. "It changed me on the inside, and I will never be the same. The fragility of life is so real. We need to cherish every moment we are given."

"Thank you for sharing your heart with me." Trent leaned in and touched her face.

"I know my perspective has changed for the better. It will no longer be all about me.

Make sure you keep me on track, will you?" Julie pleaded.

"Only if you promise to keep me on track too?" said Trent softly.

"Deal," whispered Julie.

The two kissed again and then gazed into each other's eyes for a long time. Trent knew there was more that Julie needed to talk about for her benefit, but he didn't press her. He took a bite of his bagel and washed it down with a sip of coffee.

"So, Jules, are you okay with telling me more about this weird guy that tried to kill you last night?"

Julie suspected his intentions. "Yes, thank you, Dr. Green."

"Hey, now, I'm just trying to help," voiced Trent.

Julie reflected. "Well, I was sitting on the bench at the marina and just looking at the water. I was trying figure out this whole mess. Ian and his buddies had said that the shark was headed toward the inlet, so I went to investigate. Of course, that was after my little altercations."

Trent interrupted. "Sorry, Jules, but why were you on the beach with those guys?"

"Do you want me to put a hurt on you too?" joked Julie, pretending to go after Trent.

"Please don't try it, or I'll have to ask you to leave our establishment."

"What do you mean by *our*?" The attractive police officer giggled.

"It's a long story. I'll tell you later." Trent winked and chuckled to himself.

"Anyway, Mr. Green, may I continue?"

"Sure, as you were saying?"

"I had to leave the station quick because the state police were after me and Shirley rushed me out of there."

"Why were they after you?

"Who knows? Just add it to the growing list of mysteries."

"So I gather that's why you went to the beach?"

"Yep, I was walking, praying, and thinking things through when I stumbled upon the three drunken amigos, with Billy in tow."

Trent winced. "That didn't end too well for them, I gather?"

"Nope, and I was doing them a favor by going easy on two of them, believe me."

"I bet. So go on. They saw the shark?"

"Apparently. So I make it to the marina, and I'm looking at the water, and then I think I see it circling inside the bay. Suddenly, the weirdest thing happened."

"What, Jules?"

"It was if an underwater explosion occurred. This big wave splashed up everywhere, and then the water became instantly calm."

"You never mentioned that." Trent looked perplexed.

"There are more details, believe me."

"So how long was it before the strange man showed up?" Trent sipped his coffee and intently waited.

"Well, right after that, I wanted to call you, but my phone started buzzing, and it became really hot. So hot, that I dropped it. Then all of the dock lights went out."

"Like an electrical disturbance?" asked Trent pensively.

"Yes, even the drink machine turned off over by Oceans. The next thing I know, the weird guy is behind me. I just knew it was him even before I turned around. It was so creepy, Trent."

"So what happened?"

"He demanded that I give him my cell phone."

"Why? That's so bizarre."

"Well, earlier at the station, I found some sort of microchip that fell out of my duty belt after I threw it," explained Julie, pointing to the belt around her waist snugly.

"Threw it?" asked Trent carefully.

"Yeah, it's a long story. I'll tell you later, but Shirley seemed to possibly know what it was and told me to take it."

"Once again, all roads point to Shirley." Trent stood up, poured some more coffee in both of their cups, and added cream to Julie's.

"I'm beginning to think so too, Trent."

"Do you think she knows what it was that tried to kill you?"

"Maybe so, all I know is that it's not human. It did this weird alien push-motion thing, like from *Star Trek* or *Star Wars*, that I managed to get out of."

"It became violent?" Trent swallowed his coffee slowly.

"I think it wanted my phone because I hid that chip inside of the case."

"That chip must be pretty important to someone or something."

"At this point, I was now in survival mode for sure." Julie leaned forward.

"Did it attack you then?"

"Yup, so I threw a throat punch and my hand went right through the sucker."

"Whoa, that's freaky!" Trent was on the edge of his chair.

"You're telling me. It was as if he was made of pudding or Jell-O. It made me physically sick. In fact, I remember having the same feeling when I met him for the first time at Nina's while I was having lunch with Vicki the other day."

"Come to think of it, I felt nauseous when he was in the dining room hassling Kendra," Trent recalled.

"He kept repeating the same demanding line as if it was programmed." Julie looked away in deep thought for a moment.

"What happened next?" Trent asked in order to get her attention.

Julie answered, "Before it grabbed me, I emptied my Colt completely."

"You surely had to have wounded it, didn't you?"

"Not a chance. No blood. It just kept coming and finally grabbed me by the neck and picked me up."

"It's a miracle you're alive, Jules."

"I know. I managed to cry out to God just before everything went black."

Trent reached across the table again for Julie's hand. "Jules, you don't have to continue. I've heard enough. It's okay."

Julie didn't miss a beat. "Trent, those eyes weren't human. They were so electrifying and bright blue. The face and hands were printed like a tattoo on the body to make it appear human."

"What do you mean? I'm not following you." Trent was puzzled and furrowed his brow.

"I think Shirley wants to tell us about that strange man and a whole lot more." Julie stared at the floor.

"Are you okay?" Trent was concerned. He lifted her chin up gently.

"Trent, that thing took my cell phone and absorbed it right into its body," said Julie with an intense expression.

"I believe you. I am just trying to wrap my head around all this," said Trent, looking bewildered.

"Shirley told me that she would explain things later. She rushed me out of the station before the HP showed up."

Trent scratched his head and leaned back in his chair. "Mike and I saw the state police come to the station. We kept our distance. You must have left right before they arrived."

"I did. That's when I went to the beach to clear my head. Where exactly were you guys hiding when you saw the highway patrol?"

Trent grimaced. "Well, about that…"

"About what?" Julie tilted her head slightly.

"We were up in your apartment looking across the street," revealed Trent timidly.

"What? How did you get into my apartment?" asked Julie pointedly.

"Well, we got to your place *after* it was ransacked, so getting in there was easy, unfortunately. I told Vicki and Joan that it might have been a looter, but I knew it was more than that."

"I can't believe it. Who could have…" She stopped herself.

"All the electronic devices are fried, and it must have happened just before four, according to your wall clock," Trent explained. He pulled out the photo from his shirt pocket and placed it carefully in her hand.

Julie stood up and began rolling her neck. She started pacing back and forth. She looked at the picture and then held it tight to her chest.

"It was him! It was that freak. It was that…that thing!" she whispered loudly.

"I came looking for you because you never called me back or returned my text," said Trent sorrowfully.

"I was scared and busy trying to figure things out. I got distracted. I'm so sorry, Trent!"

"It's okay, I called Shirley, and she told me where you were, so I came as quick as I could."

"This is all my fault! I let you down, I failed the town, and I failed my...my daddy." Julie cupped her hands to her face and began to cry.

Trent quickly jumped up and hugged her. "Jules, it's going to be okay. You had nothing to do with any of this."

Julie sobbed. "What is happening, Trent? Everything is falling apart!"

Suddenly, the voice of a confident elderly woman resounded from the doorway.

"Or is it?"

Both Trent and Julie stopped and looked in total surprise. Shirley Allen stood with arms crossed and a stern expression on her face.

#

"Good morning, men! Time to get up!" blurted out Jerry Foster.

"Top of the mornin' to ya lads!" followed Francis O'Reily with a loud whistle and then a hearty laugh.

Ian squinted and looked toward the doorway of the small room. Jake and Randy squirmed in their sleeping bags. Billy sat up quickly and rubbed his eyes.

"Get up, guys. We're going to the Green Sea for breakfast," called out Jerry.

Francis clapped his hands and then flipped the light switch up and down.

Randy moaned. "Please stop, man."

"Can't we sleep a couple more hours?" whined Jake.

"What time is it?" grumbled Ian.

"Time to get up and get dressed, lifesaver!" Foster shouted.

"Good morneeeng!" piped up Billy.

"Mornin' to ya, Sir Billy!" Francis winked at Billy.

"Fellas, we made it through the night. Ms. Shirley called Ms. Becky a little while ago and said that Castle Reef will be getting back to normal today."

"So why can't we sleep longer? I'm pretty sore, man," grunted Jake.

"Dude, free breakfast. Let's get up!" Randy stretched and sat up.

"Indeed, lads, we are treatin' ya to some of the best waffles in the land!" O'Reily bragged.

"So let's hurry up, fellas," coaxed Jerry, before leaving the room with Francis.

"I need some coffee," said Randy while yawning.

"I need sleep," protested Jake.

"Waffles are my favorit wit sirrup!" yelled Billy, waiting by the door.

Ian Reynolds scrolled through his texts on his phone and then quickly got dressed.

"Come on, guys, let's get going. Today should prove to be an interesting day, to say the least," muttered Ian.

They all slowly stumbled out of the guest room and into the Foster's living room.

"Good morning, guys!" Becky Foster greeted them all with a big hug.

"Let's get going troops. We're going to take a walk over to Trent's place," directed Jerry.

The Fosters and their five guests stepped outside into the sunny morning and began walking across the gravel parking lot toward Main Street. The seagulls were crying as they circled the marina, and a mild westward wind tossed all the moored boats gently.

chapter

27

Shirley, dressed in a navy-blue uniform with muted patches, walked into the suite, looking daunting and professional. She slid out another chair from the table, adjusted her attire, and then sat down.

Trent and Julie were still perplexed at how she just appeared out of nowhere, along with her demeanor. This wasn't the Shirley Allen they were familiar with.

Shirley spoke soft and serious. "You are a Kerrig. You are strong. You follow the facts. You stand for those who can't stand for themselves. You protect. You serve and you trust God."

"Yes, ma'am," said Julie, feeling intimidated by her own dispatcher and lifelong friend.

"Both of you need to focus on what I'm about to say. Do you understand me?" demanded Shirley, in a hushed yet serious tone.

Trent and Julie felt like school children, about to be disciplined by their first-grade teacher. This all seemed surreal, but they both complied and slowly nodded.

"Jules, everything is not falling apart. In fact, everything is falling into place." Suddenly, Shirley's expression changed back to its familiar warmth. Both Julie and Trent literally exhaled a sigh of relief.

"You scared us, Shirley," Julie said, cautiously.

"Well, I'm about to shed a little light on this 'everything' that seems to be looming over this little town of ours. After I finish, you'll either want to run away or you will stand and fight like a Kerrig."

Trent reached out and held Julie's hand, which now was slightly perspiring.

"Julie, and yes, you too, Trent, I'm about to give you both a little history lesson. There are a lot of skeletons in the closets of Brighton and Castle Reef. Are you up for it?" Shirley spoke plainly.

"I think my adrenaline levels are maxed after the nightmare at the marina, in addition to how you just entered this suite unannounced, dressed like a commando, but I'm up for it. I sure need to know what's going on," said Julie, in a snarky yet respectful way.

"I'm all in. By the way, yeah, I'm with Jules and still wondering how you got into my apartment when clearly the door was locked." Trent leaned in and scrunched his face.

"Someday, I'll show you both my trick," said Shirley with a wink.

"Can you show me now?" asked Trent playfully.

"Trent?" Julie raised an eyebrow and nodded toward Shirley.

"Go on, Ms. Shirley," said Trent, mouthing the word "sorry" to Julie.

"Not sure how I want to start this, but I think I need to begin by telling you something that will hopefully give you a new perspective on this town and shed light on how we can get back to some normalcy around here." Shirley took a deep breath and exhaled.

"Are you okay, Shirley?" asked Julie tenderly.

Shirley became choked up briefly and quickly composed herself. "Yes, sweetie."

"Go ahead, Ms. Shirley," encouraged Trent.

"I want to tell you a story about a woman I know very well. She was born and raised in Brighton from 1945 until 1959. One day after school, she was walking home and took a shortcut. She was attacked and raped and left for dead. She suffered several broken bones, cuts, and emotional trauma, but her spirit remained strong because of her Christian faith. She later learned that she was pregnant as a result of the rape. Her family was very devastated by the news. In the spring of 1960, her parents sent her away to a women's boarding home here in Castle Reef."

Trent's eyes widened, and he gulped. "I heard that the Green Sea used to be…um until 1986."

Shirley nodded and proceeded on. "She had her baby that summer. She worked long hours for three years, just for room and board. She continued doing housekeeping at the boarding school until she turned eighteen years old when she elected to change her name as well as her baby's name. A new start in life was exactly what this girl needed, so she decided to join the armed forces. Just before she reported for duty to the United States Navy in 1964, she met a wonderful young couple, about her age, who agreed to care for her child, since they had no children of their own at the time."

Shirley pulled out the handkerchief from her sleeve and dabbed her eyes. Tears began welling up in Julie's green eyes too as she listened to the precious lady she had admired her whole life tell this story.

"Our dear Greg and Martha Stanwick reached out and helped that young single mother, and she was forever grateful," Shirley sniffled.

"I can't believe it. Those people are amazing!" Trent exclaimed.

"Wow, that was like decades before they adopted Vicki," Julie added.

"As the child grew up, the young lady sailor visited as much as she could while on shore leave. In time, she became a decorated naval officer, with better pay, and could then devote more time to her small family. She was offered a position in Washington DC, so they moved away."

"I bet the Stanwicks were crushed," said Julie who was now intrigued with every word Shirley spoke.

"They were pretty sad, but they are strong people, Jules. Anyway, the young lady was now a woman and a very important woman at that. She was appointed to the Special Forces and other places during several administrations. She never married, believe it or not." Shirley started to laugh, which broke some of the tension in the room.

"What about her child? Was it a he or a she, you didn't say?" Trent asked.

"I'm sorry, I never mentioned that it was a boy, did I?" Shirley cackled in embarrassment.

Trent looked over at Julie and winked. Shirley gathered herself together.

"She had a son. He grew up to be a handsome young man. He too went to the United States Naval Academy in Annapolis, Maryland, and graduated with honors. He was a Navy Seal who served in the Operation Eagle Claw effort in Iran, as well as the Lebanon Civil War conflict, and ended up being a decorated veteran just like his mother. During the end of his eighth and final year in the Navy, he met the love of his life and they were married. After retiring from the Navy, he was offered a position in the Special Forces. He accepted the job, and they lived in DC until his beautiful wife became pregnant and she..." Shirley abruptly stopped and brought the handkerchief up to her eyes. She began to cry. Julie quickly slid her chair over and held her.

"Mama Shirley, what is it?" whispered Julie, who now had a lump in her throat.

"His beautiful wife died in childbirth..." Shirley couldn't continue.

Her last words hit Julie like a wave. The dots were now connected. She hugged Shirley tightly and began to weep with her. Trent watched the two ladies embrace. It was now obvious to him why this story was being told. Julie leaned back and held Shirley's face in her hands.

"Shirley? You're my grandmother?" said Julie, with tears streaming down her face.

"Jules, I'm so sorry that I never told you!"

The two women held each other rocking slowly and weeping for over twenty minutes.

Finally, through many tears and tissues, Julie turned to Trent, beaming. "She's my grandmother!"

"She is, Jules, she truly is." Trent's eyes welled up.

"I love you, Jules. Will you ever forgive me?" whispered Shirley hoarsely.

"There's nothing to forgive you for. I feel so bad for you," said Julie, carefully wiping the corners of her eyes.

"There were times I couldn't take it anymore, and I just had to let you know but stopped myself."

"Somehow, I always knew deep down inside we were connected, do you know what I mean?" Julie admitted.

Shirley wiped her eyes and then blew her nose gently. "Yes, I do. It has been so difficult. Believe me, I have ached every day since you were born."

"So why couldn't you tell me? Why didn't Daddy tell me? Or even the Stanwicks?"

"That, my dear, is a hard one to answer. It's in the rest of this story."

A look of surprise washed over both Trent and Julie's faces. They exchanged glances and turned back to Shirley.

"Um, there's more?" Julie slowly asked as she sniffled.

Shirley sighed and cleared her throat a couple of times. "Yes, there's more, Jules. Do you remember what I told you, before you left the station?"

"Yes, I do. You said this craziness we are experiencing somehow involves my dad."

Julie moved her chair next to Trent and rested her head on his shoulder. They both were intently fixed on what this amazing woman was about to say.

#

Many of the local, state and federal authorities surrounded the mansion and the entire complex of Alexander Industries. Every employee was being interviewed individually in several large tents and then being processed. Some were released to go home; many other potential witnesses stayed for further interrogation. The crime scene was the biggest the state had seen in many years. The lead team members of the state and local authorities were conferring with federal government agents, including State Highway Patrol Superintendent Neil Hillsdale, who had just arrived from the neighboring state.

"Good morning, Neil," greeted Edward Reese, FBI regional director.

"Good morning, fellas, sorry I'm running a little late," apologized Hillsdale.

"I think we are all running late, Neil. This is the most action we've had in our state in a long time," added Pete Crandall, the chief officer for the state bureau of investigation.

The state ATF director, Steven Ashley, offered Hillsdale a cup of coffee from the hot pot, sitting on the folding table at the entrance to the command center tent.

"No thanks, Steve, I've had my limit for today already, but I will grab one of these donuts here," Neil said, before entering the tent.

The men stepped inside the tent where other officers and officials were studying a large map of the Alexander complex, which was mounted on an easel. The mansion was circled in red marker along with the central part of the factory.

"He appears to have taken some sort of fast-acting cyanide with his drink last night after giving the same thing to his wife. The times of the deaths were around nine or ten hours ago, we think," reported Noah Abrams, a federal forensic specialist.

"Neil, what do you have for us?" asked Reese.

"Well, guys, we have conflicting statements from our suspects that are linked to this place and to Devin Alexander himself."

"How so?" pressed Crandall, sipping from his cup.

"Both the State Department and Congress have been notified about the dealings of JK Reynolds. He's now giving up all kinds of information on federal funds being used illegally by himself and Alexander for years," Hillsdale explained.

"What about Governor Riddick?" Edward Reese inquired again.

"He's a tough one. He denies everything. Men, I think there is a lot more to this," said Neil, stepping up to look at the map.

"Well, there was an explosion sometime last evening between 11:00 p.m. and 1:30 a.m. The lowest level of the research lab is inaccessible. We have a team trying to get in there now," said Ashley, after adjusting his ATF cap.

"Was anyone working down there during that time frame?" Reese asked.

"Only two people are unaccounted for, sir," answered Ashley.

Crandall spoke up, "Devin's daughter and her assistant is the report I'm getting."

"Cortney Alexander and a certain Terry Warren?" asked Reese.

Crandall nodded. "Yes, I believe so."

"We should be able to get into that lab soon. The elevator is working, but the doors won't budge," grumbled Ashley.

"Well, we have heard from Washington on this, fellas, and it's pretty big apparently. My team will take over with the inner layers of the investigation from this point on. State and local officials, make sure you set up a perimeter, and keep the press out please," ordered Reese in a firm yet kind tone.

"We'll have the full results back on Mr. Alexander's autopsy by this afternoon," promised Abrams.

"Thanks, Noah. Steve, let me know when the doors are open and make sure nobody goes into that lower level."

"Yes, sir." Ashley nodded to his assistant, and both men left the tent.

Reese looked over at Neil Hillsdale. "Got a second, Neil?"

Neil stepped aside and looked at the aged Reese, who smelled heavily of cigarette smoke.

"Sir?" asked Hillsdale.

"Neil, we brought you here because apparently, you have a contact within Washington that I don't have. My superiors told me that you know some things about Governor Riddick and Representative Reynolds."

"Yes, sir. We did a sting operation on JK and Riddick last night that involves Alexander and the beach town Castle Reef, somehow."

"Castle Reef? Why Castle Reef?" Reese was confused.

"We aren't quite sure. Yesterday, I was given a direct order by the governor to evacuate and shut the town down completely. Apparently, there were some shark attacks, so I did as I was instructed. However, things got really interesting following those attacks."

"In what way?"

"That, sir, I'm not at liberty to discuss," said Neil reluctantly.

"Neil, I'm not going to strong-arm you because I know you have connections to greater powers than I answer to. But can you tell me if this is more than just a corporate scandal?"

"Ed, this is definitely an onion. There are many layers. I think you're going to be busy for quite a while here." Neil pulled a pair of sunglasses out of his shirt pocket and put them on.

"Keep me posted, please?" entreated the seasoned FBI director.

"Yes, I will. You may have a high-level security clearance individual coming your way soon."

"Really? And who, may I ask, might that be?" Reese looked puzzled.

"I'm just a state police guy, remember?" Hillsdale laughed as he walked away.

Edward Reese seemed a little troubled about an unexpected visit from a high-level individual but quickly dismissed it and began radioing his team to sweep through the complex.

#

The shiny red sedan passed acres of sunbathed sorghum fields along the two-lane highway. Inside, the well-dressed woman looked at the GPS on the Volvo S60 console. She was less than three hours from Castle Reef. The many miles behind her were filled with screams of anguish, tears of sorrow, and sobs of regret. Leaving the hotel six hours ago felt merely like minutes.

Janet Reynolds had reached the very basement of her life, and it was now time to face reality and begin a different journey. She didn't know exactly what to do next, but she knew it started with seeing her son Ian. Surprisingly, she wasn't tired after being awake for over twenty-eight hours. The wealthy fifty-year-old, and soon-to-be divorced woman, was driving evenly and actually singing along to "Sometimes by Step" by Rich Mullins, which she had accidentally found on a random playlist. As tears fell from her eyes, she gripped the leather steering wheel and purposed after thirty-seven years to give God another try.

chapter

28

"Your father made a lot of enemies in other countries. He interrupted several potential global terror plots and made a lot of evil people unhappy," explained Shirley.

"Part of me wishes that he would have told me what he did for a living, but I understand he had no other option." Julie rubbed her forehead.

Shirley paused. "Your father loved your mother so much, that he requested to leave Washington and return here to raise a family. The State Department and the Defense Department stalled his request. He was about to quit, get debriefed, and return to civilian life until I stepped in."

"You stepped in?" Julie was now dazed.

"What does that mean?" added Trent.

"I think you guys forgot the part about me telling you that I was appointed to Special Forces and other defense entities during several administrations," prompted Shirley.

"You weren't? You couldn't have been!" Julie's mouth dropped open.

"Your father's supervisor? Yes, I fought for his request to come here to Castle Reef."

Julie groaned, tilting her head back. "I must be dreaming. Better yet, I think I have oxygen deprivation issues from being underwater."

"Jules, I faced a lot of resistance and opposition from my superiors years ago to get that request granted. John agreed to stay active, take special assignments, and live undercover with the strict understanding that no one, under any circumstances, was to know what he did for the government."

"No one?" questioned Julie.

"No one, not even you," said the tender grandmother, regretfully.

"So when did you come back here?" asked Julie, now feeling awkward for questioning Shirley.

"I was here for your birth, when your mother went home to Jesus. Afterward, I gave Washington an ultimatum. Either they were going to let me stay in Castle Reef and help my son raise you or I was going to quit the department too. I played the same card your dad did, I guess. I had the government change my last name and all my records again so that nobody would know we were related, with the exception of the Stanwicks and a few others."

"That was almost like thirty-six years ago," inserted Trent.

"Yes, but it feels like yesterday. Although it was top secret, I got to be with my granddaughter and watch her grow up into a beautiful woman." Shirley got choked up again.

"May I still call you Mama Shirley?" asked Julie timidly.

"Why of course, Jules, I wouldn't have it any other way." They embraced once again.

"So you aren't involved with the government any longer, are you? You must have retired several years ago, right?" probed Trent further.

"Actually, we might as well bring you both up to date." Shirley pulled out her identification wallet from her uniform pocket and opened it up so that Trent and Julie could see the fine print on the flat gold badge.

Julie slowly took it from her hands, and a look of awe came over her face. Trent's eyes widened as he sat back in his chair and grinned from ear to ear. Julie read the inscription out loud. "Department of the United States Counter-Terror Task Force, Madam Secretary, Shirley Nadine Kerrig."

There was a long moment of silence in Trent's suite. The only sound was the living room ceiling fan blades cutting through the air in the adjacent room.

"I'm sitting here in the coastal town of Castle Reef, with my grandmother, who is also the head of the Counter-Terror Task Force," mumbled the younger Kerrig, who was now totally baffled.

"That's correct," said Shirley with a half-smile.

"I never saw this coming, that's for sure," said Trent, still stunned.

"So You and Dad worked here from the station?" Julie spoke slowly.

"Yes, dear, and from our homes of course. It's a 24-7 job."

"I'm a little lost, Ms. Shirley. Can you explain how this all connects to what is going on now presently?" Trent interjected.

"Absolutely! The CTTF is a separate shadow branch of our country's military. We answer only to the President of the United States. Under my direction, John, with his team, took down many terrorist threats for more than thirty years fairly easily until he exposed a certain militia group in the Baltic States region, about four years ago."

"What do you mean? How is that connected to what's going on here and with my dad?" Julie was perplexed.

"I didn't have time at the station to tell you everything, but you need to know it now." Shirley sighed.

"I'm listening, Mama Shirley." Julie sat up.

"There is an unnamed terrorist network that is located in our neighboring state. We have been trying to infiltrate and dissolve it. This group has dealings with that same Baltic militia, according to our intel. In other words, they are working together on a hybrid version of their weapon."

"Weapon?" Julie's eyes grew big.

Shirley stood up and walked into the living room, looking out the window for a minute. She then turned around and came back to her chair.

"Trent, do you remember when you were remodeling the Green Sea Inn, and the Brighton County building inspector made sure you had the proper vapor barrier and insulation installed, according to the revised building codes?"

"Yes, I do. It was an odd request, but the inspector said it was a new county ordinance for preserving homes along the coast from bad weather," recalled Trent.

"Okay, I'm lost. What does this have to do with my dad and terrorists?" asked Julie.

"Everything, Jules, he wasn't the building inspector. He was one of our CTTF agents."

Julie gasped. "You've got to be kidding me, I remember that guy."

"That material truly does prevent damage to structures due to the ocean air and bad weather, but its primary purpose is to be a Faraday curtain."

"I know what a Faraday box is, but why a Faraday curtain on all our buildings?" asked Trent, who was now intrigued.

"This is unreal," Julie interjected as she leaned forward.

Shirley proceeded. "This curtain and the insulation are made of a synthetic, bidirectional, micro-mesh copper that allows certain radio frequencies to enter or exit all the structures."

"I had no clue. Why were they installed?" Julie shook her head.

"Most every building in this town has it in their attics or special ceiling paint to disrupt certain signals," stated Shirley.

"Why? What's the reason?" Julie's mind was now racing.

"Your father and his team acquired a very expensive and dangerous microchip from a hidden lab in an Estonia border town during one of his missions. We had to protect ourselves from all possible electronic probing by terror organizations."

Trent and Julie both gulped and looked at each other.

"I was attacked by something last night that wanted to kill me for my phone so I thought, but now I know it was for what was inside my phone case," said Julie in a dreadful whisper.

Trent reached out for Julie's hand. The room got quiet.

"You're getting close, Jules," Shirley hinted.

"You mean, they knew that my dad stole their microchip and they followed him here?" asked Julie intently.

"It's something like that, Jules, but it's more complex."

"How so?" Julie looked confused.

"We now have confirmed that there is a mole within the government who has direct connections to that same terror cell. He's right here in our area. It is of the highest national security interest to disrupt that threat."

"Threat, what threat? Is it JK Reynolds?" asked Julie, cracking a couple of her knuckles.

"Jules, it's very complicated. First, let me explain," said Shirley calmly.

"All this time, and I never knew my dad was a government agent and was up against a sleaze bag politician like JK," said Julie in disbelief.

Shirley proceeded. "Your father knew that they would come after him and the microchip. So he…"

Julie finished Shirley's sentence. "…hid the microchip in his duty belt, knowing that I would take care of it if something happened to him."

"Like I said, Jules, you're so close, but let me finish, sweetheart."

"Yeah, Jules, it's okay, let her finish," spoke Trent softly to curb her intensity.

"Sorry, Mama Shirley, I'm just amped up from all this."

"Yes. I know, Jules. I believe your father planned for this. Those operatives came and found him. They came posing as tourists, vendors, workers, and even residents. No matter how hard we tried, they began to search for that chip and set up remote transmitters almost everywhere." Shirley grimaced.

"Transmitters? For what?" Julie was puzzled.

"In order to find the microchip?" asked Trent.

"I'm afraid not just to find the microchip. They had other plans to test their new technology while they searched for it."

"This is just insane. No wonder they were quick to promote me as chief of police. It wasn't about me; it was about that stupid chip!" shouted Julie.

"Unfortunately, they succeeded for the time being." Shirley looked at her granddaughter with an expression of gravity.

Trent sprung up from his chair and ran to the suite door. "Shirley, Mike was up on the roof doing a maintenance call, and he found something strange. I'm going to my office to get it," chattered Trent, darting out the door.

"How interesting!" said Shirley, turning back to Julie.

"While we wait for Trent to get back, can I ask you something?" Julie looked directly into Shirley's eyes.

"Sure, Jules."

"Do you think those people killed my dad?" Julie asked intently.

"Um, Jules I…" Shirley became flustered.

"Or your son?" Julie sat back, crossed her arms, and waited for an answer.

#

Mike sat staring out the sliding glass doors of the Brighton General Hospital. He was just waking up after sleeping in the waiting room chair for about two hours. He heard a woman's voice thanking the receptionist and walking nearby.

"You must be Jill Sullivan?" Mike spoke up.

"Yes, I am. You must be Mike from Castle Reef?" asked the tall brown-haired woman.

Mike jumped to his feet. "Yes, it's me, Mike Rawlings, nice to meet you."

Jill extended her hand, and he shook it vigorously, smiling really big.

"Sorry if I look a wreck. I slept in this chair all night."

Jill giggled. "I know, I heard you snoring when I walked by an hour ago."

"That's embarrassing." Mike's cheeks became rosy.

"Karen is awake and has been asking for you. She said that you guys visited for the first time since the accident last night."

"Yes, we did. It was small talk, mostly. Is she okay this morning?"

"She seems to be. Her parents are up there now."

"So they saw me snoring too? Great, just great!" Mike shook his head.

"Mike, it's fine. They wanted to meet you, but they knew you needed to sleep."

"Oh well, you only get one first impression," joked Rawlings.

"You're too funny. Hey, apparently Karen starts rehab tomorrow."

"Really? That's great news!" cheered Mike.

"I was going to grab some coffee. Do you want to join me?" Jill started walking.

"Sure thing, if you don't mind." Mike hesitated and then caught up to her.

Jill and Mike walked over to the Brighton General Hospital café and ordered their coffees along with a couple of cinnamon rolls. Mike insisted on paying and politely seated Jill in her seat before joining her at the table.

"You sure are something else. Karen has found a keeper in my opinion," announced Ms. Sullivan.

"Stop! I'm just old school that's all."

"Well, there aren't a lot of men that have manners these days or know how to treat women for that matter."

"Really? Well, I can think of a bunch of men that are stand up guys and value women. My best friend Trent, for instance, is someone that is very old school," remarked Mike, sipping on his coffee.

"Well, back in Jersey, it's different. It seems like etiquette, and chivalry are out the window."

"Yeah, I know what you mean, Trent and I are both from New York City, and it doesn't get any crazier than that!"

They both laughed as they ate their rolls and drank coffee, comparing east coast stories.

After a few minutes, Jill changed the subject and became more serious. "Mike, I heard a lot of rumors on the television about Castle Reef over the past few days. Did they capture the shark that attacked Karen yet?" Jill spoke urgently.

"I'm sure they are following every procedure to make things safe," answered Mike calmly.

He realized that he couldn't tell Jill what was really going on in Castle Reef. Somehow he had to quickly find out more information from Karen about the EHF transponders and the company she worked for.

Jill sighed. "Well, this certainly wasn't the vacation we envisioned, that's for sure."

"I bet. We all need a vacation. Too bad this one became a nightmare for you guys."

"Yes, we were really looking forward to time away from our jobs."

"Just curious, what all does Karen do in her job?" inquired Mike.

"You mean at Barrington Scientific? Why?" Jill responded casually.

"I understand that she's a pretty sharp cookie. Masters at MIT, right?"

"Yup, and second in her class."

"Wow, that's amazing. How long has she been working there?"

"What are you trying to do, figure out her age or something?" Jill broke into laughter.

"I'm sorry, that was rude of me, wasn't it? I'm not a creeper, trust me." Mike put his hands over his face in humiliation.

"Hey, Mike, it's okay. I know you're trying to find out all about her and what she does." Jill grinned and finished her cinnamon roll.

"Pretty obvious?" Mike asked shamefully.

"Yes, pretty obvious. Listen, she is a very smart woman. She designed a transmitter that operates on a frequency close to the speed of light. This frequency cannot be measured because it works on a level that is virtually undetectable. She is worth billions because of her knowledge in the field of RF and EHF technology."

Mike splashed coffee down his chin and began coughing. He quickly wiped his face and then looked at Jill with wide eyes. "What did you just say?"

"I think I need to be transparent with you, Mr. Rawlings." Jill's voice got real quiet.

"What do you mean?" asked Mike who was now stunned.

"Karen is not only my best friend, but she is the lead scientist in my company."

"Your company? She's a lead scientist?" Mike's mouth dropped open.

"Yes, I'm Jill Bradford, not Jill Sullivan. I'm the founder and CEO of Barrington Scientific. I use Sullivan as my alias."

"Say what?" Mike whispered in shock.

"I'm telling you this because I was told that I can trust you, Mike."

"By who?" said Mike in disbelief.

"That's not important right now."

"Jill, I am really at a loss for words." Mike propped his head up with his arms on the table.

"It's okay, Mike, we're on the same side," Jill spoke sincerely.

"Is your mother Joan Bradford?" asked Mike in surrender.

"Yes, Mike, she is."

"Oh my, this is really making my head spin, to say the least." Rawlings wiped his hands with his napkin several times.

"By the way, my hair is really red, not brown, if that helps any." The thirty-something businesswoman giggled.

"I can't believe this. What are the odds?" The embarrassed man rubbed his temples.

"We heard about how beautiful and remote Castle Reef was from my mother, so I planned a girl's week away to have some relaxing beach time."

"I think your mother started to tell me about you last night and was interrupted," Mike recalled.

"Chances are, she was relieved, because our work is mostly top secret, and she doesn't really want to know about what we do," Jill explained.

"Is she by chance involved in any of this?"

"Hardly, she only knows that my company makes important stuff for the military and has no idea about the present situation that we are finding ourselves in."

Mike cleared his throat. "I don't have a clue what is going on either, but I'm sorry it all turned out this way."

"Well, I found out a lot of information since the attack, and it can only get better from here," remarked Jill.

"I don't think I'm quite following you." Mike felt lost.

"You don't need all the details yet, Mike, but I do have a favor to ask."

"Sure, what is it?" asked Mike expectantly.

Jill opened her purse and pulled out an envelope, placing it into Mike's hands. "I want you to give this to Trent personally. Please do not open it or let anyone see it, except Mr. Green."

"How did you know that Trent's last name was Green?" Mike hesitated.

"I didn't, but someone else I met last night did. Just deliver it to him, okay?"

"I sure will. This certainly turned out strange. I came up here to ask Karen some questions, and you ended up giving me what I needed to know." Mike became suspicious. He looked at Jill seriously. She never flinched. "Well, don't you think it's a coincidence?" Mike pressed Jill.

"Karen needs to heal so that you both can pursue a relationship together going forward. I am now fully aware of what is going on behind the scenes at the beach. Let's leave it at that, shall we?" Jill stood up.

"Yes, I can do that," Mike agreed.

"It's all good, Mike. It's going to be okay, just get that letter to Trent, please."

"I will, you have my word. Please tell Karen that I'll call her tonight."

"You bet, Mike. Thanks for the coffee and cinnamon roll." Jill smiled and picked up her purse.

Mike carried their cups and paper plates to the trash receptacle nearby. "Nice meeting you, Jill."

"Ditto, don't forget that letter."

"Yes, ma'am." Mike extended his arm. She gave Mike a firm handshake.

As Jill turned and walked past the front desk toward the elevator, Mike smiled and thought to himself, *Is this the Twilight Zone or what?*

chapter

29

"Jules, when Jerry Foster was the only one on the boat pulling into the harbor that rainy March evening, I was determined to find out what really happened because I knew it wasn't an accident," declared Shirley.

"I remember all of us being upset, but you as a mother…what did you do?" Julie asked compassionately.

"Well, after the gut punch, there was denial and anger," Shirley admitted.

"At God?" Julie asked.

"Heavens no, child! God is life, not death. I was angry at myself for letting my guard down." Shirley poked herself.

"How so?" Julie probed.

Shirley flipped her ID end over end on the table before tucking it back into her shirt pocket. "I think we were so busy trying to protect the forest that we forgot about the trees."

"Trees?" Julie seemed confused.

"Like your daddy, yourself, and all the residents." Shirley voiced her regret and then got up and walked into the living room. Julie followed her. "Jules, time will often heal wounds. There may be scars left, but you can't stop hoping and believing for the best to happen," assured Shirley.

Julie began to open up and share. "I know that now, Shirley, especially after what I experienced last night."

Abruptly, the suite door swung open and interrupted the moment between Julie and her grandmother. Trent walked in with his hands full of items that he placed on the kitchen table.

Both ladies looked at Trent and then at each other, smiling.

"Does this look familiar?" Trent held up the transmitter by its wires.

"Sure does," stated Shirley plainly.

"Mike has a friend that is in the security business back in New York, and this guy said they are called EHF antennas or something like that," explained Trent.

Shirley stepped forward. "That is a class 4 voltaic EHF transponder. It transmits and receives signals in the high end of the terahertz scale."

Julie winced. "Terahertz?"

"Say what?" Trent looked at Julie with raised eyebrows.

"It's a device that transmits signals almost at the speed of light. Our team did a sweep while we were all trying to sleep last night and removed all 3,990 of them from Castle Reef," announced the madam secretary.

"You mean, there were commandos hanging from zip lines, going through our little community all night, and we had no idea?" exclaimed Julie.

"Something like that, Jules."

Julie sat down on the couch and ran her hands through her blonde hair. Trent walked over with the folder that Vicki had given to Julie and sat down next to her. Shirley remained standing and turned in their direction.

"Hey, Shirley, not to change the subject here, but nice call on getting the Stanwicks and Joan busy on another breakfast maneuver down in the kitchen. I understand we have guests coming this morning?" asked Trent.

Julie looked at Trent then back at Shirley, perplexed. "Guests?"

"Yes, the Fosters, Francis, Billy Daily, and your friends, the lifeguards, are probably here for breakfast even as we speak," Shirley announced.

"Nice!" Trent laughed.

Julie softly elbowed Trent in the side and moved forward on the edge of the couch. "Has the Green Sea Inn now become the head-quarters for the Counter-Terror Task Force?" quipped Julie.

"I guess you could say that. All I know is that we need to stay together here until the threat is neutralized. Besides, it has a special place in my heart, remember?"

"Okay, I get it. Sorry, my bad," Julie apologized.

"In the meantime, let's finish our debriefing and bring you both up to our current status."

"It can become the police station as well, if you want, Jules," Trent teased and held up his hands in a joking manner to block Julie's elbow.

Shirley smirked, shook her head at Trent, and continued, "The transmitters were put here by the unnamed terror group's operatives. They emit a signal that not only locates the microchip they are seeking, but it also controls the existing technology that they have already developed."

"So let me get this straight, following all the facts here, that man or cyborg is controlled by those transmitters?" questioned Julie.

Shirley sat down in the matching leather chair across the room. Trent put the folder he was holding on the coffee table.

"Yes, Jules, I'm going to be as brief as possible because it's very complicated. The terror cell first designed specific technology to take out our naval ships. They sold these weapons to countries that were not friendly to the United States. We have been tracking down and eliminating these weapons for over four years. They are called Zambis."

"Oh, that's just great! Now we have zombies?" called out Julie, throwing her hands into the air.

Shirley chuckled. "I said Zambi, Jules. Z-A-M-B-I."

"Thank the Lord!"

"This type of weapon started with the invention of the torpedo in the late 1800s. It progressed through the years until, the mid-nineties, the technology boom, when artificial intelligence came on the scene. It's a code name for the weapon designed to be used in salt and fresh-waters. It's slang for the Zambezi shark or the bull shark as we know it."

"The shark! The shark that killed Charlie?" Julie covered her eyes with both hands.

"And the one that attacked Karen Anderson too," added Trent.

"The AI shark was specifically going after those people. Charlie was my superior officer years ago, and Karen is a renowned scientist in EHF technology."

Both Julie and Trent looked at each other, surprised.

Trent spoke up, "Mike went to Brighton General to find out more about what Karen knows."

"Keep in mind, they used this as a diversion," disclosed Shirley.

"The classic bait and switch?" Trent speculated.

"Accomplish a directive and then distract while another asset begins a stealth operation," confirmed Shirley.

"Dr. Hackett was onto something, wasn't he?" asked Julie.

"He knew after the autopsy, but he couldn't tell you, sweetheart."

Julie gasped, crossing her arms. "Oh wow! He's in on this too?"

"No, Jules, he's a dear friend that was waiting for me to talk to you. I'm sure he wanted to tell you his findings, but he is very loyal… to us."

Trent asked out of curiosity, "What is the robot shark made out of exactly?"

"They literally are a printed 3D image from a chemical ligand."

"What is that?" Trent questioned Shirley further.

"It's what all of these weapons are made of. It is a chemical nucleosynthesis exoskeleton, filled with electro plasma, that operates on a high frequency atomic organic battery."

"I barely made it through science class. You're right, this is way too complicated," said Julie candidly.

"So what you're saying is that these weapons are really like AI hybrids that are programmed by bad guys?" asked Trent.

Shirley expounded. "Exactly, Trent. Very well stated. They developed the technology in Europe, and it was enhanced and put into place here in the US. We now believe we've just located the lab site."

"This makes the bionic man look like a geek," Trent quickly remarked.

"You can say that again. The way, that thing grabbed me and picked me up. It was superhuman," Julie recalled.

"It wasn't human at all. These are synthetic plasma weapons that are produced in a lab and printed to look like people," Shirley added.

"The weird thing made me feel sick when I punched right through it before it took my cell phone and absorbed it." Julie's voice quivered slightly.

Trent reached over and held her hand, caressing it softly. "Are you okay, Jules?"

Shirley leaned forward. "Julie, that was the RF radiation you felt and as for the phone being absorbed, our intel sources say that it has a cavity inside it, which can hold up to twenty pounds of objects. Apparently, it was sent on many missions to steal top secret items and other assets, here and in foreign countries."

"Something weird happened before the creep came to confront me last night."

"What was it, Jules?" Shirley asked intently.

"I think I saw the shark in the marina, and suddenly, there was an explosion underwater and everything just went calm right before old blue eyes showed up."

"Well, concerning that, our intelligence confirmed that the Zambi self-destructed last evening."

"Did they find evidence in the water or something?" Trent asked.

"Unfortunately, this technology leaves no evidence. We measured the amplitude from the seismic sensors we have set up, and we knew it was the AI shark. When these weapons are destroyed, they end up being nothing but saltwater with electrolytes and minerals. That is why this technology is so dangerous in the wrong hands."

"However, as far we know, that AI zombie is still alive and well, right? And who knows where it is?" Julie was fuming.

"We are working on that right now. We should know soon."

"That's why it's always important to be on top of your game. I should have noticed this stuff. Daddy trained me to observe every situation and evaluate. Distracted by self-pity, I failed." Julie clenched her fists.

"Don't be so hard on yourself, Jules," pleaded Shirley.

Trent slid over, put his arm around Julie, and kissed her cheek. "How could you possibly know about any of this? We were all going through the motions in our everyday lives, never realizing that we were being set up," consoled Trent.

"Meanwhile, the real heroes like my dad and Mama Shirley are sticking their necks out to keep us all safe," voiced Julie, nearly in tears.

"Your father's love for you is forever. Never forget that, Jules," affirmed Shirley.

"He never got to say goodbye to us," whispered Julie.

Shirley leaned forward. "I know it hurts. He knew what they were capable of and purposely hid that microchip, worth billions, right in plain sight, entrusting it to you."

"Nothing is more deceptive than an obvious fact," said Julie, staring directly into Shirley's eyes.

"Your father faced insurmountable odds from the evil forces that are always at work in this world. My question to you, Chief Julie Kerrig, are you ready to face the storm?"

The weight of Shirley's words dropped into Julie's heart and made her realize she had a choice to make. This wasn't going away. No matter how things were going to turn out, she wasn't called to shrink back. The core values that were instilled into her life at a very young age were given for a purpose. Inside, a righteous boldness slowly began to arise. Julie took a deep breath.

"In the last twenty-four hours, I have been going ninety to nothing. I was reunited with my fiancé. I was fired by the mayor. The state police hunted me. I beat the crap out of some college punks on the beach. I was attacked by a freaky robot thing that threw me into the bay. I nearly died by drowning, only to be revived by a drunken lifeguard. Lastly, I find out that I have a grandmother, who has been right under my nose my whole life, and it turns out that she is a top agent for the Counter-Terror Task Force for our country. Yet in spite of all this, I'm alive, and I am still the police chief of Castle Reef, elected by the people to protect and serve this community!"

"Well done, Jules!" agreed Shirley.

Trent hugged Julie tightly and wiped the tears from his eyes.

"So what do you want me to do on the local level, Madam Secretary?" Julie asked.

"Well, Chief, first, I think we need to evaluate some things right now," answered Shirley.

"Is there anything I can do?"

"I am waiting for the confirmation on the lab, securing it, and then getting its operatives into custody. The situation with your phone and the microchip is a little more complicated."

"What do you mean?" Julie looked perplexed.

"The AI droid took your cell phone. Now all your personal information and contacts that were on the device are compromised. Most of that information was immediately erased by our cybersecurity team. The enemy may be able to extract some trace information, but it's more likely improbable."

"What about the microchip?" Julie did a neck roll.

"The microchip that was taken was coded to the exact specifications as the real processor chip that they were looking for."

"Hold on, say that again?" interjected Trent.

"Yeah, I'm not following you on that one," Julie agreed.

"The chip they have isn't the one they were after. The one they seized is a locator chip that pinpoints an exact location," explained Shirley.

"So let me get this straight. I was being tracked for three years every time I wore my duty belt?" retorted Julie.

"That's messed up!" exclaimed Trent.

Shirley remained calm and explained. "Your father placed that device in your belt to make sure you were always protected. When it fell out, after you threw the belt in the locker room, I had no choice but to have you keep it so that we could find you. You're family, Jules, and nothing is more important than family."

Julie took a deep breath and calmed down. "I'm sorry."

"So the Terminator took the wrong chip, and you knew that he would because it was coded to imitate the real one?" deduced Trent.

"Precisely, and that way we were able to locate where the terror cell originated from," concluded Shirley.

"That is pretty genius, but now that leaves the question you know we are all thinking," acknowledged Julie.

"Where is the real microchip that John Kerrig hid?" voiced Trent.

"Julie, stand up, please," directed Shirley.

Julie stood up and adjusted her uniform and duty belt. Shirley walked over to her and slowly reached for her service weapon.

"May I?" Shirley asked politely.

Julie raised her hands up and carefully watched Shirley. Trent leaned forward and swallowed hard.

"Nothing is more deceptive than an obvious fact," pronounced Shirley, depressing the holster lock and removing the Colt 1911.

"There's one in the chamber," Julie said firmly.

Shirley took the gun and pointed downward as she quickly racked back the chamber, ejecting the bullet and catching it in the air. She then pushed the magazine catch and slid out the clip, putting both bullet and clip into her front pocket."

"Impressive!" Julie added.

Next, the seventy-five-year-old inspected the chamber barrel. In one motion, Shirley tapped the side of her wrist watch, and several miniature tools popped out all along the circumference of the watch face. She pulled out a tiny, flat-bladed screwdriver and unscrewed one side of the handgun's stock. Inside the cover was a microchip that looked identical to the one Julie found on the women's locker room floor at the police station. Shirley carefully held it up in order for the three of them to see its miniature yellow light flashing.

"Was your real last name Bond, by any chance?" muttered Trent.

"This is the real deal, Trent. What happens now, Mama Shirley?" Julie was amazed.

"I will secure this at the station in the evidence safe, and you guys can go have breakfast with the rest of the crew downstairs," stated Shirley.

"Just like that?" Trent was baffled.

"It is important that we move forward and get back to some normalcy here. As soon as I get the green light from my team, I will make sure the town is clear to open back up," said Shirley, as she worked on the firearm.

"What about everyone else? What do we tell them?" Trent asked urgently.

"We tell them only what they need to know. We don't build community on panic. Most people will believe what the mainstream media tells them anyway," said Shirley firmly.

"You're right. People really don't stop and look at the big picture or even use common sense anymore," Trent agreed.

"You guys are the future guardians of Castle Reef, and I'll leave it at that." Shirley smiled as she dropped the microchip into a plastic thimble container and tucked it away in her duty belt.

Julie turned to Trent. "Since we're all in this together, I'm going to need your help today."

"And what would that be for?" Trent was still perplexed.

"I need a witness." Julie winked and gave Trent a smirk.

"A witness? Why?"

"She's going to go arrest Mayor Willis after breakfast," revealed Shirley with a hearty laugh.

"She read my mind, Trent." Julie took the Colt 1911 that Shirley handed her and put it back into her holster.

"Let's go get some breakfast shall we, Mr. Green?" Julie tugged on Trent's arm.

"Sure thing, Jules. Ms. Shirley, I want to thank you for sharing your heart and entrusting us with all that information."

"There's so much more to discuss with so many layers, but we can talk more about it later. Never forget, apart from my son, you both are everything to me." Shirley smiled and hugged them tightly.

"I love you, Mama Shirley." Julie kissed her cheek.

"Me too, Ms. Shirley." Trent picked up the folder from the coffee table and followed Julie to the door.

Shirley nodded. "I will be at the station if you need me."

After Trent and Julie left the suite, Shirley walked over to the living room window with her coffee to observe the empty town. She gazed down onto Main Street and caught a glimpse of the blue unmarked sedan passing by before it disappeared out of view. Shirley took notice and slowly shut her eyes.

chapter

30

The FBI tactical team moved through the empty corridor of Alexander Industries' lower level. The elevator door was finally breached after the ATF cut through its double titanium panels. The power was on, and everything looked undisturbed in the laboratory. The team searched for the two missing individuals but only found one.

"Sir, we made it in here. We could only locate one body. It appears to be DOA in a pool of water inside a large, locked, clear chamber," radioed the team leader to Director Reese.

"Take your men and comb through every possible exit and storage space a second time. Make sure there aren't any other entry or exit points," Reese ordered.

"Affirmative, sir, 10-12."

The team leader waved to the armed men to circle around the perimeter of the lab and adjacent rooms, gesturing with two fingers to his eyes to do an extra search. Edward Reese waited patiently on standby up on the ground floor as the other teams searched the large complex.

Meanwhile, in a secret room, behind the lab wall, Cortney Alexander silently stood next to a covered, lifeless humanoid that was fastened onto a vertical cart. The narrow space was sound-proofed, undetectable, and had its own living quarters. The room had a secure electronic portal door that opened into a lead-lined underground escape tunnel. This one-half-mile circular corridor gradually rose up to the ground level and opened behind a waterfall near the sixth hole of the company's golf course.

Several hours earlier, after terminating M2 and Terry Warren, Cortney discovered she'd been outwitted by her opposition. There was no remorse over Warren's death, only anger at the incompetence of Terry falling for the disguised locator chip that had been retrieved. She was determined to find the real processor microchip in order to activate M3.

Cortney, however, knew she had won a consolation prize. She was able to retrieve a few contacts off of Julie Kerrig's cell phone before it had been cyber erased remotely by her foes.

Alexander was now involved in an intricate chess match, which thrilled the warped genius. The cell phone, the locator chip, and other evidentiary items were destroyed in a bath of hydrofluoric acid to cover her tracks. Cortney would play the "missing or possibly kidnapped corporate billionaire's daughter" card until she devised a plausible scheme to appear publicly.

She had foreign ties to the media that would leak a false narrative to keep the authorities and public distracted. Money certainly wasn't an issue because the hidden assets were already in her Swiss account overseas. Now it was just a matter of time before she would personally visit Castle Reef and fulfill her plan. She began spinning her web carefully.

#

"Good morning, everyone, come on in!" shouted Vicki Stanwick.

"Hey, lassie!" bellowed the Irishman, O'Reilly.

Walking into the back door of the Green Sea kitchen, Jerry and Becky Foster embraced Greg and Martha Stanwick and immediately began comparing stories from the last few days. The lifeguards followed behind them with their heads down and eyes avoiding any real contact.

However, Billy Daily wasn't bashful; he let everyone know that he had arrived.

"Good morneeeng, Ms. Vicki! Nice to see you!"

Vicki hugged Billy. "Mr. Daily, you made my day just seeing you here."

"Looks like we got an army to feed," remarked Joan, standing alone.

Martha Stanwick instructed, with her loud, cheery voice, "Everyone, head to the dining room, we have nice big Belgium waffles with fresh maple syrup!"

"Bacon, we have bacon, men," coaxed Greg, looking at the lifeguards.

"Waffles, my fav'rit!" shouted Billy.

The small crowd left the kitchen and entered the dining room only to be greeted by Trent and Julie. There were a lot of hugs and conversation around the buffet table that had been set up by Francis. One by one, they filled their plates with waffles and all the extra sides that were made by Martha and Vicki. Joan poured everyone orange juice or coffee as needed. Greg made sure the boys had their bacon.

Julie, along with Trent, made it a point to greet the lifeguards, particularly Ian Reynolds.

"Well, good morning, Ian." Julie smiled at the unkempt and tired young man.

"Hello, Ian." Trent moved closer to the twenty-one-year-old.

"Hey, there, I mean good morning, Chief Kerrig, Mr. Green," said Ian respectfully.

"How did you sleep over at the Fosters?"

"Not too good. I mean, I had a lot to think about."

"You and me both," said Julie, nodding.

"I'm supposed to meet my mother for lunch today." Julie looked at Trent and then back to Ian.

"Not sure if they will be allowing anyone on the beach by then," she said.

"Maybe she can use her influence or something," suggested Ian.

"Let's just see how things go. I'll check into that if you want me to," Julie offered.

"Sure, that would be great." Ian filled his plate and started to walk away.

"Ian?"

"Yes, Chief?"

Julie smiled. "Thanks again for saving my life."

"No problem." Ian shuffled his feet and grinned, then walked to join his buddies and Billy at their table.

"Trent, after I arrest Willis and take him to jail, we need to ask Shirley if she will allow Janet Reynolds to see Ian, even if the town isn't opened up yet," Julie quietly shared.

"Does this have anything to with the folder I'm holding?" Trent asked.

"It has everything to do with it and more." Julie glanced over at Ian and then put a waffle on her plate, followed by a pat of butter.

The couple eventually sat down with Vicki and Joan, eating their breakfast and making fun and delightful small talk. Trent purposely kept the conversation about breakfast menu items in order to avoid any possible discussion about the present situation in their town. Julie, somewhat engaged, was multitasking in her mind and preparing for her trip to the town hall.

#

The State Highway Patrol office in Brighton was quiet after Neil had sent Linda, his personal secretary, and the remaining office staff home for the rest of the week. Only a couple of switchboard operators remained on duty. Hillsdale, who had just returned, adjusted the speakerphone on his desk and continued his conversation.

"Yes, I got the report about the out-of-state campers seeing the anomaly in the field last night. That was pretty strange," Hillsdale remarked.

"Add that to many other incidents," said the steady male voice.

"Operation Iscariot seemingly worked out well. I must say the camera microphone button on the mannequin was genius."

"I can't take credit for that one, Neil." The man laughed briefly.

"It was a little intense there for a while, but things worked out." Hillsdale sighed.

"Neil, thanks for stepping in and doing the honorable thing."

"Well, I knew something wasn't right. Even the attorney general wasn't being cooperative when I requested an investigation on some of the dealings with the governor," admitted Neil.

"No need to worry, he's being questioned as we speak."

"On another note, Edward Reese with the FBI is expecting you. So far, nothing is adding up at Alexander Industries, but I'm sure you have better insight as to what's going on there," encouraged Hillsdale.

"I'm headed there now. I believe we have credible leads and sufficient evidence to eventually complete our mission," the authoritative voice said confidently.

"I sure hope so. I can only imagine what some of those folks have been through down there, especially the police chief," said Hillsdale earnestly.

"The good guys always win, Neil. You should be clear to open up all traffic to Castle Reef this afternoon, most likely."

"That's fantastic. I will let Lieutenant Roth know. Good old Castle Reef, my wife and I love that town. You do remember that we met for the first time on the beach many years ago?"

The voice lowered. "How can I forget, it's very special, isn't it?"

"I know it is for you, sir."

There was a slight awkward pause. The man gently cleared his throat. "Neil, if there are any further developments, I will let you know. We have plenty for the press and media to go after, so don't worry about any reporters spinning conspiracy theories."

"Thank you for all you guys do," affirmed Hillsdale.

"Talk to you soon, my friend."

The call ended, and Neil stood up once again looking at his pictures on the bookshelf behind him and exhaled a long sigh of relief. Next month would be a great time to give the state his notice of early retirement.

#

Washing off the dried vomit from his face, David Willis looked at himself in the office bathroom mirror. He quickly chugged a bottle of water to rekindle the buzz from his nighttime, drunken stupor. David was now totally lost. There was no turning back.

He took his shirt off, threw it across the room, and walked to the bookshelf again. This time, in addition to grabbing another shot of whiskey from the near-empty bottle on his desk, he reached behind a stack of books, pulled out a 9 mm. handgun, and racked the slide back.

Today was the day he purposed to make someone pay for how he was treated his entire life. He didn't know who it was, and he didn't really care. Willis was sure that eventually someone would walk through his office door, and he was ready to unleash his stuffed down rage.

David sat down in his high-back office chair, took his shoes off, and waited with his finger on the trigger of the gun.

chapter

31

Shirley placed the microchip into the Faraday box behind the hidden door inside the evidence safe, along with the items that Julie had collected earlier. She made sure that these items would be undetected until they were picked up by the proper government officials.

Officers Sanchez, Caldwell, Hill, and others were never to discover these items.

The faithful dispatcher organized the station, bringing it back to the way it looked three days ago. Her double life would continue in Castle Reef, as it had for over thirty-five years. Only Julie and Trent would share her secret. They were going to be instrumental in keeping Castle Reef safe, while Shirley would strive to make the world a safer place as long as she could.

Sitting down at her desk, Shirley flipped a couple of unmarked toggle switches in a certain order and increased the numerical values on the digital display.

"Team Alpha to 613, copy?" spoke the secretary into her desk mic. There was a long silence. Shirley unwrapped a Ricola cough drop and placed it into the side of her mouth. "Team Alpha to 613, copy?

Finally, there was a short burst of static and a familiar man's voice replied. "Copy Alpha. Sorry, I'm in the middle of finishing my walkthrough up here on the Zambi Directive. I'm sending all the deceased across the state line to Hackett for evaluation. No sign of our suspect yet."

"Affirmative. Do you think it's her?" asked Shirley.

"Yes, the three murders here all point to it. We also found a DNA match on the nylon rope that was around the senator's neck from four years ago," reported the man.

"Good work. It's only a matter of time. We will be patient. Can you give me the latest update on Operation Iscariot before I let you go?" Shirley waited patiently.

"Yes, ma'am, we have a handful in route to DC as we speak. The Coastie's Jayhawk is carrying the entire package."

"10-4, I'm sure there are more," said Shirley, clicking the security system icon on her desktop computer.

"We are tracking the wife. She is thirty-five minutes outside of Brighton."

"You may have to intercept. I will let you know about that situation shortly," stated Shirley.

"Affirmative, Alpha. I will check in soon to give you the status on the third Zambi Directive when I finish my initial investigation with Team Beta," said the man confidently.

"Very good, did you speak to 717 already?"

"Yes, she will be initializing tracer software gateways into all transmitters purchased from Barrington Scientific starting immediately."

"Affirmative, great job, 613." Shirley began looking at the security camera footage over the past few days and was interrupted by another transmission from the male agent.

"One more thing," the voice became more natural in cadence.

Shirley stopped and looked at the radio panel. "Yes?" she asked expectantly.

"I had 717 pass along a note to Mr. Green by way of Mr. Rawlings."

"Do you really think it's time?" Shirley's expression was serious.

"Yes, I do. We will see what happens," said the voice as it trailed off.

"We can talk more about it tonight at 16:00 hours," Shirley said firmly.

"Yes, ma'am. 613 over, Alpha."

Shirley smiled and turned the switches back to the normal dispatch frequency configuration while continuing to look at the security footage.

#

Julie and Trent walked hand in hand down the west sidewalk of Main Street after leaving the Green Sea Inn. Trent smiled as he watched their shadows move along the concrete together. The shops and eateries looked beautiful, but they were lifeless without the owners and patrons who made them vibrant. Trent purposely crossed the street and was pulling Julie's arm to make her follow. They stopped in front of Lydiah's Bridal Shop.

"What are you doing?" Julie laughed.

"I thought you might want to do some window shopping on the way to your arrest," joked Trent, hugging Julie.

"Stop, I'm in uniform and on duty." Julie tried to let go of his hand, but Trent held it tight and kissed her.

"Nobody is here, Jules. The town hasn't opened yet," blurted Trent, with a big laugh.

"We don't know if Willis is around here!" whisper shouted Julie, as she pulled Trent's arm behind his back into a control hold.

"Ahh! Ouch! Okay! I give!" cried Trent in painful laughter.

Julie let him go, turned her blue cap around, and looked in the window with cupped hands to block the reflection of the sun.

"They sure are pretty though," she remarked.

Trent got quiet. "Sorry, Jules. It must have been hard for you to return your gown."

"Who said I returned it?" Julie turned and winked at Trent.

"Wait, for real? Are you messing with me?" he said, taking her hat and placing it on his head.

"Mr. Green, you will just have to wait and see." Julie giggled, grabbing her hat back.

"Hey, now, what does that mean?" Trent laughed, holding her hand.

They continued to walk south, past the police station, and Julie's apartment. Eventually, they turned right and headed west two blocks in order to connect to Baker Avenue, adjacent to town hall. Julie had planned this route in advance during breakfast forty-seven minutes ago.

As they drew closer to the southern side of the town hall, Julie's demeanor changed. She pulled her hair back into a ponytail, adjusted her cap, and put on her sunglasses. She checked her weapon, unsnapped her handcuff case, and tilted her head side to side, in order to loosen her neck. Trent knew it was game time, so he quietly listened for instructions. They walked up to the large sycamore in the curbed island of the parking lot.

"Trent, I want you to stay behind this tree as I go up to the main entrance, and yes, I know you have your revolver tucked in the small of your back."

"That obvious huh?" Trent was embarrassed.

"Yes, it's that obvious. I think it was the way you were sitting on the couch when we were talking to Mama Shirley that gave it away for me."

Trent sighed. "How do you spell humiliation?"

"If it makes you feel like Eastwood, you can cover me."

"That's not funny, Jules. By the way, it's a .357, not a .44, Magnum."

"Got it, Callahan." Julie kissed him on the cheek and walked casually up to the main entrance of the town hall.

Trent whispered, "Be careful, Jules."

"10-23, Dispatch, 10-12." Julie quietly spoke into her shoulder mic, turned her radio down, and removed her earpiece.

The automated glass doors were locked and did not respond. Julie had noticed that David Willis's car was still in the parking lot. She pressed the intercom button several times and tilted her head slightly, leaning toward the doors to listen inside. She heard commotion and uneven, fast-approaching, footsteps in the hallway, accompanied by heavy breathing. Acting on instinct, Julie quickly dove to her right and landed in the hedge near the entry, as gunshots exploded through the glass doors.

"Trent, stand down!" Julie shouted.

"Julie?" Trent called out.

"You're gonna pay! All of you!" screamed David Willis as he began firing again.

More glass shattered and bullets whizzed past Julie, who made herself as flat as she could underneath the thick boxwood. She continued counting the rounds being fired from Willis' gun as she was trained to do by her father. She recognized that it was a Glock 9 mm. being unloaded on her by its sound and deduced that it must have a seventeen round clip because he had already fired fifteen. Willis stepped through the empty door frame onto the shattered glass shards that crunched beneath his feet and looked around for the voices he heard.

"Where are you, Kerrig? I'm in charge!" screamed Willis. He fired another shot at the lamp post along the sidewalk, next to Julie's hidden leg.

Trent's heart was racing. He felt an urgency to act quickly because she was in serious trouble. Julie remained quiet and motionless. Any movement would be fatal, especially since Willis was now only ten feet away. Trent slowly moved to the next tree, even though it didn't fully cover his body. He stayed behind it, watching every move the crazed mayor made.

After a minute, Willis began looking in the flower beds and kicking the shrubbery. Trent took advantage of this and ran across the parking lot over to Julie's patrol SUV, and quickly dropping down, he hid behind it. He remembered her telling him years ago that whenever she left her police vehicle for any length of time, she would always put the key fob under the light bar rack on the roof, as a safety precaution. He said a short prayer and raised himself up to look.

It was there, and he had only seconds to act because Willis was now standing over the hedge that Julie was hiding under, and pointing his gun.

Willis growled, "There you are you lousy little…"

Instantly, the patrol car's alarm went off after Trent grabbed the fob and pressed the red panic button. All the lights flashed, and the horn gave continual loud bursts that echoed off the office building. Willis turned and fired the remaining bullet in his weapon into the sidewalk. He looked down in amazement, realizing the chamber was empty and then looked up only to be greeted with a full roundhouse kick in the face. Willis flew back and landed on the broken glass, unconscious. Julie rolled him over and cuffed his bloodied wrists in a matter of seconds.

"Dispatch, in custody, 10-95 after shots fired. We're clear." Julie finished speaking into her mic and took off running to her vehicle.

Trent stepped out from behind the cruiser and pressed the key fob button to stop the alarm. "That one was too close for comfort, Jules."

Julie hugged Trent tightly and kissed him repeatedly. "Are you all right? Oh my, that was brilliant, you saved my life!" cried Julie.

Trent wiped her tears with his hands. "I'm fine, honey, you were amazing! We did it, Jules. We're a team!" Trent laughed nervously, wiping tears from his own eyes.

"You remembered!" gushed Julie.

"What? The remote? Of course, you trained me well." Trent sniffled.

The couple embraced and kissed until they heard the groans from David Willis in the distance.

"Looks like we have to get our prestigious ex-mayor and ex-police chief into the back of the cruiser and over to the jail," complained Julie with a sigh.

"Let me give you a hand. Do you have any extra latex gloves?" asked Trent eagerly.

"I sure do. You can put them on while I read Mr. Willis his Miranda rights."

They walked toward the pitiful man, who was lying in front of the shattered town hall entry. Julie had now escaped death two times in the last twenty-four hours. For that, they both were thankful.

chapter

32

Chris and Jasmine Sanchez were sitting on the couch in their rustic living room, watching their favorite home remodeling show on their big screen television. Their two children were busy playing with Legos on the floor in front of them. The Sanchez's log home was just one mile outside of town, in a wooded area, that was only accessed by a remote dirt road.

Ever since the mandatory evacuation, Officer Sanchez hadn't received any calls from the police station, nor any of his family or friends. Many were afraid to contact him, thinking that they were putting themselves at risk of arrest for staying in Castle Reef. Chris had been enjoying the time off with his family and didn't think anything about it.

Suddenly, the show was interrupted. A well-dressed woman at a desk with video monitors behind her appeared on the screen.

> *Breaking News. This is Allison Glenmoore with Channel 6 News. Breaking just now, the Lieutenant Governor James Donaldson has announced that the State Highway Patrol will open the town of Castle Reef and its beaches at two o'clock this afternoon. This comes after a mandatory evacuation was issued over twenty-four hours ago due to multiple shark attacks and oddly, an underground gas line leak. The United States Coast Guard has reportedly*

caught the thirteen-foot Bull shark, responsible for the attacks. The waters appear to be safe at present time.

"Whoa! That's cool, Dad!" their oldest daughter, Metzi, shouted, when she saw the shark being hoisted out of the water by a Coast Guard ship.

In addition to the trouble on the beach, The Brighton County Public Works Authority have been working around the clock to repair the major gas line leak, in order to get the tourist town back up and running.

Jasmine looked at Chris. "I don't remember hearing anything about a gas line leak, did you?"

Chris grimaced and turned up the volume with the remote. "No, *hermosa*, not at all, unless it happened when my last shift was over."

We spoke to Evan Bryce, one of the marine biologist professors at our own Brighton State University just moments ago to get a little more insight on why authorities think the shark was there.

After conferring with marine biologists in other states, we believe that the large Bull shark was disoriented and made its way north into the Castle Reef waters because somehow its olfactory or sense mechanism was altered by water temperature change, perhaps attributed to climate change.

History and extensive research show there hasn't been a shark attack recorded for several decades in the coastal waters off Brighton County. The mayor or town officials, however, couldn't be reached for further comment, but we should have our team coverage down there soon, to get their response. Once again, the tourist town and beach of Castle Reef will be opening today thanks to the US Coast Guard and Brighton County's Public Works Authority.

In other news, Governor Riddick has been admitted to the hospital after apparently having a mild stroke. We don't have any details yet, but Lieutenant Governor Donaldson will be in charge until the governor makes a full recovery. Channel 6 News reporter Jehryn Lucien will have more on this story tonight. This is Allison Glenmoore, Channel 6 News.

Chris turned the television off, pulled out his cell phone, and looked for a text message.

He was so tempted to call Chief Kerrig or Shirley Allen.

"Nothing yet; I'll wait after lunch before I call the station," stated Sanchez, looking at his watch.

"That's a good idea, Chris. I'm sure they will let you know when they need you. Just relax, mi *guapo esposo*," consoled Jasmine.

"Sorry, you're right; it's going to be pretty crazy though with everyone coming back all at once," revealed Chris.

"That's why you do what you do, Officer Sanchez. *Eres un excelente oficial de policía*," praised Jasmine.

"*Gracias, mi bella esposa*." Chris embraced his wife.

#

Mike Rawlings finally made it back to the Green Sea Inn. On his way to the beach, he had passed several county utility trucks parked along the highway, with their flashing lights on. Approaching the roadblock, the state troopers just nodded at him when he drove past, but they stopped the other cars behind him, which he thought was odd. This whole week was odd for that matter.

Mike walked through the back screen door of the kitchen. He was greeted by the two faithful kitchen staffers, Rita McGuire and Kelly Davis, who had come to work as soon as news of the reopening of Castle Reef aired. Mike had heard it himself on the radio while driving from the hospital and was excited to see what exactly had happened to bring the chaos into order.

In his pocket was the envelope that he promised to deliver.

"Mike! It seems like forever! How are you?" Rita ran and hugged him.

Rawlings grinned. "Hey, hey, Rita! I'm great, and how are you guys?"

"Hi, Mike, how is your friend? It's Karen, right?" Kelli asked, slicing chicken cutlets.

"Yes, she's doing well, thanks. They are going to start some sort of physical therapy tomorrow."

"That's wonderful news!" cheered Kelli.

"It didn't take you guys long to get things moving in here." Mike looked around the kitchen.

"We thought we'd get a jump on things since the tourists should be flooding back here soon," Rita said, opening a package of butter.

"Most restaurants in town will likely open tomorrow, but not us!" stated Kelli proudly.

"So you guys do have gas?" asked Mike, with a serious face.

"Excuse me?" Rita giggled.

"Ha! No, I mean, are the gas stoves working?"

"Yes, they are working, and we will be serving baked beans tomorrow," snickered Kelli with a wink.

Mike was going to attempt a humorous comeback but was interrupted.

"Mikey, me boy!" shouted the Irishman behind him.

Mike turned around and was greeted by Francis O'Reily, who was holding a box of lettuce he had just retrieved from the cooler.

"Francis, you're hard at work, I see," complimented Rawlings after patting Francis on the shoulder.

"We're all in the dinin' room and upstairs workin' to get this place back together."

"Good job, Fran. I must say, I really missed your accent!" Mike laughed.

The two ladies burst out laughing also, as O'Reily just shook his head and made his way to the dishwasher area.

"Where's Trent? His truck is here," asked Mike, after settling down.

"Vicki said Julie and Trent went to the town hall after breakfast," answered Rita.

"Really? Did they say why?" Mike was curious.

"No, I think she also mentioned that they would most likely be at the police station afterward." Rita began unwrapping a packaged prime rib.

"Okay, thanks. Wow, it looks like some dishes piled up." Mike observed Francis rinsing plates and glasses.

"Yes, apparently all the Stanwicks, three lifeguards, the Fosters, Billy Daily, and even Joan Bradford were all here for breakfast," announced Kelli.

"Six people stayed here last night, including Shirley Allen," added Rita.

"The Green Sea Inn never shut down after all," said Rawlings proudly.

Kelli Davis stopped slicing. "Just like Fran said, Vicki and Joan are working upstairs to get the rooms cleaned after they finished in the dining area."

Mike scoffed. "Where are the lifeguards? Those knuckleheads should have been washing dishes instead of Francis."

"They just left to check out the lifeguard station. They took Billy with them," said Kelli, who then resumed slicing the chicken cutlets.

"Mr. and Mrs. Stanwick walked home to start fixing their front door. I guess someone tried to break in or something," Rita interjected.

Mike remained quiet and tried not to react. "Thanks for the updates, ladies. I think I'm going to make my way to my office and then help Vicki and Joan until the rest of the crew starts trickling in."

"Also, Fran is going to go over to the Foster's to get some more fish after they open up this afternoon," added Kelli.

"Okay, thanks for the updates. You know where I'll be."

The ladies resumed their kitchen duties, and Mike went through the swinging doors and into the dining room. He began to text Trent.

#

Trent and Shirley stood outside the criminal processing room of the police station looking through the two-way glass window. Julie, inside the white, windowless room, was slowly walking around the table where David Willis was sitting, restrained in both hand and leg cuffs. He was somewhat cleaned up but had a bandaged nose, two swollen eyes, and a fat lip. Willis sat wearing a bright pink jumpsuit, with his head down.

John Kerrig started the tradition of the pink jail attire seven years earlier, after researching the effects of color on violent prisoners. Conclusive studies showed pink significantly reduced the aggression of violent criminals. Julie always thought it was humorous to see so many harsh felons or unruly criminals become docile and compliant. They tagged the outfits "Pepto suits," appropriately named after the famous antacid.

"So tell me one more time, Mr. Willis, and then I will let you sleep off whatever is left in your system," instructed the police chief.

"Which part do you want to hear?" asked Willis in a defeated voice.

"How about the part when Chief John Kerrig went missing, which I'm now beginning to think you were involved with, right on up to the moment I drove my foot into your face!" barked Julie.

"I didn't kill your old man!" Willis piped up.

"Julie grabbed the back of his collar. "He wasn't my old man, punk! He was my father and don't forget it!" exploded Julie.

"Take it easy, Kerrig. I have my rights," squealed Willis.

"You don't have anything except one count of murder, four counts of attempted murder, conspiracy to commit murder, lethal use of a firearm on an officer, resisting arrest, conspiracy to commit numerous federal crimes, terrorism, assault, wrongful termination of a city employee, disorderly conduct, destruction of public property... Shall I continue?" ranted Julie.

"Okay, okay, stop!" howled the pink-dressed prisoner in anguish.

Julie started doing several neck rolls and then stopped because she remembered that she had an audience behind the glass. She took a deep breath, attempting to calm herself, and tried to look at David Willis through eyes of compassion.

"David, where did it all go wrong? What did we do to you to make you hate us?"

"What do you mean?" Willis was surprised.

"What did the Kerrigs do to deserve all this nonsense?"

The disgraced local politician sat quietly for over three minutes. Julie stood motionless and waited. Finally, Willis raised his head.

"Nothing, you did nothing wrong."

"Then why, Dave?" Julie walked up to the table, leaned over, and looked into his blackened eyes. She saw a frightened, lonely man who was trapped with no hope.

"I just wanted to be liked. I wanted to feel accepted, but nobody ever just liked me for me!" yelled Willis.

"Go on," urged the police chief.

"So when the chance came to be important and make a lot of money, I knew it was wrong, but I did it anyway." David started sobbing.

"What did you do, Dave?" said Julie strategically.

"Representative Reynolds pressured me and told me that he wanted some things done around town that he couldn't do when your father was alive. He was involved in a secret project with a company called Alexander Industries and threatened me if I ever told anyone about it. They have some weird, strong guy working for them, besides that robot shark thing."

"Dave, please continue," said Julie in a friendly voice.

"He wanted me to look the other way on financial matters and with certain contractors working here in town. We both made a miscalculation. We never thought you would be just like your father."

"How so?"

"You Kerrigs are alike. You can't be bought. You never give up. You never quit. You… You… You *always* want to do the right thing!" Willis whimpered and put his head down in surrender.

"Dave, you can do the right thing too by giving your life to Christ. Think about that for a while, okay?" said Julie with tenderness.

She motioned to Shirley, behind the mirrored glass, to open the door to the room. "Get some sleep, okay? We'll make sure you're comfortable here until you head over to Brighton County Corrections."

Willis sat very still and remained quiet. The electronic lock buzzed and the door opened. Shirley helped Julie escort Willis to one of the jail cells next to the processing room.

Trent remained by the two-way glass window, recalling everything that had just taken place. He was so impressed with Julie's technique and how she was able to draw the truth out of a suspect so easily. She truly was someone special. Before walking down the hall, Trent dried his eyes and quietly prayed for David Willis.

chapter

33

The red Volvo attempted to pull into the beach access parking lot but stopped at the caution tape. Janet Reynolds stepped out in the hot sun and walked up to the lifeguard station. As she surveyed the area, the wind picked up and blew the scarf off her neck into a patch of dune grass along the walkway. Reaching down to untangle the scarf, she heard footsteps approaching and looked up. Billy Daily stood in the middle of the wooden walkway, smiling at her.

"Hello! My name Billy Daily, I'm thurtee-five yers old, and I live here! Who are you?"

Startled slightly, Janet composed herself. "Hi, Billy, my name is Janet."

"That a perty name. You lost?" asked Billy with concern.

"Uh no, I'm looking for my son. His name is Ian."

"Ian? I know Mr. Ian! He my friend."

"You do? That's wonderful, Billy." Janet relaxed.

The friendly Daily, extended his hand, grabbed hold of hers, and started walking toward the building. Janet didn't resist but felt awkward. "I take you to him now."

Billy marched forward, pulling Janet along. They reached the building and turned the corner near the entrance. On the wooden benches were three lifeguards, all consumed with their cell phones, bathing in the sun. Ian Reynolds looked up and removed his sunglasses.

"Mom?"

"Hi, Ian." Janet nervously smiled.

"You came. You actually came just like you said you would," said Ian who was blown away, yet thrilled.

Janet's voice was shaky and became faint. "Yes, Ian, I did."

"I was going to call you and let you know that nothing is open for lunch around here. Maybe the Green Sea is. I know it's a little late for lunch," Ian apologized as he stood up.

"That's okay. I'm glad I made it here. It was tough. I had a little delay in Brighton."

Janet wiped the corners of her eyes.

Ian turned to his distracted friends. "Hey, guys, I'm going to maybe get some lunch with my mom. I'll see you later. Text me if they open up here."

Jake didn't respond.

Randy managed an affirming grunt, looked up from his phone, and did a double take. "Hey, you must be Ian's mom, right?"

"Yes, yes, I am," Janet responded cordially.

"I'm Randy, nice to meet you."

"It's a pleasure, Randy. It looks like you guys are ready to get back out there in the surf."

"Yes, ma'am. We miss it. We most likely won't open until tomorrow, though. Sorry to keep you, guys. Have a good lunch and nice meeting you, Mrs. R." Randy beamed.

"Thank you, Randy. It was really nice meeting you too." Janet smiled and waited for Ian to gather his backpack.

"I hungree. Mr. Ian buy me lunch all da time!" shouted Billy.

"Do you mind if Billy tags along?" asked Ian expectantly.

Janet paused. "Sure, Billy, you can come with us."

"Yippee! Thank you, Ms. Janut!" Billy jumped up and down.

Janet and Ian walked toward the car and Billy ran ahead of them, stopping abruptly.

"Red car look like big scareee! Red car good?"

Janet looked at Ian confused. "What did he say?"

Ian shrugged his big shoulders. "He's been talking about this big scary thing he saw the other night at the Salty Dawg Marina. Something about red lights and green lights."

"He's really observant." Janet smiled.

"He can be a pain sometimes, but most of the time, he's a pretty cool dude," remarked Ian.

They all got into the car and headed out to the Green Sea Inn for a possible late lunch.

Janet and Ian were both feeling anxious because of the many things they needed to share with each other. They did their best to conceal their emotions. Billy helped the potential awkwardness by asking several questions about her drive to the beach during their short ride. Today would be the beginning of building a healthy family.

#

The Castle Reef police station was quiet after David Willis had been secured in his holding cell. Julie was finishing up her call with the sheriff's department concerning the prisoner transport arrangements, while Shirley was culling through all the emails and voice messages, and taking notes.

Trent sat on a bench located between the locker room entrances, watching the ladies complete their paperwork and calls. He was amazed at all that went into police work and gained a new appreciation for law enforcement that he didn't have before. It was more than a badge, it was what it represented. Suddenly, Trent felt a vibration in his pocket.

"Hey, Mike, I'm sorry I had my phone on silent earlier. I'm at the police station with Julie."

"Yeah, I heard. Is everything all right?" Mike switched his phone to speaker to continue the conversation while folding towels.

"Everything is fine. It was crazy earlier. I'll tell you all about it in a little bit." Trent's voice went into a whisper.

"It must be intense. Are you headed back this way?" asked Mike.

"Pretty soon, you heard the town is open now, right?" whispered Trent, looking over at Julie and Shirley, who were still busy making phone calls and filing reports.

"I did. I saw a few cars and some news trucks. Rita, Kelli, and Fran were here when I arrived. Can you believe those guys?"

"Probably getting a jump on the cooking, right?"

"You know it. I'm helping Vicki and Joan get the rooms ready until the rest of the staff gets here."

"I appreciate that, Mike." Trent continued to lower his voice. "Listen, the reason I'm whispering is that I wanted to have a candle-light dinner with Julie tonight."

"What a great idea. Things must be moving along, eh, big guy?" teased Rawlings.

Trent turned his back. "Real funny, Mike. Listen, have Rita and Kelli plan for two surf and turfs. Tell them to make the steaks medium rare, just the way Jules likes it and include garden salads with balsamic. Maybe some mint chocolate chip ice cream for dessert?"

"Sounds like a great plan, partner. What time?"

"Let's make it for seven o'clock sharp. I wanted to give you guys the heads up in case she's around."

"Done deal. Hey, by the way, I have a special delivery for you," asserted Mike.

"Really? What is it?" asked Trent.

"It's a letter."

"From who?"

"Not sure. It's a long story, my friend, it seems pretty urgent."

"Wow! Okay, I'll be there in a little bit."

"Okay, man, I'll see you soon."

Trent ended the cell call and sat there for a moment thinking about his dinner plans and wondering why someone would give him a letter. His thoughts were interrupted by Julie calling out to him from across the room.

"Is everything okay over there, Trent?" asked Julie, studying his face.

"Sure is, Jules. I'm sorry I was just touching base with Mike. He made it back to the beach without being stopped."

"That's great, Trent," remarked Shirley.

"Some of the staff have returned and the rest of them may be on their way. I probably should get over there." Trent walked over to Julie's desk and sat on the corner.

"Does anyone know if Ian's mother arrived yet?" Julie glanced over at Shirley, who was busy on her computer.

"Yes, she did as a matter of fact, according to my sources," answered Shirley.

"And we all know about your sources," teased Julie.

"I bet Ian brought her to the Green Sea for a meal since nothing else is open," concluded Trent.

"I bet you're right." Julie leaned back and looked at the ceiling.

"What is it, Jules?" asked Trent curiously.

"I need to talk to both of them," said Julie, opening the folder that Trent had placed on her desk. She removed two documents and put them in her backpack.

"Mama Shirley, here are the copies of the records from town hall that Vicki gave me. I took the ones I needed, but these are the ones that you will need concerning the corruption involving JK Reynolds and David Willis."

"Got it, thanks, Chief. Listen, before I send this over to Washington and erase it, I want to show you something," began Shirley.

Julie and Trent were both intrigued as they watched Shirley open up a hidden window on her desktop computer.

"Officers Sanchez, Caldwell, and Hill will be here any moment." Shirley spun her monitor in Trent and Julie's direction. "This is the only footage I could find of the artificially intelligent humanoid that attacked you, Jules. It's from yesterday, right outside our station."

Julie leaned in and studied the screen. "Whoa, that's me just before I walked across the street. Is that the freak behind me? Can you zoom in on him?"

Shirley increased the magnification and pointed to the screen. "Notice the scan lines across his body? That's the RF frequency being picked up by the infrared camera."

"That's messed up! It's hard to believe we were all fooled," fretted Trent.

"Our team just concluded that it was also destroyed the same way the AI shark was: by self-detonation."

"Was the threat stopped then, Shirley?" asked Trent sincerely.

Julie stood up. "Please tell me this is over, Mama Shirley."

The seasoned veteran walked over to Julie, placed her weathered hands on her shoulders, and looked at both of them remorsefully.

"I wish I could say this was a *and they lived happily ever after* ending to our story, but it's not. You are always going to have obstacles and challenges, no matter where you find yourself in this life. No, the threat was not stopped, but we believe we have figured out who the leader is that tried to infiltrate Castle Reef and threaten our world. She is presently hiding somewhere. Her name is Cortney Alexander. She is the sole daughter of the late Devin Alexander, a.k.a. Alexander Industries. We believe she will do anything to further her cause. Killing her parents and her assistant are prime examples, just to name a few."

Trent gasped. "Oh man, that's horrible!"

"She has many connections here and overseas, who are still active. We are going to need your help, and we need you to be vigilant, but it is very important that you don't let this consume your lives. I can't emphasize that enough. Do you understand me?" warned Shirley.

"Yes, ma'am," said Julie. Trent nodded in agreement.

"Despite all this, we made the decision to open up our community for two reasons. First, we need to curb the suspicion of the media and the public. Secondly, we must to show strength against any terrorists by continuing to function as a healthy society."

"I understand, Ms. Shirley, but how can we help you? We can't just ignore all this and let you and your counter-terror teams do everything," questioned Julie.

"You're right, we can't. I know you've probably been wondering who will take over the mayor's position, right?" asked Shirley.

"It has crossed my mind," Julie answered with a raised brow.

"Honestly, I didn't even think about it," muttered Trent.

"Well, there's an old friend of ours, Neil Hillsdale, who is considering the position we offered him."

"You mean Hillsdale, as in State Police Superintendent Hillsdale?" Julie asked carefully.

"The one and only. He's retiring and wants to make a change. That will definitely take some pressure off of you, Jules," said Shirley, smiling.

Julie sighed. "Wow, that's a game-changer!"

"Listen to me. This is my life. I've been doing this longer than you both have been alive. It's all I do, and I accepted that fact many years ago." Shirley looked directly at them. "I never had the opportunity to receive the blessing of falling in love and experiencing the type of relationship that you have with each other. Don't ever take that for granted." Shirley dabbed her eyes with her handkerchief.

Julie reached out and held her grandmother tightly. "Thank you, Mama Shirley, for all your prayers and preserving all that is good in our family and…"

"…in this town," Trent finished her sentence.

Shirley spoke slow and emphatically. "Listen to me, Jules. Now, as your grandmother, not your dispatcher. I want you to take the rest of the day off, as well as tomorrow, and spend it with Trent."

Julie shook her head. "Mama Shirley, the town is just opening up and there is a lot to…"

"Look at me, Jules. Please take the time off. I'm asking you to do it for me," Shirley insisted.

Julie swallowed hard and then inhaled. "Okay, I'll do it," she breathed out.

"That's my girl!" Shirley beamed through watery eyes.

The automatic doors in the entry hall opened, and the sound of men talking ended their deep and emotional conversation. The three of them wiped their eyes and moved away from each other. Shirley sat down at her desk, quickly deleted the video footage, and put her handkerchief back into her sleeve. Trent and Julie both nodded at each other and smiled. The officers came in and stood in the middle of the room. Sanchez and Caldwell finished their discussion about firearms and then turned to greet everyone. Officer Hill looked into the corner past Shirley's desk.

"Where's Judy?" Hill asked.

"Whoa! Hey, she's gone," Caldwell joined in.

"She was given a new assignment," Julie spoke up.

"How so?" Sanchez asked with a grin.

"We transferred her to Brighton because she was receiving workplace harassment," heckled the police chief.

"Hey now!" Sanchez called out and then burst into laughter."

"On a serious note, gentlemen, we have a prisoner in our holding cell," Julie revealed.

"Who is it, Chief?" asked Caldwell.

"Our *ex*-mayor," said Julie with a saddened face.

"What happened?" Sanchez was curious.

"The pressure of the evacuation and things in his personal life were probably too much for him. One of the charges was a 10-56."

"Poor guy. Is he sober?" Hill asked.

"Sleeping it off. County will be by today to get him."

"Hey, boys, the chief has your assignments over here," announced Shirley, in order to change the subject.

The men started looking at their clipboards that Shirley handed out. The officers began discussing the notes they were given among themselves. Shirley stepped away and walked up to Trent and Julie.

"Go on you two, I got this," Shirley whispered.

"Are you sure, Mama Shirley?" mouthed Julie.

Shirley waved her hands to shew them out the door. Julie took her cap off and hung it on the wall rack. She unfastened her duty belt, removed her firearm, and put it into her side cargo pocket. Trent smiled at Shirley and put his arm around Julie. They were starting to walk out the automatic doors when Julie stopped to look back at her grandmother and smile. Mama Shirley returned the gesture by blowing her a kiss.

chapter

34

The air-conditioning inside the Green Sea Inn felt wonderful, as the outside temperature had risen considerably. Janet, Ian, and Billy had just been seated at a large round table inside the empty dining room.

"Welcome back, Ian and Billy! And you must be Mrs. Reynolds? Hi, I'm Kelli," greeted the energetic kitchen worker.

"Hey, Ms. Keleee! I kno yu!" Billy shouted and clapped his hands.

"Nice to meet you. I'm Janet." The exhausted lady attempted a smile.

"Sorry, there was nothing else open in town yet, I figured you guys might be serving lunch since Billy, and I had waffles here this morning," mentioned Ian.

"I heard that they made you breakfast. I also heard through the grapevine that you're our hero too." Kelli beamed.

"Hero? What do you mean? Ian, what does she mean?" questioned Janet.

"It's nothing, Mom, really," muttered Ian.

"Nothing? Come on, Ian, you saved the police chief's life, and it was nothing?" announced Kelli.

"Yes, yes! Mr. Ian kiss Ms. Julie reeel long!" Billy yelled.

Ian did a face palm as Billy giggled and patted him on the back.

Janet looked at Kelli with a confused stare. "Is this true? What happened?"

"Apparently, the chief was attacked at the marina last night and thrown into the water. Ian saw it happen, dove in to save her, performed mouth-to-mouth, and revived her."

"Oh my word! Ian, that is wonderful! Why didn't you mention this?" his mom asked.

"He's quite a guy. You have a great son, Janet," praised Kelli, pulling out her notepad.

"I'm proud of you, son." Janet reached for his hand and then slowly drew her arm back.

"Thanks, Mom." Ian reached halfway and stopped, then glanced at his mother, and quickly looked away.

"Well, you guys must be starving! I tell you what, right now we only have two choices—a grilled chicken sandwich or a hamburger. Either selection comes with chips or fries, and of course, a drink as well."

"I love cheee burger and friiies!" Billy blurted out.

"Okay, Billy! A cheeseburger it is with french fries and an orange soda, right?" asked Kelli knowingly.

Billy nodded his head fast and smiled.

"I'll have the same, please," said Ian softly.

"Will do, and for you, ma'am?" Kelli smiled at Janet.

"I'll just have the grilled chicken, no bun, and ice water is fine."

"Do you want me to throw some fresh veggies in with that?" Kelli scribbled on her pad.

"Yes, thank you," said Janet politely.

"I'll grab your drinks and get these orders going. Again, welcome to the Green Sea Inn."

Kelli grinned and walked into the kitchen.

The three of them sat quiet in uncomfortable silence, for what seemed like an eternity before Billy spoke up.

"Hey, Ms. Janut?" Billy asked.

"Yes, Billy?"

"Guess what?"

"What?" the weary woman responded.

"Chicken butt!" Billy burst into laughter.

Janet and Ian started snickering and eventually caved into full laughter, even howling a long time together over the funny awkward moment.

"Mom, I want to apologize for saying all those things to you and treating you that way on the phone—it was wrong," lamented Ian.

"I am the one who needs to apologize. I'm a terrible mother and I…" Janet broke down.

"Mom, it's okay, please don't do that," whispered Ian.

Ian slid his chair over next to his mother and put his arm around her for the first time in many years. Billy was moved to tears and got up and hugged both Ian and Janet from behind.

Kelli was about to bring them their drinks but witnessed the moment unfolding and slowly retreated back into the kitchen.

Janet sobbed. "I was never there for you, Ian. I don't know what to do. My life is falling apart."

"We can work on this together. I'm not going anywhere. Can we start over?" pleaded Ian.

"Yes, I want to so bad. Our family is a mess. Your father was arrested, and I want out. I want normal."

The weight of her words hit Ian like a large wave. However, for the first time in his life, instead of resisting the blow, he rode on top of it and let it carry him until it diminished.

"Mom, we will get through this together. I'm not going anywhere," said Ian with confidence.

Janet wiped her eyes with a napkin and patted both Billy and Ian on their arms.

Eventually, Kelli came out and served them their lunch. She was quiet and courteous, respecting their privacy. Seeing that perhaps Ian and his mother might need to talk further after they finished eating, Kelli came over and asked Billy to help her in the kitchen. Janet nodded with a silent "thank you."

"So here we are. Do you know what happened with Dad?" asked Ian with a troubled look.

"It's bad, Ian. He was involved in some pretty serious stuff. I'm sure we will find out more details soon enough." Janet sipped from her water glass.

"The paparazzi and the media will be all over this one. I think we need to stay here and live in the condo until I finish college," suggested Ian.

"That did cross my mind," affirmed Janet.

#

Julie's police cruiser traveled down Main Street, only a few blocks from the Green Sea.

Sitting in the passenger seat, Trent watched Julie carefully and noticed she was still working despite agreeing to take time off. She found herself listening carefully to the officers on the radio while looking at all the storefronts and alleys as she drove. Julie would never totally unplug, and it was futile to try and change her. It was in her blood; she truly was just like her father.

"Hello, Jules?" Trent waved his hand.

"Huh? What?" said Julie, somewhat startled.

"Earth to Julie, this is ground control to Major Tom," joked Trent.

"Hey, you, you better be nice, or I will take you back to the station and put you in that cell with Mr. Willis," taunted Julie.

"Ha! Seriously, I wanted to tell you how impressed I was with your interrogation and professionalism back there with Willis."

"Well, thanks, Trent. That means a lot, especially coming from you." Julie smiled and assessed the amount of traffic and the number of news vehicles parked along the street.

"Can we go on a date?" asked Trent awkwardly.

"What?" Julie laughed loudly.

"Yeah, just you and me by candlelight," continued Trent.

"Where, silly?" Julie glanced at Trent.

"Well, I know of this great restaurant just a block from here."

Julie was about to speak, and then she stopped herself. She turned her head to the left and focused on the vehicle that was passing her.

"Hold on, Trent!" shouted Julie.

She swerved and turned the cruiser 180 degrees while accelerating.

Trent held on to the interior roof handle with two hands.

"Dispatch, unit 1, 10-80, dark-blue Chevrolet heading southbound Main Street. All units be advised." Julie reached up and turned her lights on, keeping the microphone in her hand.

Shirley's voice came over the speaker. "10-4, unit 1."

Trent looked ahead and saw the dark-blue car outrunning them and abruptly turning into a side alley.

"Dispatch, I believe it's 613 Nitro Hacksaw Jackson, copy?" Julie reported.

"Copy, unit 1. Units 3 and 5 are 10-76," said Shirley, in a serious tone.

Julie turned into the same alley and looked thoroughly at the yards and houses while driving along the packed sand path.

"Come on! Where did it go? This is a dead-end!" demanded the frustrated police chief.

"It's like it just disappeared. What did the driver do wrong?" Trent exclaimed.

Julie remained silently concentrating, as she turned the cruiser around at the end of the alley. "Now that's impossible, it had to be here!" she groaned.

"I saw it turn too, Julie. Man, that's weird," added Trent, looking out his side window.

"Dispatch, 10-20 on the 10-37." Julie exhaled long and eventually pulled back onto Main Street.

Julie and Trent listened to Sanchez and Hill call out several street names as they doubled back around the area looking for the illusive vehicle.

"What do we do now, Jules?"

"We let those guys handle it," said Julie, sighing slowly.

"Are you sure?" Trent asked.

"That car has been seen around town ever since all this crap started. I can't help but think it's somehow involved." Julie looked straight ahead in deep thought.

"That's creepy." Trent glanced over his shoulder.

"Sanchez may find it. I'll let him investigate. We just have to keep our eyes open and do the best we can."

"I'm proud of you," remarked Trent.

"For what?" Julie questioned.

"You have just unhooked, and let someone else carry the load," affirmed Trent.

"That's what I'm supposed to do, right?" Julie laughed.

"Yep, but most of the time, you don't. I know you, Jules."

"You're right, but I guess it's time for me to start."

"You'll always be a great cop, Julie, but I value you as a person more than anything else."

Julie kept her eyes on the road and wiped the tear that was forming in her eye. She reached for the volume knob of the police radio and turned it all the way down.

"So you were saying something about a candlelight dinner?" Julie asked, slowly pulling into a parking space in front of the Green Sea Inn.

Inside, a few more people were now seated in the dining room, in addition to Janet and Ian Reynolds. Most of the servers and hotel staff hadn't shown up yet, and Mike Rawlings had his hands full at the front desk. A couple from out of town had just arrived and was ready to check into a room for the weekend.

"Hi, folks, welcome to the Green Sea. I'm Mike, and I don't know what I'm doing!" The maintenance director chuckled.

The husband and wife looked at each other nervously and smiled.

"Seriously, I just fix stuff around here and make sure you have hot water and ice. Our front desk clerk is on her way, and she will get you checked in as soon as she gets here. In the meantime, I could try."

"We just drove in from Oklahoma. We heard the news about the shark attacks while we were traveling and attempted to contact you several times," said the husband, mildly distressed.

Mike panicked. "Wow, so sorry, hey um… Let's see…"

"Regardless, we came anyway," added the wife.

Suddenly, the sound of the front door opening rescued Mike from the awkward moment he was having. The couple turned around to see Trent and Julie stepping inside, holding hands.

"Whew, it is getting toasty out there. Hi, folks, welcome! My name is Trent Green, and this is Julie Kerrig, our chief of police," said Trent, in an over-polite manner.

"Hello," the couple said in unison with a look of bewilderment on their faces.

"Hey, Trent, they just got here and…" Mike mouthed the word "help."

"Let's get you guys checked into your room!" Trent walked around behind the counter, and quickly began typing in their information as they gave it to him.

"Just so you folks know, Trent here is the owner of the Green Sea," Mike said with a nervous laugh.

"There you are, you're all set," said Trent confidently.

"Wow, that was fast! Thank you. We were getting a little scared there for a moment. We just got finished telling Mike that we had been trying to call here to confirm our reservation," explained the wife.

"I apologize, our system was down due to the evacuation, but everything seems good to go now." Trent looked past the couple at Julie, who gave him a flirtatious wink.

"We heard. So glad they got that shark! We sure were looking forward to our vacation in this quaint beach town," the husband remarked.

Trent cleared his throat calmly after being distracted by Julie. "Well, we are glad you're here, and I want to give you both a complimentary stay due to all the inconvenience you had."

The surprised woman gasped. "Oh my, we certainly don't expect that, sir!"

"It's the least we can do. And please, call me Trent," he insisted.

As she stood there waiting, Julie noticed Ian Reynolds and his mother sitting at a table, engaged in conversation. She caught Trent's attention again, and indicated that she was going to approach their table.

Trent nodded and then looked at the weary travelers. "Here's your ID and your two keys to room 115. Would you like some help with your luggage?"

"Oh, heavens no! We don't know how to thank you," expressed the satisfied husband.

"It's our pleasure," assured Trent. "Please let us know if you need anything."

The couple grabbed their bags and headed upstairs very content. Mike watched them carefully until they were out of sight and then looked over at Trent.

"Man, I just about blew that one. Sorry, I'm the wrong guy for the front desk. My social skills leave a lot to be desired," confessed Mike.

"No worries, bro. It all worked out."

"Mary should be here any minute. I'm amazed people are starting to come back to the beach so fast."

"It is summer after all, and we live in a great spot. Unfortunately, it made the news, and now everyone and their brother may be coming to check out Castle Reef." As he was speaking, Trent noticed Julie across the room. "Looks like Julie will be busy for a while. Hey, didn't you tell me that you had something to give me?" asked Trent expectantly.

"How could I forget? Sorry, man." Mike reached into his back pocket, pulled out the envelope, and handed it to Trent.

"I was told to give this to you by Jill, Karen's best friend, who just so happens to be her boss and Joan Bradford's daughter. Wrap your head around that one!" Mike acted out a mind-blowing emoji.

Trent took the envelope and started opening it. "I thought her last name was Sullivan?"

"Go figure. Hey, buddy, I gotta get moving on some work orders, my friend. Call me if it's a ransom letter. I'll be upstairs sanitizing that ice machine," jeered Rawlings.

Trent smiled, shaking his head, and began to read what was inside the envelope.

#

Janet and Ian Reynolds stopped talking to each other as soon as Julie had reached their table. Julie could tell the conversation was emotional due to their bloodshot eyes.

"I apologize for the interruption. How are you, Ian?"

"Hi, Chief," said Ian, wiping his eye with his shirt sleeve.

Julie reached out to shake Janet's hand. "Hi, I'm Chief Kerrig."

"Hello, I'm Janet, Ian's mother."

"It's so nice to meet you, Janet. Your son saved my life, and I will always be forever grateful." Julie smiled at both of them.

"I heard about that, and I'm so glad you're okay." Janet put her hand on top of Ian's forearm.

"Do you mind if I have a seat?"

"I'm sorry, that was rude of me. Of course, please join us," invited Janet.

"Thank you." Julie slid a chair out from the table, hung her backpack on it, and sat down.

"I apologize for the little mess here. We have a guest who ate with us and is now busy helping in the kitchen," said Janet with a half-smile.

"Billy Daily came along with us. He's washing the dishes," shared Ian.

"That is wonderful, and I think it is fitting that everyone is here together," Julie said.

Ian and his mother gave each other a confused look.

Julie continued. "I just came from the police station and what I'm about to share with you is very important."

"Is this about JK?" Janet speculated.

"Mom, let her talk," voiced Ian.

"I finished booking Mayor Willis a little while ago. This will become public knowledge very soon during his arraignment.

Unfortunately, it also involves your husband, Janet, and of course, your father, Ian," said Julie reluctantly.

"I don't understand. What is this all about?" Janet became uneasy.

"Yeah, Chief?" asked Ian nervously.

"Janet, I'm sure you were briefed in Brighton before you got here, and I know you were probably in the process of telling Ian some of the details," stated Julie calmly.

"Yes, sort of, I was about to, but why are you involved now?" wondered Janet.

Julie carefully chose her words. "Mayor Willis's arrest shed light on a lot of illegal activity that involved State Representative Reynolds, but in the middle of it all, we found something very interesting that you need to know. Given the circumstances, I'm glad that Ian is here with you, Janet, not only as a witness, but as a member of your family."

"Witness to what, Chief? Can you tell us please?" begged Ian.

Julie gathered her backpack and opened it. She removed the two documents and placed them on the table in front of Janet Reynolds.

Julie began, "In 1980, the AACWA was signed into law. It is a law to initiate programs in order to assist unwanted babies and foster children within each state. It is known as the Adoption Assistance and Child Welfare Act."

"I'm still not following you, Chief Kerrig," said Ian with hesitation.

Janet put her head down slowly, stared at the table, and folded her hands tightly.

"In front of you are signed legal documents consisting of DNA test results and a 1985 birth certificate of one William Joshua Reynolds."

A hush seemed to come over the entire dining room. Janet's ears began to ring. Ian felt sick to his stomach. Julie waited long for their response.

"I knew it was him when I saw him today for the first time. I always heard Ian mention him in passing every time he came to the beach, but today when I saw him, I just knew," lamented Janet, as tears welled up in her eyes.

"Mom, what are you saying? I don't..." Ian looked at Julie bewildered and ran his hands through his hair.

"It was the summer of 1984, and I was only fourteen. Your father was eighteen at the time. He was a lifeguard just like you. He always wanted to be popular and have his way. We did something very wrong."

"This isn't happening right now," moaned Ian.

"After finding out that I was pregnant, I was ashamed and didn't want to be labeled as a tramp. JK wanted me to have an abortion, but I couldn't do that. I couldn't end an innocent life. So I spent a whole year here."

"Where?" Ian swallowed hard.

"Right here, Ian. This place used to be a women's boarding home for unwed mothers and runaways. I had my baby on March 9, 1985. The home closed the following year and remained vacant until Mr. Green made it into what it is today." Ian's mother sobbed.

Julie slid the folder closer to Janet. Ian leaned over to look.

"Billy is my brother? He's... He's my older brother?" Ian began to cry.

"I never got to see him after he was born. My parents took him and put him into foster care. Your father's family made sure that his name was changed and all ties to us were severed. I just stuffed the pain and the hurt down inside of me all these years. I'm sorry that I never told you, Ian," she spoke through her tears.

"Mom. I love you." Ian hugged his mother tightly and wept in her arms.

"I will never stop loving you or Billy," cried Janet.

After several minutes, Julie helped escort Janet and Ian back into the kitchen to see Billy.

The entire kitchen staff paused and witnessed a touching family reunion. Everyone hugged them as they left for Billy's apartment to gather his things. They would be living in the beach condo for many months until the Reynolds estate was settled.

chapter

35

Evening had settled and Castle Reef was alive once again. The news was spreading fast that the town, and the ocean waters were now safe. Traffic steadily increased, mostly due to all of its returning residents. Many business owners were busy getting their shops and stores ready for the weekend tourists that were soon to arrive. The Green Sea Inn was no exception. The dining room, now buzzing with new and local patrons, was nearly full. Even the front desk was engaged in taking numerous reservations online and over the phone.

Meanwhile, Trent was in his office finishing up several calls with his food suppliers. He was both nervous and excited because he knew that seven o'clock was quickly approaching.

Julie was upstairs getting ready and had agreed to meet him at their reserved table. It felt like it was his first date, and the letter he had read earlier wasn't making things any easier. He made one more important phone call before heading to the dining room.

"Hey, Shirley, sorry to bother you," whispered Trent, looking out into the busy kitchen.

"Hi, Trent, you are never a bother," replied the familiar, friendly voice.

"I'm just about to have dinner with Julie for the first time in three years, and I was kind of thrown for a loop by a letter that was given to me a few hours ago. Do you know anything about it?"

Shirley chuckled softly. "Yes, Trent, I know all about it."

"What should I do?" he asked anxiously.

"Well, that's up to you and how you want to go about it," said Shirley with a noticeable exhale.

Trent listened carefully, while turning a little felt-covered box he had retrieved from the old safe, end over end on his desk.

"Our girl has been through a lot these past three days, and for that matter, the last three years."

He hesitated. "I guess that's what makes it so hard."

"Trent, my suggestion is that we pray about it and trust God to show you the right thing to do. You'll know what to do."

"You're right. I just needed a little confidence booster from Ms. Shirley," said Trent fondly.

"I'm Mama Shirley to you, Trent. You're family," Shirley said boldly.

"Almost." Trent chuckled, tapping on the box.

"I'll be praying for you both," said Shirley tenderly.

"Thanks, Mama Shirley. I will call you soon and let you know how it goes."

"I will be waiting. Enjoy this memorable night, Trent."

Trent tapped his cell phone screen once, pushed himself away from his desk, and stood up. It was almost time to meet Julie. He opened the small box and looked at the diamond ring he had given her almost four summers ago. Carefully putting it in his pocket, he left his office and made his way through the kitchen.

"We got you covered, boss-man," called out Rita from the stove.

"I appreciate it, and I'm sure she will too," answered Trent, noticing the fresh lobster tails on the cutting board.

"We are excited for you guys. Have an enjoyable evening," said Kelli, who was busy preparing a large bowl of greens.

"Thank you, everyone, for all you do here," expressed Trent.

The two ladies and all the other kitchen staff members smiled and continued working as Trent made his way to Mike's office.

#

"Vick, I don't know why I'm nervous, but I have butterflies." Julie leaned over her phone, as she brushed her hair in front of the bathroom mirror.

"This is exciting, Jules. Look how far you've come," encouraged Vicki Stanwick who was also on speakerphone.

"I guess. I tried to take a nap this afternoon, but my mind kept racing again."

"The candlelight dinner is going be wonderful, Julie. It is beautiful to see you both together again."

"Trent really has done so much for me, that's for sure."

"You're not the only one," Vicki agreed.

"What do you mean?" Julie began slipping on her boho sundress.

"He sent Mike and two of those lifeguards over to my parents' house to help Pops repair the front door."

"Really? What a guy!"

"Not only that, he bought all the lumber and stuff to do it."

"He's great at taking something that's broken and rundown and making it beautiful once again." Julie realized how profound her words were as they left her lips.

"You there, Jules?" Vicki waited.

Julie shut her eyes, raised her hands to heaven, and thanked God silently. "Yes, Vicki, I'm here. I am really here," rejoiced Julie.

"You go, girlfriend! Love ya, Chief Reef. I can't wait to hear all about it later."

Julie sighed. "You're my BFF."

"Bye, Jules." Vicki ended the call.

Julie finished putting on her lipstick and took a moment to look into the mirror one last time. "Okay..." She paused. "Okay, Julie, you got this!"

#

It was 6:58 p.m., and Trent rubbed his hands together in nervous excitement. After changing his clothes quickly in Mike's office, he sat at the table in his khaki pants and blue chambray shirt waiting for the love of his life. The flickering candle reflected in his eyes as he faced the stairway anticipating Julie's grand entrance.

Kendra, the designated server, came by to fill both water glasses and see if Trent needed anything. He neglected to hear her because his full attention was fixed on the beautiful woman now approaching his table. He could literally feel his pulse bouncing against his shirt collar.

"Is this seat taken, sir?" said the lady, moving her long blonde hair to the side.

"If your name is Julie, it is," replied Trent, with a slight falter in his voice.

Trent jumped up and moved behind to pull the chair out for her. As he did, he caught a whiff of her intoxicating perfume, which instantly transported him back in time. Sitting down, Julie adjusted her sundress, looking over her shoulder and then up at Trent with a big smile.

"Thank you for doing all this."

"It's my pleasure, Jules. It's been a long time coming." Trent sat down.

"Everything looks so nice. You weren't kidding. Candlelight and the works," complimented Julie.

"Yep, and guess what's for dinner?" boasted Trent.

Julie beamed. "No, you didn't?"

"Your favorite!" said Trent proudly.

"Surf and turf, medium rare?" asked Julie eagerly.

"Of course!" He reached out and held her hand.

"You went over and above as usual."

"You look so beautiful. It's going to be difficult to stay focused," teased Trent.

"Stop, you're making me melt. You know, I could really get used to living in that apartment of yours up there," whispered Julie.

"I had you in mind throughout the whole renovation."

"I bet you did." Julie winked.

"What about your place? Did you want me to fix it up for you?" baited Trent slightly.

"Actually, in all seriousness, I was thinking about asking Mr. Haywood, the owner, if he would consider selling the old building. I would like to remodel it and make it a place for unwed mothers to stay or for women who may need a new start in life."

"What a great idea! Kind of like what this place used to be," said Trent.

Julie looked outside at the cars and people walking past the large windows and nodded.

"There are plenty of people in this world that need a second chance or at least a lift in life," she said, looking into Trent's eyes with great expectancy.

Trent did his best at suppressing his emotions and remained silent. He smiled, took a sip from his water glass, and swallowed slowly.

"I feel tonight will be a night that we will cherish for many years," whispered Julie.

"How so, Jules?" Trent cleared his throat slightly.

"Is there something you want to share with me before we eat all that wonderful food you prepared?" asked Julie, with a hint of skepticism.

"Ha! You are like this 24-7 detective, body language reader!" Trent laughed.

Julie giggled. "It's in my DNA, I can't help it."

"Right, so much for the unhooking," Trent joked.

"Hey, now, let's just call it woman's intuition then," conceded Julie.

"Good one, Jules," snickered Trent, noticing Kendra coming back to the table.

"Hello, Chief Kerrig," greeted the server cordially.

"Tonight, just call me Julie," she answered with a wink and a smile.

"You bet, Julie! Are you ready for your salads?" the young server asked.

"Bring us everything, Kendra. I think we're ready, right, Jules?"

"Yes indeed!"

They both watched Kendra walk to the kitchen.

"She's a good kid," mentioned Trent, trying to fill the space.

"Okay, Trent, what's going on?" pressed Julie with a grin.

"Well, I've been thinking things over, and I wanted to talk to you about our future," said Trent carefully.

"Is there something you want to ask me in particular?" teased Julie.

Trent fidgeted. "Perhaps…"

"I know one thing. I couldn't sleep this afternoon because I kept thinking about us having dinner together. This is truly a perfect evening," said Julie, reaching for both of Trent's hands.

"After we eat, maybe we can take a walk down to the beach?" suggested Trent more confidently.

"If you insist," Julie teased.

At that moment, Kendra arrived with the dinner tray on her shoulder. She quickly set up the tray stand and began serving. The sizzle of the steak and lobster distracted Julie, but not Trent. He knew the evening had only just begun.

chapter

36

The breeze was gentle and warm, and a swath of orange light flickered on the bronze-tinted beach. The outlines of Trent and Julie stood together motionless, their arms wrapped around each other, as they faced the full moon that was rising over the ocean.

"Thank you for a wonderful evening that I'll never forget," said Julie with a long sigh.

"Jules?" Trent asked. He gently stretched out her left arm.

"Yes?" Julie replied, with the moon reflecting in her green eyes.

"I don't know how to really ask you this again…"

"Yes, Trent, I will marry you."

Trent stammered, "You… You will?"

He quickly took the engagement ring that was in his front pocket and started placing it on Julie's left ring finger. She shivered with joy and began to cry instantly. They embraced instantaneously and kissed each other. As they held their hands together, they both noticed once again, the heart-shaped tattoo that formed on their entwined forearms. Many passionate kisses were exchanged as the sun continued slowly setting behind them. Trent wiped Julie's tears off her cheeks with his thumbs and held her face in his hands.

"Can we…" Trent began to ask.

Julie finished his sentence. "Get married real soon?"

Trent laughed and kissed her again. "You took the words right out of my mouth."

Julie looked intently into his eyes. "I love you, Trent Green, and I can't wait to be your wife."

"I love you, Julie Kerrig! I knew you were the one when our eyes first met."

As they hugged again tightly and spun around, laughing, Julie suddenly caught a glimpse of an eerily familiar car parked sideways in the distance by the lifeguard station. Her heart sank, and she pulled back from Trent's embrace.

"I can't believe it!" Julie said in horror.

"What is it, Jules?"

"I thought we were the only ones here?"

Trent turned around. "Who is it?"

"It's the blue mystery car. The one that disappeared today." Julie's eyes were fixed on the parked vehicle.

"Are you sure?" Trent stepped forward.

"Yes, that's it. There's no mistaking it."

"Do you think it might be one of the agents with the CTTF that's watching out for you?"

"Maybe, I don't know, but I'm going to find out." Julie started walking briskly toward the parking lot.

"Jules, hold on. I think you need to wait." Trent started jogging to catch up.

The car remained parked, and the setting sun made it appear even more ominous the closer they got. Julie was now in a full-on run, and her sundress resembled a parachute swirling behind her. In midstride, she managed to pull out the Colt 1911 from the side of her concealed holster shorts.

"Jules, slow down. Hold up, will you?" Trent recognized her intense determination and knew it was useless to stop her.

Closing in on the parking lot, Julie could hear the car quietly running. No other vehicles were present, only the mysterious dark-blue four-door. Julie turned her head slightly sideways but kept her eyes fixed on the mystery vehicle, while maintaining a two-handed grip on her weapon. She took a deep breath and exhaled slowly. Trent eventually caught up and was ten yards behind.

"Trent, call Mama Shirley and tell her to dispatch Sanchez or Caldwell here right away."

"But, Jules, I think you need to…"

"Trust me, Trent, just do it now please!" ordered Julie.

She made it into the parking lot and came to a halt. Trent slowed down to a walk and pulled out his phone. Julie slowly approached the car from behind and kept her gun drawn with a firm, stacked thumb grip. Seeing the license plate, that plainly read *613NHJ*, it confirmed all her suspicions.

Julie placed her hand on the back right quarter panel and decided to proceed cautiously along the passenger side of the car, in order to use the sun to her advantage. Raising her weapon in one hand, she firmly knocked on the window.

"Castle Reef Police! Open up and show me your hands!" Julie shouted.

The car just remained parked and running. There was no movement or noise from within the vehicle. Julie only saw herself and the orange glow of the sun reflecting on the dark glass.

"Let's go, driver! Castle Reef Police! Show me your hands!"

Julie was now becoming impatient and at the same time a little uneasy. She could only hear the car engine quietly idling and Trent's voice talking on the phone in the distance. Tapping on the glass again, Julie demanded, "I'm going to ask you one more time to open up your window and show me your hands!"

Julie was now perplexed at the lack of compliance. She thought perhaps the driver was asleep or possibly dead. The door handle was locked. She knew she had to wait for Sanchez to show up or she could possibly end up in a compromising situation.

"Julie?" Trent called out from several yards behind her.

"Move back, Trent, and give me the status on back up," shouted Julie, aiming her firearm.

"Backup is on the way!" Trent replied and retreated to the lifeguard station.

Then it happened. The passenger's electric window slowly began to lower. Julie's heart began to race as the dark tint and sun's reflection disappeared. She stood at a slight angle, pointing her weapon and slowly moved forward.

"Put your hands on the top of the steering wheel where I can see them!" commanded the police chief.

The driver slowly put his hands on the wheel. She saw a pair of hands that looked oddly familiar, especially the wedding band. Julie felt that her heart was about to leap out of her chest.

This can't be true. Is this for real?

Julie stepped sideways and slowly looked into the car with her finger on the trigger. She saw a familiar old leather Bible, with a cross on its cover, lying on the passenger seat. Then it finally hit her. She realized the license plate matched the writing on the back of the first page of that Bible, her father's Bible. 613NHJ? It was JHN 3:16 backward! She could hardly breathe.

Julie gazed upon a large framed, middle-aged man, who turned his head and leaned over to look at her with his tear-filled green eyes. There was a long pause as they studied each other's faces. Only the sound of the rolling waves could be heard in the distance.

"Daddy? Is it really you?"

"I'm here, Jules."

"Oh my, Daddy!" Julie opened the door and dove into his arms.

From fifty yards away, Trent waited and then heard multiple cries of joy and tearful laughter. He exhaled with great relief, raised his phone, and confirmed with Shirley that her granddaughter was finally reunited with her son. As he slowly began walking toward the vehicle, he smiled and thought to himself, *Julie was right. Tonight would truly be a night that they would cherish for many years.*

Acknowledgments
and Resources

Helpful Links:

Let Them Live: *letthemlive.org*

Fellowship of Christian Peace Officers-USA: *fcpo.org*

Cornerstone Fellowship: *cornerstonefellowship.tv*

Through The Word: *throughtheword.org*

Andrew B. Sampsel: *andrewbsampsel.com*

Special thanks to:

Marlene Sampsel

Barbara Van Brunt

Pastors Allen & Lisa Nolan

All my co-workers in ministry

ABOUT THE AUTHOR

Andrew Sampsel became intrigued with writing when his high school English teacher required her students to express their thoughts and stories in a weekly journal. These 'green books' provided an outlet for his imagination and eventually paved the way for him to use many art forms in ministry. Andrew, the creative arts/technical director at his local church, is married to Susan, the love of his life and his inspiration. They have two beautiful children and three adorable grandchildren.

CPSIA information can be obtained
at www.ICGtesting.com
Printed in the USA
BVHW080542130722
641931BV00001B/30